The Walled Orchard

The Walled Orchard

Volume Two in *The Walled Orchard* series

Tom Holt

St. Martin's Press
New York

Library of Congress Cataloging-in-Publication Data

Holt, Tom.
    The walled orchard / Tom Holt.
       p.   cm. — (The walled orchard series ; v. 2)
    Sequel to: Goatsong.
    "A Thomas Dunne book."
    ISBN 0-312-05990-6
    I. Athens (Greece)—History—Fiction. 2. Greece—History—
Peloponnesian War, 431-404 B.C.—Fiction. I. Title. II. Series:
Holt, Tom. Walled orchard ; v. 2.
PR6058.0474W35   1991
823'.914—dc20   90-27106
                                                         CIP

First published in Great Britain by Macmillan London Limited.

First U.S. Edition: June 1991
10 9 8 7 6 5 4 3 2 1

For Theo Zinn and Denis Moylan; with thanks

Translator's Note

Readers who are not familiar with the first part of this work, known since Roman times as the *Inaccurate Histories* and attributed to Eupolis of Pallene (translated in this series under the title of *Goatsong*), may benefit from the following brief dramatis personae:

Eupolis, son of Euchorus; (relatively) successful Comic dramatist and member of the (moderately) wealthy Cavalry class of Athenian citizens. After losing his father as a boy and his grandfather and most of the rest of his family shortly afterwards in the Great Plague of Athens, which he survives with no ill-effects apart from damage to the muscles of his face and loss of a finger, he goes to live with –

Philodemus, son of Daemon, his honest and sympathetic Heavy Infantry class uncle, who brings him up with his only son, the admirable –

Callicrates, son of Philodemus, who retrieved Eupolis from his grandfather's house during the Plague, and who becomes Eupolis' surrogate elder brother and guardian angel. Despite their love and guidance, Eupolis is ill-advised enough to rescue from a fate worse than death (abduction in the aftermath of a drunken party by Aristophanes, q.v.) and subsequently marry –

vii

Phaedra, daughter of Theocrates, an extremely beautiful but incorrigibly foul-tempered girl, whose good opinion of her husband does not survive the wedding night; and when Eupolis returns from his first taste of military service on a routine tax-gathering expedition to Samos, where he wins a laurel crown by killing, albeit inadvertently, an enemy warrior and saving the life of his dependent Little Zeus (q.v.), he finds that Phaedra has spent large sums of his money on a large and horrible house in the City, which he refuses to live in. His unsatisfactory marriage leads Eupolis to throw himself into the improvement of his lands and the pursuit of his dramatic career; and this soon brings him into conflict with –

Aristophanes, son of Philip, the leading Comic poet of his time; and their professional rivalry rapidly develops into all-out hatred, not helped by Aristophanes' seduction of Phaedra and the success of Eupolis' second play, *Maricas*, after the abject failure of his first play, *The General*. Meanwhile –

Cleon, Nicias, Demosthenes and Alcibiades, the leaders of the Athenian state, have been getting on with the Great Peloponnesian War against Sparta, which has been in progress for most of Eupolis' life. Cleon's early death at Amphipolis gives the brilliant but unsound Alcibiades a chance to make his bid for overall leadership of Athens, and during a truce in the War proper, he proposes the annexation of the fabulously rich island of Sicily. A huge army and navy are assembled for this purpose, but on the eve of their departure the many small statues of the god Hermes which litter the streets of Athens are vandalised by upper-class drunks (including Aristophanes, and witnessed only by Eupolis). The Athenians, in a wave of superstitious horror, vote to have Alcibiades (whom they incorrectly assume to be responsible) put on trial for sacrilege as soon as he gets back from leading the Sicilian Expedition.

Also involved are:

Euripides; the great avant-garde Tragic dramatist;

Socrates; the philosopher and professional teacher of oratory;

Little Zeus son of Diogenides; Eupolis' gigantic and devoted follower; a descendant of an illustrious but poverty-stricken family, he feels himself forever in Eupolis' debt as a result of Eupolis' neighbourly act of subsidising the reclamation and development of his extremely small holding of land;

Alexander and Jason; princes of a semi-barbarian kingdom in Thessaly, whose principal affectation is a love of the Athenian theatre, and who acted as Eupolis' hosts when he was sent there on a State diplomatic mission;

Pericleidas; a Sicilian dried fish magnate who sat next to Eupolis in the Theatre during the performance of *The General* (q.v.).

Scene: Athens and Sicily, in the fifth century BC. The Peloponnesian War is in its tenth year and Eupolis is in his early twenties – by Athenian standards, on the threshold of middle age. Although they are by no means reconciled to each other, Phaedra and Eupolis have composed an armed truce in their marriage, brought about, like the truce in the War, by the exhaustion of the participants.

The text followed throughout by the translators is the Oxford Text, edited by Dickson and Mayerbeer (1917), except where amended by the Budé edition of Follett and Lascariot (1963). Finally, the translators wish to thank Professor Lise-Ellen Pentangeli for her inspired insights into the notoriously obscure incident of the Veteran of Himera, although they would stress that all errors which remain are entirely their own responsibility.

S. Sigmundarsen
J. Casimir
University of Chicopee Falls, Iowa
1989

The Walled Orchard

Chapter One

We Athenians despise optimists, but we occasionally perpetrate unintentional optimism in the sacred name of shrewdness. For example: Dexitheus the bookseller commissioned me to write the history of my times for three hundred drachmas, at a time when History seemed to be the coming thing and paper was cheap. I settled down to my task and was happily scribbling away when he came to me and suggested that, since my life had clearly been so fascinating and packed with incident, it would be a good idea to publish my history in two volumes. Being somewhat oversceptical as a result of this long and fascinating life of mine, I assumed that he wanted to sell two volumes at a drachma each rather than one long one at one drachma three obols, and agreed. After all, it suited me fine, since I anticipated that Dexitheus would be left with a lot of copies of my first volume on his hands and would abandon the idea of a second, and that I would therefore get three hundred drachmas for half the work.

Well, nothing definite has been said about the matter, but I believe Dexitheus still has plenty of Volume One taking up space in his barn at Cholleidae and getting nibbled by mice; but he has just come bounding back asking me how far I've got with Volume Two, and making vague breach-of-contract noises when he hears that I haven't actually started yet. What his clever little soul is saying to him is that if enough people buy Volume Two, they'll want to buy Volume One to catch up on the first part of

1

the story, and then he'll have some space in his barns again to put his winter barley in once it's cut.

Personally, I think Dexitheus' reasoning is somewhat flawed, but far be it from me to argue with a man as depressingly litigious as Dexitheus of Cholleidae. I only mention this sordid little detail as an illustration of the Athenian character, and in particular my fellow citizens' obsession with cleverness.

You will understand the relevance of this if you've just finished reading Volume One, and recall that I broke my narrative at the point at which the great Sicilian Expedition was about to set sail. But I don't suppose you have, so in order to do my duty by Dexitheus and the Muse of History, I will now give a very brief epitome of what is contained in the first roll. Once you have read this, you will immediately want to read it, and so before I begin I must just tell you that Dexitheus' stall in the Market Square is just to the left of the shield-maker's stands as you come in from the Acropolis past the Mint. Say Eupolis sent you.

I, Eupolis of Pallene, the Comic playwright, was born thirty-eight years after the defeat of the Persian fleet at Salamis, and eleven years before the outbreak of the Great Peloponnesian War between Athens and Sparta. I lived through the plague which killed the celebrated Pericles, catching the disease myself but being cured of it by the God Dionysus, and in my twentieth year I presented my first Comic play at the Dramatic Festivals, which came third out of three. I was not put off, and eventually won first prize with *Maricas*, which is undoubtedly the best Comic play ever written. By this stage I was married to one Phaedra daughter of Theocrates, whose temper was so filthy she made Medusa look like a kitten. At first we didn't get on terribly well, but shortly before the start of this volume she had had her very beautiful face kicked in by a mule, leaving her looking as well as sounding like Medusa, after which her behaviour towards me became rather less ferocious.

While all this was going on, Athens had been getting further and further into the Great Peloponnesian War;

2

and, after the short, brilliant and disastrous career of the celebrated Cleon, had fallen under the spell of the celebrated Alcibiades. This Alcibiades had hit on the idea of conquering the fabulously rich island of Sicily as a means of replenishing our depleted exchequer, and had so filled the heads of his fellow Athenians with his idea that everyone, even I, wanted to be part of it. A great expedition was organised, and a huge army was raised, in which every man in Athens except me and a few people with only one leg seemed to be enlisted. I was livid at not being allowed to go, but on balance this didn't seem to worry our leaders terribly much. Then, the night before the fleet was due to sail, a group of drunks (including my rival Comic poet and evil spirit Aristophanes son of Philip) smashed up all the little statues of Hermes in the City, causing a wave of superstitious hysteria. I was about the only eye-witness to this, by the way. For some reason which defies logical analysis, the Athenian people decided that Alcibiades was behind the sacrilege; but, not wanting to be deprived of their treat, voted that Alcibiades should continue to lead the Sicilian Expedition, subject to his coming back to Athens after it was all over to be impartially tried and executed for blasphemy.

If that is not a complete summary of Volume One it will do to be going on with, and I think you have a general idea of who everyone is. Various other points to note, such as the fact that Aristophanes and I had been generally getting in each other's way and on each other's nerves since childhood, and that Aristophanes had an affair with my wife before her face got kicked in, will no doubt emerge from context, and you will guess without my having to tell you that the Callicrates who occasionally crops up was the son of my uncle Philodemus (who looked after me since I was orphaned by the plague as a boy) and general guardian angel, and that the curious person named Little Zeus was a hanger-on I acquired in the course of my boyhood as a result of a rash promise to plant out his tiny and unproductive holding of three acres in vines for him as soon as the War was over. I certainly won't insult your deductive powers and general knowledge of Athenian history by telling you who Nicias and Demosthenes are, or how I came to be quite comfortably off and a member of the cavalry class by virtue of inheriting land from relatives who died in the plague. Now then, about Alcibiades.

Chapter Two

Alcibiades was not a fool. He jumped ship as soon as he could and hurried off to Sparta, where they were very pleased to see him. The Athenians consoled themselves for his loss by holding his trial *in absentia*, which was almost as much fun as if he had been there. They didn't get to hear him speak, of course, which was sad, but on the other hand they were able to find him guilty (which might have been tricky had he been present) and so prove conclusively that it was indeed he who mutilated the statues.

The fleet carried on, with Nicias now the overall commander, and at home we waited anxiously for the news of the fall of Syracuse. But weeks passed, and no news came, and so we forgot about Sicily and started grumbling about how empty the City was these days, and how difficult it was to get together enough people for a dinner-party. The weeks turned into months, and still no news, until everyone in the Market Square was convinced that Nicias had finished in Sicily and moved on to the Golden Isles or the Islands of Perpetual Rain.

The money that our loyal Sicilian allies promised us didn't arrive, either, and we soon found out why. You remember that Alcibiades' messengers had been entertained in private houses where everything was made of silver; well, the Sicilians had been clever there. A week or so before the messengers arrived, they had been all round the cities requisitioning every silver object they could find, and every single piece of coined money, and they had put on a special show for their Athenian guests. Then, when the messengers moved on to the next city, the silver preceded them, and the Sicilians prayed that the Athenians wouldn't wonder why the silverware in Egesta looked so very like the silverware in Catana. As for public treasuries, they had covered the floor with figs and stones, and spread the coined money very thinly over the top, except for the areas near the doors.

After we had got over our initial fury at being outwitted by the Sicilians, we decided to put the whole thing down to colonial high spirits and forget about it; after all, the treasury of Athena in the Acropolis was full of coined silver, and it wasn't as if we were spending the money; rather, we were investing it, and a few hundred talents was a cheap price to pay for mastery of the world and the destruction of Sparta. But that, together with the Alcibiades business and the lack of reports of glorious successes, set people worrying about the project in a way that they had not worried before. But nobody, not even the most paranoid of us, thought for a moment that the expedition should be recalled; only that someone somewhere ought to be punished for something at some time. This was so close to our normal state of mind that we soon stopped discussing it. Then a letter arrived from Nicias which was quite different from his earlier, utterly uninformative despatches.

There is an art to writing military despatches, I suppose; my favourite is one supposed to have been sent by a Spartan officer later on in the War, which went something like, 'Ships all sunk. General dead. Soldiers starving. Haven't the faintest idea what to do next. Advise.' Nicias' letter was longer than that, but not much more cheerful.

According to his letter, he had spent the time since his arrival in Sicily building walls. I knew from my own experiences in Samos how much the military mind loves a good wall, especially if it goes nowhere and gets under the feet of the infantry. It gives a man a sense of achievement to be able to point to a wall and say, 'I built that'; and since (according to Nicias' letter) there was nothing else he could hope to achieve in Sicily, I could understand why he had occupied his time in that particular way.

The truth behind Nicias' letter was that he was in a hopeless mess. Because he had been his usual cautious, painstaking self, he had given the Syracusans plenty of time to sort out their internal problems (they killed a few people, I believe, which seemed to solve everything) and they had presented a united and resolute front to the invading army. They also had promises of help from our enemies in Greece, and the Spartans were sending them a general. The worst thing about it all was that there were rather more Syracusans than we had been led to believe, and they were by no means incompetent when it came to the arts of land and sea warfare. Nicias' only intelligent colleague, a brave and fairly honest man called Lamachus, had been killed, and the General could see no way of achieving his mission without substantial divine intervention – a plague, say, or a large-scale earthquake. Obviously the sensible thing was to call it a day and go home; but if he tried that, he would be in court on a capital charge before he had time to take off his helmet. His only chance of being around to taste the next vintage was if he was actually recalled; then at least he could say (at his trial) that he had been just about to trample the towers of Syracuse level with the mud when the *Paralia* had drawn up on the beach with his marching orders.

So, being Nicias, he tried the tactic he had used the first time, and which had gone so disastrously wrong. He begged to inform the people that, in order to do the job he had been sent out to do, he needed twice as many ships and twice as many men, and every four-drachma piece in Attica and the Empire, plus a colleague or two to help him with the command, plus could he please come home now, because his kidney trouble made it impossible to do his job properly? He realised that if the forces he had requested were sent to him, Athens would be emptied of men, almost entirely without any form of shipping larger than a lobster-boat, and bankrupt; but if Athens wanted Sicily, that was what it would take.

Oh my beloved city. You listened to the letter of Nicias, you made a few speeches, you coined a few clever phrases, and you sent Nicias everything he had asked for, except his recall. I think it was only then that I realised the true extent of your power and your wealth and your resources of ships and men, and your imperishable stupidity. To have mounted an expedition like the first fleet would be beyond any city or confederation of cities today; but to raise and man a fleet bigger even than that, and to send it out on the strength of a single letter from an idiot – that was an act of such magnificent folly that no man can ever blame you for it. It surpasses even the lunacy of the Persians. And to wage this war thoroughly, to the death, to the last drop of blood, you called on the brilliant Demosthenes, your ablest general, and sent Eupolis son of Euchorus, of the deme of Pallene – and five thousand or so others – to help him do it.

'For God's sake, woman, stop fussing,' I said to Phaedra as I prepared to set out for Piraeus, 'and don't worry, please. We'll be back before you know we've gone.'

'You keep saying don't worry,' she said, packing my ration-bag tightly into my shield, 'and I'm not worrying at all. If anyone's worried, it's you. Now are you sure you've got everything?'

'Of course I've got everything.'

'Spare blankets?'

'Yes.'

'Clean tunic?'

'Yes.'

'Needle and thread?'

'Yes.'

'Spare helmet liner?'

'Oh hell, no. I knew I'd forgotten something.'

She grinned triumphantly. 'I've packed it in with your food. It'll smell of cheese rather a lot, but you won't mind that.'

'You bitch,' I said, 'you did it on purpose.'

I looked out of the door. The sky was growing pink, it would soon be dawn.

'Hector didn't call his wife a bitch when he went out to fight,' said Phaedra.

'But Andromache was a sweet, loving and good wife,'
I replied, 'and you're a bitch.'

'That would account for it,' she said.

I frowned. 'Don't you want to have the last word,
Phaedra?' I said. 'That's unlike you.'

She smiled. 'I'll have it when you come home,' she
said. 'I'll pass the time by thinking of nasty things to say
to you when you come back. Oh, Eupolis, you do look
silly in your armour.'

'I feel silly,' I said, shaking my head to make my plume
nod. 'Whoever first thought of putting bits of horsehair on
top of helmets has a lot to answer for. Be good.'

'I will,' she said, 'then I can be bad when you get
home. You will come home, won't you?'

'Now I say "Yes" and you say "Pity"?'

'That's right.' She kissed me, and pulled my helmet
down over my face. 'Now get on, or you'll be late, and
I'd be so ashamed if my husband was the only man in
Athens to miss the boat.'

Then she pushed me out of the door and slammed it,
and I walked away as quickly as I could, without turning
my head.

On my way to Piraeus I bumped into Callicrates –
literally, since my helmet had fallen down over my eyes,
and I couldn't see where I was going. For a moment I didn't
recognise the man in armour on the hem of whose cloak
I had just trodden; but as soon as he cursed me for being
a clumsy idiot I recognised his voice.

'Callicrates!' I said. 'What are you doing dressed like that?'

'Is that Eupolis under that chamber-pot?' He lifted the
helmet up. 'I was just coming to find you. I thought we
could go down to Piraeus together.'

I stared at him. 'Are you coming to Sicily too?' I asked.

'That's right,' he said. 'Late addition to the list this
morning. They wanted to make up the numbers.'

I was so delighted I hardly knew what to say. 'Why,
that's marvellous!' I cried. 'I'm so pleased.'

Callicrates frowned at me, just as he used to when
I was young and did something stupid. 'Why?' he said.
'What harm have I ever done you?'

'But don't you want to go, Callicrates?' I said, mystified. But he only shook his head, so that the plume on his helmet nodded.

The nearer we came to the docks, the more crowded the streets became; and I have never seen such a curious spectacle. It was like a cross between a pageant and a funeral. There were dancers and flute-players and women handing out garlands, and next to them wives and mothers dressed in mourning, wailing and shrieking as their men tried to prise their fingers off the hems of their cloaks. There were sausage-sellers, and jobbing poets, and painters with trestle tables offering to do a five-minute portrait of the departing hero on a wine-jar or oil-flask for a drachma, and next to them old women from the country selling charms to avert evil; and spear-polishers and crest-makers and while-you-wait shield menders, and fortune-tellers and sprat-sellers (in case anyone had forgotten to bring his rations); and creditors waiting for their debtors, and moneylenders, and men offering to take short leases on land, and landlords wanting their rent, and merchants buying options on shares of loot, and old soldiers promising to tell you everything there is to know about Sicily for an obol. And, directly underneath the most magnificent plume you ever saw in your life, Aristophanes son of Philip, giving last-minute instructions to his Chorus-trainer about the two plays that he had committed to him in case he wasn't back in time to see to them himself.

Callicrates and I avoided him as best we could – he was in a different regiment sailing on a different ship – and took our places in the line for our names to be pricked down. As I stood there, I saw a head towering over all the others. It was topped by a battered green helmet that had probably last seen action when Themistocles was General, and it was reciting a passage from the *Seven Against Thebes* to a somewhat restless audience.

I asked Callicrates to keep my place for me, and went to see. Sure enough, there was Little Zeus, in fine voice and a suit of armour that was far too small for him. As soon as he saw me he broke off in mid-strophe and called out my name in a voice that must have shaken the trees on Parnes.

'What are you doing here?' I asked. 'I thought you went with the first fleet.'

'The idiots,' he said passionately, 'the wretched, miserable fools at the Polemarch's office, wouldn't let me go. They said my armour wasn't good enough, would you believe.'

'Well,' I said, 'it's not exactly pristine, is it?'

'This is my new armour,' he said coldly. 'It cost me twenty drachmas and a yearling goat, every last coin I had. A complete waste of money, I may say – there was nothing at all wrong with my old armour, nothing at all. The helmet belonged to my great-great-grandfather, who wore it before the Persians came.'

I couldn't think what to say to that. Luckily, I didn't have an opportunity to say anything.

'But I look upon it as an investment,' Little Zeus continued. 'At last, I promise you, I'll be able to pay off my debt to you. On my word of honour.'

'I do wish you'd forget about that— ' I started to say.

'And you're really coming too?' he continued. 'You're sailing with us?'

'Yes,' I replied.

'That's the best news I've heard all month,' said Little Zeus. 'Now I know everything will be all right. And we're in the same regiment, of course; why didn't I think of that before? It'll be just like that time in Samos, when you killed the enemy champion and saved my life.'

People were looking round and pointing, and I could feel my face burning with embarrassment. 'Keep your voice down,' I muttered, but it was too late.

'What's that you said?' asked one of the men next to us. 'Is this bloke some sort of hero then?'

'Was that Pericles' campaign in Samos?' asked another.

'Who is he, anyway?' said a third. 'Hey, Crito, come over here. There's a man here killed a general in Samos and saved the entire fleet.'

I made an attempt to slip away, but it was too late. Little Zeus was answering questions from all sides, confirming that I was indeed a hero, and that they were all lucky men to be in the same regiment. It was several weeks before I was able to live it down.

In case any of you have ignored my earlier excellent advice and haven't yet secured a copy of the first half of these memoirs of mine (Dexitheus informs me, by the way, that he still can't see the floor of his barn for copies of it, but that the mice seem to enjoy it tremendously, which is one of the nicest things anyone has ever said about anything I've written), I should make it plain that I didn't actually kill a general in Samos. I did kill a Samian of sorts, in circumstances that would have been very funny but for the blood and loss of life, and anybody with the sensitivity of one of those thick-skinned Egyptian animals, who live in rivers and whose name escapes me for the moment, would have taken particular care to see that the subject was never mentioned in my presence again. But that was Little Zeus for you.

We boarded the ships, and stowed our equipment as best we could, and waved and shouted to the people on the quayside; and then we were off. We were going to Sicily.

Except that we went the long way round. First, we had to meet up with Demosthenes, who was chasing round Laconia with the Operational Fleet; and, Demosthenes being Demosthenes, he couldn't resist a few little diversions on the way.

The idea was that we should raise a few troops here and there, on the principle that you can never have enough men, so we scooped up some Argives, who didn't really want to come but didn't like to refuse; then, since we happened to be passing Laconia, we stopped off and spent a pleasant few days chopping down olive trees, rooting up vines, and generally getting our own back for what the Spartans had been doing to us since we were all children. It's a strange feeling for a farmer to destroy vines and trees. At first, you don't enjoy it at all, but after a while you get into the spirit of the thing and it becomes immensely entertaining. I got the feeling that I was venting my fury not only on the Spartans but also on the recalcitrant, perverse and incomprehensible Spirit of Nature, which torments anyone who lives by growing things. 'Take that,' I found myself saying as I put an axe to a fig tree, 'that'll teach you to get blight and leaf-rot for no readily apparent reason.'

While we were there, we also fortified a little isthmus as a safe haven for runaway helots, and then sailed on towards Corcyra, stopping on the way to sink a Corinthian ship at Pheia and take on more heavy infantry at Zacynthus and Cephallenia, while Demosthenes went off collecting light infantry in Acarnania. Do I sound, by the way, as if I know where all these places are? That would be misleading. The fact that I have been somewhere does not necessarily mean that I know where it is, or anything about it at all. The truth is that we Athenians are not great geographers, although we claim to be. In Assembly, we listen gravely to the Great Men discussing the strategic value of Caulonia, or the implications of the situation at Syme for the route to Cnidus, and we vote for whoever speaks best; we haven't the faintest idea where Syme is, any of us, but not one of us would admit this for a second.

After Corcyra, then, we went to the Iapygian Promontory, the Choerades (which, I am reliably informed, are islands quite close to the Iapygian Promontory), and Metapontum, which is somewhere in Italy. On the way we gathered a great host of outlandish-looking people, including a number of Italian savages, before dropping in at Thuria (I have not the faintest idea where Thuria is). There, or somewhere quite like it, we landed and had a parade, marched about for a while until the locals politely asked us to go away, and then sailed on to a place called Petra. At every place we stopped we took on yet more reinforcements, until nobody could quite remember who we had with us, let alone why. But in the end I think we had about seventy-three ships, seven or eight thousand heavy infantry (Athenian and foreign) and goodness knows how many light-armed troops, savages as well as Greeks, when we sailed up to Nicias' camp outside Syracuse one fine morning. We were feeling supremely confident after our journey, which had been more like a holiday than an expedition, and we felt that not even the gods could stop us now.

The shore was lined with men waiting to greet us. We saw the flash of their shields long before we made land, and immediately started waving and shouting. Some of the men on the deck with me were looking out for friends and relatives, others were searching for the piles of loot and captured weapons which we all expected to see; everyone else was looking out for the smoke of the cooking-fires. Because we had taken on more troops than we had expected in Italy and all those other places, the supplies of food had started to wear a little bit thin; and although we were by no means hungry, none of us would have refused a large meal by that stage. And what we had seen of Sicily from the sea – one enormous wheatfield, trimmed at the edges with vineyards and topped off with the olive groves that go right the way up the few mountains they have on the island – was enough to make anyone salivate, let alone men like us who scratched about in the dust on the side of the mountains of Attica. The general consensus was that we would be greeted with tureens of pea soup, followed by roast mutton with mountains of white bread, huge square chunks of cheese and heaped dishes of beans, washed down with neat wine and milk. A considerable minority wanted to add roast thrush, tunny and eels, but the rest of us were not convinced, despite their eloquence.

But when at last we were close enough to see the men on the shore, we started to worry. They didn't look like a conquering army somehow; more like a crowd of slaves just coming out from a shift in a big workshop, or down the silver mines. Only a few ran out to meet us; the rest just stood and watched, without moving, as if we were a vaguely interesting spectacle but nothing to do with them; and those that did come seemed to be shouting something about food, and which ships were carrying it, and did we need any help unloading it? So instead of jumping out into the sea and wading or swimming ashore, we waited until the ships had stopped moving and the taxiarchs told us to disembark.

I recognised a face among the men standing on the

beach – Callippus, a man from Pallene from whom I had once bought a diseased goat – and as soon as I had answered to my name I slipped out of line to talk to him. I greeted him cheerfully and asked him how things were.

'Terrible,' he said, without any visible emotion – he seemed totally uninterested in any of what was going on – 'particularly after the sea-battle yesterday.'

'What sea-battle?'

'I forgot, you won't have heard,' he said. 'The Syracusans heard you were coming and attacked us, twice. The first time they didn't get very far, but yesterday they hammered us. For God's sake,' he suddenly shouted, 'they don't fight *fair*.'

I stared at him. 'What do you mean?' I asked.

'You won't believe this,' he said, lowering his voice. 'The Syracusans kept us fooling around all day, sending their ships out and then drawing them back, until our men had got thoroughly bored and gone back to base for their dinner. Then they come roaring out, this time for real, and our men rush away from the cooking-fires on to the ships, starving hungry – the Syracusans timed it beautifully – and try to get into some sort of order. There's a god-awful mess, and while the ships are fighting each other in the proper way, they send out hundreds of little boats full of javelin-throwers and archers and shoot up the crews of our ships, while we just flounder about like beached whales and can't do a thing about it. They sank seven ships and damaged I don't know how many more. It was total chaos. Did you ever hear the like, Eupolis? You just can't fight these people, on land or sea. They don't stay put and they don't fight *properly*; they just shoot at you and run away.'

'Don't worry,' I said soothingly. 'We're here now. Demosthenes won't take any of that stuff, you'll see.'

'Sod Demosthenes,' said Callippus, 'what can he do? These men are savages. They don't fight like we do. They're really vicious, I tell you; they aren't interested in winning battles, they're interested in killing people without getting killed themselves. It's inhuman.'

15

'Demosthenes will make them fight,' I said. Callippus laughed sourly and shook his head.

'Did you bring any food on those ships?' he asked. 'We're starving to death here.'

'You can't be,' I replied. 'For God's sake, you're the besiegers.'

'Tell them that,' he said, waving his hand in the direction of Syracuse. To be honest with you, I hadn't really looked at the city – that sounds very strange, but I hadn't. I looked now; it was just a city, with walls and a gate. 'Do you know they hold regular markets in there? With merchants and fishmongers and sausage-sellers and everything? We're down to a couple of pints of flour a day out here. They throw their crusts over the wall for us, and we actually go and pick them up.'

I felt as if whatever I was standing on had suddenly given way. 'You're exaggerating,' I said. 'It can't be as bad as all that.'

'It's going to get worse,' said Callippus, grinning unpleasantly, 'with you lot to feed as well. I take it you haven't brought any food.'

'We thought . . . for God's sake, this is the richest country in the world. Where's all that wheat and cheese?'

'Good question,' replied Callippus. 'But Nicias has managed to get the whole of Sicily against us, somehow or other.'

'Can't you bring anything in by sea?' I asked.

'Of course,' said Callippus impatiently. 'We get things from Catana and Naxos, just enough to keep us from starving. No more.'

'But this is terrible,' I said.

'Yes.' He grinned again and walked away, like a man going to a funeral. I went back to our ship and told my friends what I had heard. They had been told the same, many times over. Meanwhile, Nicias' men had got bored with us and had mostly wandered away, making us feel like fools.

I remember one time someone got up a rumour – completely untrue – that the King of Somewhere Else had sent the Athenians a present of a million bushels of wheat,

16

and it was being handed out to all adult male citizens in the Market Square. Of course, I jammed my feet into my sandals and sprinted off as fast as I could; and sure enough, there were crowds of people milling around with big jars on their shoulders. The only thing that was missing was the wheat, which (like the King of Somewhere Else) did not exist. Even when the point sank in, we stayed there for some time – the general feeling was that the Archons ought to open up the granaries to compensate us for our disappointment. Anyway, that was what it was like, that day we landed in Sicily.

So there you are, commander of a huge and useless army; your men are demoralised and have nothing to eat, the enemy is in a strong defensive position with no incentive to come out and fight, and has just beaten you at sea. What do you do? Attack, of course.

Demosthenes had seen that the only way to break into the city of Syracuse was by going over the slopes of Epipolae, which is a large rocky hill, roughly triangular, on the other side of the city from the sea. It wouldn't be easy; but we would either take the city or prove that the job was impossible – and either way, we would all soon be going home.

So, after a miserably hungry night, we set off early next morning to damage such olive trees and vines as Nicias' men had overlooked, down by the river Anapus; apart from a few bored-looking light infantry, we saw no enemy soldiers and had a pleasant enough time – we even caught a couple of skinny-looking goats, which we converted into an approximation of food. I was particularly struck by Little Zeus' attitude to the laying waste of crops, bearing in mind his Herculean efforts to squeeze a living out of the hide of Mother Demeter. After the first hour or so, he seemed to go absolutely berserk; he had got hold of a big double-headed axe from somewhere, and he fell upon a small plantation of fig trees like mad Ajax killing Agamemnon's sheep. So strenuous were his efforts that he quite wore himself out – and he broke the axe, missing the trunk of a tree with the head and so striking the shaft against the wood and

17

smashing it in two. When I asked him what had got into him, he confessed that he hated fig trees; he always had, and he always would.

What with the goats, and smashing things up, and stretching our legs after all that time on board ship, we all came to the conclusion that fighting under Demosthenes was much better than work. In fact, the only man who didn't seem to be enjoying himself was Callicrates, who was always far too sane and well balanced a person to come to any good end in this life.

While we were busily occupied in this manner, Demosthenes had been attacking the outlying fortifications of the Syracusan position with battering-rams, without any success at all. Most people are terrified of battering-rams; the noise of them, and the way they make the ground shake, and the fact that, being tree-trunks, they cannot be killed. But the Syracusans were quite blasé about it all; they threw burning torches on to the hide canopies that protect the men operating the ram from arrows, and then shot the men down as they ran away. It was all rather humiliating; and when Demosthenes sent some heavy infantry forward to try and recover the rams before they were burnt to ashes, they shot arrows at them too, until the weight of arrowheads in their shields made them too heavy to carry, and they had to withdraw. A few men were killed; but they were Zacynthians and Corcyreans, so nobody was unduly upset about it.

In fact, Demosthenes had only done these things – ravaging the countryside and making his attack on the outer defences – to satisfy himself that they were pointless, and to make the Syracusans think that he was as unimaginative as Nicias. What he really had in mind was something utterly Athenian in its daring, novelty, and sheer ambition. He had made up his mind, as soon as he first set eyes on Epipolae and learned that the Syracusans had three large camps up there, to attack the position by night. After all, nobody had ever done such a thing before, so it would be totally unexpected. In the dark, the Syracusans' local knowledge would be useless; and, above all, so would their arrows, javelins and slingshots, about which he had heard

18

so much. Once we were inside the wall, the enemy would be utterly terrified, not knowing where we were or what we were up to, just as the defenders had been at Troy when the Greeks came out of the Wooden Horse. We would keep in touch with each other by shouting secret passwords, and this would terrify the Syracusans even more.

When we were told of this, we didn't know what to think; but the sheer cleverness of it all so caught our imaginations that we could scarcely wait until nightfall. Although most of us were exhausted from all the work we had done during the day, we couldn't sit still to rest, for we were all too excited. One thing was certain; this was quite unlike any other campaign anyone had ever been on before. No marching all day with a heavy sack on one's back, or building endless walls for no very good reason, or tramping up and down outside impregnable walls wishing one was somewhere else. There was a feeling of being involved in something very special and important, and everyone was talking, very quietly and intensely, to everyone else – not just their neighbours and friends and relatives, but people from the other side of Attica whom they had never met, or even to the foreigners. We all suddenly felt that Demosthenes was a friend of ours, someone we knew personally – and still our leader, of course; in charge and somehow incapable of failure. It was like being a child again, and being in one of those gangs of herd-boys who elect a king and execute daring raids on other people's orchards; there was that same thrill of taking part in something daring and exciting, with a strong dash of danger about it but no real fear of death or injury. It's hard to imagine grown men feeling that way. Perhaps it was because the whole City seemed to be there; it felt more like a festival or a holiday than a military expedition, with so many of one's friends and neighbours present. There were plenty of strangers, of course, but you felt that you were bound to know someone who knew them. As it started to get dark, we lit our camp-fires and moved around like an army going to bed, and as we did so we kept running across people we knew, friends and distant cousins and the like; I met five or six men who had been in choruses of mine, and many neighbours, and (needless to say) Aristophanes son of Philip. He was creeping furtively round the back of a tent with what looked like a baby in his arms, and when I called out his name he jumped high in the air.

'For God's sake,' he hissed, as he recognised me, 'what did you want to do that for?'

'What have you got there, Aristophanes?' I demanded. 'You're acting very strangely.'

'Since when have you added informing to your list of accomplishments?' he muttered. 'Go and play with the Syracusans, there's a good boy.'

It suddenly occurred to me that Aristophanes' baby might be a wineskin. 'Let me guess what you've got under your cloak,' I said loudly.

'If you must know,' he said, 'it's a dead play. One of yours, by the look of it. You know, stunted, off-colour, never expected it to last as long as it has. I'm going to give it a decent burial, if there are any compost-heaps in Sicily.'

'Give me a cupful and you can bury it in peace,' I offered.

'Vampire,' replied Aristophanes. I held out my cup and he filled it.

'Where did you get this from?' I asked.

'Sicily,' he replied. 'Haven't you got anything better to do?'

I drank the wine and left him to it. Then Demosthenes himself came hurrying by, in his red cloak and gilded armour, and I stepped aside to let him pass. He turned his head as he went past and said, 'Hello, Eupolis,' just as he had that day in Athens, when I went to see the Council. Before I could reply he had passed on, and I stood watching him in the light of the camp-fires; a man always busy, always doing something, always striving to be the best, as a true hero should. 'Where the hell are those stone-masons?' I heard him shouting. 'And has anybody seen the Chief Carpenter? Come on, I haven't got all night.' Other men came running up to him, and their cloaked backs hid him from me. Then someone called my name from inside one of the tents. I put my head round.

'I thought I recognised you,' said Nicias. 'It's a long time since we met.'

I didn't know what to say. Ever since we arrived in Sicily, Nicias had been a sort of bad joke that nobody could resist repeating, me least of all. It was very strange to see him, joint General of this mighty enterprise. He looked very ill, and he wasn't wearing his armour. He was sitting on a little cedarwood stool with a pile of wax tablets on his lap, obviously working out some tiny discrepancy in the lists of supplies that nobody but he would have worried about.

'Good evening, General,' I said. 'Aren't you coming?' I must have made it sound like a party, for he shook his head and said he hadn't been invited.

'I'm to stay here with the reserve and look after the camp,' he said, and to my amazement there was bitterness in his voice. 'It's just as well,' he went on. 'I would only be in the way. Demosthenes would be sure to consult me on points of tactics, and what could I say to him?'

I was in much the same dilemma, and so I kept silent and fiddled with the buckle of my sword-belt.

'It won't work,' he said at last. 'Demosthenes is a fool.'

That was more than I could stand. 'You should know,' I blurted out – for I was an Athenian and a voter, and I could say what I liked. 'It's just as well you're not coming,' I went on. 'Much better to let Demosthenes save your skin for you.'

He wasn't angry or even offended. 'Is that what your chorus will say when you get home?' he asked. 'That Nicias let the bull out of the pen, and Demosthenes had to get it back for him? Shall I tell you something, young man?'

'If you like, General,' I said insolently.

'The Athenians elected a fool,' said Nicias slowly, 'for a fool's errand, and the fool made a mess of it, for he could do nothing else. Then the Athenians elected a clever man for the fool's errand, and he will be a greater fool than the experienced fool, since he does not know the work. They should have left the fool to fall over and break his neck.'

21

I began to feel very uncomfortable. There was obviously something very wrong with Nicias, to start him off talking like a drunken oracle, and I didn't want to know. I backed away and hurried off, feeling as if I had just seen a ghost. Soon after I ran into Callicrates and Little Zeus, and we filled in the rest of the time until the first watch, which was when we were due to set off, by looking for Aristophanes' wineskin. We found it in the end, as it happened, stuffed under a thorn bush, but by then it was too late to do much about it; so we emptied it out and filled it with water, and put it back exactly where we had found it.

Chapter Three

Oddly enough, I rarely have nightmares about Epipolae now. Shortly after my return I used to have them all the time, but they faded after a year or so and were replaced with a composite nightmare that dealt with a wide variety of issues. While they lasted, however, they were extraordinarily vivid, and were some of the few dreams that I have ever been able to remember after I have woken up. This is highly relevant to the account I am about to give of that adventure; for after all these years I cannot reliably distinguish between my actual recollections of the geography of the battle and the slightly amended and amplified version in the nightmare. So if one of you knows the place well and objects that I have put in a sheep-fold where no sheep-fold has ever stood, or littered an otherwise bare escarpment with gratuitous and wholly unfounded olive trees, I must ask you to keep your erudition to yourself. My Epipolae bears the same relationship to the real Epipolae as, say, Homer's Achilles bears to the real man, whoever he was. The loss in accuracy is more than adequately compensated for by the author's exquisite handling of the theme, and all alterations are strictly necessary for legitimate literary purposes.

Shortly after the first watch we received the order to move out, and we dragged our way up the steep sides of Euryalus, trying to make as little noise as possible. The sound of a large and excited army making as little noise as possible is quite deafening on a quiet evening, particularly if you are terrified, as we all were, and the prospects of getting such an enormous gathering of people past the enemy without being noticed seemed poor, to say the least. But I suppose we must have managed it somehow; certainly I saw no sign of any Syracusan forces. Mind you, I had enough trouble seeing my own feet, despite the relatively bright moonlight, so I am hardly qualified to pontificate on this point. Every time that I, personally, trod on something that made a noise or dislodged a loose stone, I expected to hear a roar of enemy voices all around me, but it was not so. Whether I would have been able to hear an enemy attack above the noise of several thousand Athenians trying to be quiet is another matter entirely.

We didn't so much attack the Syracusan fort that was our primary objective as trip over it. In fact, we went past it twice looking for it and had to turn back, and the man next to me, a part-time carpenter from the north of Attica, was muttering something under his breath about sending someone down into Syracuse and asking the way when suddenly there it was, a vaguely circular pile of heaped-up stones like an overgrown goat-pen, outlined against the dark blue sky.

I had been expecting something slightly grander – the taxiarch had talked about 'forts', and I had conceived a picture of a miniature Persepolis, with castellated walls and gateways flanked by carved lions – and the sight of this ramshackle structure cheered me considerably. Anyway, I think Demosthenes was so delighted at finding the wretched thing, after all that frantic searching, that he abandoned his siegecraft (he was, as you will remember, the expert on assaulting fortified positions), yelled out something like 'Right, let's *get* the bastards!' and went scampering off in the general direction of the wall. We followed him as best we could; and since it appeared that it was now permitted to make a noise, we started screaming and whooping like a Chorus of Furies.

I can well imagine how those Syracusans must have felt. They were almost certainly asleep; and you know what it's like when you're woken up unexpectedly and asked to take some frightfully important decision. Your mind refuses to operate; you stand there trying to collate certain preliminary facts, like who you are and what is going on. Then, as soon as a coherent scheme of action forms in your brain, you follow it, however inappropriate it may be. The Syracusans' reaction, as it happens, was perfectly logical; they ran like hell. Unfortunately for them, they ran straight into a detachment of our forces under the general Eurymedon which had got separated and come up on the other side of the fort, apparently still trying to find it.

From what I have heard since, it seems that the Syracusans assumed that the mob of soldiers milling about below them were reinforcements of their own from the city, and so ran to meet them. The Athenians, for their part, took the men coming towards them to be Athenians sent out to find them – certainly they had no idea that they were Syracusans, the results of their searches for the fort having led them to believe that the species was extinct in those parts. So each unit trotted eagerly across to the other and asked it what was going on; and I am told that they had been chatting away for some time before one of the Syracusans noticed that the man he was talking to spoke with a funny accent and stuck a spear clean through him.

After that there was a disorganised sort of a fight, in which matters were not helped by the fact that by this stage nobody knew who anyone else was; then most of the Syracusans slipped away and ran down to the main Syracusan camps to wake up their colleagues. As soon as the taxiarchs managed to part the Athenian and Corcyrean contingents, who were beating hell out of each other under the impression that the other was the enemy, the detachment hurried up to the fort to see if there were any Syracusans left in it. Regrettably, Demosthenes had in the meantime got to the fort, discovered the way in (after several exasperated circuits), found it unoccupied and occupied it. Thus when the victorious Athenians came dashing up and found it full of human beings they quite naturally assumed that the position was still being vigorously defended and attacked it with arrows and javelins. Since we Athenians are not terribly handy with such weapons little actual harm was done, and the mess was quickly sorted out by the general Menander, who was about the only person on our side who could cope with the darkness. He was a great sportsman in peacetime, and his favourite occupation was long-netting hares at night, which trains a man for this sort of work.

My part in all this was fairly straightforward; I simply followed the man in front of me as if I was Eurydice being rescued from the Underworld by Orpheus, found myself inside the fort just as Eurymedon's men came charging up at us, and sat down under the wall with my shield held over my head until somebody told me that it was safe to come out. Since several javelins and a large rock had come sailing over my part of the wall in the last few minutes I needed quite a deal of persuasion, which eventually the taxiarch administered with the toe of his boot.

Demosthenes had by now realised that night-fighting was rather different from day-fighting, and held a quick conference with his officers. It was no good (he said) just blundering about and hoping to identify the enemy by their Dorian accents. Not only was this method both time-consuming and unsoldierly, it was also unreliable, since many of our allies spoke in the Dorian dialect, while many of the Syracusans' allies spoke Ionian like us. What we needed, Demosthenes said, was a password, and the password would be *Victory!*, unless anyone had a better suggestion. The officers agreed that *Victory!* would do to be going on with and set off to tell the men. There was a great deal of sniggering from the soldiers, which did not bode well for the rest of the operation, and we reformed into files and set off to attack the Syracusan camps. By this time I had located Little Zeus and Callicrates, and we practised saying the password together until we were word perfect.

I think Demosthenes' idea had been to come down on the Syracusan camps without any warning and massacre them in their beds. This would have been a good idea had it worked, but unfortunately it required the presence of the Syracusans in their camps to be one-hundred-per-cent successful, and by this time the Syracusans had left their camps and come out to find us. In this they were not entirely successful. For our part, we had no trouble at all in finding the first Syracusan camp, and we charged it, in perfect formation and with remarkable cohesion, only to find there was nobody there. Of course, I had had many similar experiences of dropping in unexpectedly on empty houses after dinner-parties, and was not unduly distressed; I knew perfectly well that we would all meet up later on at someone else's place. But Demosthenes seemed rather put out, and so we stayed where we were.

I gather that the Syracusans eventually got tired of looking for us, accused the survivors from the fort of making the whole thing up, and went home to bed. By this time, Demosthenes had resolved to go out and have another shot at finding the enemy, and the two armies bumped into each other a short way from the camp. We charged – what we charged I am not quite sure – and met with surprisingly little resistance. It transpired that we had missed the enemy completely, and as we were coming back the Syracusans charged us. Unluckily for them, they didn't know the password, and so we were able to identify the mass of heavily armed men running towards us and throwing javelins as the enemy and beat them off. Of course when I say 'we', I am speaking collectively; the celebrated Eupolis was wedged in the middle of a file and only vaguely aware of what was going on. For a short while I was very frightened, for I could hear the screams of men being hurt and I had never heard that sort of sound before. Apart from my experience in Samos (which was entirely different) I knew nothing about what it was like in a grown-up battle, and I suddenly realised that a great many people were in danger of serious injury. I was reminded of the time when I had seen a nasty accident in the street – some men were knocking down a house and some bricks fell on to a group of men walking underneath; one of them was hit on the head and screamed quite horribly until they took him away, and it unnerved me for days afterwards. I found my first experience of an infantry action similarly distressing, and when the enemy had gone away I found that I was shaking all over. I particularly remember seeing a man who had had his hand cut off – accidentally, by one of our own men, which can't have made it any more pleasant for him – and being struck by the unreality of it all. He looked so strange without a hand on the end of his arm where a hand should be, and he was shouting and sobbing quite terribly, saying that this couldn't be happening to him, since he had a farm to work and nobody to help him. I felt a sort of impulse to say that he should be used to running the place single-handed by now; I'm glad I didn't say it, but somehow it was very difficult not to. I suppose my terror was turning into jokes inside my head, which is what usually happens to me when I get frightened. Of course, the Spartans are great ones for this sort of humour (although they are rather better at it than me), and everyone says that it proves how brave they are, that they can crack jokes in the midst of suffering and death. I think it proves exactly the opposite; but I may well be wrong on this point.

Well, as soon as the Syracusans had gone away – they had got considerably the worst of the encounter – we pulled ourselves together and went plunging off after them. There was a great shouting of orders from our officers, and for all I knew these may have been very good, sensible and constructive orders; but I couldn't hear a word of them through the padding of my helmet, and neither, I suspect, could anybody else. Nor could we see any signals or even the other parts of the army, let alone the enemy; so we did the logical thing and followed the men in front of us. As a result, I suppose, the front of our lines was pushed forward and stumbled onwards in no particular direction, and soon the detachment I was with began to have a horrible feeling that nobody knew where we were or what precisely we were supposed to be doing. We blundered on, yelling out the password at the tops of our voices; and I guess that the Syracusans must have worked out the significance of the word *Victory!* bellowed loudly and with no great conviction by the all-conquering Athenian army, because they started shouting it too, from all sides. As soon as we heard it, we were delighted and moved off in that direction to meet up with our own men, only to find small but ferocious groups of the enemy rushing down on our flanks and rear and making our lives distinctly uncomfortable. Thereafter we took the shouting of the password as conclusive proof of the shouter's hostile intent, and charged immediately. The result of this was some extremely bitter fighting between the Athenians and the Athenians, which the Athenians eventually won.

They tell me that it was the enemy's Theban allies who turned the battle, standing up to a powerful Athenian force and driving them back. If this is so, all credit to the Thebans, who are by and large a race of homicidal maniacs and quite capable of heroic action. Personally, I don't believe there was any need for valour on the part of the enemy; their contribution to our defeat was, it seems, largely peripheral. As well as the password and the impossibility of hearing orders, there was the incredible mix-up over the Victory Song. As you know, whenever an army wins an action (and quite often when it doesn't) it sings the Victory Song, and all Greek nations use more or less the same words and tune; but Dorian-speaking nations such as Syracuse naturally sing in Dorian, and Ionian-speaking nations like Athens in Ionian. Now our Argive and Corcyrean allies were Dorian speakers, and quite early on they pulped a contingent of the Syracusans' Siceliot allies – this was by no means difficult, as the Siceliots are a timid people – and lost no time in striking up the old, familiar melody. The Athenians behind them (of whom I was one) heard the sound of delighted, bloodthirsty Dorian singing, naturally assumed that the Syracusans had won a crushing victory over the men in front, and immediately formed themselves into a posture of belligerent terror. The Corcyreans, having disposed of all resistance in front of them, quite properly fell back on their own lines, and were greeted with an Athenian charge of considerable force – that was us, all resolving to die like men – accompanied by the Victory Song in Ionian combined with frequent reiterations of the password. The Victory Song confused our stout-hearted allies at first; but as soon as they heard the password they knew that the men coming towards them must be enemies, and retaliated with all their remaining strength. To add to all this, as soon as the taxiarchs had managed to part the two sides and formed them up to march onwards, one bright spark of an officer contrived to march his company off the edge of a cliff, with fatal results for most of his men.

As soon as the news of that percolated through, most of the Athenians came to the conclusion that the expedition was no longer a good idea and that the sensible thing would be to go back to the Athenian camp as quickly as possible. Unfortunately, this proved to be rather more difficult than anyone imagined. To start with, nobody had the faintest idea where they were, and few people were willing to go blundering about in the middle of a battle asking the way home. There was also the small matter of the Syracusan army, which had been in just as much of a mess as we were, but which had somehow gathered itself together and was now busily engaged in killing Athenians. I believe that by this stage the Syracusans had chosen a password of their own, but had intelligently decided not to go about shouting it at the top of their voices. As a result, the only Athenians to hear it didn't live long enough to communicate it to their fellows, and the Syracusans were able to distinguish between friend and enemy, to a certain extent at least.

The unit I was with was one of the first to start moving out, and by immense good fortune we set off in roughly the right direction. We tramped along at a great rate, firmly ignoring any human voices from any direction, and eventually found ourselves on the path that we had originally come up. Unfortunately, there was a solid line of men blocking it, and although in the moonlight it was impossible to make out anything beyond silhouettes, it stood to reason that any contingent blocking the only escape route from the battlefield was quite likely to be Syracusan.

By now, our taxiarch in charge of our unit (a man from the east coast called Philo) had gone completely to pieces and refused to have anything more to do with the exercise of command in the Athenian army. This suited the majority of us, who had not been unduly impressed with his achievements so far, and we held a sort of impromptu Assembly, at which various opinions were voiced. Two main parties quickly evolved; those in favour of attacking, and those who supported the idea of trying to get round the side of the enemy line without being noticed. The pro-attack lobby pointed out that there *was* no way to get round the enemy, since they straddled the narrow strip between two steep and rocky slopes, and anyone trying to go round would almost certainly fall to his death. The opposing faction, to whom I devoutly belonged, replied that the Syracusans were mighty warriors and invulnerable and would certainly kill us all if we attacked and, further or in the alternative, these people would probably turn out not to be Syracusans at all but Athenians, as had been the case all night, and that it was a terrible thing to kill one's fellow citizens. Much to my regret, the pro-attack lobby won the day, and we lumbered off at a slow charge to break through the enemy line.

In the event we went through the Syracusan line like a stick through soft clay and made a pretty horrible mess of those fools who tried to stop us. As I'm sure you know, fighting in those days was more a matter of pushing and shoving than skilful manipulation of weapons offensive and defensive, and besides outnumbering the Syracusans we were so frantic with fear and general unhappiness that nothing much short of a mountain could have stopped us. Most of the enemy broke and ran before we got to them, and those that didn't were simply rolled into the ground and trampled to death. In fact, I can remember treading on a man myself – I hope he was Syracusan, though of course many of our men went down too, tripping over or being shoved, and they were killed just as surely. The man I trod on had lost his helmet, and I looked down just before I got to him, to see his face staring up in terror at me. There was no way that I could avoid him without risking being pushed down myself by the great mass of men behind me, so I looked away and pressed on. As my foot landed on his face I heard a loud crack, even through my helmet, which

I think must have been his nose. I think he screamed too, though it may have been someone else.

I was nice and snug in the middle of the formation, and although I had been separated from Callicrates, Little Zeus was beside me, as he had been all evening. He had been taking the whole thing in his enormous stride, apparently only upset because he had not hitherto had a chance of saving his benefactor's life and so paying off at least part of the great debt he felt he owed me. It should have been reassuring to me to have such a large and strongly built companion, but it wasn't, somehow. We had reached the path that led down from Epipolae, which was confoundedly narrow, and were starting to feel relatively secure when the formation seemed to bump into something and tried to stop. This was, of course, impossible; we had picked up a fairly considerable momentum by now, and the threat of being trampled made any movement other than trotting forward extremely hazardous. What had happened was that we had run into the back of another Athenian unit; but of course we weren't to know that, especially in the middle and rear of the column, where you can't see a thing except the back of the neck of the man in front of you. We all assumed that the front of the column had been charged by the enemy, and started pushing with all our strength. It was about then that the real and actual enemy, who had reformed behind us after we had pushed through them, and of course knew all about the narrowness of the way down, came thundering up behind us and started carving up the rear of the column. There was absolutely nothing that any of the Athenians could do about this, particularly the ones being carved up; we were all wedged tightly together, with no hope of turning round or using our shields or weapons. Instead we instinctively pushed forward against whatever was in front of us, while the impetus of the enemy attack behind us hit us like a hammer striking a piece of metal on an anvil. The man in front of me lost control of his spear, and I was jolted forward on to the butt-spike of it with such force that the spike went clean through my breastplate. I had no idea whether or not it had also gone clean through me, and no real way of finding out, since I couldn't move my arms. What I did know was that if anyone else pushed me from behind I would undoubtedly be spitted like a thrush, and this would do me no good at all. Since the only part of me which I could move was my head, I used it to bang on the head of the man in front to get his attention, and tried to explain the damage his spear was doing; but of course I couldn't make him hear me. Just in time the idiot must have realised that his spear sticking out like that was a public nuisance and pulled it free; a moment later, I felt a terrific thump between my shoulder-blades and was hurtled forward, so that my nose ended up buried in the hair of the plume of the man in front.

I lost my footing and went down, instinctively trying to roll up into a ball and feeling that this was my just punishment for trampling on that man's face. But the whole column had by now come to a dead halt, and apart from some fool standing on my ankle I came to no harm. The men in our rear had finally realised that they were being attacked by Syracusans and were desperately struggling to turn round. Most of them managed it at last, but only by ditching their shields and spears (which would have been useless anyway in that terrible crush), and managed to keep the enemy off them by grabbing hold of the shafts of their spears and pushing them aside. Fortunately, there was no room to draw a sword, let alone use one for its ordained purpose; and, anyway, by now the Syracusans' progress was halted by the mound of dead or near-dead bodies that had been built up by their enthusiastic efforts. The whole extended column – two Athenian units and one detachment of Syracusans – had come to a standstill, with no realistic prospect of ever getting disentangled. To add to the confusion, another force of Athenians trying to get away from the battle had come up behind the Syracusans, and was happily demolishing them just as they had demolished us.

What had been holding everybody up was another Syracusan force, quite a small one, which had earlier been sent to block the path. Into this the Athenian unit in front of ours had run, and up till now they had been unable to shift the enemy in front of them, because of a similar build-up of dead and wounded men to the one which was now guarding the rear of my unit. Eventually, however, this dam had been burst by the sheer weight of people pressing down on it, and the Syracusan unit must either have broken and run or been pushed out of the way down the slope. Whatever it was that happened, the column started to move. The result was, of course, total and utter chaos, with everyone scrambling over each other in their hurry to get down to the level ground. I had just managed to lever myself back on to my feet when I was knocked over by someone hurrying past. I grabbed at Little Zeus to break my fall; luckily he was quite stable on his feet and was able to drag me on with him until I could get back into my stride. I dropped my spear, of course, but at that moment I could conceive of no more useless item of equipment in the entire world, and was heartily glad to be rid of it. I did, however, cling on to my shield, which I felt might well come in useful at some later stage in the proceedings.

What happened then I do not know. Part of the column in front of us came to a sudden halt – I think the path got narrower a little further down and this had caused a bottleneck – while the rest of us kept moving. As a result, Little Zeus and I were stranded and unable to move, while men from the ranks behind us came surging past us down the hill. I was uncomfortably aware that the enemy weren't that far behind, but there was nothing I could do without risking being trodden into the mountainside, so I stayed where I was. After a while I saw my first close-up view of the Syracusan enemy *en masse*, and it did little to cheer me up. It was possible to tell them from the Athenians this time from the way in which the Athenians of our unit were hitting them and they were hitting back. I drew my sword and tried to turn towards them, but I confess that fighting was the last thing in my mind at that moment.

Then a man – an Athenian rushing down the path – tripped and collided with me, nearly knocking me over again. He grabbed hold of me to steady himself, and his helmet fell off. It was Aristophanes, the son of Philip. I

34

cannot pretend that I was pleased to see him, since he had knocked most of the breath out of me and the Syracusans were nearly on top of us now, being driven down on to us by the Athenians above them. I tried to push him aside but he wouldn't let go of the rim of my breastplate, which is what he had grabbed hold of, and we wrestled there for a moment; me trying to fend him off with my shield, and him refusing to be fended. He had both hands on me – he had discarded his shield and spear – and apparently saw me as a sort of altar at which he could take refuge. Just then, the Syracusans started washing round us, and one of them aimed a blow with his sword at Aristophanes' bald and unprotected head.

I often wish, for the sake of the development of the Athenian Comic drama if for no other reason, that I had minded my own business at that point. If the Syracusan had killed Aristophanes, Aristophanes would of necessity have let go of me, and I could have joined in the escape with no further interruptions. But, like a fool, I put up my sword to parry the blow, and the weight of it jarred every muscle in my body. Aristophanes saw what was going on and let out a loud shriek, which seemed to do something to the Syracusan; I don't think he would have bothered us any further if my fellow poet had kept his mouth shut. As it was, the Syracusan took another mighty swish, this time at me, and succeeded in cutting the plume and plume-holder clean off my helmet. I tried to hit back but couldn't reach him. Then Aristophanes compounded his many felonies by letting go of me and running for his life. I lost my balance and lurched forward, received a dreadful glancing bump from the rim of the shield of another fugitive, and saw my Syracusan letting loose a third blow at me which I was in no position to parry. I felt it glance off the side of my helmet, shaking the brains up inside my head until they must have started to froth. The Syracusan realised that I was still alive and must have come to the conclusion that I was immortal, for he made no further attempt to do me violence and I was able to put my shield between his sword and my merrily vibrating head. As far as we were both concerned, the encounter was at an end.

That was when Little Zeus decided to intervene. He had had troubles of his own to contend with, I think, and had only just become aware of the risk to his beloved Eupolis. Anyway, here at last was his chance to save my life, and the mere fact that I was no longer in any sort of danger wasn't going to stop him doing it. He jumped on the Syracusan with a roar like a lion and lunged at him with his spear. The Syracusan tried to get out of the way but wasn't quick enough, and the spearpoint went through his forehead and out the other side, splashing a fair quantity of his brains over me. Little Zeus jerked his spear free, waved it jubilantly in the air, and set up a shout of triumph that must have been audible on the other side of Sicily. In his excitement he quite failed to notice the other Syracusan standing immediately behind him, at least until he stabbed him in the throat. Little Zeus fell silent in mid-yell – I think his windpipe was severed – and collapsed in a heap. The Syracusan left his spear in the wound and was swept away down the path before I could even think of trying to attack him.

I stood there for a moment, with another man's blood and brains all over my face, wondering what on earth was going on. I felt completely numb and detached, as if I was invisible, like one of those gods in Homer who goes unseen through the throng of battle. Everyone knows that he and his friends and the people he knows will die sooner or later, and after a while the thought recedes to the back of your mind, being a problem that must be faced when the time comes. But you feel that you at least have a right to some notice of such an event, to give you time to prepare your mind for it. Now during the course of that night it had frequently occurred to me that I myself might get killed; but the thought that someone else, Little Zeus or Callicrates or any of my other friends, might get killed had not occurred to me at all, and the sheer surprise of the thing left me totally bewildered. I honestly have no idea of how I got down off Epipolae that night. I don't think I had any trouble with the enemy; I'm sure I would remember something like that. I think I just stood there for a while, then walked away down the path. My brain wasn't functioning at all. I can't claim to have been shocked with grief; I'm not sure I was particularly horrified, although I was by no means used to such spectacles. I simply do not remember what I felt; it's as though the contents of my mind had been wiped away, as marks are wiped off a marble floor with a wet cloth.

Eventually, I suppose, I got back to our camp. I remember arriving there, and I think there were people with me. Anyway, Callicrates was standing by the gate, with a deep cut over his left eye but very much alive. I remember being pleased to see he was still alive, but only moderately; nothing seemed to matter very much just then. It was exactly the feeling I had had during the plague, when I came out of the house and found everybody was dead; it must have been seeing Callicrates standing there that reminded me of it, I suppose. It was almost as if all the time between the plague and this moment had been some sort of dream from which I had just woken up, and that I was on my own again, set irremediably apart from everyone else by the mere fact that I had survived.

Callicrates had come running up to meet me – he was limping, I remember, and it looked as if running was painful to him; I wished he wouldn't do it – and hugged me fiercely. I didn't hug back; I just stood and stared at him.

'Eupolis!' he said. 'Are you all right?'

This seemed a very strange question to me, given that I was so obviously immortal. 'Of course I am,' I replied. 'Why shouldn't I be?'

'You're covered in blood,' he said.

'Oh, it's not mine,' I replied. 'Somebody that Little Zeus killed. That reminds me, Little Zeus is dead. He'll never enjoy his five acres now, poor sod.'

Callicrates stared at me. 'Are you serious?' he said.

'Of course I am,' I replied.

'You said it like you were telling a joke,' Callicrates said.

'He's dead all right,' I told him. 'Saw it with my own eyes.'

For a moment I thought Callicrates was going to be very angry with me – for being so callous, I suppose

– and then I imagine he must have understood how I was feeling, though how he could understand it I don't know. Anyway, neither of us said very much after that; except that I noticed that it was a rather pretty sunrise, and quoted the recurring line in Homer about Dawn, the rosy-fingered, which I detest and which always jars on me when I hear it. I washed my face and hands very carefully, as if it was something else besides dried blood I was washing away, and used a stone to beat out the jagged edge in the middle of my breastplate where the butt-spike had gone through it, so that it wouldn't cut me. Of course, the spike hadn't gone through to my skin at all; how could it? I was immortal after all. I went out to draw my rations and heard that some other friends of mine had been killed too, but the news meant nothing to me; it was like hearing that they had had a moderately good crop of silphium in Libya this year or something equally remote and meaningless.

The rest of the army trickled back in during the course of the morning; our losses had been heavy, since many of our men had gone off in the wrong direction and been ridden down by the enemy cavalry as soon as it was light enough for the cavalry to come out. I remember hearing that one very small allied contingent from a non-Greek city somewhere in the far south of Sicily had been completely wiped out except for a single man, and that for days afterwards he wandered round the camp looking completely lost, since there was no one left alive who could speak his language. I knew how he felt.

Chapter Four

The next day, heralds from the Syracusans came to announce a truce for collecting our dead without hindrance, according to the custom. They also thanked us for the vast amount of armour and weaponry which we had donated to the Syracusan war effort when we ran away; if we had any more, they said, they would be delighted to receive it, for although they now had more than enough for their own needs, including the construction of the appropriate trophies, they could always sell any surplus to their allies the Spartans.

I think the disaster at Epipolae must have turned Nicias' brain for a while. For Demosthenes, who was no fool, saw that we no longer had any hope at all of capturing Syracuse, and that the best possible thing for us to do would be to go home while we still could. The Syracusans were clearly feeling quite unbearably cocky after their victory, and would probably make some attempt to fight us at sea, where we still had a theoretical superiority. But Nicias would have none of it; he said that he wasn't going home without orders from Athens, since he would undoubtedly be tried and executed as soon as he set foot in the City and he was too old and too tired to defect to Sparta. Besides, he had reliable information from Syracuse that the oligarchic faction there (which was still quite strong) was seriously alarmed at the Democrats' ascendancy after the victory, and would be prepared to help us in any way we wanted. How Nicias had heard this, given that it was only a matter of hours since the battle, nobody knew; but he was adamant that he wasn't leading his army back, although Demosthenes could do what he liked. The two of them argued away for hours, with their junior colleagues Menander and Eurymedon contributing such helpful comments as 'There are good arguments on both sides' and 'Don't ask me, you deal with it.'

So we stayed where we were, and whiled away the time by collecting and burying our dead. That was a miserable business, as you can imagine, but for some reason it distressed me far less than it did my fellow soldiers. I did keep well away from the spot where Little Zeus was killed, but otherwise I just got on with the job, which was very hard work, as anyone who has done it will testify. But I do remember that instead of the rather splendid and dignified ceremony which the Athenians generally use when burying their fallen comrades, we simply dug a series of big round pits like granaries and pitched the bodies in; and that we hadn't dug them deep enough, and that in the end we were so sick of the thing that we couldn't be bothered to dig an extra pit to accommodate the left-over bodies, so we just crammed them in as best we could and covered them over with cairns of stones to keep the dogs off. A lot of people, Callicrates among them, weren't at all happy about doing it that way, but for my part I couldn't have cared less.

I didn't even have the heart to kick Aristophanes' head in for him when I saw him the next day, although properly speaking it was my duty to do so. Needless to say, he had got deeply involved in the Impeach-the-Generals Campaign, which was preparing the prosecution and condemnation of Nicias, Demosthenes, Menander and Eurymedon for when we got home. There is invariably such a campaign whenever an Athenian army takes the field; it frequently starts before the first battle has been fought, and in extreme cases has appointed its chairman and governing body before the troop-ships have left Piraeus. Anyway, Aristophanes was in his element, going over the proposed list of charges with some experienced political litigants and polishing up his speech for the prosecution; they had drawn lots for it and he had only got Eurymedon, which must have been a disappointment to him. I rather fancy he had set his heart on prosecuting Nicias or Demosthenes, both of whom he had, in his time, fearlessly championed in the Theatre. Anyway, Aristophanes had the nerve to deny that he had so much as seen me in the battle, let alone been saved from death by my intervention.

Several days passed, and I think Demosthenes managed to talk Nicias round, saying that whatever happened to them their first duty was to the men under their command, whose safety must come first. That was the sort of talk to give Nicias, and soon there was a healthy rumour going round that we would soon be on our way home. As you can imagine, there was general rejoicing at that. The entire army had had enough of Sicily and even the Great Peloponnesian War itself; I think the reaction was so strong because of the tremendous feelings of hope and expectation with which we had all set out, and which had now turned into abject despair. Men started talking about the enemy again (no one had mentioned them since the battle) and a few fire-eaters were already talking about teaching the bastards a lesson next time. As the rumours grew more and more substantial, and only the hardened pessimists refused to believe them, the camp started to come back to life and be recognisably Athenian once again. Assured that they would soon be safe at home, men started saying that it was a shameful thing to be running away like this, and that what they should really do was stay and give it another go – preferably by daylight, and unquestionably at sea, where there had never been the remotest threat to our supremacy. So eloquently did they express this view (being Athenian) that some people were actually convinced by it, and said as much to Nicias. That set him off again; was it his duty to make one last attempt to salvage the pride and good name of his city? Could he be a party to such a monumental act of cowardice? Had the ships' captains made their weekly rations returns? And so on.

But I assume we would have gone, had it not been for the eclipse. That was a stroke of bad luck, I think.

41

Because, as I have told you, quite a few idiots had talked themselves into thinking that we ought to stay and fight at sea, the eclipse was widely taken to be a sign from the Goddess that we were being dishonourable in giving up the fight after one reverse. The longer it went on, the more people started to mutter, and Nicias (who was very superstitious) was quite unnerved.

Now I have my own theory about eclipses, which is as follows. Obviously they are signs from the Gods; I don't have anything to do with the blasphemous fools like Socrates who say that they are natural and meaningless. But my argument is that there is only one sun, and that when there is an eclipse, the sun must be blacked out all over the world. It is therefore highly presumptuous and arrogant of any individual person, group or nation to hold that this particular eclipse is a sign to them as against anyone else. For all we know, the eclipse might be a sign from Hera to the Ethiopians, or Poseidon warning the Odomantians of an impending earthquake. In addition, it is only reasonable to expect that when the Gods choose to warn us they will use several different methods at the same time; an eclipse and a flight of birds, and possibly a prodigy and a malformed sacrificial victim as well, simply in order to let the recipients of the message know that it is intended for them. Otherwise the system would break down completely; people who have nothing to fear would immediately break off whatever they happen to be doing at the time (which cannot be the will of the Gods) while the intended recipients of the warning would take no notice, having learned from experience that the majority of eclipses never have any special significance for them at all. Unless the Gods so arrange things that all the nations of the earth get into trouble and need warning at exactly the same time, I think my explanation is the only rational one.

Be that as it may. The Athenians took this particular eclipse as a positive order from Athena herself not to abandon the expedition, and so the expedition was not abandoned. Nor was it prosecuted with anything remotely resembling enthusiasm, mind you; it just lay dormant for a while as Nicias and Demosthenes went back into emergency session to work out between them, in addition to their more immediate difficulties, the purposes of the immortal Gods.

For their part, the Syracusans had no doubt whatsoever about the significance of the eclipse. It told them, in no uncertain terms, that unless they got a move on and finished off the Athenians while they had them on their knees, they were going to be in severe trouble before too long. It is not inconceivable that this interpretation was the right one. The Syracusans bustled about with their ships, deliberately practising the various standard naval manoeuvres in full view of our forces. Opinions on the quality of the sea-power of our enemy differed in the Athenian camp. Some of us, myself included, believed that they were demonstrating a high degree of skill and expertise which ought finally to dissuade us from any further involvement with them, especially by sea. Those of us who knew or professed to know anything about naval warfare were of the opinion that the Syracusans knew as much about the science of fighting at sea, both theoretical and practical, as various domestic animals of their acquaintance. As might have been expected with a gathering of Athenians, a suitably ingenious compromise was reached between the exponents of both interpretations; namely that the Syracusans were indeed a formidable enemy at sea as well as on land, and that the inept display they had mounted for our benefit was designed to lull us into a false sense of superiority which would provoke us into a disastrous battle.

After a few days of training, they attempted a minor amphibious assault on part of our line, and succeeded in running off many of our small number of cavalry horses. Encouraged by this, they followed it up with a full-scale attack by land and sea. When the order came for our men on land to form up I pushed my way into the front rank, since I was keen to test my immortality theory, which had become something of an obsession with me since the night-battle. I can honestly say that once it was clear that there was going to be a battle, all fear left me; I seemed to feel a sort of morbid calm, and as we marched out towards

43

the enemy I suddenly understood why. They couldn't kill me; I was dead already. I had been dead for days, ever since Epipolae. Arguably I had been dead ever since the plague, except that at the time I had been too young to understand, and had never stopped moving long enough for rigor mortis to set in properly. I said as much to Callicrates, who looked at me most strangely and asked about the blow on the head I had received from the Syracusan whom Little Zeus had killed, so I could see that he could not understand.

The naval part of the battle was an utter disaster for our side, its only redeeming feature being the death, through his own incredible ineptitude, of our general Eurymedon. The defeat was not really mitigated by the fact that our land forces won a comparative victory (in which I, incidentally, played no part at all, since my section of the line was not engaged), in that we managed to prevent the Syracusans from burning those of our ships which they had not contrived to sink, and which had run for the cover of the shore.

It was this defeat, I think, that finally broke the spirit of our army. An Athenian believes in his navy as men believe in gods; and it was as if some ill-natured person – Socrates, say, or Diagoras the Melian – had just conclusively and irrefutably proved that the Gods do not exist. After the battle was over, everyone in the camp seemed utterly dejected. There was no panic or hysteria, just a total acceptance of the defeat. It was far worse than it had been after Epipolae; then, there had been fear and anger and considerable pain, but people had at least been busy, what with burying the dead and plotting against the Generals and looking after the wounded and having bad dreams at night. Now, nobody seemed interested in any form of activity. The dead bodies of our men bobbed up and down in the water of the harbour, but nobody could be bothered to take a boat out and pick them up. Nobody muttered about Nicias or Demosthenes. The wounded men were left to look after themselves, and many of them died – did I mention that our camp was in a fever-trap? – and nobody had any dreams at all, not even dreams of home. I tried to explain to everyone that this was in fact perfectly natural, since they were now all dead too. But such was the general apathy that nobody could be bothered to argue; and when Athenians refuse an argument, you can be sure that something is wrong.

A day or so after this, I was eating my meal (a pint of barley porridge and four olives) in solitary silence when someone came running into the middle of the camp waving his arms and shouting. Several people asked him mildly to stop, since they were trying to sleep, but this only seemed to encourage him. Finally, someone thought to ask him what the matter was, and he replied that the Syracusans were blocking the entrance to the harbour.

It took about half a minute for the significance of this to sink in; then there was the most extraordinary display of panic that I have ever been fortunate enough to witness. I expect you've seen an ants' nest when the woman of the house pours boiling water into it; well, that's the nearest thing I can think of to the Athenian camp at that moment. I was utterly fascinated by the sight, and I remember thinking that all the dead people had suddenly come back to life; which was rather pointless, because if the Syracusans blocked the harbour they would all be dead again very soon. Now I come to think of it, I didn't panic at all; I sat there speculating what a good Chorus scene this would make – like that scene in the *Agamemnon* where the Chorus suddenly loses its unified voice and collapses into a group of gibbering individuals. No one had ever done it in a Comedy; it would be hell on earth to rehearse, of course, but the effect would be spectacular. Then I remembered that I wouldn't be going home to Athens after all, and there would be no more plays, if the Syracusans succeeded in blocking the harbour. It seemed a pity, but not much more.

Apart from myself, the only person who didn't seem to be panicking was a small, round man who was sitting in front of a fire eating a very thin sausage. His tranquillity and the sausage seemed to draw me to him, and I walked over to his fire and sat down on my helmet beside him. He looked at me and returned to his meal, and neither of us said anything for a while.

45

'You don't seem worried,' I said at last.
'I'm not,' he replied with his mouth full.
'Everyone else is.'
'You're not.'
'Yes, but I'm dead.'
'Well, there you are, then. Your worries are over.'
He sounded like a man from the hill country, and I asked him where he lived. 'Here,' he said.
'No, but before that,' I asked.
'Can't remember,' he replied. 'Been here so long,' he paused to swallow a lump of gristle, 'that I just can't recollect.'
'How long have you been here?'
'A very long time.'
'Tasty is it, that sausage?'
'Be even better with a dab of honey. You got any honey?'
'No.'
He had very big hands and forearms, and I guessed that he had once been a smith. He had that way of talking to you without looking at you that is unique to the trade. 'So you're not worried, then,' I said.
'No.'
'Why not?'
'Nothing's going to happen,' he replied.
'What makes you think that?' I said. 'The enemy are blocking up the harbour. That means they aren't going to let us escape. They mean to wipe us out to the last man.'
'They won't manage that,' he said.
'Don't be too sure.'
'They never manage to kill everyone,' he said. 'There's always one or two that get away. There was two men escaped from Thermopylae, so the story goes.'
'And you reckon you'll be one of the survivors.'
'That's right.'
'Why you?'
'Why not?'
Why not indeed? 'Trade you a bit of that sausage for an onion.'
'Don't like onions. Never did. Only thing that grew where I used to live.'

'Before you came here?'

'That's it.'

I leaned forward and pitched a small log on to the fire. All around us, the Athenian army was winding itself up into a thick knot of terror.

'I used to write plays,' I said. 'For the Festivals.'

'Comic or tragic?'

'Comic.'

He looked at me again, chewing vigorously. 'I used to like the Comedies,' he said. 'Never went much on the Tragedies. Couldn't see any point in making up sad stories. Gets you down, that sort of thing. Me, I always look on the bright side.'

'I can see that.'

'The one I used to like best of all,' he said, 'was that Eupolis. He was funny, he was. I liked him.'

'Really?'

'He's dead now, of course.'

'Of course.' I smiled. The smith went on eating his sausage. 'Are you dead too?' I asked.

'Don't talk soft,' he replied. 'Do I look like I'm dead?'

'I just wondered.'

'There's nothing in this world,' he went on, 'that can kill me.'

'Really?'

'Nothing at all.'

'I feel like that sometimes.'

'I don't feel, son,' he asserted firmly, 'I know.'

'That must be a comfort to you.'

He broke off a very small piece of sausage and offered it to me. 'You want to know why I know?'

'If you like.' I popped the sausage into my mouth and chewed. It was obviously home-made, probably out of cormorant.

'When I was a boy,' said the smith, 'my whole family got drowned in a ship. Not me, I swam ashore. Odd, that, 'cos I can't swim. So I get myself apprenticed to a smith, only he gets killed by robbers, and his wife and his sons too. Not me. I hid behind the anvil till they went away. So there I am a blacksmith, with a forge of my own and a

47

little bit of land to scratch away in, and I've just got married and had a family when along comes the plague and kills the lot of them, except me. Well, this is a bit of a facer, but I'm not one to complain, I get on with my business, and now I've got a bit more land that came from my wife and I'm really quite comfortable, except my neighbours won't have anything to do with me. They say I'm unlucky, which is a bit of a joke. I must be the luckiest person in the whole world by now.

'And then I get called up to do my bit in the war, and they put me on a ship, and this ship sinks and I'm the only survivor. I get ashore and fall in with some of our lads, and what happens but the whole lot of them get killed by the enemy – don't ask me which enemy, mind, 'cos I've forgotten. Anyway, there I am in the middle of nowhere wondering what old Death's got against me, when I get picked up by the enemy and taken along to the slave market, where I get sold to a Phoenician and bundled on board his ship. But I had no worries. I knew that ship was going to hit a rock and sink, and I'd be the only survivor; and I was right, too. Laugh? I nearly wet myself. Anyhow, I got back to Athens all right and carried on with my trade, and I've done all right for myself, got myself into the heavy-infantry class and everything. Then when old Demosthenes gets his fleet together he sends out for all the smiths he can get, and they pick me up, though I'm way over the age limit, and here I am. I'm telling you, son, I didn't want to come on this. I really don't fancy being the only survivor out of this lot.'

He made a vast encircling gesture, taking in the whole enormous camp. I shuddered slightly. I could see his point.

'You came the same time as I did,' I said. 'I thought you said you'd been here a long time.'

'It feels a long time, son. Nice talking to you.'

He got up, stretched his arms, and walked slowly away. I spat out the taste of the sausage into the fire and sat quietly for a while thinking of nothing much; then, for the first time since I could remember – that is, since I got off the ship – I started to compose verse in my head. It

48

was good, too, I realised, and I closed my eyes, so that the words would take in my mind and not blow away. I find that my mind is like a threshing-floor. Unless I close the doors of my eyes, the wind carries off the grain and the chaff together.

I found that I was turning the old smith's story into a protagonist's speech, for a play called *The Long Sufferer* or something like that. The plot would come later, or maybe there wouldn't be the usual sort of plot, all politics and the usual jokes. That didn't matter so much; it could just be a play about this extraordinary lucky-and-unlucky man, and how he saw the world, how it was unbelievably cruel to everyone else and unbelievably kind to him. I sat there and built that speech like you would build a wall, first one layer, then another one on top of it; or a pile of apples which has been heaped up too much, and the slave keeps on putting on more and more, so that you stand there waiting for it to collapse, but it doesn't. It was a good speech, as funny as anything I had ever done, and as I heaped misfortune on to misfortune for this extraordinary character of mine, I forgot completely where I was or what was happening.

Then a taxiarch was standing over me and shouting something, and he wouldn't go away, so I picked up my helmet and my shield and went where he told me to go, still hammering out the words of my speech, like the slaves at the mint hammering coins and tossing them into jars. I joined a long queue of men leading to a ship, and I got the impression that the army was being embarked for a big sea-battle, to fight as marines. But just as I was coming to the head of the queue they shouted out that there was no more room; so I sat down on my helmet again and got back to work. I was left in peace for a while, then someone else pushed me into another line of men. I lifted my head after a while and looked out over the harbour, as I groped in my mind for an article of clothing that scanned long-long-short, and saw our fleet moving out from the shore. All the ships were riding very low in the water, and every inch of them was crammed with soldiers. I commanded my mind to hold the speech and started to count the ships, for I had never seen

49

so big a fleet in all my life. There were a hundred and ten.

Nicias appeared from somewhere and started to make a speech to us. He explained briefly what was happening; he had embarked as many men as possible on the ships, and they would try and break down the barrier the Syracusans had put across the mouth of the harbour. If they succeeded they would disembark and the ships would come back for us, and we would all go to Catana. If they failed, we would have to go to Catana on foot.

Then he started talking about honour and our city and freedom and so on, and my mind was just about to wander back to my speech when someone yelled out that the Syracusans were setting sail, and we all craned our necks to see what was going on. Out by the mouth of the harbour we could see the enemy fleet, and there seemed to be a depressingly large number of them, fanning out like the fingers of a hand.

'Oh, for God's sake,' someone shouted, 'they're sailing straight into them.'

He was right. Our ships just went ploughing on, while the Syracusans opened up to receive them. I think Demosthenes (who was commanding) reckoned he could split the enemy in two, break the barrier, and get out into the open sea, where he would be able to turn. The enemy would follow, and he would turn quicker than they expected and be on to them before they could form. It was a typically daring Demosthenean plan, but it was obvious that it wasn't going to work. The Syracusans were too strong to brush aside like that, and our fleet had started to move too late. The enemy ships closed round us like fingers round a stone, crushing our ships closer together. It was brilliant work on their part. At least forty of our ships were trapped in the middle of a huge block, utterly useless, while all the enemy ships were spread out like a net; their ninety ships were engaging only seventy of ours, and ours were jammed and unable to move. They were the rocks and the Syracusans were the waves. In that enclosed space, of course, all our superior skills and seamanship were useless; the Athenians are open-sea fighters and need masses of space to execute their dazzling turns and sail-throughs. But in the harbour it was solid demolition work, like a land-battle on sea. Now I assume Demosthenes had foreseen this, which is why he crammed the larger part of his land forces on to the ships; but of course that was useless too, since the bulk of his forces were trapped on the ships in the middle and could do nothing. But what was worst of all was the way the Syracusans were fighting this land-on-sea battle. The normal way these affairs go is for the opposing ships to grapple on to each other and board each other for an infantry fight. But the Syracusans had rigged up rawhide shields over their ships so that our grappling-hooks would simply slide off; they drew their ships up alongside ours, just far enough apart so that our soldiers couldn't jump aboard their ships, and let loose volley after volley after volley of arrows, javelins and stones. There was absolutely nothing our men could do; there was nowhere for them to take cover since they were all packed tightly on to the ships like horses in a horse-transport. They stood there and the Syracusans shot them, clearing our ships one by one.

'Somebody stop them, for God's sake,' shouted a man near me. 'That's not fighting, it's just killing.'

For a while I couldn't understand; then it started to make sense. It was basically the tactic Cleon had used at Pylos, when his light infantry with their slings and bows had conquered the invincible Spartan heavy infantry, who had no bows and so could not shoot back. I started to laugh, for it struck me as unbearably comic that our own cleverness should be used against us in this way, until somebody got very angry with me and threatened to kill me if I didn't stop laughing. I tried to explain the joke to him, but he couldn't grasp the point. Meanwhile, Demosthenes and his squadron had managed to break a hole in the ring of enemy ships and was running for the shore as fast as possible. The Athenian ships in the centre followed him as best they could, pouring out of the gap he had made like water out of a punctured skin; but the Syracusan reserves were waiting for them and hit them as they came out, and there was a quite awful mess

51

until the Syracusan ring was broken somewhere else and ships started pouring out of there too. Because there was so little room for manoeuvre, particularly with empty or sinking ships all over the place, neither side was able to do anything much; there was just a horribly confused jam. It reminded me irresistibly of a net that has just been drawn up and landed in the bottom of a boat; and the ships were all the fish, heaped on top of each other and thrashing and wriggling furiously.

It seemed to go on like that for hours and hours. I don't know what you would call it; it certainly wasn't a sea-battle. The ships didn't ram each other, they collided, and you could hear the oars being broken off, like the branches of a falling tree; and you could hear the screams of the oarsmen as the handles of their oars were driven back and through their bodies, or they were crushed against the side of the other ship. And then one of our ships would break free and make a dash for the shore, with half its oars broken, perhaps, or a great hole in its side; and our men on the shore would cheer it on so desperately that you imagined that if that one ship got away we would all be saved. And sometimes it made it to the shore, and sometimes a Syracusan ship would catch up with it and rake it with arrows, shooting the oarsmen dead at their oars, so that our ships would suddenly lose speed and come to a pathetic halt or drift round in a circle, struggling like a bird with a broken wing. And some of our ships managed to outrun their pursuers, broken oars and all, and dash across to where they thought they could see a force of Athenian infantry on the shore who would protect them; and they would flop up on to the beach like so many tunny-fish, only to discover that the men they had seen were Syracusans and not Athenians. When they discovered that, they didn't even bother to fight, but simply allowed themselves to be cut down where they stood. And whenever one of our ships was lost, all the men round me would shriek and yell and throw themselves on the ground as if they were completely mad.

Eventually the Syracusans withdrew. I heard afterwards that they had run out of arrows and felt they could achieve nothing more. Our ships were able to limp back to the shore, and every single one of them had dead men on its decks. But just as the battle was dying away, we saw a Syracusan ship being driven towards us by two Athenians; it had somehow got separated from the others and allowed our two to get behind it. The encounter between these ships was a remarkable sight, considering the wretched state they were all three of them in; it was like a fight I once saw between three decrepit old men, who hardly had enough life between them to keep from falling over; yet they were lashing out wildly at each other with their sticks and dealing their puny blows as if they were the Achaeans at Troy. As the ships drew nearer to us, the men around me fell silent, watching the attempts of the Syracusan to break away from its pursuers. For my part, I must confess, I wanted them to succeed, for I could make out the expressions on the Syracusans' faces as they came close in to the shore trying to turn, and they looked so pitiful that I could see no earthly point in their being killed, now that everything had been so conclusively decided. But for once that day the Athenians prevailed, and the enemy ship, after several desperate attempts to turn, ran aground on the beach and was unable to move. As soon as it came to rest, the men around me let out the most ferocious whoop of pure pleasure that you could possibly imagine and splashed out into the shallow water. In a matter of minutes they had turned every man aboard that ship, living and dead, into so many cuts of butchers' meat; including a couple of our Corcyrean allies, whom the Syracusans had fished out of the water earlier on. I distinctly heard these men yelling out who they were, but nobody took any notice, and I was reminded of a bad day in the Assembly or the Law Courts, when the voters get an idea into their heads and refuse to listen to the opposing view.

Just one more thing. A few hours after the battle I went down to the shore to pick up some driftwood for a fire, and I saw the body of a man floating peacefully in the water a few yards out. The shape of the body looked familiar, and my curiosity was aroused, so I waded out and had a look. It was the lucky-and-unlucky blacksmith. There was an arrow wound in his forehead and the fish had already started on him, but it was unmistakably him; and it might just have been the relaxation of the muscles in death, but I would swear he was smiling. As I walked back to the camp with my driftwood I tried to remember the speech I had been composing just before the battle started, but it had completely slipped my mind.

Chapter Five

A week or so ago, just before I started scratching this
narrative down on wax – wax isn't what it was, by the
way; in my young days, it never used to crumble or flake
the way it seems to now, and you could melt it down and
use it over and over again – I found I couldn't remember
some detail or other and decided that I had better check
it; so I walked up into the Market Square to Dexitheus'
stall, to see if he had any copies of a book I had heard
about which dealt with the matters I was concerned with.
I found the book I was after and persuaded Dexitheus to
let me have a look at it for nothing – you will remember
that Dexitheus is the lucky entrepreneur who has secured
the right to copy this great work of mine; and I persuaded
him that it was in his own interests that all the facts in it
should be accurate – and then partly since I had nothing
else to do that morning and partly to irritate Dexitheus, I
stood for a while browsing through some of the other books
he had there, including one about this Sicilian expedition
I am currently describing. As I stood there reading it to
myself, a little old man (I would say he was about my age,
or maybe a year or so younger, but bent up with arthritis)
obviously overheard the words I was saying from the book
and came up to me.

'What was that you said?' he asked me.

'It wasn't me,' I replied, 'it was this book. It's by . . . ' I
turned back to the head of the roll ' . . . Pheidon of Lepcis,
whoever he is.'

'What was it you just read, then?'

I looked back over the page. 'He says that in the great battle in the harbour between the Athenians and the Syracusans, the Athenians lost fifty ships, either sunk in the fighting or rendered useless, and the Syracusans forty. And he says that his authority for this is Sicanus, the Syracusan commander, who counted the wrecks himself and was regarded by both friend and foe as a truthful man.'

'Well I'm buggered,' said the old man. 'Did we really sink forty of the bastards' ships? It didn't seem like it at the time.'

'Were you there too, then?' I asked. And then, quite suddenly, I recognised him and was able to call him by his name: Jason son of Alexides of Cholleidae. Then I introduced myself.

'You owe me seven drachmas,' he replied.

The first and last time I had seen him was on the evening after that battle. He was sitting in front of an evil-smelling fire fuelled mostly by discarded helmet-plumes (which seemed to be rather significant in the circumstances) playing knuckle-bones against himself. To cheer myself up I asked if he wanted a game. He asked if I had any money and I said yes, some, so he proposed stakes of two obols a point. Those were quite high stakes in those days, but since I could see little point in dying rich I accepted and we started to play. Of course he won every point and took off me every last obol that I had, plus the seven drachmas alluded to above. When he found that I couldn't pay the whole amount he was most upset and called me all sorts of uncouth names, and started demanding that I put down my sword and armour as security for the debt. At this point I left rather hurriedly. But he followed me all round the camp, whining on about his seven miserable drachmas, until Callicrates and some of his friends came up and chased him away.

I mention this incident for three reasons: first, because it makes a moderately light-hearted opening for a rather miserable part of my story; second, in the hope that one day Jason son of Alexides will hear this being read and feel thoroughly ashamed of himself; thirdly as a comment on the profound bad taste of the Fates, who allowed men like me and this poisonous Jason to get out of Sicily alive but struck down so many good men there.

To return to my story. After the battle in the harbour the only question that remained was how, if at all, we would be able to get away. Although honest general Sicanus may have been aware that the Syracusans had lost forty of their ninety ships, no one on our side knew that, and when Demosthenes suggested to the crews of our ships that they might like to consider having another go at a break-out the following morning he barely escaped with his life. So it was decided that we should burn our remaining ships and march off over land to Catana, which at the moment represented a sort of earthly paradise to every man in our army. In fact our ships never did get burnt; the man whose job it was thought it was someone else's job, and they were left neatly lined up on the sand for the Syracusans, who thus ended the war, as they had started it, with exactly ninety warships.

The next problem was when we should leave. Demosthenes was for setting off straight away. Defeat had not addled Demosthenes' brains to the same extent as it had those of his colleagues, and he could see that if we set off immediately, not only would the enemy not have time to send out units to cut the roads, but our soldiers would not have an opportunity to burden themselves with all the useless junk that any army, given the chance, insists on taking with it, to the great detriment of its average marching speed. But Nicias flatly refused to budge without first taking full inventories of our supplies and making detailed calculations as to what we would need to get us to Catana without having to rely on finding food by the way. Demosthenes realised that, in his present near-hysterical state, the only thing that would calm Nicias down was a good five-hour burst of heavy book-keeping, and let him have his way. This was a disastrous mistake, of course; but I believe that Demosthenes had a genuine though misguided affection for Nicias, who was suffering the torments of the damned immediately after the battle, and could not bear to overrule him in anything.

So it wasn't until three days after the battle that we finally left that horrible, fever-stricken slaughterhouse of a camp, and there wasn't a single man in the army (except me) who wasn't heartbroken to leave it. For a start, most men were leaving wounded friends there – there was no possibility of taking our wounded with us – and those few who weren't were leaving friends and relatives unburied. Then there was the natural and instinctive fear of leaving a place that was apparently safe and going out into a world that was quite definitely hostile, which was made infinitely worse by the fact that we were leaving our ships behind. An Athenian soldier regards his ships as a small child regards his mother; so long as they are there he cannot truly lose hope, but once he loses sight of them he starts to panic and lose his wits.

Now I come to think of it, there was one particular ship in that fleet which had assumed an almost divine aura; it was obviously quite old, to judge by its design and the way it had been built, and the legend quickly grew up in the camp that it was one of the ships that the celebrated Themistocles had built all those years ago, just before the Great Persian War, and that it had seen service at the immortal victory of Salamis, when it had sunk the ship of one of the Persian admirals. Although this was obviously ludicrous most of us believed it, and by some strange chance it was virtually the only one of our ships not to suffer damage or casualties in either of the sea-battles; in fact, it had sunk a Syracusan ship by ramming in the second battle, and was one of the last of our vessels to retire from the fighting. As a result, we believed in this ship as if it was our patron God, and the thought of leaving it was the last straw for some of our people. In the end, we put the most seriously wounded men into it before we left; and oddly enough most of them survived and got back to Athens, since both the ship and its contents were bought by a rich Syracusan slave-trader who was secretly pro-Athenian. He sent doctors to look after the men, and when the war was over and the State had no further use for the ship, he had it dragged inland to his estate and set up on a platform outside his house, with a carved pillar next to it setting out its remarkable history. There it stayed for a good ten years, until a slave accidentally set light to it and damaged it beyond repair; whereupon it was broken up and the serviceable timbers used to build a cheese warehouse.

The army (I use the term loosely) that trailed away from that camp was over forty thousand strong; larger than the Greek army that defeated a million Persians at Plataea during the Great War. A large part of our force was made up of allies, of course, but it seemed to me that the entire male population of Athens, or all that was left of it, was present in that army, and I was reminded of nothing so much as the end of the final day of the Festival when all the plays have been dreadfully bad.

I marched with Callicrates and his two closest friends, Myronides (who was a distant cousin of ours) and Cyon, who had been in a Chorus of mine. For an hour or so we marched on in silence. Now I come to think of it, nobody had said anything much for days; there had been none of those busy conversations or animated discussions that are a sure sign of the presence of more than one Athenian, ever since the night-battle on Epipolae. The whole camp had been quite unnaturally quiet. But Cyon, Callicrates' friend, was one of those almost irritatingly cheerful people who cannot be miserable for long, and after a while he started humming one of the chorus-songs from the play of mine he had been in, and after a while I joined in too, since the song was one of which I was particularly proud. It was all about Demosthenes, as it happened, and a rather sordid business deal he had got mixed up in many years ago – something about a shipload of seasoned timber from somewhere in the north that he had an interest in – and parts of it now seemed strangely topical; something about Demosthenes being reluctant to abandon his beautiful ship riding on the wine-dark water of the harbour. Anyway, the men around us took up the tune, as marching men will do, and when we came to the end we started at the beginning again. As we sang, we quickened our step to keep in time with the music, and soon we were striding purposefully along roaring out this song of mine about the petty dishonesty of our great general, who was marching boldly at the head of the column, as he always did. I guess the Syracusan outriders who had been following us ever since we left the camp must have thought we had all finally gone quite mad.

But this euphoria didn't last long, and when the song died away we were soon trudging along in silence once more. It wasn't a cheerful sight, that column, and matters were not helped by Nicias son of Niceratus. Noting the despondency of his soldiers, he took it upon himself to hobble up and down the line cheering us along and saying a few words of hope and encouragement in his inimitably grave and pompous style. This was, of course, profoundly embarrassing to every man in the army. For a start, his illness had got much worse since the battle and he now moved very painfully (which many men found quite remarkably funny); furthermore, I don't imagine there were that many men there who would willingly have given an obol to save Nicias' life, after the mess he had got us all into. But he was still our general; and so not many men yelled at him or threw stones as he passed. They simply looked the other way, and spoke loudly to their neighbours to drown out what he was saying, until Demosthenes came rushing down from the head of the column to protect his friend from self-induced humiliation. As soon as they saw Demosthenes, the soldiers started cheering, which only made matters worse for poor old Nicias. For my part I was sorry for him; he was an idiot, and would probably prove the death of all of us, but he had been my producer for *The General* (another disaster, I remembered) and so I felt a degree of loyalty to him. Unfortunately, I couldn't help bursting out laughing when he shambled up to our part of the line and launched into one of his tirades, since he repeated, almost word for word, that celebrated rigmarole of his about men, not walls and ships, making up a city with which he had reduced our rehearsals to a state closely resembling death. My laughter set off the men around me (who didn't know the joke but who desperately wanted to laugh at something) and poor Nicias shot me such a look of pure hatred that I wished the ground would swallow me up. Then he gave up trying to encourage the troops and was helped back to the head of the column. Every man has his evil spirit – some person who always seems to be involved, actively or passively, in his worst misfortunes. Aristophanes has always been mine, and I think that I may have played the same role for Nicias.

I can't remember when we first saw the enemy. As I think I said earlier, there had been Syracusan horsemen watching us ever since we left the camp, and the number seemed to grow all the time, though nobody could say that he had seen them come. But I remember looking up and thinking, There's a lot of them now, where did they all come from? and I think Demosthenes must have had the same idea, because he reorganised our line of march with the baggage-train and the more inadequate parts of our army in the middle and the rest of us forming a sort of hollow square around them. It was a highly intelligent arrangement, now I come to reflect on it, except that we should never have taken so much stuff with us in the first place. It wasn't food we were carrying with us; for all Nicias' fussing over wax tablets, there simply wasn't very much food in our possession.What was slowing us up was such things as supplies of arrows and sling-bolts for the archers and slingers (we had no significant force of either), shovels, trowels, adzes and similar tools necessary for building walls and other operations connected with siegecraft, chains for binding prisoners-of-war, and other essentials such as plunder (not a large item) and the personal possessions of the dead (a very large item).

I do remember, however, that it was two days after we left the camp that the Syracusans first attacked. We were all heartily sick of marching by now; we were hungry and tired and our feet hurt, and many men were sick with fever and dysentery (marching in the company of men with dysentery is not to be recommended as a pastime). I was fortunate enough to stay relatively healthy, but I'm afraid that I showed far less fortitude and courage than many men who were genuinely sick, until I was shamed into pulling myself together by Cyon. He had the fever quite badly but never complained; and once, when I had been whining for several hours about how thirsty I was, he left the line and ran over to the river, which was on our right for a large part of our march, and brought me back water in his helmet. I drank it all and handed the helmet back to him, and then Callicrates started shouting at me and calling me all the names he could think of. Cyon told him to leave me alone, but Callicrates had clearly had enough of me and wanted to say his piece. Of course, when I realised how selfish I had been I tried to apologise, but Cyon wouldn't listen.

That was just before we reached the river Anapus, where the Syracusans were waiting for us. At first we were very frightened, but as we looked around we could see no heavy infantry drawn up in line of battle, only mobs of light infantry and a few cavalry. At once we began to feel better, since every Greek knows that light infantry, being composed of men from the lower orders of society, is rather less dangerous to a force of heavy infantry than a mild shower of rain. We pressed on and waited for the enemy to run away, as we knew they would.

They didn't. They stood their ground until they were within range of us, and loosed off a volley of spears and arrows. Now one expects such things in a battle, but the unwritten rule is that the shooting of arrows and throwing of spears is primarily for the benefit of the thrower or shooter, to make him feel better and not quite so left out of the general fun. They are not meant to be serious contributions to the blood-letting, for the very good reason that a stray arrow can kill a brave man just as easily as it can kill a coward, and that sort of indiscriminate slaughter is downright immoral. The invariable practice therefore, ever since the Great Lelantine War between Chalcis and Eretria in which men first fought on foot instead of from chariots, has been for the light infantry to do their stuff in as cursory a manner as possible. There is generally no actual punishment for hitting someone, but it is regarded as the worst possible sort of clumsiness and makes the perpetrator feel particularly stupid.

After about the third volley, it dawned on us that the enemy were not doing it right. They were shooting and drawing back in relays, and inflicting quite serious losses on our heavy infantry. Demosthenes quickly decided to send out sorties to chase them away, but when he did so they would shoot and retire, not running for their lives as they should have done but pulling back just fast enough to keep clear of our men, so as to draw them forward until their line became disorganised and they were left unprotected by the shields of their neighbours. Then they would dart forward, loose off another volley and repeat the process all over again. Our sorties were very severely handled in this fashion, and Demosthenes called them off. But the only result of this was to encourage the Syracusans, who came in ever closer, until some of our men lost their tempers and broke ranks to go charging off at them; and those men did not come back.

I can't begin to describe the feeling of cold terror that this inspired in us. We had never heard of anything like this, for we could see no way to defend ourselves. It is one thing to accept and come to terms with the fact that you are probably going to die; it is another thing to have demonstrated to you well in advance the manner in which you are going to be killed, particularly if that manner is both new and humiliating and there is nothing at all you can do about it. I think some of us had been relying on a heroic death in battle to make up for the ignominy of being caught up in the worst military cock-up in the history of the City of Athens, and the sight of those Sicilian peasants darting backwards and forwards with bows in their hands like a lot of deer-hunters was more than they could stand. Our men started shouting and cursing at the Syracusans, and throwing things at them. At first they threw stones – they generally missed – and then swords and sandals and helmets and anything they had, which set the enemy laughing. This made matters worse, and there were a number of suicidal charges by individuals and small groups.

Then, almost as a sort of blessed release, we saw enemy heavy infantrymen forming a line on the other side of the river. I don't think any army has ever been so pleased to see the enemy in the history of warfare. There were tears of joy on Demosthenes' face as he ordered us to charge, and we went through that river and through the enemy line like an arrow through a rabbit. Unfortunately, not many of the enemy stayed to meet us, but those we managed to get hold of were chopped up so fine you could have made sausages out of them. But afterwards the light infantry came back, and stayed with us every step of our way until nightfall.

Although we were all exhausted, very few of us slept that night. We started off very early the next morning, I suppose in the hope that we might outrun the enemy; but they were with us again by mid-morning, and their attacks were exactly like those of the previous day. In the end we were forced back to the place we had camped the night before. The food had run out now, and the enemy cavalry made it impossible for us to go out and look for any. The next day we set off even earlier, and reached the blocked pass where we had been turned back the day before. There were heavy infantry waiting for us there, and we ran at them with a will; but the Syracusans had lined either side of the pass with vast numbers of archers and javelin-men who were able to shoot at us from above at short range without our being able to do anything to them, and I was reminded of that time on Samos when a handful of herd-boys with slings had briefly neutralised our column. We gave up trying to force the pass, and fell back over the dead bodies of our own men, both that day's and the previous day's losses. Then, just to add to the misery of it all, it started to rain very heavily, and through the rain we could just make out the Syracusans building a wall at the other end of the pass.

'This is fun,' said Cyon next to me. 'The buggers can't be doing with all this walking about, they're penning us in to murder us.'

But Demosthenes wasn't standing for that. He led the attack himself and threw down the wall, and we went desolately back to our campsite for the second time. The next day we set off in a different direction through open country, but this didn't help matters very much. They still came at us ('For God's sake,' Callicrates kept saying, 'they've got to run out of arrows soon. There isn't that much bronze in the whole world!') and there seemed to be more of them every day. I think that the Syracusans had their heavy infantrymen at it now, throwing and shooting side by side with the serfs and peasants, which was a striking tribute to the levelling power of patriotism but no fun at all for us. We struggled on like idiots for the rest of that day and camped where we could.

But Demosthenes wasn't finished yet. In the middle of the night the order came round to light as many camp-fires as we had fuel for, leave everything except our weapons, and move. Callicrates, I remember, suddenly became very cheerful as we discovered that we were now marching in a different direction; no longer towards Camarina but straight for Catana, which, as I seemed to remember, had been our intention in the first place.

'The only reason they've been chasing us,' he said, over and over again, 'is that they've been afraid we were just pulling out to reform and would come back again. Now it's obvious that we're going home, they'll leave us in peace. They're civilised people, they don't want to kill us just for the hell of it. What earthly good will forty thousand dead Athenians do them?'

Put like that it sounded very reasonable, and I felt greatly relieved. Needless to say, this march by night was not a pleasant experience, bearing in mind what had happened the last time we went out after dark in this war. But Demosthenes had got things sorted out, and had rigged up a simple but efficient system of communications based on runners to keep the army together. Unfortunately, Nicias refused to co-operate – God knows why – with the result that his part of the army got separated from Demosthenes' force and went wandering off on its own. I heard afterwards that Nicias had got it into his head that if he separated from Demosthenes and made a run for it, he might get to Catana while the Syracusans were busy butchering Demosthenes' force; and it's certainly true that Nicias' men got quite some way ahead of us. But I refuse to believe that Nicias would deliberately have done such a thing, and I prefer to think that it was simply confusion and ineptitude.

Be that as it may; the army was now split into two parts, which made us that bit more vulnerable. We thought we would move more quickly without the rubbish we had been carting with us before; but now we had a large number of wounded men with us – the arrow attacks wounded many times more men than they killed, and since the wounded men invariably died sooner or later it made relatively little difference, except that the presence of so many dying men did little to improve our morale – and we refused to leave them behind. Many men attributed our present misfortunes to abandoning our wounded at Syracuse, and they were determined not to make the same mistake twice. So we didn't move significantly faster.

When it became light and there was no sign of the enemy, there was such a feeling of jubilation in the army that you would have thought we were safely home in Attica. We soon reached the sea, and the sight of it cheered us up still further. We may not have had any ships, but we were still Athenians, and the sight of all that blue water somehow made us feel nearer home. We joined a main road, and gradually our speed increased. The general opinion was that Demosthenes would head down this until he came to a river called Cacy-something (I'm hopeless at place names more than two syllables long); he would then turn up country in the hope of meeting up with the savages who were on our side. Apparently they had plenty of cavalry and light infantry, and they hated the Syracusans, and would see them off in next to no time.

The sheer exhilaration of not being chased or shot at made many of us act as if we were drunk; we had had the Syracusans on our backs for four days, and the effect was cumulative. Now that we couldn't see them any more we started singing and scampering along, speculating as to what they were up to and whether they were missing us. We wished we could see the expression on the faces of their mighty generals Hermocrates and Gylippus the Spartan, when they came out to play and saw nothing but an empty camp; and no way of knowing which way we had gone. Being Syracusans, we reckoned, they would immediately accuse Gylippus of letting us escape on purpose (they did, as it happens) and cut his head off (they didn't). We imagined what they were saying to each other right now; for example:

Gylippus: Well, you had them last.
Hermocrates: I'm sure I had them a minute ago. Hell, I'm always losing things; bits of string, old oil-jars, battles . . .
Gylippus: Where did you have them last? Have you looked in your other pocket? I'm sure I gave them to you to look after.
Hermocrates: We could ask Sicanus, he may have seen them. Hey, Sicanus . . .

We came to the crossing of the river Whatsitsname and found that there had been a battle. The Syracusans had built a wall across the road at this point, and obviously Nicias' men had been through it, since it was smashed down and the ground all around it was littered with bodies. There was no way of knowing whether they were dead Syracusans or dead Athenians, but we naturally assumed they were Syracusans. We started cheering and yelling and waving our spears in the air as if we had just won the victory ourselves, and suddenly it seemed to us that we might get away after all. Nicias had left some men behind, and they said that he had pressed on towards the river Erineus, which was a little way further on; he had been talking with some friendly natives, who had assured him that it would be better to turn in there, since that would be a better way into the mountains. The thought that there were friendly natives to give such advice was marvellously reassuring, and we set off towards the Erineus.

We were marching more slowly now, as if the urgency had gone out of it, and we realised we were extremely hungry. And sure enough we came across a large farm with five full barns, and nobody at home except a crazy old woman, whom the family had presumably left for us to kill. Since it was nearly time for the main meal of the day, we stopped and sat down to eat. I remember the buzz of conversation that rose from the army, for the first time in many days; it was like a hive of bees excited by the warmth of the sun after a long period of rain. Someone found where the farmer had buried his wine-jars and we helped ourselves. It was almost like one of those picnics City people love to take up into the country round Phylae. And then we saw them behind us, the Syracusan cavalry. I will never forget how quiet it suddenly became, as everyone, nearly twenty thousand men, stopped talking and eating and just stared at them. It was so quiet that I could hear a hoopoe calling in the far distance, and the wind sighing in the trees. I don't know why, but I knew that this was where it would end. I tipped out the rest of my cup of wine and dusted myself off.

I think Demosthenes was as shocked as the rest of us; but he quickly pulled himself together and tried to form us up for battle, for he intended to fight here and have done with it. But as he paced up and down shouting his orders in that reassuring, slightly harassed voice of his nobody moved; they couldn't be bothered, there was no point. We did finally get up and shuffle morosely into formation, more to please him than with any intention of making a fight of it; but by then the Syracusans had brought on their Chorus, so to speak, all ready for the big number. There seemed to be more of them than ever, an endless line of men, a sort of grey and brown shape.

Demosthenes had noticed a large walled orchard beside the farmhouse, and he reckoned that the walls would provide good cover against the enemy arrows. I don't know how he planned to get out of it, but perhaps he wasn't thinking that far ahead. He led us off and the Syracusans made no effort to stop us; they simply marched parallel to us, watching us as a dog watches a mouse. They waited until we were all safely inside. Then they attacked.

I don't know if you've ever been caught out in a really severe shower of rain, when the water comes hurtling down so hard that it hurts your face when it lands on it, and you take shelter under a tree or a rock, which covers half of you but leaves the other half to get completely soaked. Well, that's what it was like behind this wall, with the Syracusan arrows and slingbolts coming down on us for hour after hour. Not that it was a downpour, after the first few volleys; more a sort of drizzle, since they had given up wasting their arrows on the walls and trees and were only shooting at such targets as presented themselves. Unfortunately Demosthenes had made a slight miscalculation, as to both the size of the orchard and the height of the walls. As a result of this slip (a mistake anyone could have made) we were crammed together so tightly that we could barely move, and the walls were just that little bit too low to offer full protection. Therefore the Syracusans had plenty of targets throughout the day, although they frequently wasted time and arrows shooting men who were already dead. We put our shields up, of course; but quickly they became so riddled with holes as to be useless; and besides, we were too tired and miserable to bear the weight of them.

I had managed to stay close to Callicrates and his friends, and we were huddled together in the same place, right under the wall itself. Being small, I was able to get rather more of my body behind cover than most people; but Callicrates was rather exposed, since he had made room for me. Once I saw an arrow bounce off his helmet and I was terribly frightened for him, but he swore loudly and I knew he was all right.

As the day wore on we all started to suffer agony from cramp, since it was scarcely possible to move; and even if our movements had not been so hindered by the conditions I don't suppose anyone would have dared to shift from where they were. After we had been there about three hours, I nudged Callicrates with my elbow.

'Callicrates,' I said, 'I want to ask you something.'

'Well?'

'You remember when you first found me, after the plague?'

'Yes.'

'What were you thinking, then?'

He twisted his head and stared at me. 'What a peculiar question,' he said. 'I don't really know, to be honest with you. If you remember, I was just back from my tour of duty with the army in Messenia. Philodemus sent me out to find out what had happened to your family, and I found

69

all of them dead except you. I suppose I was feeling pretty shocked; the City was a really horrible sight, in the plague.'

'As bad as this?'

I heard him laugh faintly. 'I don't know. This is rather nastier for me, but it's all men dead and dying here; back then, what really got to me was the women and the children. I think you're brought up to accept that men might die before their time, but women and children are supposed to be protected from that sort of thing. I think the plague was worse, because it was so arbitrary and meaningless. This may be a defeat for us, but it's a victory for them. Someone's getting some good out of this. But the plague . . . '

'I think this is worse,' I said. 'Maybe because I'm old enough to understand now, and I was only a child then.'

Callicrates sighed. 'I never thought I'd have any trouble deciding what was the worst thing I'd ever seen in my life. It's a terrible thing having a choice.'

I laughed faintly. 'I don't know,' I said. 'I mean, it all just seemed to happen. One moment we'd just arrived, and we were going to eat up Sicily and then press on to Carthage and the Tin Islands. Then we lost a battle, and the worst that could possibly happen was that we'd have to go home without taking Syracuse this year. And then there was the sea-battle, and everyone was depressed because we would have to walk to Catana, but there was never any doubt that we'd all get there safely. And now look at us. What happened?'

Callicrates thought for a while, then he said, 'We're lucky men, you and I. We've been present at the moment when the world changed.'

'What's that supposed to mean?'

'Think,' he said gently. 'Out there is an army made up of small men, three-acres-or-less men, or men without any land at all. And in here is an army of ten-acres-or-more men, big men. And the little men out there have beaten the big men; well, that may have happened before, though it's not supposed to. But if you think, the Spartans have been beaten by their helots once or twice; that's not the unique thing here. What's new, what's going to change the world, is that once they've beaten us they don't let us go.' He paused to wipe the sweat out of his eyes; it was getting terribly hot. Then he went on, 'They're going to destroy this army, whatever it takes. I've been thinking about it, since we got cooped up in here, and I can't think of a single instance where it's happened before.'

I couldn't quite follow his line of argument, but I didn't say anything. It was just nice to hear him talking, in that explaining voice that made him sound so intelligent and authoritative. It was like the old days, when I was a boy and he would explain politics to me.

'That's the real point about all this,' he went on. 'Those men don't want to win a battle and set up a trophy and be big heroes. They want to kill us, and they want to do it as efficiently as possible. They know they'll never be heroes; they haven't got enough money to be heroes, they can't afford the armour. But they've got hate. I never knew one nation hate another like that. There won't ever be a peace between Athens and Syracuse, like there's peace between Athens and Sparta every so often, and they join forces to thump the Persians, and the Athenian envoys come back from Sparta and say they're not bad fellows actually, they get drunk just like us and they sing quite well, for foreigners. No, we made a mistake coming here. After this, fighting wars just won't be safe any more. And when that happens, God only knows what'll become of Athens.'

'But didn't we hate the Melians when we killed all of them?' I said. 'And what about the Mityleneans? We voted to wipe them out, only we thought better of it the next day.'

Callicrates didn't answer. I nudged him, and he didn't move. I looked at him, and there was an arrow right through his windpipe. I nudged him again, and his head fell forward on to his chest. It's extraordinary how floppy a dead body becomes. I remember thinking how funny it was; just like a rag doll, which you shake up and down and the arms and legs just flop about. And it was so very strange that I hadn't even heard the arrow hit him. I wondered how that could be, and I wanted to ask him, since he was in an explaining mood. Callicrates always knew the answer to everything.

Since I no longer had anyone to talk to, I nestled down behind my shield and tried not to think for a while. I could hear that damned hoopoe again – obviously that bird wasn't afraid of anything. Perhaps it was asking us to go away and leave it in peace, in that peremptory way animals have. We used to have a cat who would yowl at you when you walked into a room, as if you had no right to be there. It used to aggravate me beyond measure, that cat. And if I could hear the hoopoe, how come I hadn't heard the arrow that killed Callicrates? That was just typical, I thought, I always miss the big event, the moment when they light the sacred flame, or the longest javelin-cast ever at the Lady's Games. I've got up at crack of dawn and trudged all the way into the City to see it, and stood about in queues for hours to get a seat, and then when the moment comes I'm looking the other way or unsealing my wine-jar or something, and the first I know about it is the big shout.

I can't remember how long I was there for after that. My mind seemed particularly clear and sharp, but there was nothing to think about. Then the man on the other side of me turned and looked at me, and I recognised his face.

'Hello, Eupolis,' he said, and I felt as if my whole skin was on fire. 'I told you I would meet you here.'

'So you did,' I replied. 'I had forgotten.'

'You've had other things on your mind,' said the God Dionysus, and he smiled. 'Well, this is supposed to be our last meeting. I expect you're glad to see me.'

'I don't know,' I replied. 'So this is the walled orchard, is it? I've wondered about it a lot, over the years.'

'Is it how you pictured it?' asked the God. Once again his voice seemed to come from all round me. It echoed inside the bronze shell of my helmet, and I could hardly hear myself think.

'No,' I confessed. 'But you didn't explain, did you? You just said the walled orchard, and left it like that.

And I've been in plenty of other walled orchards since then, in Attica and places. I've even got one on my estate at Phylae.'

'This is the walled orchard,' said the God, 'where the old Chorus dances off and the new one comes on. It's a pretty Comedy I've given you to produce, though your Chorus,' and he made a sweeping gesture with his arm, 'look as if they don't want to dance any more. I think it's time they left the stage. They've done their best, I suppose, but they didn't understand the words they were saying. What can you do with a Chorus like that?'

I felt a tiny spurt of anger, despite the presence of the God. 'They danced as well as they could,' I replied. 'Perhaps it's really the poet's fault, for giving them such difficult lines. If the Chorus can't understand them, what will the audience make of them?'

Dionysus laughed, and I thought my head would split. His laughter rolled out over the tops of the trees like thunder, and echoed in the mountains above us. 'Now then,' he said. 'What you must do is this. I don't want my best poet getting killed here in Sicily, so I want you to hop over this wall and run for your life. Catana is over there,' and he pointed. 'Find Pericleidas the fish-merchant; he lives in a big house next to my shrine by the little gate, he'll look after you. I think we may meet again after all, Eupolis son of Euchorus of Pallene. Look for me in a house by the Propylaea, the day after anchovies sell for three drachmas a quart in the Market Square. And remember, look after my favourite poet. I don't want him getting hurt, understood?'

And then he turned back into the man who had been there before, who was also dead; I could see an arrow sticking through his ear. He must have been killed while I was talking to the God.

I took a pinch of dust between my fingers and dropped it over Callicrates' head by way of burial; I didn't have a coin to press into his hand for the ferryman, since I had gambled away all my money with the odious Jason. Then I picked up my shield and made sure my sandals were tied tightly, since I didn't want to trip up, and climbed over the low wall.

My legs were so stiff after being cramped up all day that at first I could scarcely hobble. But when the first arrow hit me, bouncing off the side of my helmet and giving me the fright of my life, I found I could suddenly run quite freely. Actually, I wasn't in the least afraid of being killed, but I reckoned it would be disrespectful to the God to put his clemency to the test by standing there like a straw target while the Syracusans bounced arrows and slingbolts off me.

There was a wide gap in the Syracusan line not too far away from the wall (they had been coming closer and closer all day) and I ran straight at it. Several things hit me as I ran but none of them slowed me down, and I kept well in behind my shield. As I sprinted through the gap I heard a horse coming up behind me, and I remember wondering how Dionysus was going to get me out of this. When the sound was so close that I guessed the horseman was almost on top of me, I turned, dropped down on one knee (just as they tell you to) and put my shield up to cover me. It was a manoeuvre I could never get right on the parade-ground, but just for once I had no trouble at all with it.

The horseman was there all right. He pulled his horse's head round to come up beside me on my right, where my shield wouldn't cover me, but the stupid animal stumbled over something and he lost his balance for a moment. I could see his left armpit and ribs were unprotected, for he was pulling hard on his reins to control the horse, and I stood up and prodded at him hard with my spear. The spearhead went in as far as the socket, just as if there was already a hole there for it to go into, and as he slid off the horse's back I let go of the shaft. As easy as that.

There was no point walking when I could ride, especially since there were other horsemen approaching; so I grabbed the horse's reins and tried to get up on his back. But it was a big horse and I am not tall, and he kept moving about; in the end I had to jettison my shield. This is supposed to be a great dishonour to a man, but just then I couldn't care less. I had finally made up my mind to abandon the horse and keep on running when I managed to get the upper half of my body over his back and scramble into position.

I should have been in a great hurry just then, what with the enemy cavalry closing in round me and everything; but I took a moment to look at the face of the man I had killed. There was a look of such complete and utter disgust on his face that I couldn't help laughing. 'Oh, for God's sake,' he seemed to be saying, 'there has to be some mistake here.' I knew how the poor sod felt; it was truly rotten luck on his part. But how was he to know he was up against the God of Comic drama? I spat on his face for luck – I was feeling a bit full of myself, understandably enough – and pulled the horse round.

I gave him a ferocious kick and he broke into a trot, which wasn't nearly good enough, so I kicked him again and called him by several epithets that Comic poets usually reserve for rival dramatists. These seemed to do the trick, and he burst into a nice easy gallop. He was a good horse, now I come to think of it, though at the time I had no very great opinion of him.

There were at least two Syracusan horsemen after me, but I wasn't greatly bothered. 'Come on, Eupolis,' I remember saying to myself, 'you aren't taking this thing seriously enough.' But my soul refused to listen; after all, what was there to be afraid of? I was totally detached, no longer human.

The horse seemed to know where he was going, and after what seemed to me a grossly inadequate chase my pursuers reined in and turned back. I galloped on for a while, then slowed down to a gentle canter. When I looked round, I could no longer see the farmhouse, or even the tops of the olive trees in the walled orchard. There was nobody except me on the Elorine road, and it was drawing on towards evening on the sixth day since the battle in the harbour.

I drew up to let the horse drink from a little stream, and I found my mind was still sharp and clear. I had a good idea of where Catana was; to get there I would have to go in from the coast and round the mountains near Acrae; I daren't cross them, since Syracuse lay just below them, at the other end of the Anapus river. After that I would have to pass Leontini on my right and cross the Simaethus, before

75

making my way through the flat plains to Catana. Going that way, the distance could not be less than a hundred miles, and all the great cities I would have to pass on the way were allies of Syracuse. My other option was to try and join up with Nicias' men, who were presumably not that far ahead of me up the road. But my soul wasn't interested in that idea. Anywhere where there were substantial numbers of Athenians in this country was not likely to be safe.

The best thing, then, was to make for Catana. I looked up to my right at the mountains, and thanked Dionysus that I had been brought up in the hill country at home. A man can live off the land quite easily in the hills, if he knows how, and can make himself difficult to find. In the plains you can't help being noticed – which is why the plainsmen are so sociable, I suppose, while hill people tend to be more withdrawn and suspicious. I took off my helmet and breastplate and dumped them under a fig tree. They were battered and dented, and I wasn't sorry to be rid of them. I was tempted to get rid of my sword as well, but it had been in the family for many years and I would need something for cutting wood and sharpening sticks. I wrapped my cloak round it so that it wouldn't be too obvious, and tried to remember how you do a Dorian accent. That was another stroke of luck; I had written many Comic Dorians in the past, Spartans and Megarians and the like, and since I'm a bit obsessive about getting my dialects right I had taken trouble to listen to as many Dorians as possible, and practised speaking Dorian at home, which used to aggravate Phaedra no end. I couldn't pass for a Syracusan, of course, or any other sort of Sicilian; but I could probably get by as a Corinthian, and I knew the names of the streets in Corinth from the stories my grandfather used to tell us about his visit there on a diplomatic mission.

This pleasant and reassuring train of thought was suddenly interrupted by the sight in front of me of a man in infantry armour, with his helmet down over his face, running towards me as fast as his legs would carry him. Behind him was a mob of herd-boys, yelling and screaming and waving sticks and stones. One or two of them had swords as well, which they had presumably picked up from dead Athenians somewhere. The running man was plainly an Athenian, and the herd-boys were after his blood. It was rather comic in a way, since the eldest boy couldn't have been much more than twelve years old; but there were at least ten of them, and there was no doubt in my mind that if and when they caught the soldier they could and would kill him. I felt a tremendous lack of enthusiasm about getting involved, but in the end I kicked the horse and rode forward.

'Hey,' I called out in my Corinthian voice, 'what's going on here?'

The Athenian stopped and turned, and the boys stopped too. 'He's an Athenian,' said the tallest boy after a moment, 'and we're going to cut off his head.'

'You can if you like,' I said, as casually as I could manage. 'Bit of a waste, though.'

'Waste?' said the tallest boy.

'Use your brains, son,' I replied. 'They're worth good money, Athenians.'

The child frowned; this had not occurred to him. 'Are they?'

'Forty or fifty staters, easy,' I said. 'You won't get anything like the full price, mind, because this island'll be swarming with Athenians for sale in a day or two. But forty staters is forty staters. It's up to you.'

'Will you buy him?' asked the child hopefully.

'I would if I had forty staters,' I said. 'Only I haven't.'

'I'll take thirty,' said the child decisively.

'I haven't got thirty staters, either,' I said. 'I haven't got so much as a half-stater' – I nearly said obol, but I remembered just in time – 'for the ferry. All I've got with me is this horse.'

'All right,' said the child, 'I'll take the horse.'

At this his colleagues started to protest vehemently, but he shut them up by clouting them with the flat of his sword. 'Well?' he repeated.

'Go to hell,' I said. 'This horse is worth twenty Athenians. And anyway, who said I was interested in buying Athenians? How would I get him home, for a start?'

'We'll tie him up for you,' suggested a smaller child.

'Then how would I transport him, without the horse? Talk sense.'

The tall child thought for a moment, and the other children gazed at him in confident expectation. 'Twenty staters,' he said, 'and that's my final offer.'

'Tell you what I'll do,' I said wearily. 'His armour's worth fifteen on its own. You take that, and I'll give you this ring and bracelet for the meat on the hoof. There's ten staters weight of fine silver in them, not to mention the workmanship.'

'All right then,' said the boy sullenly. 'You lot, get his armour off.'

The other children obeyed this order with relish. They were none too gentle about it either. For my part I pulled off the ring and bracelet. They had been a present from Callicrates. I leaned over and handed them to the child.

'You won't die poor, will you?' he said nastily.

'No, but you might,' I replied. 'You were going to cut his head off, remember?'

They tied a long strip of rawhide round the Athenian's hands and neck and handed it to me. I took it and wrapped it round my wrist, and kicked the horse.

'Which way are you going?' said the boy.

'Acrae,' I said.

'Straight up from here's the best way,' replied the boy, 'and turn left up that cleft in the mountains. That'll take you straight there over the top.'

'I know,' I replied. 'Come on, you,' I snapped at the Athenian, 'or you'll feel my boot up your arse.'

'What are you doing in Acrae?' the boy called after me.

'Wouldn't you like to know?' I shouted back, and rode off away from the road towards the mountains.

As soon as the children were out of sight I jumped off the horse and started to untie the rawhide. It was the first time I'd seen the face of the man whose life I'd saved. I recognised him.

'You're a total arsehole, Eupolis, you know that, don't you?' he said savagely. 'Why didn't you just give them the fucking horse?'

I should have guessed when I saw the bald head emerge from under the helmet. I should have guessed when the God told me to look after 'his favourite comic poet' rather than to look after myself. I should have known he didn't mean me.

It was Aristophanes the son of Philip.

Chapter Six

'Admit it,' Aristophanes said. 'You're lost.'

'If I'm lost,' I replied, 'which I'm not, it would be because I did as you suggested and turned right at the top of the hill instead of left, as those children said I should.'

'If you had turned left,' replied the son of Philip, as if talking to an idiot, 'we would now be in Acrae. We do not want to go to Acrae. They would kill us if we went to Acrae. We want to go the other way. Therefore it was necessary for us to turn right, to avoid going to sodding Acrae.'

'Perhaps,' I conceded, 'what you say is true, although I would be prepared to point out the basic fallacies in your argument if I wasn't so bloody thirsty. But let us assume that you are right. That still doesn't mean we're lost.'

'I think it's my turn to ride the horse now.'

'You don't get a turn. I bought you, remember. I was robbed.'

It was the morning of the second day since the walled orchard, and I had had more of Aristophanes than I could take. One thing was certain. He wasn't going to ride my horse. I would hamstring the animal first.

Aristophanes had been with Nicias' men, and shortly after the armies split up he had got lost in the darkness. He had finally managed to make his way on to the Elorine road, but had slightly misjudged which direction he should take. He had therefore been walking back towards Syracuse for quite some time when he met up with the murderous children. When I asked him how grateful he was to me for saving him from them, he looked extremely surprised and asked me what I meant. Surely I hadn't imagined that he was frightened of a bunch of kids? I pointed out that he was running away from them. Had he been playing a game with them, I wondered? He gave me a scornful look, and said that since they were obviously intent on starting a fight, and since he, having at least some vestiges of decency about him, could hardly start beating up twelve-year-old children, however vicious they might be, the only course open to him was to retreat. Then I had shown up and started interfering. He couldn't do anything then, of course, for fear of blowing my cover as a stage Corinthian. In fact, if anybody had saved anybody's life, he had saved mine. For a while I was at a loss for a reply to this, but then I thought of one. I told him he couldn't ride the horse. I might be under orders from the God to look after this scumbag, but I was damned if I was going to get blisters in the process.

To do him credit, Aristophanes took this very well; and apart from trying to pull me down from the saddle every now and then, he had accepted the situation like a man. Luckily, I had woken up before he did that morning, and was up and mounted before he had opened his eyes. What he had taken an objection to was my very sensible idea that we should continue in the character of master and slave. He couldn't do a Dorian accent to save his life – I auditioned him very carefully, and he was utterly hopeless – and so we desperately needed some reason why a Corinthian should be taking an Athenian towards Catana. The only possible explanation was that he was my slave and that I was taking him to Leontini to sell him at the market there, where there wouldn't be such a glut of Athenian prisoners and I might be able to get a respectable price. And if we were going to play master and slave, it stood to reason that the master would ride the horse and the slave would walk. Aristophanes couldn't think of a (sensible) objection to this, but he continually complained about having to have the rawhide round his neck. It was degrading, he said, and it was giving him a sore throat. Also, he objected, what if I got carried away with my role and actually did sell him as a slave in Leontini? He wouldn't put it past me, and I had to confess that the thought had crossed my mind. I was triumphantly vindicated, however, when we were stopped by a detachment of Syracusan cavalry, although the son of Philip couldn't see it.

'They didn't ask us what we were doing or anything,' he said. 'They just wanted to know if we'd seen any Athenians.'

'There you are,' I replied. 'We were so convincing they didn't feel the need to ask.'

'When I get home I'm going to prosecute you for enslaving an Athenian citizen.'

'When you get home you're going to pay me forty staters.'

'You thieving sod,' he said. 'You only paid ten.'

'I've got to take my profit, haven't I?'

'You're only making the jokes because you're riding the horse,' he said.

By sticking to the slopes of the mountains and keeping the peaks on our right, I knew that we couldn't go far wrong. You may legitimately ask how I came to be such an expert on the geography of south-eastern Sicily; well, I had managed to get a look at a map after the sea-battle. It was a big thing, engraved on a bronze plate and bearing the name of the celebrated geographer Histiaeus, and I found it on the shore, all wet. I imagine it had been in one of the Syracusan ships which got sunk, since I knew perfectly well that no one in our army had such a thing. Eventually Callicrates insisted that it should be handed over to the Generals, but not before we had memorised its contents. Thanks to that map, I was fairly confident that I knew where to head for, and if my estimate of the distance was anything near right, I reckoned that it shouldn't take us more than a week, barring mishaps. All in all, I was reasonably happy about that side of the problem. What worried me was getting there. We had no food and no water, no money and nothing to trade except

Aristophanes' cloak and my sword; neither of which we could sell without arousing suspicion.

'We could sell the horse,' Aristophanes suggested.

'No, we couldn't,' I replied firmly. I had become very fond of that horse. 'If things get really bad we might eat him, but otherwise we'll keep him. Understood?'

'No.'

'Besides,' I went on, 'the last thing we want to do is go into any form of town, village or settlement. That would just be asking for trouble.'

'You're enjoying this, aren't you?'

It was a startling accusation to have to face, and I didn't reply. But there was a degree of truth in it, at that. After the utter helplessness of the sea-battle and the march, it was exhilarating to be one's own master again, to be free. It was almost a pleasure to be daring and take risks, just so long as the risks remained reasonably theoretical.

'There's always plenty to eat in the hills,' I said, 'if you keep your eyes open. We shouldn't have any trouble.'

'Such as what?'

'Berries,' I replied airily. Last night we had eaten the bread out of the dead cavalryman's saddlebag. There wasn't any more. 'Wild figs. Wild olives. That sort of thing.'

'Correct me if I'm wrong,' Aristophanes said, 'but don't figs and olives and berries generally grow on trees?'

'Yes indeed.'

'And can you see any trees? Anywhere?'

'Strictly speaking, no. But we're a bit high up here.'

'So why don't we go a little further down?'

'Because,' I said, 'it's nice and even up here and I can ride the horse. Also it's likely to be cultivated land further down, and that means there'll be people.'

'In other words, we're going to starve.'

'Be patient,' I said. 'There are also rabbits, hares, deer and wildfowl up in the hills. We aren't going to starve.'

Aristophanes expressed grave doubts about this, but I persuaded him that I was right by pulling quite sharply on the rawhide, nearly choking him.

'Sorry,' I said, 'accident.'

As the day wore on, however, and I started to feel

steadily hungrier, I began to wonder if my confidence was well located. We had found several wild olive trees by this time, but there were no olives on them, this apparently being the off year. We found a hive of bees, and we finally succeeded in breaking it open (after being stung rather too often for our liking) but although there was plenty of wax in it there was no honey. We also saw a hare, but the hare saw us first.

'All right,' I said, 'what do you suggest?'

'I suggest we go down the hill,' Aristophanes said.

I considered this. 'Let's compromise,' I said. 'Let's go down the hill later.'

'How much later?'

'This evening, when it gets dark. It might be a bit easier then.'

That evening, we went down the hill. It wasn't a pleasant feeling, coming off our nice empty hillside, where there had been nothing to see except a few goats, into fields and terraces which seemed full to overflowing with chatty farmers. Actually, I don't suppose we saw more than three people, and only one of them spoke to us. He asked us the way to Acrae. But it was still nerve-racking; and when we saw a village up in front of us, I felt decidedly uncomfortable and wanted to turn back. As for Aristophanes, he was plainly terrified. He was sweating profusely and at every sound he would jerk his head round and stare wildly. I think it was the sight of his obvious terror that made me decide to press on.

I cannot for the life of me remember the name of that village; which is strange, because I can picture it in my mind so vividly that you would think I had lived there for thirty years. It had what I suppose might loosely be described as a street, lined with a number of impressively built but dilapidated houses, and at the head of the street was a little brick and thatch shrine. Aristophanes had completely lost control by now, and was quite insistent that we should go and take sanctuary in this shrine. I was not in favour of this proposal. To begin with, I doubted very much whether sanctuary would work in this armpit of the earth, since it is not exactly reliable in places like Athens and Sparta. But even if it did, I could see no prospect of us ever getting out of the shrine once we had gone into it, and I had no great wish to spend the rest of my life, which might be quite long given the history of longevity in our family, in a thatched hut in Sicily. I suggested that we go to the smithy instead, to see if we could get a cup of water and sell the horse.

'Sell the horse?' Aristophanes gasped.

'Oh, so you're not deaf after all. I thought you didn't have holes in your ears?'

Now you don't realise it, but that was a remarkably witty thing to say, since in those days slaves used to have their ears pierced as a way of marking them out from free men. Well, I thought it was funny. Aristophanes didn't; he just told me to keep my voice down. But he was obviously pleased that we were going to sell the horse.

There were about six men at the smithy, and the usual cluster of boys and youths who love the sight of other people working, and they all turned and stared at us as we walked diffidently into the firelight. There was a quite harrowing silence for what can only have been a minute or so (but which seemed longer) during which time I tied the horse's bridle to a tethering-post. Then I tried to make conversation. Unfortunately, somebody had secretly built a mud wall across my throat which stopped the words getting out, and for a while all I could do was gurgle. Finally, I forced myself to say something like, 'Good evening, friends, my name is Eupolidas of Corinth, I'm a merchant passing through on my way to Leontini and I'm taking this Athenian slave with me to sell in the market there, only I dropped my purse with all my money in it somewhere in the hills and so I've got to sell my horse.'

There was another long, long silence, during which the blacksmith laid down his hammer and wiped his hands thoroughly on his tunic.

'Going to Leontini, are you?'

'That's right.'

'Wouldn't do that if I were you.'

'Oh?' I tried to look unconcerned. On reflection, I don't think I made a tremendously good job of it.

85

'No.'

'Why not?'

'They don't like Athenians there.'

'You mean I wouldn't get a good price for my Athenian slave?'

'I mean you wouldn't get a lead stater for your Athenian head.'

That was what I thought he had meant. At this point I should have drawn my sword with a flourish and done something brave, but instead I just melted, like a hunk of cheese left negligently in front of the fire.

'Not in Leontini you wouldn't,' the smith went on. 'Out here we couldn't give a toss.'

I stared at him as if he had just grown an extra ear. 'Oh,' I said, or something equally brilliant.

'Nothing to do with us,' said a large man sitting on a three-legged stool beside the hearth. 'I mean, anyone can see *you're* not dangerous.'

Now you might be affronted by that, but just then I thought that was the nicest thing anyone had ever said about me. I relaxed slightly.

'Mind you,' went on the smith, 'we could probably get a price of sorts for the two of you. Not a lot, of course, but something. Well, for him, anyway.' He pointed at Aristophanes with a pair of tongs. I pointed out, in a voice robbed of conviction by extreme terror, that there would be little point in this, since the market would soon be flooded with much higher quality Athenian slaves, and that he might well find himself stuck with us, eating our heads off at his expense and virtually unsaleable. He gave me a funny look, as if a cut of meat on his plate had just sat up and told him there was too much vinegar in the marinade, and stroked his chin thoughtfully. There was another silence, and I was starting to get nervous again when a little bald man poked me in the ribs with his stick and said, 'So you're Athenian, are you?'

'Yes,' I said.

'Right,' said the old man. 'Entertain us.'

He stretched out that word *entertain* as if it was a piece of dough for a honey-cake and for the life of me I couldn't understand what he meant by it, although some horrible alternatives went through my mind. But the other Sicilians seemed to approve of this idea, and the smith, who was clearly the nearest thing that village had to a First Citizen, told the cluster of boys to run and fetch their parents.

'I know you Athenians think we're just a lot of animals and Cyclopses,' the smith said, 'but we're not. We like the finer things in life, when we can get them. Tell you what we'll do; you give us a good show and we'll give you . . . ' He considered for a moment. 'We'll give you five staters each and a jar of wheat-flour and maybe a few onions. And we'll let you keep your horse. But if we don't like you, we'll sell you to the bosses at the stone quarries. They aren't fussy about the quality of their labour, since it mostly ups and dies on them after a week or so. We'll get maybe thirty staters a head. So are you gonna give us a show or not?'

I still couldn't see what he was driving at. 'What sort of a show?' I asked. The Sicilians laughed.

'We don't care, do we, lads?' said the smith. 'Just so long as it's Euripides.'

Then, suddenly, as if the sun had just risen, I remembered that fat Sicilian who had sat next to me in the Theatre at the performance of *The General*, my first (and worst) play. He had said that the Sicilians were obsessed with drama, and although I had assumed he was exaggerating, as all idiots do, perhaps I had been wrong.

'Euripides?'

'Yeah, of course Euripides. Who else is there worth a dead pig?'

'You wouldn't rather have some Comedy?' I said. 'I know plenty of Eupolis.'

'Never heard of him,' said the large man. 'Aristophanes, yes, I've heard of him. But not who you just said.'

Aristophanes stepped forward; he hadn't opened his mouth up till then.

'It so happens,' he said grandly, 'that I am Aristophanes the poet.'

'You?'

'Me.'

'Well,' said the large man, 'I think your plays stink. Especially the way you bad-mouth Euripides. Euripides is an artist.'

'As it happens,' I said quickly, 'I know Euripides quite well. I think he's our greatest living playwright, and I would be delighted to recite a few lines from his very latest play.'

This was a stupid thing to say, since I knew nothing by Euripides at all, except a few of the really silly bits that every Comic playwright has to know for the purposes of parody. But I knew for a fact that Aristophanes can't keep a speech in his mind for five minutes (unless it's one of his own), so I resolved to try my luck as a Tragic poet, for the first time in my life. As you know, I can improvise verse, and Tragic parody is easier than Comic verse, if anything; if you get into difficulties you just lament, or invoke the Gods, or say that dying is good, but not being born in the first place really beats cock-fighting. These sentiments generally come in ready-to-use units, and while you're getting those past the gate of your teeth your mind is concocting the next few lines.

'What play would that be?' asked the smith.

'*Thersites*,' I said. 'You'll love it, it's a honey.'

'Never heard of it,' said the bald man. 'When was it on?'

'Last Lenaea,' I replied desperately. 'That's why, I suppose. Best thing he's ever done.'

Aristophanes stared at me but I kept myself from meeting his eyes and tried to herd together a few suitable Euripidean clichés. The smithy was full of people now, and there were others hurrying out into the street. When I reckoned that there was no space for any more I gave a signal for silence and stood up.

'Ladies and Gentlemen,' I said, 'I would like to perform for you now— '

'Speak up, will you?' shouted someone from the back.

'Ladies and Gentlemen,' I yelled, 'I would like to perform for you now the debate between Odysseus and Thersites from Euripides' *Thersites*, as it was recently performed in the Theatre of Dionysus in Athens.'

I took a deep breath and plunged in. I was horribly aware that I was composing for my life – I had heard rumours about the stone quarries of Syracuse, and I didn't want to find out whether they were true or not – and that I was by no means qualified to impersonate the celebrated Euripides. To get a little divine assistance, which I felt badly in need of, I started off with a full-blooded invocation by Odysseus to Lord Dionysus. This was difficult; in Comedy you have to be rude about Dionysus, but in Tragedy you have to be terribly polite about all the Gods. Also, I had somehow to stop myself drifting absent-mindedly into Tragic parody. Even a Comedy caesura would give me away, or a misplaced spondee (which you never get in a Tragic line); yet these metrical devices were second nature to me, and I tended to use them without thinking.

I didn't dare look at the audience. If I was laying an egg, the first I wanted to know about it was the blacksmith putting the fetters round my ankles. I just pressed remorselessly on, trying to act the lines as well as say them (I was supposed to be acting another man's work, remember), and kept my eyes rolling and my head moving, like the really hammy actors do in the Theatre. I guessed the Syracusans would like that.

The theme of my debate was Mercy versus Expediency. Odysseus wants to kill a group of Trojan prisoners, to terrify the Trojans. Thersites objects; it may be a really good idea, tactically and politically, to chop one's fellow man now and again, but it's not the sort of thing that pleases the Gods. Since the Gods order our affairs and are quick to punish the wrongdoer, surely Mercy is the true expediency? To which Odysseus replied that by stealing Helen the Trojans have made themselves into the enemies of the Gods, so ripping open a few Trojans would surely not offend them. Thersites then embarks on that old Euripidean nonsense about Helen not being stolen at all; in fact she was spirited away to Egypt, and a replica shaped out of cloud accompanied Paris to Troy. The Gods have punished the Trojans already, making them suffer the horrors of war for the sake of a handful of vapour; and they are punishing the Greeks in the same way for being so warlike as to launch the biggest armada ever seen on the pretext of recapturing Helen but really to carve out an empire for themselves. Well, now both Greeks and Trojans have had a rough time of it, and surely the killing ought to stop.

Well, as you can see this was all blatantly topical stuff, directly designed to speak to the hearts and minds of my audience; then the horrible thought struck me that this *Thersites* of Euripides was supposed to have been written at a time when the Sicilian campaign was no more than a warped little notion at the back of Alcibiades' mind. I changed tack quickly, and started giving Odysseus some clever things to say, all about the integrity of the Gods (dramatic irony) and the nature of Truth. Finally, after several false starts, I managed to find a convincing way to round the thing off, and drew the debate to a close. My mouth was as dry as paper, and I was trembling like a bad case of fever.

Now all authors love applause; there's nothing like it in the whole world. It's a strange thing, the effect it has on you. You can be a dyed-in-the-wool oligarch like that fool Pisander and regard the People as utter scum; or you can be aloof and intellectual – Agathon, say, or Theognis – and pronounce that the man in the street has no culture whatever and is entirely incapable of understanding the brilliance of your work; but the only approbation or praise you value is that of all the oarsmen and sausage-merchants and bath-attendants and carpenters and stone-masons and itinerant harvesters and olive-pickers packed on to the benches in the Theatre. You don't know – or care – what it was they liked; it could have been the costumes, for all you know, or the way the actors delivered their lines (not at one of my plays, probably). But that applause is the thing; that's better than all the compliments in the world from the young men at the baths or the old men at parties. You wouldn't reckon much to your average fishmonger or barber or caged-bird-seller as a dramatic critic; but when his hands join in clapping or he laughs at your joke about the eels, which you've been up all night fiddling with and still don't think is right, then you value his opinion above that of Cratinus himself. And what all this is leading up to is that those swinish Sicilian peasants applauded – how they applauded! – and I can't think I ever tasted anything so sweet. They jumped up and down, and they whistled, and they shouted, and I forgot entirely about the stone quarries and just glowed. Which was odd, considering that Tragedy is not my thing at all and that my performance was not even particularly good Tragedy, now I come to think of it.

The smith belted his anvil a couple of times with a lump-hammer to restore order, and silence fell over the smithy.

'Not bad,' said the smith. 'Now let's have some Euripides, or it's the stone quarries for you.'

I never met a more perceptive man in my life. I could see from his face that he wasn't bluffable; and I couldn't think of any way out of it. So I said, 'I don't know any Euripides. Sorry.'

Aristophanes let out a sort of wailing noise and buried his head in his hands. 'You cretin,' he said. 'You had to be clever, didn't you?'

'All right,' I said, 'you give them some Euripides, if you're so damned smart.' Just then, I thought of Little Zeus, and his *Persians* and his other extracts from The Poets. If anyone could have saved us here it would have been him. That depressed me even more, but I couldn't help smiling, as I always did when I thought of that dear idiot.

'What are you grinning at?' said the smith. He gave me an idea. I straightened my back and resolved to make one last effort.

'You,' I said.

'Me?'

'Yes, you,' I replied, 'the whole lot of you. You don't know you're born. Here you have, delivered into your hands by an overgenerous God, the two greatest Comic dramatists Athens has ever known . . . '

'Who are you then?' asked the little old man.

'I,' I said, 'am Eupolis. Now you haven't heard of me, I know, but that can only be because you've got enough wax in your ears to make candles for the whole of Sicily.

I can see it from here, actually. Don't you *ever* wash?'

That got a good laugh, and I could see I was in with a chance. I took another deep breath and went on.

'You have here,' I said, 'not only the immoral – sorry, immortal – Aristophanes but the even more immortal (and immoral) Eupolis, whose name will be remembered in Athens when the works of Euripides and Aeschylus – and, of course, Aristophanes – have long since been scraped over to make paper for a fishmonger's accounts. You have these two giants of Comedy at your disposal; you may command them to be as funny as humanly possible, or you'll send them to the stone mines. And what do you want them to do? You want them to recite you Tragedy. Gentlemen – I use the term loosely – would you try and squeeze oil out of a grape? Would you milk a stallion? Let us make you laugh.'

There was a cheer you could have heard in Naxos, and I let it run for a moment. Then I held up my hand for silence.

'Well, blacksmith?' I asked. 'What about it?'

'Go ahead,' he said equably. 'Make me laugh.'

'No problem,' I said, and cleared my throat. Unfortunately, that was when my mind went completely blank. I couldn't have scanned an anapaest to save my life. You may judge of my desperation from the fact that I grabbed Aristophanes by the cloak and pulled him on to his feet.

Now Aristophanes is very much a wax-and-stylus dramatist; he thinks by writing, and he's hopeless at improvisation. But I think he realised that this was absolutely our last chance, because he started straight into a dialogue scene. I recognised it as a bit out of his *Two Blind Men*, which is in my opinion the biggest load of tripe ever foisted on a long-suffering audience. Still, words were being said, and my mind slowly started to work. When it came to what I judged was my cue, I was able to nip in with a couple of lines with a joke in them, followed by a rough paraphrase of what I vaguely remembered the character in the play saying. I must have got it completely wrong, because Aristophanes gave me a startled look and for one dreadful moment I thought he was going to dry up; but he threw me back another joke that more or less scanned, and I could see he was improvising too. I had another two or three lines ready and we started to gather a little momentum. There was a slight problem, of course, since each of us wanted the other to be the straight-man; and there was a sort of wrestling-match for the feed which I eventually won.

I can quote you every line from that dialogue, word for word. It was between Aeschylus and Euripides, about which of them was the better poet. They go through all the old chestnuts about each other's works, and then they fight it out on points of metre and prosody. This was to both our advantages, since when we felt ourselves drying up we could quote a snippet or two of the original plays, which gave us a chance to think up the next joke. It tickled the audience, too, since it made them feel immensely erudite, and they followed all the technical stuff like schoolboys – which shows that they really did know their Tragedy, at that. The finale, like the rest of it, was my idea; Aeschylus would have it that Euripides' iambics are so lazily composed that you could fit any old phrase, like 'lost his oil-bottle', into them at any point. Euripides is furious, and starts firing off his best-known quotable lines, the sort of lines that people fire at you in support of the thesis that they don't write 'em like that any more. I was Euripides and Aristophanes was Aeschylus, so all he had to do was fit in 'lost his oil-bottle' at the appropriate point. My job was to find immortal lines from Euripides that could be subjected to this indignity, and this was not easy, since the charge of sloppy versifying was – is – totally unfounded. Still, I managed it somehow, and we got the biggest laugh that can ever have been heard in Sicily outside of a human sacrifice.

Does that sound familiar, by the way? If it doesn't, it certainly should. That scene, word for word, was reproduced by my dear friend Aristophanes son of Philip as his own unaided and original work in his most successful play *The Frogs*, together with a garbled recollection of our (mostly my) wisecracks on the subject of who should ride the horse, which he served up, boiled and hashed, as his opening scene between Dionysus and Xanthias. Our wonderful Greek language has many synonyms for the phrase 'thieving bastard', but none of them seems quite adequate to describe the depths to which that man is capable of sinking, so I shall leave the facts with you and allow you to find your own form of words.

When the laughter had died away and those incapacitated by it had been led away to be calmed down with hot wine and cold water, I turned to the smith and said, 'Well?'

He thought for a minute and then said, 'Me, I'd rather have had some Euripides, but I guess that'll do.' Why does everyone want to be a comedian?

We must have made a hit, because there was actual competition among those Sicilian peasants – who wouldn't normally give you the dandruff from their collars – as to who would give us a bed for the night, a decent meal, fodder for the horse, food for the journey, and even – incredibly – money. Aristophanes got extremely drunk and made quite a nuisance of himself with our host's daughter, so we were very nearly killed after all; but I was too exhausted to do more than eat and smile gratefully, and then sleep. I was certainly too tired to be frightened any more, stone quarries or no stone quarries.

Just before I went to sleep my host came to see me. After spelling out in graphic detail what he would do to both of us if Aristophanes laid another finger on his daughter, he told me that a neighbour of his had just come in from the Elorine road, and had passed a certain farm with a large orchard. He had stopped to ask what was going on there, and he was told that there had been a great battle between the Athenians and the Syracusans. Not that it had been much of a battle, he had been told. Nearly twenty thousand Athenians had gone into the orchard, but only six thousand had come out on their feet; and all of those were now in chains, together with their general Demosthenes, waiting to be marched on to the slate quarries, where Demosthenes would be beheaded and the rest would be kept until they were sold or died. They had taken all the money from these men, and it had filled four shields. Then the army had moved on to deal in the same way with the other Athenian army, under the celebrated Nicias.

I thought of Jason of Cholleidae, and wondered if he was still alive. If so, he hadn't managed to keep my money after all. Then I thought of what Callicrates had been saying, just before he died.

'Why did they stop shooting and take prisoners?' I asked. 'Did the man say?'

'They ran out of arrows,' replied my host. 'Otherwise they'd have killed them all. Sleep well.'

Chapter Seven

The next morning, fairly early, we set off again. Aristophanes said that, since he had a hangover and was in great pain, he should ride the horse, but I persuaded him that this would not be a good idea by kicking him in the head, which seemed to satisfy him, because he didn't raise the subject again for at least an hour.

Our host had advised me that the best way to keep out of sight would be to ride along the side of the mountains about half-way up (which is what we had been doing up till then); that way we wouldn't come across the farmers in the fields or the shepherds up on the top, and so long as we stayed well away from the Acrae side we should be more or less safe. Considering Aristophanes' conduct with regard to this man's daughter I was in two minds as to whether we should take his advice, but I couldn't think of an alternative, so we did. He said we should make Catana in three days, or less if we got a move on and didn't get lost. We had been given more than enough food to last three days, and just over twelve staters in small coin; mostly Syracusan Arethusas, which are acceptable all over Sicily. Somehow this good fortune worried me; apart from our brief brush with the stone-quarrying industry, things were going rather too easily. This fear was starting to get to me by midday, and so preoccupied was I with it that I communicated it to Aristophanes. I should have known better.

'It's all right for you,' he said. 'You're riding the horse.'

96

I said something vulgar regarding the horse, and went back to my worrying. Perhaps anxiety has prophylactic powers, I don't know; but we managed to cover quite a few miles that day without running into any sort of trouble. We found a little hollow in the side of the mountain to stay the night in, and while Aristophanes was taking his sandals off and giving me a detailed description of the condition of his feet, I unpacked the saddle-bags, tethered the horse and went to sleep.

I knew as soon as I woke up that something was wrong. 'Aristophanes,' I said, 'where's the horse?'

'I don't know,' said the son of Philip. 'He'll be long gone by now. You might find him, I suppose, but I very much doubt it. He'll probably have gone off down the hill to the village. I think he liked it there.'

I frowned. 'And how do you think he managed that, bearing in mind that I tied him securely to that tree-root last night?'

'Easy,' replied Aristophanes. 'I untied him, about an hour before dawn.'

'Why?'

Aristophanes shrugged. 'Because I was going to take the horse and ride on ahead. I'm sick of walking. But I tripped over something in the dark and he got away. I was going to tell you, so that we could go after him, but you looked so peaceful sleeping there that I didn't want to wake you up.'

'Well, that's bloody marvellous,' I said. 'Now neither of us can ride the bloody horse.'

'That's what I call democracy in action,' said Aristophanes. 'If I can't have him, neither should you.' I threw a stone at him, but I missed.

We no longer had the horse to bicker about, so we bickered about who should carry what. You will already know what we said if you have ever seen or read *The Frogs*, since Aristophanes filched that too; so I won't bother to repeat it.

We had been walking for maybe three hours when Aristophanes started to complain that he was feeling feverish. I assumed that this was just another variation on

97

the luggage theme and ignored him; but so persistent was he that I had a look at him, and saw that he was showing alarming symptoms of fever. This was the last thing we needed, and I confess that I lost my temper and started shouting at him, although not even Aristophanes would deliberately catch fever just to spite me (or not in Sicily, at any rate). He asked me several times what I intended to do about it, and I replied, truthfully, that there was absolutely nothing I could do except keep well away from him to avoid catching it myself. He seemed greatly offended by this, so to make it up to him I let him tell me the plot of the play he had left behind in the hands of a producer, with instructions to update the topical bits should they become outdated by the time the play came on. It was, he kept insisting, his masterpiece (every play he writes is his masterpiece, according to him), but it sounded pathetic to me – all about a city in the sky and blockading the Gods. But I didn't tell him so, since the fever was getting worse by the hour, and he was starting to ramble in his speech. He went on talking, however, losing his place and going back to the beginning over and over again, until I could cheerfully have brained him with a rock to shut him up. In the end there was nothing for it but to stop and let him rest.

When he was lucid again, I gave him a cup of water (we had very little left, and we hadn't passed a spring or a pool for a long time). He drank it quickly, spilling quite a lot. I gave him some more.

'Aristophanes,' I said, 'I expect you'll suggest to me sooner or later that since you obviously can't make it to Catana and there's no point in us both dying in this miserable place, I ought to abandon you and try and get through on my own.'

'Get stuffed,' he replied. 'You let me die, I'll kill you.'

'I thought you'd say that,' I replied, 'it's a quote from one of your plays. In that case, we've got a choice. I don't know the first thing about what to do when a man gets fever. We can either try and press on and get you to Catana while you're still curable, or we can wait here and hope the fever breaks. What do you think?'

'I think you're a complete bastard,' said Aristophanes with conviction. 'Just get me safely to Catana, will you?'

'So you want to carry on, do you?'

'No,' he replied firmly. 'Get me off this god-forsaken hillside and under cover. If I die, my heirs will sue you for every obol you've got.'

Shortly afterwards he went off his head again, and I could see he was clearly in a very bad way. There was a funny side to it, of course; both of us had survived the Athenian camp, where men were going down with fever wherever you looked, only to get caught with it out on the clean, healthy hillside.

I suddenly got it into my head that it was going to rain, and that could be disastrous. So I draped the food-sacks round Aristophanes' neck and hoisted him on to my back – he was so heavy I could scarcely walk – and set off in the hope of finding some sort of cover. It was nearly dark when I saw a little stone building with light coming from it, surrounded by some of the scrubbiest looking vines you ever saw. I wobbled over to it as quickly as I could and kicked the door hard.

'Go away,' said an old man's voice from inside.

'Open this bloody door, or I'll kick it in,' I said ingratiatingly, and after a while the door opened a crack and a long, pointed nose appeared.

'What do you want?' said the nose.

'This man is dying of fever,' I said. 'I claim the sanctuary of your hearth, in the name of Zeus, God of guests and hospitality.'

'We haven't got a hearth,' replied the nose, 'just a tripod and a hole in the roof. What do you think we are, millionaires?'

That was a tricky one, since Apollo is the God associated with tripods, and Apollo couldn't care less about guests and hospitality. However, I snatched my mind away from the theological niceties of the thing just in time to put my foot in the door.

'I'm a desperate Athenian warrior escaping from a battle,' I said. 'If you don't let me in, I'll chop down all your vines.'

The nose said something unpleasant and opened the door. Now that I could see the rest of him, he turned out to be an extremely old man, once very tall but now bent almost double with age and rheumatism. I felt awful about forcing my way in on him so violently; but this remorse soon departed, for he was a singularly nasty old man.

'There's no food,' he said quickly. 'All my food is *buried*,' he spat the word out triumphantly, as if he had foreseen my coming with the help of some mysterious divinatory art. 'You'll have to kill me first.'

'I've got some food,' I replied. 'All I need is somewhere where my friend can rest until the fever breaks. I'll pay you,' I added brilliantly.

'Pay me?' His little round eyes lit up. 'Silver money?'

'Genuine silver money.'

'Let's see it.'

'Can I put my friend down first?'

He nodded irritably, as if making a great concession. I shifted Aristophanes on to a pile of goatskins on the floor and straightened my back. Sheer bliss.

'Let me see the money,' said the old man.

I took out the linen purse I had been given in the village, turned my back and took out a Syracusan two-stater piece. It was not too badly worn and had no holes or banker's cuts on it; a persuasive coin. I showed it to the old man. He stared at it.

'So that's what they look like,' he said in wonder. 'I'll be seventy-three come the vintage, and I've never seen one of them before.'

I waited for a moment, to give him a chance to fall under its spell, and then said, 'If my friend gets well, you can have it. For your very own.'

That seemed to have a remarkable effect on the old man. He started moving round the house at a terrific speed, tipping out the contents of jars and poking up the fire on the little tripod until it roared. He was mixing something up in a little pottery mortar, and as he did so he sang a song in a language I could not understand. Then I realised he was not a Greek at all but a Sicel, one of the savages who lived in Sicily before the Greeks came. I have had little to do with non-Greeks in my life (apart from Orientals and Scythians, and you quickly get used to them) and he fascinated me from that moment onwards.

At last he seemed satisfied that his concoction was ready. As a finishing touch, he grabbed hold of the she-goat that was standing peacefully in the corner of the room and squeezed a little drop of milk out of her udders into the mortar; then he put it on the grid on top of the tripod to warm through. 'We'll have your friend up and about again in no time,' he panted (for he had exhausted himself with all that running about). 'Just let me see that coin again.'

'Later,' I said. He scowled horribly, and took the mortar off the tripod. Bending low over Aristophanes, he started smearing the stuff all over his face. Luckily, the son of Philip was barely conscious and didn't seem to notice.

'Give him a few hours, he'll be good as new,' said the old man.

'That's not saying much.'

'You what?'

'Forget it.'

The old man frowned, then shook his head. 'I know everything there is to know about fever,' he said proudly. 'Get it myself every year. Nothing to it.'

'That's good to know,' I said. 'Now then, I'm going to need a horse or a donkey or something.' I jingled the coins in the purse. 'Can you help me at all?'

The old man seemed to undergo an inner torment. He seemed to hear the voices of the little coins, imploring him to obtain them and look after them; but of course he had no donkey, and no way of getting one. He gave me such a pitiful look that I regretted raising the subject. Then a smile started to spread over his face, originating somewhere behind his ears and drawing his lips apart, revealing a startling absence of teeth.

'Sure thing,' he said. 'You wait right here.'

He scampered out of the house and disappeared, leaving me feeling highly perplexed. After a while I sat

101

down beside Aristophanes and looked at him carefully. There was sweat pouring out of him, and he was starting to shift restlessly and moan. I wanted to pour water on him to cool him down, or at any rate do something, but I didn't like to interfere. Whatever the stuff was that the old man had cooked up, it seemed to be having an effect.

I must have fallen asleep – I was exhausted myself by then – because the next thing I remember is the old man shaking me violently. At first I couldn't remember what was going on and I was greatly alarmed.

'I got you a mule,' he said. 'Come and look.'

I dragged myself to my feet and followed him out of the house. Tethered to a dead fig tree was the most wretched-looking animal I have ever seen outside a silver mine. You could see at a glance that it still had all its ribs, but apart from that there was little to recommend it.

'This is my neighbour's mule,' said the old man proudly. 'I just bought him. You can have him for four staters.'

I burst out laughing – not as a negotiating ploy but out of pure hilarity. The old man scowled and said all right, two staters. Still sniggering helplessly, I excavated two staters from the purse and gave them to him. When he felt the coins in his hands, he looked like Prometheus receiving fire from heaven.

'Hang on,' I said. 'If you haven't got any money, how could you buy a mule?'

'We don't buy and sell with money up here,' he replied scornfully. 'Money's for keeping. I gave him two hoes and a bushel of figs.'

'You were robbed.'

'That's a good mule,' he whined defensively. 'He'll keep on going all day, and doesn't need much feeding. I've known him since he was foaled, poor brute.'

'You'd better come and look at my friend,' I said. 'He's not well.'

The old man sniggered, and for a moment I felt terribly suspicious. But when we went back into the house, Aristophanes was sleeping peacefully.

'That old poultice never fails. Even works on Greeks,' he added, full of wonder. 'I always thought there'd be more malice in a Greek than it could draw out, so I put in more of everything.'

'He'll be all right, then?'

'Soon enough,' said the old man proudly. 'Mind, if you hadn't brought him to me when you did, reckon he'd have died on you.'

I nodded gravely and gave him the four-stater Arethusa. He took it like a mother receiving her baby from the midwife, sat down on a jar by the tripod and played with it for a while, rubbing grease from his hair on to it to make it shine.

I suppose I should have been sleepy, but I wasn't; and the old man showed no signs of being tired. For a crippled man, in fact, he was unbelievably active. When he had gazed his fill on the profile of our Lady Arethusa, he turned to me and said, 'So you're a soldier-boy, are you?'

'Sort of.' It was many years since anyone had called me a boy.

'Athenian, you say?'

'That's right.'

'That's in Greece, isn't it?'

'Yes.'

He shrugged, as if to say that it was too late to do anything about that now. 'So who're we fighting, then?'

'Us.'

'You what?'

'You're fighting us. The Syracusans against the Athenians.'

He looked at me as if I was mad. 'The Athenians against the Syracusans?'

'Yes. I'd have thought you'd have known.'

'We don't get news here,' he said, and his voice suggested that he didn't hold with news. 'Why?'

'Why what?'

'Why are the Athenians fighting the Syracusans?'

'They felt like it.'

That seemed to satisfy him, for he went back to studying his coin. I was feeling hungry, so I opened the food-sack and poured out some flour into my bowl. 'Have you got any water?' I said, looking pointedly at the three-quarters-full pitcher on the floor.

'No,' he replied.

'If you give me some water I'll give you some flour.'

He picked a wooden bowl off the floor and handed me the pitcher. I gave him some flour.

'What about him?' I said, nodding towards Aristophanes.

'In the morning.' The old man was mixing up his porridge. 'Have you got any honey?'

'No, but I've got an onion.'

'An onion!' Was there no end, his expression suggested, to this man's wealth of strange and delightful luxuries? I cut the onion in half with a small knife that was lying on the floor, and threw half to him. He caught it and bit into it as if it was an apple. 'I used to grow onions till maybe three years ago, but then the seed died.'

'Why didn't you get some more?'

'All the seed died in the neighbourhood,' he replied. 'Maybe they've got some over to Acrae, but I haven't been there in forty years.'

'They've got some at the village a day or so back from here.'

'The hell with it,' said the old man. 'So the Athenians are fighting the Syracusans?'

'That's it.'

'Foolishness, if you ask me. I was a soldier once,' he said, as if he had suddenly remembered after a long time. 'But we were fighting the Carthaginians. That was a long time ago. When I was eight years old.'

'Wasn't that young to be a soldier?'

'We were men earlier then. That was when there were kings in Sicily, in old Hiero's time, or was it Gelo, I forget. That was when the Persians were fighting the Greeks,' he said, as if revealing some great secret. 'But we were fighting the Carthaginians. That was a long time ago,' he added.

'It must have been,' I said.

'It was a big battle,' he said. 'Don't rightly know how we came to have any part of it. I was a slinger, and two of my brothers with me, and my father and my two elder brothers, they were archers. Good ones, too. We went out – oh, must have been two weeks from here, with that old king Hiero or Gelo, and you never saw anything like those

104

Carthaginians. They were strange people, all black-skinned some of them, like olives. We won, too, but my father and my brothers, they got themselves killed and I got my back all messed up, when a chariot ran over me, and that was my fill of the wars right enough. But those Carthaginians – well, I wouldn't have missed seeing them. Did you ever hear of that war?'

'That was the Battle of Himera,' I replied.

'Himera,' he repeated. 'I never knew that before. Himera, you say?'

'That's right.'

'Well I'm damned. I never knew it had a name.' He shrugged again. 'Never too old to learn, hey?' Then he nodded forward and fell asleep. I took another look at Aristophanes and then lay down beside him and closed my eyes.

When I woke up next morning, the old man was exactly where he had been the night before, and I realised that he had died in the night. I found a mattock under a pile of rags and dug a grave outside the door – it was terribly stony ground, and I blistered my hands. Then I laid his body in it and put the four-stater piece in his hand, for the ferryman; it was just as well, I thought, that I had come along when I did, or he would have been stranded on the wrong side of the river for ever. Then I closed up the grave and sprinkled a little flour over it. It was the first time I had ever conducted a burial all on my own, but I think I got it right. After I had done everything I could think of, I went into the house and let the she-goat out.

Aristophanes was sitting up and yawning. 'What's going on?' he said sleepily. I turned on him angrily.

'Now look what you've done,' I said. 'You're nothing but bad luck.'

'The hell with you,' he said. 'I'm starving. Where are we?' I told him. 'That's a stroke of luck,' he said.

'What do you mean, a stroke of luck?'

'Well,' Aristophanes explained patiently, 'all we have to do is find where he buried his food, and we'll have plenty to get us to Catana.'

Just then, I could have killed Aristophanes. 'Get out of

105

my sight,' I shouted. He stared at me, and went outside.
A moment later he came back in again.

'What the hell's happened to the horse?' he said.

'You turned him loose,' I replied, 'remember?'

'No. Why should I want to do a thing like that?' Then he
seemed to notice something. 'Eupolis,' he said, 'what's all
this muck all over my face?'

'You threw up,' I said. 'You'd better wash.'

'Where's the water, then?'

'There isn't any.' I gathered up the food-sack and
went out to see to the mule.

Oh God, that mule. You know what the Pythagoreans
say about the souls of the dead returning to this world in
the bodies of animals; well, that mule must have housed
the spirit of someone who didn't like Comic dramatists
– some Athenian politician, say, or an oversensitive Tragedian – because it took against the two of us from the
very first moment. This was very strange, since it was
obvious from one look at the animal that we were the
first human beings ever to go out of our way to supply
it with such commodities as food and water. But perhaps
it was a diehard Syracusan patriot; at any rate, we got no
co-operation from it whatsoever. In particular I remember
its charming habit of stopping dead in its tracks for no
discernible reason and making the most extraordinary
noise I have ever heard outside a play by Carcinus. It
was also lazy, vicious and lecherous, and had it not
been a reincarnated politician, I could have sworn it
was the embodiment of one of Aristophanes' protagonists
– Philocleon, maybe, or Strepsiades.

But Aristophanes was blissfully happy just because he
was riding and I wasn't, which at least took one problem
off my mind. He was still weak and not much use for anything, but at least he didn't look as if he would die at any
moment (which was how I managed to tell him from the
mule). Now that he was riding at leisure, like a gentleman,
he started up an unending stream of conversation, which
I was unable to take much part in owing to fairly continu-
ous shortness of breath. He told me what was wrong with

Athens, the conduct of the War, the Attic Comic drama, my plays, my marriage, the state of the mountain tracks in Sicily, the mule, the weather, my personality, his intestines, the Athenian commanders in Sicily, the Syracusan commanders in Sicily, Sicily itself, the Gods and the food, with frequent cross-references and recapitulations. By the time we reached the river Terias (which was as far as we could go in the mountains before crossing into the plain) I knew his opinion on every conceivable subject as well as or better than he did himself. I can honestly say that, with the exception of the second book of the *Odyssey*, which they made me learn when I was a boy, I have never learned anything less useful or with more suffering.

We differed in opinion as to how we should tackle the final leg of the journey to Catana. My view was that we should get down to the coast as quickly as we could, then press on and have done with it. There was, I argued, a reasonable chance that anyone we met once we crossed the river Symaethus would be either friendly or indifferent, probably indifferent, and that our one main problem would be to get past Leontini in one piece. Aristophanes, on the other hand, was not worried about Leontini, but doubted very much whether our food and the mule would last us as far as Catana. He therefore wanted to go into Leontini, sell the mule, buy another mule and more food, and stroll onwards to Catana without undue haste. All the Sicilians we had met so far had been helpful and friendly, he said, and since we had money there was no point in starving ourselves and making ourselves ill just for the sake of excessive caution.

I flatly refused to go into Leontini, and Aristophanes refused, equally flatly, to make a dash for the coast. The only possible compromise was to make a stroll for the coast, and that, needless to say, was what we decided to do.

I am not saying that that was the silliest decision ever reached. For example, you may remember that Theseus decided that it would be perfectly feasible to abduct the Queen of Hell, and Icarus saw no reason why he should not fly just that little bit higher and thus enliven his flight to

107

Greece with a better view of northern Crete. I still maintain that it was the silliest decision in living memory, and will need sworn evidence from at least two reputable witnesses before I change my opinion.

We spent our last night on the mountain bickering, and set off early the next day across the plain. It was impossibly hot that day, and the mule had probably remembered something nasty Aristophanes had said about its foreign policy in its previous existence, for it stopped and started as often as a sacred procession in a thunderstorm. We were soon in open country, following what was clearly a main road, and the passers-by (who we met far too frequently for my liking) all seemed to stop and stare at us as we made our irregular way towards the little village on the horizon. I cannot say what most aroused their suspicion, but the fact that we were shouting at our mule in the Ionian dialect must have made them curious, to say the least. Whatever the main reason was, they must have felt sufficiently uneasy to mention us to the cavalry captain at the village, who was out patrolling for stray Athenians making their way to Catana.

We didn't know that, of course, when we made our way past a little grove of trees, arguing with each other about what to do next. Our minds were taken off the problem by the sudden appearance of three men in armour blocking our way.

My first reaction was to scream with terror and run. But one of the men dashed forward and grabbed the bridle of the mule, and said, 'Please God, are you Athenians?' He said it in Ionian.

'Yes,' said my moronic comrade, 'Aristophanes son of Philip at your service. Are you Athenians too?'

I took another look at the three men. They were dirty, ragged and starving. It was a fair bet that they were Athenians. Their spokesman thanked the Gods volubly, and begged us to tell them where Catana was, and whether we had any food.

'Catana is over there,' said the son of Philip, 'and we have plenty of food for all.'

I tried to object to this last statement, but Aristophanes

108

would have none of it, and very shortly we had all retired into the grove and eaten the last few husks out of the grain-bag.

Our three compatriots were Nicias' men, and they had had a rough time of it. After they had devoured everything there was to eat except the mule (to which, as far as I was concerned, they were welcome) they told us their story. Nicias and his command were either dead or captured; they had been caught by the Syracusans and harried down to a river. Because, by that time, the whole army was out of its mind with thirst, the men had thrown down their weapons and crowded into the river to drink, and the Syracusans had shot them while they drank. But the Athenians went on drinking, although the water by now was fouled with blood, and fought each other for possession of it. When the Syracusans had emptied their quivers they charged, killed as many as their stomachs would allow, and took the few survivors prisoner. But fifteen neighbours from Eleusis had managed to fight their way out. Of that number, these three had made it thus far. The other twelve were giving the crows of south-eastern Sicily a rather inadequate meal – inadequate since ten of them had died of starvation. The remaining five had been on the point of giving up themselves when they found a goat wandering on the hillside. After spending their last reserves of energy cornering this goat, they killed and ate it; but the local goatherds saw them and ran down to the village nearby, where a cavalry patrol was resting after a large meal. The cavalrymen came thundering up the hill and killed two of the Athenians, who had eaten too much on empty stomachs and were unable to move; but the three had fought back and driven the cavalrymen off with rocks and their bare hands, and run for their lives. They now had no idea where they were and were desperately hungry again, and they were sure that the cavalry were after them, and would be upon them in the next few hours. So they thanked us tearfully for our food and our companionship, but urged us to get away as quickly as we could.

I was all in favour of this; but Aristophanes wouldn't

listen. I think he had decided that it would be a glorious thing to save the lives of his fellow citizens, who had been fortunate enough to step under his shadow in their hour of trial. He was feeling decidedly cocky, as I have told you, and had come to regard this escaping-through-Sicily business as pitifully easy for a man of his intelligence and talents. He declared that he would not abandon them now, and that if they did exactly what he told them, he would bring them safely to Catana. They stared at him for a moment, then clasped him by the knees and called him their saviour; a scene which I found highly distasteful.

Of course the idiot hadn't the faintest trace of a plan of action, but he wasn't going to admit this to his worshippers. Instead, he ordered them to take off their armour and bury it, which they did most scrupulously. After all, Aristophanes explained as they were scraping over the hole, the enemy were looking for three armed men; they were not looking for five unarmed men and a mule. This appeared to strike our companions as a piece of tactical brilliance worthy of the celebrated Palamedes.

Well, a little later the sun set, and Aristophanes led out his little army. By then he had thought of a plan, and it could have been marginally worse. Aristophanes knew that in Athens a drunken rout is given a wide berth by all sensible people. What better way out of our difficulties than for us to pretend that we were a bunch of drunken revellers, staggering home from a heavy day's drinking at some far-flung shrine? All we needed was a few props – a couple of wine-jars, a wreath or two, maybe a pinewood torch to shove under the noses of any passers-by – and these we could pick up and improvise on our way. The true brilliance of the scheme – according to Aristophanes – lay in the fact that although it is hard to speak a foreign dialect convincingly, it is not too difficult to sing it, particularly if you sing it as if you were drunk.

So there we were; five desperate fugitives singing the only Dorian song we all knew (the Hymn to Apollo by the Corinthian poet Eumelus) as we lurched through the Sicilian landscape trying to remember what it feels like to be drunk. Now I am a fair man, and will not deny credit where it is due, even if it is due to an idiot; so I must tell you that we quite obviously convinced the various travellers we met on the way. They took one look at us and bolted, some of them shouting opprobrious names at us as they ran. Perhaps I should not have been as surprised as I was at the time by the success of this ruse; it is a general rule of human nature that people will implicitly believe that you are drunk if you sing and stagger about. They want you to be drunk; it makes it possible for them to despise you on sight.

What Aristophanes hadn't bargained for (and I suppose there's no reason why he should have) was the edict recently passed by the people of Leontini, as a result of various disturbances in their city, making public drunkenness a criminal offence punishable by a substantial fine. Accordingly, when we reached the outskirts of the village, we were met by the cavalry patrol and the magistrate, who arrested us. The following dialogue took place between Aristophanes, who was riding the mule at the head of our little procession, and the magistrate.

Magistrate: I arrest you.
Aristophanes: Whaffor? We haven't done anything.
Magistrate: For being drunk in a public place.
Aristophanes: That's not a crime, is it, lads? I said, that's not a crime.
Magistrate: Where are you from?
Aristophanes: Leontini. Best little city in the world. Born an' bred in—
Magistrate: You don't sound like a Leontine to me.
Aristophanes: Oh.
Magistrate: You sound like Athenians to me.

That was enough for Aristophanes. He panicked, swiped desperately at the magistrate with his torch, and kicked the mule savagely. Considering his previous experiences with the mule, he should have known better; that miserable animal immediately stopped dead in its tracks and let out a succession of roaring noises that must have woken up

111

half of Sicily. This magistrate – a brave but foolish man – grabbed at its bridle and got the torch in his face for his pains. The cavalrymen drew their swords, and the three Athenians drew theirs and wrapped their cloaks round their arms.

Now I had deliberately chosen to stay at the back of the procession, in case sudden flight should be necessary, and I took to my heels at once. A cavalryman started to follow me, but one of the three Athenians lashed out at him and hit him just above the knee. He howled with pain and rode away, and I don't know what became of him after that. I had turned round, and I saw the cavalrymen chopping those three Athenians down, as a forester clears brushwood. I was all set to make a dash for the nearest cover when I remembered that it was my God-given duty to protect Dionysus' favourite poet. Very, very reluctantly I drew my sword and ran back.

Aristophanes, for once in his life, had done something sensible. He had fallen off the mule. He was thus out of the way of the cavalry when they were busy with the Eleusinians, and by the time I had returned to the battle he had climbed under the mule and was hiding. Now the cavalrymen had not seen me come back, and the magistrate (who was, I suppose, about sixty years old and had just been hit with a burning torch) had stepped out of harm's way and had his back to me. I grabbed him by his hair and put the sword-blade across his throat, and announced in the loudest voice I could muster that I had a hostage and was a reasonably bloodthirsty person. It was not a heroic act, I'm afraid, but then, I am not a hero.

The cavalry captain was clearly embarrassed by this. He was, I think, a local man, possibly something or other in village politics; anyway, he appeared unwilling to risk the life of the magistrate, and called his men off Aristophanes. The son of Philip scrambled out from under the mule and dashed over to where I was sheltering behind a very frightened magistrate.

'All right,' said the captain nervously, 'let him go.'

'Why?' I enquired.

112

'Because if you don't, I'll cut your head off, that's why,' explained the captain.

I pulled the magistrate's hair sharply, which made him squeak like a mouse. 'Be fair,' I said. 'You're going to cut my head off if I let him go. I've always wanted to kill someone in regional government, now's my chance.'

'Let him go and your lives will be spared,' said the captain. The effect of this offer was spoiled slightly by the fact that his troopers – there were ten of them – were ostentatiously waggling their swords at us, and I shook my head.

'Well, what do you want, then?' said the captain, exasperated. 'I can't say fairer than that, can I?'

'Try,' I replied.

'If you think you're going to get away with this— ' said the captain. I gave the magistrate a tiny shove. He obligingly screamed.

'Go away,' I shouted. 'Quickly. Now. Save yourself the trouble of divisive local elections.'

There was a cavalryman who must have been related to the magistrate, or a friend of his, or something like that. Anyway, he pulled up his horse and rode away towards the village. The captain was furious, but he knew he was beaten. 'Let him go and we'll pull back,' he said.

'Piss off and I'll let him go,' I replied. 'Deal?'

'You won't get away with this,' said the captain.

'Oh, I don't know,' I replied. 'Did you ever read *The Telephus*?'

The captain stared at me. 'What?' he said.

'*Telephus*. Very bad play by Euripides. Perhaps it's before your time, I don't know.'

The captain looked at me, and the magistrate, and my Thracian sabre (which, as I think I mentioned before, is a very businesslike-looking implement), thought carefully, and said, 'Yes, I've read *The Telephus*. So what?'

'You will remember,' I said, 'that the hero in *The Telephus* tries this stunt and gets clear away. If some verbose idiot out of Euripides can do it, why can't I?'

I have no idea why, but this exchange seemed to help the captain make up his mind. He got off his horse, signalled to his men to do the same, and started walking backwards towards the village. I started walking backwards in the opposite direction. When I reckoned we had gone far enough, I gave the magistrate a hearty shove and sprinted off as fast as I could go.

It was quite some time before I dared stop running and look round. There was no sign of any cavalrymen; also, no sign of Aristophanes. I threw the sword on the ground and swore. Despite my ludicrous and entirely uncharacteristic bravado, I had failed to save Aristophanes. I sat down on a rock and put my sword away; I no longer cared about the enemy, or anything very much. The recollection of the episode with the magistrate and the absurd threats I had made and the inane things I had said had taken all the spirit out of me and I wanted to go to sleep. I had just made up my mind to go back to the village and give myself up when a very frightened-looking Athenian Comic dramatist came pounding down the road towards me.

'Where the hell have you been?' I shouted. 'God, I was worried about you.'

He didn't stop running; he just carried straight on past me, and I remember thinking, Oh God, the cavalry, and chased after him. Eventually he slowed down and stopped. I came up beside him.

'You lunatic,' he said. 'You nearly got me killed with all that— '

I was tired, I was scared, and I was past caring; but I was not made of stone. I kicked the son of Philip very hard. He gave me a startled look and whined, 'What did you do that for?'

The expression on his face was so comical that I couldn't help laughing. My laughter did not seem to impress Aristophanes very much; he urged me to pull myself together and reminded me that we were quite some way from Catana. That made me laugh even more; I don't imagine Aristophanes has ever had a more receptive audience. In the end he raised his eyes to heaven with a gesture of despairing incomprehension and asked what he had done to deserve all this. I forced myself to stop laughing, grabbed him by the arm and marched him off down the road. We were lost, without food or transport, going in the wrong direction, and the whole of Sicily would soon be out after our blood, but we were still alive. Not bad going, I reflected, for a pair of comedians in a world that undervalues Comedy.

Chapter Eight

We spent the night in a drainage ditch and woke up at sunrise. I suppose I had been hoping that our problems would evaporate overnight, but they were still there when I opened my eyes; and I felt extremely frightened. My trusty comrade was still asleep, curled up in a ball like a little puppy or something equally helpless, and I woke him with my foot.

'Where the hell are we?' he moaned.

'I don't know,' I replied. 'I don't think this is the road we came up yesterday.'

'How would you know?' he grumbled.

'Because we didn't see this ditch yesterday,' I replied.

'What does that prove?' replied the son of Philip.

'Besides,' I went on, 'this is a drainage ditch, right?'

'Could be,' said Aristophanes cautiously.

'Of course it is, you idiot. Now it stands to reason that it drains into something, or leads out of something. Agreed?'

Aristophanes looked at me. 'You've been seeing too much of Socrates,' he said.

'Agreed?'

'If it makes you feel good, yes.'

'Now what could that something be except the river Terias?' I said. 'And the Terias goes to the coast, just above Trotilus. Agreed?'

'You, of course, know where Trotilus is,' said Aristophanes.

'Correct. It's about a day's walk from Catana. I don't know which side the Trotileans are on, but maybe they don't either.'

'What has this to do with the fact that we have no food left?'

Now that was a good question, which I answered as best I could thus. 'Listen, you,' I snapped, 'I've had just about enough out of you to last me the rest of my life. You and nobody else got us into this mess, and I'm going to get us out of it, if I can. But if you interfere just once again, then so help me I'll cut your tongue out.'

'You've really got a way with words, son of Euchorus,' said Aristophanes. 'So what do we do now?'

'We follow this ditch to its logical conclusion.'

'Up it or down it?'

I looked up at the sun. 'This way,' I said, pointing north. 'Then we follow the river down to the sea. Then we go north along the coast to Catana. Then we go home. Simple.'

After maybe half an hour we reached the river Terias, and this cheered us both up considerably, since something had gone right at last; also we hadn't seen any Sicilians. In fact, the absence of people was quite remarkable, and I couldn't think of a reason for it. But quite suddenly it was explained.

We hadn't gone far along the river-bank when we saw a party of people coming in the opposite direction. They had seen us, and so there was no point in trying to hide. As we got closer we saw that it was a man and his whole family, dressed in their best clothes and carrying baskets decked out with wreaths.

'They're going to a Festival,' said Aristophanes brilliantly.

The family, which consisted of the man and his wife, two old women and three small children, waved to us cheerfully as we came closer to them. Aristophanes looked at me and said, 'What do we do now?'

'As little as possible,' I replied. 'Keep your mouth shut.'

They were within shouting distance now, so I shouted.

'Keep back, for pity's sake,' I shouted. 'Plague. We've got the plague.'

'What plague?' replied the man.

That threw me for a moment, but I couldn't be bothered to think of anything clever. 'Get away from us,' I yelled, as loud as I could. 'Go away or you're all dead!'

The Sicilians stared at me but didn't move. 'Where are you from?' they asked. I made a quick guess and said, 'Leontini.'

'There's a plague in Leontini?' shouted the man. 'Since when?'

'It's the Athenian plague,' I said. 'Athenians brought it there a day or so back, they were escaping from the war or something. The whole city is like a slaughterhouse. Don't go near it, whatever you do.'

'But the Festival,' said the man. 'We're going to the Festival.'

I shook my head violently. 'Keep away,' I said. 'Go home, don't let anyone near you. It's the Athenian plague.'

The man shook his head in perplexity. 'Where are you going?' he said.

'To the sea,' I replied.

'Why?'

'Why not?'

'Sorry?'

'I said, why not?'

'Oh.' The man looked at his family. One of the old women had started jabbering at him and all the children were crying. 'Well, thank you,' he shouted. 'Do you need food?'

'Yes,' I replied. 'Very much.'

'There's bread in this basket,' he said, pointing to the basket he was carrying. 'I'll leave it here for you.'

'Thank you,' I shouted – I was nearly hoarse by now. 'Please go away, before you catch it. It's very contagious.'

The man put down the basket and ran, followed by his family. When they were safely out of sight we fell upon the basket. There were five freshly baked wheat Festival loaves in it, and two honey-cakes. Good honey-cakes too, as I remember.

'I wonder whose Festival it is?' asked Aristophanes with his mouth full.

'Search me,' I replied, 'I expect it's Demeter or Athene. It wouldn't be Dionysus at this time of year.'

'Well, whoever it is, it's a stroke of luck,' he said. 'I was starving.'

'You amaze me, were you really?' I licked the last of the honey off my fingers. 'Right, let's press on, shall we?'

Not long afterwards, we came to a farmhouse. It was completely deserted except for a sleeping dog. Everyone was away at the Festival. After making sure there was nobody about, we kicked open a door and went in.

There is a story about old Alcmaeon, the founder of the illustrious Alcmaeonid clan of Athens. The story runs that he founded the family fortunes by doing a favour for the celebrated Croesus, King of Lydia, the richest man who ever lived. His reward was that he could go into the King's treasury and take as much gold away with him as he could carry. Well, when Alcmaeon went into the treasury his eyes nearly burst in his head; there was gold everywhere – gold cups and plates, gold armour, gold rings, gold tripods, gold statues, gold everything. But as soon as he had calmed down a bit, Alcmaeon realised that the most efficient way of carrying gold was in the form of gold-dust, of which there were many full jars. So he tied up the legs and sleeves of his gown to make a sort of sack out of it, and emptied a whole jar of gold-dust down his chest; then he poured gold-dust into his hair, which was thick and curly and well-oiled; then he found two big gold jars, as heavy as he could carry, and filled those with gold-dust. Finally he took a handful of gold-dust and popped it into his mouth. Thus laden, he staggered out of the treasury to his quarters and collapsed. He nearly died from swallowing gold-dust, but his servants managed to make him throw up in time.

That was how we felt when we broke into that farmhouse. There were jars of every kind of food, wine, and oil. There were fresh clothes, and newly made boots, and leather hats. Everything a man could reasonably want was there for the taking.

'It's like paradise,' Aristophanes said.

Then it occurred to me that it wasn't like paradise at all;

119

it was like my house in Pallene, except much smaller and less affluent. Ordinary people lived here, farmers, people who worried about having enough to eat in a bad year. There we were, two rich men of the Cavalry class, who had lived our whole lives surrounded by the sort of wealth these people could never aspire to; and this ordinary house was more desirable to us now than anything we could think of.

Our first instinct was to loot the place; but we calmed down after a while and took fresh clothes and five days' food. We felt like gentlemen, for all that, in clean woollen tunics and cloaks and boots and big leather hats, with walking-sticks and a sword for Aristophanes, and linen satchels for our food. We also found a razor and a mirror and trimmed our hair and beards – you have no idea what pleasure that gave me. Needless to say, Aristophanes went one stage further and ferreted out the family's purse. There were twenty staters in it, and he refused to put any of them back.

'What we need now,' said Aristophanes, 'is a horse.'

'You're never satisfied, are you?'

'No,' he said truthfully. 'I'm an Athenian, aren't I?'

He had a point there. Nicias and Demosthenes had failed, but here were two Athenians carrying off the wealth of Sicily. Somehow I felt a little better about plundering the house after that. A little better, but not much.

As we left, I closed the door behind me as best I could, and looked round. I saw two things: one good, and one bad. The good thing was an outhouse with its door slightly ajar, and inside it was a cart; a small two-wheeler ox-cart, just like the ones we use at home. Its storage capacity consisted of one of the big grain-jars they use on the corn-ships. A man can hide in one of those, I thought to myself, no problem at all. The family had obviously gone to the festival in the donkey-trap.

'Aristophanes,' I said, 'I've had an idea. Do you think this household keeps its ox in a pen?'

'Certainly.'

'Do you think you could find it for me?'

'All right.'

While he was away, I pulled out the cart and tested

my theory. I was right. It was a bit of a squeeze, but perfectly possible. Then Aristophanes came back, leading a large white ox by a halter. We got it into the shafts after a while, and I put the harness on it.

'What's the idea?' said Aristophanes.

'Get in there,' I said, pointing to the jar.

'No fear,' replied Aristophanes.

I pointed to the bad thing I had seen, which was getting closer; a cloud of dust on the road, about a mile away. 'Do you know what that is?' I asked.

'Oh God,' said Aristophanes, 'it's those damned cavalry.'

'I should think so,' I replied. 'Now be a good fellow and get in the jar.'

He got in the jar, and I closed the lid. Then I went into the house and grabbed two large pots of green olives, and dashed back out to the cart.

'Aristophanes,' I called out.

'Yes?'

'Mind your head.' I lifted the lid of the big jar and poured in the olives. 'Sorry,' I said. Then I dumped the olive-pots, closed the farmhouse door behind me, and climbed up on to the cart.

The cavalry overtook me shortly after I had joined the main road. It was the patrol we had encountered the previous night; there was no mistaking them. I knew what a gamble I was taking. I had staked both our lives, and the future of Athenian Comedy, on a wash and a shave, a big leather hat, my ability to do regional accents, and eight medimni of green olives.

'You,' shouted my old friend the cavalry captain. 'Pull over.'

'Sure,' I replied. 'What's the trouble?'

'Is that your place back there?' asked the captain, pointing with his sword at the farm behind us.

'No,' I replied, 'it's my cousin's place, but he's over to the Festival in Leontini.' I was sweating so much that I could hardly see. I had risked a Syracusan accent instead of a Corinthian one. It was my big day for taking risks.

'Why aren't you at the Festival, then?'

121

'Not my Festival,' I replied. 'We had our Demeter last month in Syracuse.'

This was a desperate effort on my part. I had seen a small terracotta Demeter inside the house, newly wreathed; and I remembered someone in the camp outside Syracuse telling me how he had watched their Demeter Festival. God knows why I took the risk; but it worked. The captain nodded, and didn't look too closely at my face. 'Visiting?' he said.

'That's right,' I replied. 'First chance to get out and about since the war. Taking a few olives up the coast for my cousin. They're starting to sweat already, and he didn't want them to stand until after the Festival. What are you boys after?'

'There's a couple of dangerous Athenians loose,' said the captain.

'Athenians,' I replied. 'Well, that's a bit of news. Wouldn't have thought there were too many of them left.' And I sniggered.

'Have you seen two men, ragged-looking, on foot?'

'Tall one and a shorter one? Bald-headed, both of them?'

'That's it.'

'Couple of men answering to that were round our place this morning,' I said. 'Wanted food, offered to buy a mule. They had money, but we didn't like the look of them. Talked funny. They went back the way they came, so far as I could make out.'

'When was this?'

'Maybe an hour after sun-up, maybe later. And they were Athenians, you reckon?'

'We think so, yes.'

'And dangerous?'

'They threatened the magistrate and injured one of my men.'

'That's bad,' I said. 'That's very bad. Hope they stay clear of me, that's all. Could you spare a couple of your boys to ride me up to the coast?'

The captain shook his head. 'Sorry,' he said. 'But you've got a sword, you should be all right.'

I felt as if someone had just pulled my heart out

122

through my ear. I didn't look down, but it was obvious that the captain could see that confounded Thracian sabre on its baldrick round my neck. Had he recognised it? I doubted very much if such swords were common in that part of Sicily. My soul cursed me for a feckless idiot, but I managed to keep my face straight.

'That's strictly for ornament,' I said. 'I'm not what you'd reckon to call a fighting man myself. I leave that to you boys.'

The captain laughed. 'Thanks for the help,' he said, and pulled his horse round.

'You make sure you catch those Athenians,' I replied. 'I don't feel so good now about leaving my cousin's place unattended if there's Athenians about. Mind,' I added, 'I wouldn't much fancy being there if they took it into their heads to break in, so perhaps I'm better off where I am.'

The cavalryman laughed again, and led his troop back the way they had come. For a moment I was afraid he would turn in to the farm – which was what I would have done in his place – but he rode straight past it and out of sight. I dropped the reins and started to shake all over. This was not my line of work, I said to my soul; and for once my soul agreed with me. But (replied my soul) you mustn't worry about it. Nothing can happen to you, today or for ever. You have been chosen to survive. You survived the plague. You survived the war. You have survived through Sicily. The old smith who could not die died. The veteran of Himera died. The Eleusinians who did not starve died. Everyone except you and the son of Philip has died and the son of Philip is protected by the God, as the old heroes were at Troy, and so he doesn't count. You are quite probably going to live for ever.

I met various other travellers that day, but none of them was any bother. By now I was firmly convinced that I was a Syracusan farmer visiting my cousins near Leontini. My name was Pelopidas son of Temenus, and I had fifteen acres mixed cereal and grazing on the slopes of Epipolae, with a few vines on the other side of the mountain. My wife, Callistrata, was a big woman with a bad temper, but we had two fine sons, Leon and Gigas, and

Gigas had been taken as apprentice by a well-established potter in the City. He would do well, if he worked at it. We also had a daughter, Theodora, but she died of a cold when she was ten. During the war we lived in the City, which was uncomfortable, and I had done my bit in the fighting. I missed out on the Epipolae business, but I was in at the kill at the walled orchard, when we stomped on those Athenians once and for all. I didn't want to put in that last part, but I couldn't help it. However much I sought to rewrite my life, I couldn't leave that out.

It was probably just as well that I wasn't called on to play this part I had composed for myself, since it was probably riddled with inaccuracies. But I must confess that I enjoyed being Pelopidas son of Temenus. He was on the winning side, for one thing, and this was his country, for another. He might not have the wealth and talents of a Eupolis, say, or even an Aristophanes, but nobody was after his blood and he didn't really care all that much if he never did get to Catana. God, I envied him.

That night, I carefully unpacked Aristophanes, who was not happy. He had a whole day's recriminations stored up for me when I finally extracted him from the jar, and he seemed to get most of them past the gate of his teeth in the first five minutes of his liberty. I took no notice of him, however; I was bored with him now, and regarded him as nothing more than a piece of inconvenient and perishable merchandise that I had to deliver to Catana. I hid him under the cart and went to sleep, and dreamed, at first, of being Pelopidas son of Temenus. But that turned into a dream about the walled orchard, the first I had had, and I woke up drenched in sweat and shivering. This convinced me that I had the fever, and worrying about that kept me awake for the rest of the night.

When Aristophanes woke up, we breakfasted on half a Festival loaf each, a cup of wine, a sausage and a handful of figs, which was the best meal we had had since we arrived in Sicily. It was a lovely morning, warm but not too hot, and there was a spectacular sunrise over the mountains behind us. We washed in the river, and then I told Aristophanes that it was time for him to get back into the jar. Much to my surprise he refused.

'Those olives stink,' he said. 'If I get back in there I'll die.'

'Please yourself,' I said. 'Only if you don't get back in there, I'm afraid I'll have to kill you.' I drew my sabre in a matter-of-fact sort of way and laid it across my knees. Aristophanes stared at me.

'I'm sorry,' I said, 'but there it is. I can't afford to let you go wandering off on your own. They'll see you're an Athenian, and then they'll come looking for me. So I'll have to kill you and bury you in . . . ' I looked round quickly ' . . . under that pile of rocks there. I'll give you a stater for the ferryman, but that's my best offer.'

Aristophanes opened his mouth but no words came out; and I suddenly realised what I had said. I hadn't been joking; I would have done it. That was a horrible feeling.

I stood up, and Aristophanes cowered visibly. 'So are you going to get into the jar?' I asked.

'Yes,' said the son of Philip. 'Right away.'

'Good man,' I said. 'We'd better tip the olives out first. Give me a hand with the jar, will you?'

We tipped the olives out and put the jar back in its mounting, then Aristophanes climbed in and I put the olives back on top of him. 'Can you breathe?' I asked. He assured me that he could.

'That's fine,' I said. 'Right, time to go.' I put the lid back on and backed the ox into the shafts. He was a good ox, docile and well behaved. I liked him. Then I took up the reins and we were off again.

We reached the sea just before evening, and the sight of it made me feel like a small child once more. It was huge and beautiful and friendly, and on the other side of it was Athens in Attica, and Pallene, and my house there, and my steward and his wife, and my grey horse with the black tail, and my house in the City, and my wife. I hadn't so much as thought about Phaedra since I set foot in Sicily; and now that I had remembered that she existed I couldn't for the life of me remember what she looked like. I dismissed the thought from my mind, and went back to being Pelopidas.

Only a day away from Catana. Would the olives keep fresh that far?

I had stopped for the night and was just about to let Aristophanes out when a party of men leading donkeys came up the road behind me. There were about ten of them, and I saw they were farmers taking their produce to the city. That city could only be Catana.

'Evening, friend,' said one of them, a tall man with a lot of fine grey hair. 'Going to market?'

His voice was warm and friendly, and I smiled as I replied, 'Sure. I've got olives in the jar here.'

The man wasn't so friendly now, and I realised that I was still being Pelopidas, purely from instinct. My Syracusan accent had become so good that he recognised it instantly. The trouble was, of course, that the Catanians hate the Syracusans like poison. I would have laughed if I wasn't suddenly so frightened.

That's the way it goes with fool's luck, said my soul inside me, and I could hear a horrible sort of smugness in its voice, as if it had known it would all end in tears. You muddle your way right across Sicily and manage to get out of the most horrific scrapes without really trying; then, as soon as you've got your act together enough to pass for a Syracusan, you run in with a bunch of Catanians who'll tear you limb from limb for not being an Athenian. That'll teach you to be so damned lucky.

'Just where exactly did you say you were from, boy?' said the grey-haired man. 'Maybe I didn't catch it the first time.'

'I'm from Pallene,' I replied in my normal voice – only it didn't come out normal. 'Pallene in Attica. I'm an Athenian.'

The grey-haired man scowled and said, 'Don't you try being funny with me, stranger. Are you going to tell me the truth, or do I have to beat it out of you?'

I tried to dig down into my mind for some way out of this mess; but there was nothing left. 'Oh, for crying out loud,' I said, 'I'm an Athenian, can't you see that? I'm one of Demosthenes' men. I was in the battle at the walled orchard, but I got away. I stole this cart outside Leontini

126

because there were cavalrymen after me and I needed to fool them. I pretended to be a Syracusan just now because I didn't know I was in your country.'

The men muttered darkly to each other; they weren't convinced. I didn't know what to do.

'I don't believe you,' said the grey-haired man. 'I reckon you're a Syracusan spy, and I'm going to take you in. Get him, boys.'

'Hold it, hold it,' I shrieked. 'You're making a really silly mistake here. Look, I've got another Athenian in this jar-contraption here. He's my friend, we escaped together.'

The grey-haired man stared at me. 'In the jar?' he said.

'Yes,' I shouted, 'in the bloody jar. Get him out if you don't believe me.'

They cut the jar loose and tipped it on to the ground. There was a minor cascade of olives, and out came the son of Philip, looking extremely put out. He tried to draw his sword, but they took it away from him and tied his hands together.

'Athenian my arse,' said one of the men. 'He tried to kill me.'

'He couldn't hear you, he was in the jar,' I said. 'He thought you were the enemy.'

The grey-haired man didn't like that. 'Do we look like the Syracusans?' he said angrily.

'He couldn't see you either,' I replied frantically, 'because he was in the sodding jar. Don't you ever think?'

'Don't you talk to me like that,' said the grey-haired man. 'You're lucky we don't string you up right now.'

'Oh, do what you like,' I said miserably.

'I might just do that,' said the grey-haired man. His companions seemed to agree with this, and one of them uncoiled some rope from his donkey. Just then, I remembered something. I remembered the fat dry-fish merchant who had sat next to me during the performance of *The General*. I remembered that his name was Pericleidas son of Bellerophon and that he said he was from Catana. I could have wept with pleasure.

'Will you listen to me, just for a moment?' I said. 'I have

a friend in Catana who'll vouch for me. Pericleidas son of Bellerophon, the dry-fish man. Do any of you know him?'

'Sure I know him,' said one of the men, 'I sell him tuna in the season. You know him?'

'I met him in Athens.'

'If you know him,' said the grey-haired man, 'where does he live?'

I was about to explain that I had only met him in Athens and couldn't be expected to know where he lived when suddenly I remembered that I knew exactly where he lived. The God had told me, in the walled orchard.

'Next to the shrine of Dionysus,' I replied, 'by the little gate.'

'That's true,' said the man who knew Pericleidas, 'that's just where he lives.'

'Proving nothing,' said the grey-haired man. 'Everyone knows that.'

'I didn't,' said one of his companions. But the grey-haired man ignored him.

'Take me to him,' I said. 'He'll know me.'

The grey-haired man thought for a moment. 'Who's that?' he said, pointing at Aristophanes.

'He's my friend,' I replied. 'Like I told you.'

'Does he know Pericleidas?'

'No,' I replied. 'But not many people in Athens do. Look, can we get on, please?'

The grey-haired man thought again, then nodded. 'You'd better hope Pericleidas recognises you,' he said, 'or so help me I'll string you up myself.'

They bundled me and Aristophanes on to the cart, and we spent the rest of that day bouncing along the road to Catana. It was not the way I had intended to arrive there, and somehow it didn't feel right. My main nightmare was that Pericleidas was out, or abroad peddling his misbegotten fish. That would be just my fool's luck, and then they would string us up and make us into sausages.

A crowd gathered round us as soon as we entered the city, and we soon attracted the attention of a magistrate and some soldiers. When asked what he had got in his wagon, the grey-haired man said he didn't know; they said they were Athenians and that Pericleidas could vouch for them; but if he couldn't, they were Syracusan spies and should be hung. The magistrate thought this was eminently reasonable, and walked in front of us through the streets. As we passed, some people cheered and others threw stones; this is what is known as hedging your bets.

The cart jolted to a halt and we were hauled out. It was quite dark by now, but there were plenty of torches round us, and the whole proceeding looked like a cross between a wedding and a sacrifice. The magistrate came over and addressed us both.

'Right,' he said, 'this is Pericleidas' house. We'll see what he has to say.'

He knocked loudly on the door and called out Pericleidas' name. As I waited for what seemed like for ever while the slave came down and opened the door, I reflected bitterly on my fate, which now rested on an idiot of a dry-fish merchant I had met once in the Theatre. This could only happen to a Comic poet, I said to myself, and considered, not for the first time in my life, whether I had chosen the right profession.

'What is it?' said the slave. He was startled by the sight of so many people. 'My master is having dinner.'

'He's needed to vouch for these men,' said the magistrate. 'They say they're Athenians.'

'I'll fetch him,' said the slave. He disappeared into the house, and there was another eternity of a wait, with the good people of Catana whispering inaudibly around me. Then Pericleidas the dry-fish man appeared, exactly as I remembered him, except that he was a trifle fatter, and his hair was quite grey. But what if he didn't remember me?

'Are you Pericleidas son of Bellerophon?' asked the magistrate.

'Sure I am,' said Pericleidas, clearly bemused. 'You know perfectly well who I am, Cleander, you had dinner here last night. Why did you bother to ask?'

This got a good laugh from the audience, and the magistrate frowned.

'Pericleidas,' he said, 'I have to ask you if you recognise these men. They say they know you.'

Pericleidas shrugged. 'What have they done?' he said.

'Never mind that now,' said the magistrate, 'just see if you can identify them for me. Can you do that?'

'I'll do my best,' he said, and turned to Aristophanes. 'I'm sorry,' he said, after an agonising moment, 'I've never seen this man before in my life.'

There was a gasp from the crowd, and muffled cheering. Then he turned to me. He looked at me, blinked, and looked again.

'Well?' said the magistrate, 'do you know this one or don't you?'

'I don't know,' said Pericleidas. 'Hell, Cleander, you know I've got a rotten memory for faces.'

That was enough for me. 'Pericleidas,' I said, before anyone could stop me, 'do you remember going to Athens and seeing a play called *The General*?'

Pericleidas blinked. 'Yes,' he said, 'I remember it well. But surely – aren't you the young fellow who was sitting next to me? Yes, I'll swear you are. You're the young fellow who wrote the play.'

'Is my name Eupolis?' I said.

'That's right,' said Pericleidas, relieved. 'You're Eupolis, the playwright. I'm terrible at faces, but I never forget a name. Yes, this is Eupolis, I can vouch for that.'

'Are you sure?' said the magistrate. 'You said yourself— '

'No, it's him all right,' said Pericleidas. 'If I'm right, he's missing a bit of one finger.'

Now my hands were tied behind my back and he couldn't have seen them. The magistrate ordered his men to untie me. I didn't dare look down, in case my missing finger had suddenly grown back, just to spite me. 'All right,' said the magistrate, 'I guess you're who you say you are. But who's this?' He pointed to Aristophanes, and the crowd, who had been bitterly disappointed, started to hope once again. 'You don't know him, do you?'

'We never claimed he did,' I said quickly. 'But I can vouch that this is Aristophanes son of Philip, an Athenian citizen.'

'Not *the* Aristophanes!' exclaimed Pericleidas. 'Why,

sir, are you Aristophanes who wrote *The Acharnians* and *The Two Jugs*?'

'Yes,' said Aristophanes. For once, there was no smugness in his voice, only relief.

'Then I can vouch for him too,' said Pericleidas.

'No, he can't,' said the grey-haired man, 'he's just said he couldn't.'

The magistrate made an angry gesture. 'The hell with it,' he said. 'Look, Pericleidas, will you be responsible for these two?'

'It would be an honour,' said Pericleidas, gazing at Aristophanes as if he had just seen a vision of a god. Not at me, you understand. Just Aristophanes.

'That's good enough for me, then,' said the magistrate. 'All right, folks, the party's over. Go home quietly, it's after dark.'

The crowd drifted away, and Pericleidas hustled us both inside.

'Stratylla,' he shouted, 'come here quick, and we'll need hot water and towels. We've got company.'

I honestly can't remember any more about that night. I think I must have fallen asleep on my feet, or something of the sort, because the next thing I remember was waking up in a bed, with light coming in through the window. For a moment I was confused; then I remembered what had happened, and that I was in Catana, safe, in a friendly house. In the bed next to me was Aristophanes son of Philip, snoring. I looked at him and realised, with a great surge of joy that nearly took off the top of my head, that I was no longer responsible for him.

Chapter Nine

Don't you hate it when you're listening to a story or a poem; and the hero has just got himself out of a scrape by the tips of his fingers in Argos, say, or Crete, and then the scene suddenly changes to Tempe or Phocis, and there's our hero, sitting in a nice clean tunic with his hair newly curled and his beard trimmed, having a bite to eat with the King and planning his next adventure? I do. I feel cheated. I want to hear how he got all the way from Argos to Phocis, which is probably more difficult in practical terms than duping the three-headed giant or escaping from the man-eating bull. Particularly since the three-headed ogre turned out to be incredibly gullible, or the hero was so laden down with magical hardware, pressed into his hand by some helpful god or other, that the whole Spartan army wouldn't have stood a chance against him. No, what I want to hear is how he managed to hitch a lift on a ship without any money, and what he did for food and water as he crossed the mountains, and how he got past the King's doorkeeper without a sealed pass and three chamberlains to vouch for him.

I am no Milesian cheapskate; I will not fob you off with an implied challenge to your imaginative powers. Before we return to violet-crowned Athens, I will give you a short account of our stay in Catana and the trip home.

At first, Pericleidas was thrilled to have the celebrated Aristophanes under his roof, and for three days we were treated like princes. Everything that twenty years' accumulated proceeds of the dry-fish business could provide for our comfort and delight was showered upon us, and the only thing demanded of us in return was theatre talk. But neither of us could find very much to say to gratify our host's modest, if eccentric, requirement. It was as if we had forgotten what it was like to be Athenian literary lions. Even Aristophanes could find very little to say about his own prodigious talents and triumphs, and I was quite useless. All I seemed able to remember was the Athenian expedition to Syracuse; it was as if I had been born the day I landed in Sicily, and the things I had done before that were heroic tales of the old days, when the world was young and the Gods still appeared openly to men. Although I pretended to, I couldn't bring myself to believe in this mythical place called Athens in Attica, where they did nothing all day but grow food, write plays and talk to their friends about the weather and politics, and nobody died. The real world, I knew in my heart, was not like that at all. In the real world, terrified men marched down unknown roads and were trapped in orchards, or slept in ditches while the cavalry searched for them; and sooner or later this holiday would be over and I would have to put on my muddy old boots and cloak and go back to work.

In this mood, I freely admit, I wasn't fit company for a stage-struck tuna baron. The only thing I wanted to talk about was the War – God, how I wanted to talk about that to someone; even Aristophanes. I tried once or twice but he put his hands over his ears and yelled until I went away. Most of the time, in fact, he spent drinking himself into a coma, which seemed to work well enough for him. But when I tried it, I fell asleep and dreamed about the War, and that was no good at all. And then Pericleidas would come bounding up, certain in his mind that at last we were ready to talk about cosy chats behind the scenes at the first rehearsal of *The Wasps*, and what Agathon said to Euripides about Sophocles.

I asked everyone I could about what had happened to the Athenians, and tried to find any other survivors who had made it to Catana. I found them, quite a few in fact; most of them hospitably locked up by the Catanian authorities, who regarded them as a public nuisance and were trying to negotiate a cheap price with a Phoenician slaver for the hire of a ship to send them back to Athens. But I heard that Nicias and Demosthenes were dead, and that most of the men who had been captured by the Syracusans had died of cold and starvation in the stone quarries. By all accounts, seven thousand men had survived the two massacres, in the orchard and the river bed, out of forty thousand who had left the camp. Of these, about four thousand lived long enough to be sold off, mostly to Phoenicians. Very few of those, I was told, were Athenians. A Corcyrean I met who had been in the quarries and had escaped said that the Athenians there had given up quite early and refused to eat, or had caught the fever and died. They had no will to live, he said, since they believed that their City was already dead. I also found out that the man who owned the farm with the walled orchard in it was called Polyzelus. He was a decent enough man, by all accounts, and when he came home and found his home knee-deep in bodies he was profoundly shocked and had to be taken away and looked after by some relatives. When he had recovered, he had to find some way of disposing of fourteen thousand dead Athenians, and for a long time he didn't know what to do. All this time the Athenians were not smelling any more wholesome, and his neighbours were starting to complain. In the end, he hired every slave and casual worker in the district and got them to dig an enormous hole in a marshy part of his property where nothing would grow anyway, and shovelled the dead bodies into it until it was full. Then he raised a big cairn of stones over it, and set about recovering the quite phenomenal cost of this operation from the Syracusan government. By all accounts, the legal complications beggared all description, and he or his heirs are probably at it to this day.

After three days, Pericleidas came into the room where we slept and said, in a rather embarrassed manner, that he had arranged a passage home for us. We thanked him profusely. This seemed to make him feel worse. He explained that the ship we were going home on was one of his. We thanked him again. He explained further that all his ships were cargo ships laden with dried fish; they were therefore not immensely comfortable. We said that that didn't matter; going home was the important thing. Actually, said Pericleidas, wretchedly, there was only enough room on these fish-cruisers of his for a *working* crew. He hated to impose like this, but . . .

So that is how, when anyone in a poem or a reading purports to give an account of what it is like to sail a ship on the open sea, I can stand up and tell him he's a liar, because I have done it myself, and it's no fun at all. You get very wet working a ship, particularly if you haven't the faintest idea what you are supposed to be doing and the rest of the crew are muttering about you being bad luck and how they ought to throw you overboard before you bring on a thunderstorm. Oh yes, we were also chased by pirates in the Straits of Rhegium. They were very enthusiastic, those pirates, and were just about to catch up with us when one of the crew had the wit to shout out that our cargo was nothing more valuable than dried fish, and to throw a jar over the side to prove it. The pirates picked up the jar, opened it, and stopped following us, which must be a very significant comment on the quality of Pericleidas' stock-in-trade.

And then, after a long and exhausting journey, we saw Cape Sunium on the horizon and heard the ship's captain saying, with evident relief, that this was where Eupolis and Aristophanes were getting off. For two pins, in fact, they would have landed us at Sunium; but we persuaded them to take us into Piraeus by giving them the remainder of our Sicilian money.

As we cruised round the Attic coast, I suddenly started to feel sick. That was not the motion of the ship – I had got over that after the first couple of days of our voyage; it was a sort of fear, that Attica would not be what it had to be, in order for me to stay sane. Attica had to be a happy ever after, a place where the story could end. I had tried to picture it in my mind while I was in Sicily, but no image would come; and I had put together a rather unconvincing reconstruction to take its place. This Attica was half an enormous theatre filled with laughing people, backing on to a maze of cosy little streets, and half a sort of pastoral idyll, jammed permanently at the end of the olive harvest, with carts creaking down narrow lanes. The reason why I chose the olive season was that I could remember what an olive cart looked like; it had two wheels, an ox between the shafts, Aristophanes in the storage-jar and cavalrymen all round it. The cavalrymen seemed a little out of place in Attica, but that couldn't be helped. Now if this phantom Attica didn't exist, what was I to do? I realised, as we sailed on from Sunium, that I really didn't want to go home; that was the very last thing I wanted to do.

Aristophanes was also very quiet. We had spoken very few words to each other since we reached Catana, and we seemed rather embarrassed to be in each other's company, as if each knew a terrible secret about the other and didn't trust him to keep his mouth shut. In my case of course, I did know quite a few things about the son of Philip that would, if made public, utterly destroy him in Athenian society, and I felt sure that he had invented a corresponding number of calumnies about me; but although we said nothing to each other about it, we seemed to have reached an agreement that when we got home, we were going to have as little to do with each other as possible.

But of course you don't want to hear all this; you are asking yourself why, if we were coming from Sicily, we passed Sunium before reaching Piraeus. Well, if you had used your head you would have realised that our captain wouldn't want to go further down the Argolid than he absolutely had to, what with the War and everything, and had thus sailed straight from Methana to Sunium across open water. He then backtracked from Sunium to Piraeus, intending to go back the way he had come after that. The result of this complex manoeuvre, besides bad temper on everyone's part, was that we didn't make Piraeus until about half an hour before dawn.

I don't know what exactly I had been expecting; whether I had assumed that the Polemarch and the Council would be there to meet us, with garlands and honey and flute-girls, or perhaps a more modest delegation led by one of the lower ranking magistrates, or perhaps just a few friends and relatives. Instead, there was nobody to be seen anywhere, not even the usual crowd who lounge about the docks waiting for someone to spill a jar so that they can dart across and steal the contents. The only living creature was a dog, whose barking brought the toll-collector out, and he was only interested in separating the captain from his harbour dues, and took no notice of us whatsoever.

When I say us, by this time I mean me. As soon as his feet touched Attic soil, Aristophanes was off like a startled polecat, without a word to me, the captain or anyone. He just muffled his face in his cloak and vanished, I think in the general direction of the City; but I couldn't say for sure. I felt it would only be polite to thank the captain for putting up with me on the voyage, so I did this. The captain made no reply, so I shrugged my shoulders at the world in general, pulled my cloak round me, and started to walk towards Athens.

Of course the old Long Walls between Athens and Piraeus are no longer there, and I suspect that many of you who are reading this will not remember them. That morning, they seemed to go on for ever, and although I had walked that way hundreds of times in my life, they seemed very foreign and unfamiliar to me as I trudged along under them. I don't know why, but I got it into my head that the City was actually empty, and that all its people were now in a hole in a marsh on the estate of Polyzelus. It was a very eerie sensation, I can tell you, and I didn't like it at all. But when I was half-way to the City I saw a man hurrying up from the opposite direction, and to my overwhelming joy I recognised him. In a way it was like seeing a ghost, but he was real enough – Cleagenes the corn-merchant, who I had done business with a few times.

'Hello, Cleagenes,' I shouted.

He peered at me (he was short-sighted) and replied,

'Hello, Eupolis. I haven't seen you about for a couple of weeks now. Have you been in the country?'

I stared at him. 'Come off it,' I said, 'I've been in Sicily with the army. I've just got back.'

Cleagenes gave me a curious look. 'Don't be funny at this hour of the morning, Eupolis, there's a good lad. The army isn't back yet.'

Back yet? 'Honestly, Cleagenes,' I said, 'that's where I've been.'

He frowned. 'Have you come back with a message for the Council or a letter from Nicias or whatever?' he asked. 'If so, you'd better— '

'Nicias?' I said. 'Nicias is dead.'

'Dead?'

'Dead.'

Cleagenes pondered this for a moment. 'That's not very funny, Eupolis,' he said at last. 'I suppose you're just going home from a party with some of your peculiar friends. Take my advice, lad. Go home and sleep it off before you offend someone important. Some people have got sons at the War, you realise.'

Cleagenes bustled away, leaving me standing with my mouth open. But there was nothing to be gained by gawping (as my grandfather used to say), so I pressed on into the City towards my house. I saw a few people out and about once I had passed through the gate, but I didn't stop and talk to any of them. Something told me that the best move at this stage would be to keep my head down until I had managed to find out what was going on.

It was easy to rationalise, of course; obviously, the news of the disaster had not yet reached the City. This was hard to credit; surely someone in authority at Catana should have sent a letter or something. But probably someone had left it to someone else, or it was still on its way, or the ship it was on had been sunk or stopped off at Methana to do a little business.

Then it occurred to me that, if I was right, the son of Philip and I were the only people in the whole of Athens who knew about the destruction of the fleet. That was not a pleasant thought. Now it was clearly my duty (I couldn't count on Aristophanes to do anything useful) to go and tell someone about it, such as the Polemarch and the Council. But would they believe me? Of course not. Cleagenes the corn-merchant hadn't believed me, so why should the Polemarch? I would probably find myself in the prison for starting seditious rumours or something of the sort.

But I couldn't just go home, take my boots and hat off, and pretend I had never been away. Leaving to one side the fate of the City, which was now totally defenceless and at the mercy of the Spartans (who undoubtedly knew), there was my peace of mind to consider. I couldn't keep a forty-thousand-corpse secret to myself; I would burst, like the frog in the fable. Perhaps I could tell someone else who would tell the Council for me; someone they would listen to.

I was walking along thinking like this when a man touched me on the shoulder and said, 'Is that you?'

I turned and looked at him. It was Philonides the Chorus-trainer. I said nothing.

'Eupolis,' said Philonides, 'I thought you were away at the War.'

'I was,' I replied.

'When did you come back?'

'Just now.'

'This morning?'

'Yes.'

He studied me carefully; I wasn't usually this taciturn, he was thinking, perhaps I was ill. 'Have you been wounded?' he asked. 'Is that why you're back?'

'No,' I replied. 'I'm all right.'

'So what are you doing in Athens?' It was extraordinary, I thought. Here is a man I know, being friendly in a normal sort of a way, and I suddenly don't know how to talk to him. 'Glad to see you, of course. And how's the War going?'

'The War's over,' I said.

He broke into a smile. 'Already?' he said. 'I knew we could rely on Demosthenes to get it finished. He's hot stuff, Demosthenes, whatever they say down at the Baths.'

139

'We lost,' I said. 'Demosthenes is dead.'

'Dead?'

'Yes,' I snapped, 'dead.'

'Oh God,' said Philonides, and he seemed to sag, like a punctured wineskin. 'So Nicias is in charge of the army?'

'Nicias is dead too.'

'Nicias as well?' Philonides stared at me. 'But that's impossible.'

'No, it's not.'

'Then who's in charge of the army, for God's sake?' he said. 'Not that imbecile Menander. I couldn't bear it. Or Eurymedon, for that matter. The man's a fool.'

'There is no army.'

'I beg your pardon?'

'Watch my lips,' I said. 'There is no army. Got it? They're all dead. All except maybe two or three hundred.'

For a moment his mind rejected the statement; then he believed it. 'The whole lot?' he said.

'The whole lot.'

'So what about the fleet?' he demanded. 'Where's the fleet?'

I smiled, I can't say why. 'At the bottom of Syracuse harbour,' I replied. 'Most of it, anyway.'

He stood there for a moment, a totally empty man, a shell of a man, a man with no contents. His mouth was wide open, and I noticed how straight and white his teeth were for a man of his age. He clearly didn't have anything to say, so I reckoned it was up to me to keep the conversation going.

'I was lucky,' I said. 'I managed to get away to Catana with Aristophanes the son of Philip. He's probably at his house by now, getting drunk I shouldn't wonder. Go and ask him if you don't believe me. How did his play do, by the way; the one he left with you?'

'It came second.'

'Second?'

'Yes.'

'Oh well.'

'*All* of them?' he said. 'That whole army?'

'Yes.'

We stood there for a moment; there was no hurry about

anything. Then Philonides said, 'Have you reported to the Council?'

'No,' I replied. 'I'm on my way home. I badly need a wash and a shave.'

'That can wait,' he said. 'Look, my nephew Palaeologus is a Councillor, we'd better tell him first.'

I shrugged. 'I don't mind,' I said. 'Shall we get Aristophanes to back me up?'

'Good idea,' said Philonides. He was excited, talking quickly; this self-imposed task was something he could keep between himself and what he had just heard. 'Look, my place is on the way, I'll send the boy round to Aristophanes' place – you're sure he'll be there?'

'No,' I said, 'he didn't say where he was going.'

'Oh well, never mind. We'll send the boy anyway. Then we'd better get over to Palaeologus' house.'

So that was what we did. The whole thing struck me as vaguely comical; after all, I reasoned to myself, if our army were dead now, they were likely still to be dead after I had had a wash and a shave, and probably would stay dead until I had had something to eat. But I didn't want to say anything to Philonides; I felt it might upset him.

Palaeologus the Councillor wasn't unduly pleased to see us; he had been up late the night before, he said, and he had a headache. I offered to go away and come back later, but Philonides shut me up. He said he had some terrible news. I objected that I was the one with the terrible news, and would he please stop upstaging me. He got rather upset with me at this and told me to be quiet; in fact, he was getting rather hysterical. Palaeologus the Councillor looked at me, since I appeared to be rather more in control of myself, and asked me what was going on. I told him.

'Oh God,' he said. 'Oh God in Heaven.'

'So you believe me, do you?' I asked. 'I thought I'd have difficulty convincing you.'

Palaeologus shook his head. 'We'd heard news already,' he said. 'Well, sort of. We didn't believe it.'

He explained. Two days ago, an Aeginetan scent-dealer had landed at Piraeus with a cargo of myrrh. He had sailed non-stop from Methana, and he was tired, and he wanted a shave, so he went over to a barber's shop he knew just off the Market Square. While he was being shaved he started making conversation, the way you do in a barber's shop.

'Sorry to hear about your bad luck,' he said.

'What bad luck?' said the barber.

'In Sicily,' said the Aeginetan. 'It's all over Methana. I'm sorry for you, really I am. It was a rotten thing to happen.'

'We haven't had word from Sicily for a while now,' said the barber. 'Things going badly, are they?'

'I should say,' said the Aeginetan. 'Your whole army's been wiped out.'

The barber stared at him for a second or two, then ran out into the street, still holding his razor, and started yelling at the top of his voice, 'The army's been wiped out! The army's been wiped out!' Now it happened to be just before Assembly-time, and so the magistrates and the archers were out, getting the red rope ready. They saw this lunatic running up and down, waving a razor and yelling, and arrested him.

He told them what he had heard and pointed to his shop, where the Aeginetan was sitting waiting for the rest of his shave. The magistrate marched into the shop, saw that the man was Aeginetan, and arrested him for spreading malicious rumours. He and the barber were in the prison at this very moment awaiting trial. The Council had been told, as a matter of routine, but they had ignored it. But what convinced Palaeologus was the fact that he knew (now he came to think of it) that I had been with Demosthenes' army, because he had happened to see me at the dockside when he came to wave off his brother-in-law, and someone had pointed to me and asked him who I was.

Then Aristophanes arrived, looking very irritated at being disturbed, and confirmed what I had said. So we had to go down to the Council Chamber and wait until the Council could be summoned, and then the Councillors grilled us for what seemed like hours, asking all manner of trick questions to try and catch us out. This made

Aristophanes livid, and he asked if they were calling him a liar, but I realised that it was just Athenian instinct and answered their questions as best I could. Then we were shoved into a little room – me, Aristophanes and Philonides – and the door was bolted on us. We asked why we were being locked up like this, but nobody answered.

'Well,' I said, 'this is cosy. So what's been happening in the City while we've been away?'

Philonides didn't answer, and we sat there for a while staring at the walls. Then Aristophanes asked how his play had got on. Philonides told him it had come second.

'Second?' said Aristophanes, with disgust.

'That's right, second.'

'That's bloody typical, that is,' he said. 'You realise that the parabasis was a thorough condemnation of our Sicilian policy? God, we deserved to lose.'

After two or maybe three hours someone came and let us out. They told us to go straight home and stay there, and not to say anything to anybody. There would be widespread panic, the man said, and it was the Council's job to make the announcement.

We were bundled out by the back way, past the ash-heap, and escorted home by archers; hardly a hero's welcome, I thought, but then, who cares? It was nice that some things, like the Council, were still the same. I wondered how long it would last.

The archer knocked on the door for me; I imagine he thought I might try and communicate a coded message if I knocked myself. The slave opened the door and stared at me, and the archer more or less pushed me through the door.

'Hello, Thrax,' I said to the slave. 'Is your mistress here, or is she in the country?'

'She's here, asleep,' said the slave. 'We thought you were in Sicily.'

'I was,' I replied, 'but I've come home. It happens quite a lot, you know. Go and wake her, will you?'

He went scampering off, and I drew my sword and put it back over the lintel, where it belonged. It made quite an attractive ornament.

Now I assume that you are all educated people and know your *Odyssey*, and your *Thebaid* and *Little Iliad* too; so I can't describe this next scene as I would wish to, in the interests of dramatic effect, because you would object that I had stolen it from the classics. This business of not appearing to copy one's predecessors is a very real problem for a writer, and when all the most obvious approaches to a particular scene have been blocked by the previous efforts of the great masters, he often finds himself reduced to describing what actually happened. The only form of literature that seems to be immune from this difficulty is Tragedy, of course, but the Tragedians' minds are too lofty and elevated to worry about that sort of thing. At times, I feel, they live in a world of their own. But the poor, long-suffering historian has this concern as his constant companion, sitting by his elbow as he writes, and saying, 'No, no, you can't do that, it's been done before; you must have them coming *down* the hill and turning left'; or 'You must be crazy putting in a battle here; we had a battle in the last chapter that was exactly the same.' Now your historian may start off with all manner of lofty ideals, such as recording for all time the clear essence of what actually happened, but he soon gets this beaten out of him by the people he reads his work to while he is writing it. Take the celebrated Herodotus, for example. Now when he was writing his histories, he spent years traipsing all round the world asking old men what their grandfathers remembered, and writing down their answers on wax, and when he got home he sorted through these facts and eliminated the inconsistencies and accounted for the errors in chronology arising from the fact that in some places a generation is reckoned at thirty-three years and in other places at forty years, and at last sat down and wrote his history. Then he read it to his wife.

'Are you out of you mind?' said she. 'You can't expect anyone to listen to that.'

'Why?' asked Herodotus.

'Well,' said his wife patiently, 'it all sounds so . . . well, so *true*, if you see what I mean.'

Herodotus thought for a while; then he saw what she was getting at. He went back to work with a vengeance. He increased all the distances he had so carefully measured, and doubled the numbers of Persian soldiers which he had so painstakingly recorded; he took out the account of how gold dust is refined in the desert by the use of sieves and running water, and replaced it with a ludicrous fairy-story about pygmies and giant ants; and he invented a whole new section about Scythia, which was the one part of the world he hadn't been to, and claimed that he had travelled the length and breadth of the country and seen all these fictional wonders with his own eyes. Finally, he lodged his original draft in the temple of Athena, in case the Council should ever need accurate information on any of these places or subjects, and gave readings from the revised version which were, of course, a spectacular success.

But I see, on looking back through what I have written up to this point, that I have given a factual and quite personal account of what happened to me in Sicily – written, it seems, on the assumption that my readers will be interested in the deeds of one single man who was not himself particularly important, which is of course a highly doubtful assumption to make. As a result, I have left myself no option but to describe what follows, including my meeting with Phaedra, as truthfully as I can after so many years, or else go back and rewrite what has gone before, putting in nice little snippets of geography and fable and scattering about gods and miracles, just as we interplant barley in the empty ground between the rows of vines in a vineyard. I would have no objection to doing this if it were up to me; but that tiresome man Dexitheus the bookseller was nagging me for a completed manuscript this morning when I went down to the Market Square to buy fish, and so I had better press on; and if what follows seems to you to be too realistic, you must blame him, not me.

I was putting my sword back over the lintel, as I have told you, when the door to the inner room opened and there was Phaedra. I assumed it was Phaedra; but if I had been a

145

witness in a trial and the prosecutor was asking me if I was absolutely sure I would have had to qualify my statement, because I couldn't just then remember what Phaedra was supposed to look like. What I saw was a woman of average size in her middle to late twenties, with untidy hair and the clear signs of a badly set broken jaw. As I looked at her, I could find no memories, recollections, associations in my mind about her; neither love nor hate, nothing binding me to her or repelling me from her, and I had this extraordinary feeling that it was open to me either to accept her as mine or reject her as spurious, as if she was one of the stray goats that we round up on the hills from time to time and do our best to identify. If I accepted her now – it was almost like a second wedding-day – then I would be bound to her for life. If I rejected her, I could turn my back on her and be done with her for ever.

I am and have always been indecisive. I prefer to be forced into decisions rather than to make them freely and calmly; this makes it possible for me to blame the Gods when things go wrong. So I did not take either of the two initiatives open to me then; to throw my arms around her and kiss her, or to ignore her completely. I waited for her to say something.

'Eupolis?' she said. 'Is that you?'

'Yes.'

'What are you doing here?'

'I've come home.'

Neither of us moved, and it suddenly occurred to me that I had no idea how long I had been away. Perhaps it was less than a month since we had left Athens, or perhaps it was two years. I had no idea. I had no idea what season of the year it was – ploughing, harvesting, vintage – or how long it was since we had been together last, in this room, when I still had all that expensive armour of mine which by now must have been auctioned off in some dusty square in Sicily.

'You've come home?' she said. 'What's happened? Nobody said the fleet was back . . . '

Then she ran across and put her arms around me, somewhat clumsily; rather as an enthusiastically friendly dog jumps up at you and knocks the breath out of you. 'Oh, you're back,' she said, and pulled my head down and kissed me. But, contrary to my expectations, that kiss was not decisive; I still did not feel committed, one way or another.

'So what happened?' she demanded. 'Did you desert? I'll bet you did, you coward. At the first sight of the enemy, you said to yourself, "That'll do me," and you didn't stop running till you reached the ships. And now everyone'll point to me in the street and say "There goes the coward's wife." Do you want something to eat?'

'No,' I said.

'Well, I expect you're still full of Sicilian wheat. And what were the girls like there? Were they cheap? Of course you spent so much on them you haven't brought me back a present, not so much as a pair of bronze earrings. Your beard needs trimming. And what have you done with your armour? You can't have thrown it all away.'

'I have, actually,' I said.

'Eupolis,' she said, 'what's wrong?'

I wanted to tell her, but I couldn't. Now that I was home I didn't know what to do, like a seasonal worker after the vintage is over.

'There is something wrong, isn't there?' she said. 'You look just like you do when one of your stupid plays flops. And then you're hell to live with for a fortnight, and I daren't buy myself anything. What's happened? Where's everyone else? Did we win?'

'No.'

'Don't say you've abandoned the War and come home empty-handed. I knew that Demosthenes was nothing but a crook. They'll put him to death for this, you mark my words. And high time too.'

'They won't get the chance,' I said. It was as if what had happened, to the army and to me, was a sort of secret which Phaedra would have to prise out of me. If she managed it, she had won.

'I wish you'd tell me what's going on,' she said. 'Have you really deserted? Or have you been injured and sent home? Eupolis, are you hurt?'

'No,' I said, and I looked at her, dispassionately, for the first time since we met.

I remember the first time I realised what I looked like. I was playing out on the hillside at Pallene with some other boys, and there was a little stream that ran into a pool during the season, before the sun dries up all the water there. We were sitting round this pool throwing stones at the frogs, and one of the boys was telling a story he had heard from his grandmother. It was the story of Narcissus, and I couldn't understand the point of it. The prince looked into the water, they said, and saw this beautiful youth and fell in love with him. I couldn't bear not getting the point and interrupted.

'Amyntas,' I said, 'who was the beautiful youth? And how could he breathe underwater?'

Everyone laughed and called me names, but I didn't care. 'You don't know, do you?' I jeered. 'This is a silly story and you've just made it up.'

Everyone laughed again, and Amyntas explained that if you looked at calm water, you could see your reflection.

'What's a reflection?'

'It's a picture of you.'

'My father has a picture of my mother,' I said. 'He had a vase painted with her as Penelope, though it doesn't look a bit like her. But no one's ever painted me.'

'It doesn't have to be painted,' said Amyntas. 'It just happens. Look in the pool there.'

I knew better than that, of course; this was just a trick, and they would push me in and hold me under until I started gurgling. But on my way home my curiosity got the better of me, and I stopped and looked at the water in the watering-trough in our yard. There, sure enough, was a picture. It was a horrible little boy, with a squashed-up face and big ears, and I hated him, because he frightened me. I burst into tears and ran home, and my father asked what had upset me. I told him, and he laughed.

'Well,' he said, 'there's nothing you can do about it, is there? You're stuck with that face, whether you like it or not.'

'Can't you make it better?' I asked.

'Only Zeus can do that,' he replied.

So every night I prayed to Zeus to make me look better, and every morning I went and looked in the watering-trough, and I was still the same. For a long time I couldn't understand why Zeus hadn't answered my prayers, for I had prayed very hard and even sacrificed my pet grass-hopper to him. Then it came to me in a blinding flash of inspiration that he must be away visiting the Scythians or the Ethiopians and couldn't hear me, and so I would have to wait until he got back. I must have forgotten to pray to him after that, for my face stayed as it was, or perhaps got worse.

Anyway; as I looked at Phaedra then I had that same feeling; that she was as much a part of me as my face, and that only Zeus could do anything about it.

'How's my son?' I asked, and that was honestly the first thought I had given him since I left Athens. Even now that I had remembered him, I felt no great interest in him. He was like some unsightly present that a friend has given you, and you only remember to get it out and put it on display when the friend is knocking on the door.

'He's fine,' Phaedra replied. 'He's with the nurse at the moment. Shall I send for him?'

'No, that's all right,' I said. 'So long as he's well.'

'There is something wrong, isn't there?' said Phaedra.

'Yes,' I replied.

'What?'

'Let me take my boots off first.'

'The hell with your boots,' she said irritably, and I smiled.

'But my feet are hot,' I said. 'I want to take my boots off.'

'Then take your wretched boots off, if it means so much to you,' she said. 'Only tell me what's the matter. I want to know if you're going to be arrested or not.'

I put my arms round her. She felt familiar, as if she belonged. She pushed me away.

'Not now,' she said. 'Tell me what's going on. You can be really irritating at times.'

I sat down and pulled off my boots. 'Thrax,' I called out, 'bring me my sandals, would you? And I wouldn't mind a bit of bread and some cheese, if there is any.'

'Honestly,' Phaedra said, 'I don't understand you.'

'I know,' I replied.

She scowled. 'I don't know why I put up with you, really. I mean, this is ludicrous. Tell me what's going on.'

I wished that I could; but there was no way that I could tell her now. I had handled the business very badly, but that was nothing new. Thrax brought me the bread and cheese and I ate it.

'Are you going to tell me?' said Phaedra. 'Or do I have to go to the Market Square and ask?'

I put down the plate and brushed away the crumbs. 'Phaedra,' I said, 'how would it be if . . . ' I couldn't finish the sentence; it wasn't necessary, and it would sound ridiculous. I had meant to say something like ' . . . if we start again from scratch', or something like that, but of course we wouldn't be doing that. Impossible.

'If what?'

'Nothing,' I said. I knew I was home, then. 'Phaedra, the army's been wiped out.'

'What did you say?'

'The army, Phaedra,' I said. 'It's been wiped out. They're all dead.'

She stared at me. 'Are you mad?' she said.

'No,' I replied, 'but I don't know why. Phaedra, it was horrible. Nicias and Demosthenes too, all dead, every one of them. There's just a handful of us left.'

'I don't understand,' she said. 'For God's sake try and talk sense.'

'The Syracusans won,' I said. 'They destroyed our army. Destroyed, killed, wiped out, massacred, put to death, eliminated, decimated, there isn't a word for it. I escaped and got away to Catana. Me and Aristophanes, son of Philip. I think there are a few hundred other survivors too. But the rest of them are all dead. I got us to Catana and we came back on a cargo ship. The others aren't coming back.'

For a moment I felt the whole weight of it pressing on me; you know how it is when you get the toothache very badly, and you think that you just can't bear the pain of it any more. It was as if having Phaedra there was thawing me out, and in a moment I would melt and fall to pieces, and everything would come out in a rush, like being sick. My soul within me was demanding that I tell her everything, now, just as it came into my mind, so that I could get rid of the poison under the abscess and be well again. You fool, said my soul, unless you get rid of it all now, with tears and the comfort of her arms holding you, you will never be clear of it. But I held myself together for that little time, and turned back the words from the gate of my teeth; and then I was outside it all again, someone who saw it happen rather than a participant. And in that time I grabbed hold of Phaedra's hand, but I didn't do more than that, although I was tempted to bury my head in her and hide under her arms. I realised that I didn't want to get rid of this unique possession, this great secret that the God had entrusted to me. Like a miser with a pot of coins I wanted to hide it away where no one could get at it.

'Oh, Phaedra,' I said, lifting my head and looking into her eyes. 'I've seen the most extraordinary things while I've been away.'

Phaedra was marvellous, just then. She wanted passionately to make me tell her exactly what had happened – how would you have felt, in her position? But she sat there and waited while I fought it out with my soul, even though I was closing the gate on her as well as the world. If I had melted then, as I almost did, if I had lost my balance and she had caught me, our whole lives would have been different after that. It was then that I knew that she did understand me, in some undefinable way beyond communication by words or gestures.

'Is there anything you've got to do?' she asked. 'Like notifying somebody or something?'

'I've done that,' I said. 'You don't mind just keeping me company for a minute or so, do you?'

She didn't smile, or hug me or anything. 'Of course not,' she said. 'If you're sure it's me you want.'

'There isn't anyone else,' I said. 'They're all dead.'

'Callicrates?'

I nodded. She said nothing. She knew that if he was

still alive I would have talked to him, told him everything. But there was no one left alive I could tell it to; not until my mind had broken it down and digested it, and made something out of it.

'Promise me you won't ask me about it,' I said. She smiled.

'All right,' she said. 'You're back safe, that's the main thing.'

'I'm glad you think so,' I replied.

'Oh, it would have been an awful nuisance if you hadn't,' she said, getting up and pushing her hair back behind her shoulders. 'Lawsuits and inheritance problems and who gets what. All your money would have been tied up for ages, and I would have had to marry your nearest male relative. Of all the laws Solon ever passed, that must be the silliest.' She paused for a moment. 'Who is your nearest male relative, by the way?'

'I don't know,' I confessed. 'I think they're all dead.'

'So long as it's not that horrible cousin of yours, Nicomedes, the one with the big hairy arms and no neck. I couldn't fancy him at all.'

'He wouldn't exactly be overjoyed,' I retorted. 'I believe he's quite fond of his wife, and he'd have to divorce her.'

'Isn't she that skinny woman with those enormous elbows?'

'Habrosyne,' I replied, dredging the name out of the silt at the bottom of my mind. 'She isn't a thing of beauty, I'll grant you. But at least she doesn't spend all her husband's money on carpets.'

Phaedra looked down quickly. 'Oh, that,' she said. 'And that's all the thanks I get for getting you the best bargain you'll ever make. Just look at the weave.'

'What was wrong with the old one, for God's sake? It had years left in it.'

'I don't know why I bother,' said Phaedra. 'I should just put rushes down on the floor, like they do in Pallene.'

'If you swept the place occasionally,' I said, 'we wouldn't have to get expensive new carpets every five minutes.'

'I bet Nicomedes isn't so petty about money,' she

replied. 'Perhaps you'd better go back and get killed.'

'If you spent Nicomedes' money like you spend mine, he'd break both your arms.'

'Just shows what a low-class family I married into,' said Phaedra, triumphantly. 'You don't know how lucky you are.'

'True,' I said. 'If I hadn't a wife who makes life unbearable at home, I'd never have taken up writing plays.'

'And that's another thing wrong with you,' said Phaedra. 'You steal my jokes for your plays.'

'Rubbish. You've never made a joke in your life.'

'Are you saying I've got no sense of humour?' she said angrily. 'Just because I don't laugh at your puerile efforts at Comedy?'

'You wouldn't recognise a joke if it bit you.'

'I'm unlikely to come across one in this house.' She giggled. 'Except in there,' she said, pointing to the inner room. 'Now that's quite comical sometimes. Most of the time, in fact. And before you say anything,' she added quickly, 'that's not an invitation.'

'Good,' I said, 'I'm far too tired.'

'You usually are, thank God.'

'No,' I said, 'usually it's just an excuse. But today I mean it.'

'Are you sure?'

'Yes.'

'Please yourself.'

I leaned back in my chair and closed my eyes, stretching my feet out until I could feel the leg of the cauldron with my toes. But it was not as if I had never been away. It could never be that. Still, tomorrow I would go to Pallene, and after that to Phylae, and then I would come back to the City again, and take up some new occupation, such as composing Comedies. Something quiet and safe, where I wouldn't have to hide from the cavalry any more. I looked across at Phaedra just as she retreated into the inner room and slammed the door. She wasn't perfect, not by a long way, but she wasn't a Sicilian cavalryman, and that was the main thing.

Chapter Ten

'And now, Eupolis,' you are saying, 'will you please get on with the story, and stop bothering us with all this nonsense about your wife and your complicated mental state? We get enough of that sort of thing at home, thank you very much; what we want from you is entertainment. What happened next in the War?' Be patient. I've had enough of the War for the time being, and I want to put in something now that will impress my grandchildren. Yes, little ones, the silly old fool actually knew the celebrated Tragedian Euripides, whose plays you have to learn when you really want to go catching grasshoppers. The longest sustained conversation I ever had with Euripides . . . Well. First I must tell you what happened when I next met the celebrated Tragedian Euripides.

The news of the disaster had broken, and the City was in a state of complete panic. Scarcely a day passed without a rumour starting that the Syracusan fleet, crammed to bursting-point with bloodthirsty Sicilians, was only one day away from Piraeus in search of vengeance, and it was the general consensus of opinion that if the City walls were still standing in a month's time, it would only be because the Spartans wanted them as a defence against the Persians. You could get any money you asked for food, particularly grain, as people started hoarding, and quite a few families sold up their land and sailed off to the Black Sea, where they reckoned they would be safe. As for me, I took no part in the general panic. I had used up all my fear for the season, and had none left to fritter away on mere rumours. It would, of course, be a suitably ironic ending to be killed by the enemy here in Athens, after flogging all the way across Sicily to get home, but I felt that it would be too great an expense of energy even for the Gods to destroy Athens completely just to round off my personal story.

When I saw how buoyant the market for grain and other foodstuffs was, I set off for Pallene to find out how much I could spare for sale, and to see to the ploughing and manuring, since it was already the beginning of October. My vintage had taken place without me, and perhaps as a result we had made a larger than average amount of wine, and the harvest had been no worse than we had all expected at the start of the season. Now I always like to start ploughing early, since that way you can plough more often, and if possible I like to get the fodder vetch in before the end of September. This year, however, there had understandably been a shortage of seasonal workers and my steward had decided to leave the vetch and start the main ploughing. That was sensible, but since I had nothing better to do I decided to get on and see to the vetch myself; for it pains me to run short of fodder and have to feed good barley to mules and donkeys. So as soon as I had taken stock of what we had in and what we would need for ourselves, and sent off the surplus to the City, I put on my short cloak, got out a rusty and broken old plough which wouldn't be needed for the main work, harnessed up a mule, and set off for the low terraces. It was pleasant to be working again, and I was making a better job than usual of keeping my rows straight, and in addition some promising verses were starting to come together in my head, so I was annoyed to be interrupted by a pair of travellers who called out to me from the road.

'I thought it was you,' said the elder of the two. 'I had forgotten you had land out here.'

I recognised who it was: Euripides, and his cousin Cephisophon. I knew them both only slightly, and it was some time since we had last met. But these were guests worth stopping work for.

'Come down to the house,' I said, 'if you're not in a hurry. We're drinking up the year before last's vintage to make room, and we could do with some help.'

Euripides smiled and agreed. It turned out that he had been visiting relations half a day to the north and was quite tired after his journey. Of course as a Comic poet it is my duty to make nasty remarks about our leading Tragic authors, and so I had frequently insinuated that Euripides was no enemy to a cup or two of wine; but I was surprised to find out that I hadn't actually been slandering him at all. I made a mental note and asked him how he had been getting on. Was he writing something at the moment?

He shook his head. 'No,' he said, 'not just now.' He sounded rather bored with the subject, and it occurred to me that he probably didn't enjoy writing any more. I always find that hard to understand, but apparently it is an occupational hazard with Tragedians. 'Your olives are shaping up well,' he said.

'They won't get much bigger now,' I replied. 'Too dry. So you aren't planning to present anything this year?'

'No,' he said. 'I saw your people were manuring quite thickly down on the levels. That is yours down there?'

'Yes.'

'We always save the best of our manure for the higher ground,' said Euripides, 'and you're much higher up here than us. How much do you give it per acre?'

'What?'

'Manure.'

'Oh.' I thought hard. 'I can't remember offhand,' I replied, rather ashamed of myself. Euripides looked down his nose at me. Just as I was about to die of shame, I remembered. 'At a rough estimate,' I said, 'we reckon that what we get each year from one ox will do two and a half acres or thereabouts. But we aren't very scientific about it; it's more a sort of instinct.'

'Instinct,' he said. 'I see. And do you rot it or use it neat?'

'Oh, neat, of course,' I said.

'Really?' He seemed surprised. 'So what are you getting back, per acre, in an average year?'

'What?'

'Barley.'

'Oh.' I had thought we were still on about manure. 'Fourteen medimni, fourteen and a quarter if we're lucky. Depends a lot on the rain, of course. This year we didn't get twelve.'

'Fourteen?' said Euripides, clearly shaken. 'As much as that?'

'What are you getting?' I asked.

'Eleven,' he snarled, 'and that's if we're lucky. What about your vines? What does that come to, per acre?'

'Around thirty metretes, sometimes more.'

'Olives?'

'We do quite well with olives,' I said. 'We usually make four per acre, and more if it rains.'

He stared. 'You can't be serious,' he said. 'Four metretes the acre, in this god-awful country?'

I didn't like to ask him how much he was getting. He looked quite upset. To calm him down, I said how much I had liked his last play.

'Never mind all that,' he said, 'what are you doing that I'm not? Thirty met to the acre in wine; it must be as weak as water.'

'You're drinking it,' I said, affronted, 'you tell me.'

He apologised, and I accepted his apology. 'How often do you plough?' I asked.

'Three times, maybe four if there's heavy dew,' he said. 'More than that and we'd have to take on casual workers.'

'We plough five times, and six does no harm,' I replied, for this was my pet topic. 'It works the moisture down into the soil, you see.'

'You probably have more men than me,' he muttered. 'And like I said, I don't take on casuals.'

'Neither do I,' I replied. 'You ought to try a fifth ploughing. The fifth ploughing only takes a tenth of the time of the first, and it really does make a difference.'

'Writing anything this year?' he asked, slightly defensively I thought.

'Don't think I'll have time,' I replied, 'what with the vetch and the fenugreek to get in.'

'Fenugreek?' He stared at me as if I was mad. 'What earthly good is that stuff?'

I told him about fenugreek, and lupins too, and to give him his due he listened. But when I started up on my favourite theme of all, beans, he seemed to lose patience and said it was time he was on his way.

'Well,' I said, 'any time you're passing. And I hope you do try a fifth ploughing this year. Let me know how you get on.'

He assured me that he would, picked up his hat, collected Cephisophon (who had been helping shift my wine-surplus all this time) and started to leave.

'By the way,' I called after him. He turned. 'I thought you'd like to know, your stuff is really popular in Sicily.'

'What?' He seemed puzzled.

'Your plays,' I explained.

'Oh,' he said, 'that.'

'Yes indeed,' I assured him, and I briefly told him about the village where we had given our extempore recital. It didn't seem to please him in the least, and he was quite short with me as he left. But a year or so later he sent me a charming little bronze bowl with Triptolemus on it, as a thank-you present, and said that I had been quite right about a fifth ploughing and using less manure; he was now clearing twelve and a half medimni to the acre, and had high hopes of seeing thirteen in a couple of years' time. But I don't think he ever made a serious effort to grow beans.

While I was busy with my vetch, I started work on a new Comedy. It virtually crept up on me when I wasn't looking, for I had not intended to enter anything for a while; but before I knew where I was I had thought of a splendid entry for a chorus of sheep, and after that there was no stopping me. Of course I needed a Message, and I couldn't really think of one. The City was a very different place now, after the disaster, and the old themes no longer seemed appropriate.

It was a difficult time. As soon as the news about Sicily broke, our enemies became extremely animated and talked very loudly about finishing us off once and for all.

Our so-called allies, which means our subjects, were all on the point of rebellion, and as winter came on King Agis of Sparta set out with his army. But for some reason he didn't attack the City; instead he went around trying to collect money to build a fleet. We were building a fleet of our own, of course, and we cut out all useless expenditure so as to be able to afford it. Luckily, the Festivals were spared, and I pressed on with my play. I was back in the City now, and I saw quite a lot of Philonides and his friends, since I wanted him to present the play when the time came. The Chorus of sheep had been scrapped in favour of a Chorus of shipwrights, and I had high hopes for the piece come the spring.

I was so wrapped up in this work that I didn't take any notice of what was happening in the City. Now, quite naturally, the Athenians wanted to punish someone for what had happened in Sicily, but they were unable to do this since Nicias and Demosthenes were both dead and Alcibiades was in exile. They tried and executed a taxiarch who had escaped and made his way home, on some charge of general cowardice, but that wasn't really enough to make them happy, and so they looked round for a worthier scapegoat. Such a person was difficult to find, since the fault lay with the voters in Assembly; but then some ingenious person hit on the idea of blaming the whole thing on the people who had damaged the statues, the night before the fleet sailed.

Don't laugh, it's true. The movement gathered an incredible amount of momentum, and was soon completely out of control. There was a spate of accusations, and the men who had fostered the crisis in the hope of getting rid of various political opponents began to worry in case they got caught up in the general frenzy.

Now I knew the truth behind the whole thing, of course; I had been a witness, if you remember, and had barely escaped alive. 1 certainly knew who at least some of the perpetrators were; Aristophanes son of Philip, for example. I had no intention whatsoever of turning informer myself, as informing is a very dangerous business and only to be resorted to if you are desperately short of money.

But Aristophanes and a few others knew that I had seen them at their work that night, and this cannot have been any comfort to them. As soon as she realised what was happening, Phaedra urged me to get out of the City until things had settled down. But I was still preoccupied with my play and wanted to stay in town so as to be able to talk things over with Philonides. I had abandoned the shipwrights now; I had struck on a truly brilliant idea.

My Chorus was to be made up of all the various regions of Attica, with each region unmistakably dressed in an appropriate costume. The Chorus-leader would be my own deme of Pallene, in a costume made up of mountains and goats, and the plot would be that all the great statesmen of the past return to earth to advise us in our hour of greatest need – the whole lot of them, from Solon to Pericles. I toyed with making that Solon to Cleon, but I rejected it, which was cowardly of me. If only I could get it right, it would be my best play by far; it would deal with not just one theme but every theme. Of course with so much meat in it, the funny bits would have to be just right, but I felt that I could deal with that, if I tried my best.

It was about this time – please don't expect me to be more precise than that – that Aristophanes son of Philip came back into my life. He was, as I have told you, horribly implicated in this business with the statues, and to be fair to him he was in danger of being put to death or exiled for something so completely trivial that it must have been hard for him to take his problems seriously. The strange thing was that, apart from the participants themselves and a few eye-witnesses like myself, nobody actually did know who had smashed up those confounded statues. As you no doubt remember, it was the night before the fleet sailed; so everyone was either asleep or drunk. We Athenians are privileged to live in a city where the sound of nocturnal breakages is so commonplace as to be unworthy of attention, and I imagine that most people took no notice. This mystery, however, added the little spark to the affair that turned it into a raging fire. The average voter took it to be the symptom of some all-embracing conspiracy; and we Athenians love a conspiracy. Of course the absence of anything remotely resembling an established fact in connection with the business allowed the creative imagination of my fellow countrymen to run away with itself; there was simply no limit to what they could convince themselves of, given time and the encouragement of like-minded people. I honestly believe that if I had had the wit to start a rumour that the frogs from the marshes did it, under orders from their paymasters, the frogs from the swamps round Syracuse, in order to prevent our ships from coming into Syracuse harbour and so getting in the way of their annual mating, then everyone would have believed it and a great deal of trouble would have been saved; except of course for the frogs in the marshes, who would have been massacred to a frog.

There were debates about it in Assembly, of course. Now one of the great things about a democracy, which anyone considering setting one up in their native city should bear in mind, is that the voters really do believe that anything is possible. If there is a food shortage, for example, it's no use explaining to them that there is no food to be had; that the Spartan fleet is blockading Byzantium and we can't get so much as a grain of wheat past them, or that the Public Treasury is so empty that you can see more floor than coins. They won't believe you. What you must do is blame somebody. You must get up on your feet and say, 'Antimachus is responsible for the corn shortage; he's done a deal with the corn factors to create an artificial shortage, and he's lining his own pockets while your wives and babies starve. I propose that Antimachus be prosecuted.' Then, when all the voters have gone rushing off like happy children to lynch Antimachus, and only a few of the old and confused are left, you propose the motions necessary to do what can be done in the circumstances, bribe the few remaining voters present to vote in favour, and then get on with the job. This is rough on Antimachus, of course, but it's a fair proposition that if he's a politician in the public eye then he's had it coming to him for a long time, so in the end the system works.

After the news of the Sicilian disaster, of course, the Athenians' belief in their own omnipotence was badly shaken. At first they were rather too preoccupied with panicking to reason the thing out, but when whole weeks had passed and still the Spartans weren't sacking the Ceramicus they stopped feeling subdued and argued thus. We ordered Sicily to be conquered (said the Athenians). It wasn't. Now anything we order done is as good as done unless some one of us deliberately sabotages it, and since we are omnipotent, only we ourselves can stop ourselves doing something. We must therefore punish the saboteurs. Now the Generals, Nicias and Demosthenes, cannot be punished, since they are dead already. But we can do anything, including punishing the guilty. It therefore stands to reason that they can't really have been to blame, especially since they died like heroes, and heroes don't go around sabotaging things and bringing about their own deaths. The only possible saboteurs were the young men who damaged the statues. They must therefore be killed. Before they are killed, it is desirable that they be found. Therefore we must find them. The fact that we cannot presently find them can only be explained by a conspiracy. Therefore we will kill the conspirators.

Which is what they proceeded to do. Their test for finding out whether someone was in on the conspiracy or not was brilliantly simple. They knew that any conspirator, when questioned, would automatically deny any knowledge of the conspiracy. So when a man was standing his trial, and the prosecutor asked him what he knew about the conspiracy and he said 'Nothing at all', they hauled him off to the prison and stood him a large hemlock. If, however, the accused was clever and said, 'As it happens, I do know who was involved in the conspiracy; it was Lysicles and Phaonides and the rest of that crowd from the Gymnasium', then they would exterminate the Gymnasium set, and the informer as well, on the grounds that if he knew about the conspiracy and hadn't told anyone before now, he was to all intents and purposes a conspirator himself.

The really odd thing about all this was that of all the people they killed, none of them actually did have anything to do with the smashing-up of the statues. Now you would have thought that, in what was effectively a random sample of the political classes, at least one of the smashers would have drawn the short straw, so to speak. But they seemed immune, and I was able to feel relatively secure. I say relatively; in context, that meant that I felt reasonably confident that if I started a bowl of porridge and ate quickly, I would probably stay alive long enough to finish it. My personal nightmare was that one of the actual smashers would be caught in some general sweep, lose his nerve and confess, giving such plausible corroborative detail that even my idiotic fellow citizens would believe him. And then of course my name would be mentioned as being someone who was actually there, and the next thing I would know about it would be an alarming feeling of numbness around the toes.

When the party was just starting to get exciting, and the juries were working flat out, in shifts, to clear the backlog of cases, a gentleman by the name of Demeas came round to see me one evening. Now Demeas was one of the masters of a trade that has now almost died out, although there are sporadic efforts to revive it; he was a professional informer. He made a reasonable living out of it – his main work was reporting contraband goods in return for a percentage of their value, and let me tell you that he had an almost supernatural ability to tell, just by looking at them, whether goods were contraband or not. I am told that he had been apprenticed in his youth to the great Nicarchus, perhaps the leading informer of all time, and that may explain where he got his instinct from. Now when this business with the statues came up, Demeas set to work with a degree of enthusiasm which should serve as an example to skilled tradesmen everywhere. He was, however, slightly hampered by a shortage of raw materials. Just as you cannot make fine pottery without glaze, you cannot bring a successful prosecution without witnesses; and since the mortality rate among witnesses in this affair was almost as high as that among defendants, most of the professional witnesses had been used up or had retired, and for once there was no rush of amateur talent to take their place. In the normal course of events, an Athenian loves being a witness, particularly in a treason trial. It gives him a chance to participate in the downfall of a leading public figure (which gives one a feeling of pride and something to tell one's grandchildren), as well as the opportunity to speak in public, which no Athenian not cursed with a cleft palate can resist. But with so many witnesses being promoted from the supporting cast to the leading role, so to speak, it was getting difficult to find anyone remotely plausible, even for cash in advance. Hence Demeas' visit to me.

When a person with so much standing in the community as Demeas had comes to call on you, you don't keep him hanging about on the doorstep, particularly if there are people about who might see you. Nor do you refuse to listen to whatever it is he has to say; for if you do, you risk finding out a great many things about yourself that you never knew before.

'Eupolis,' said Demeas, putting down his cup and stretching out his toes towards the fire, 'I believe you know Aristophanes the son of Philip.'

'Yes,' I said.

'You were with him in Sicily, weren't you?'

'Yes.'

'So I'd heard.' Demeas nodded approvingly. He was a short man; for some reason all the great informers are – Nicarchus was a tiny little chap, by all accounts. Demeas had broad, round shoulders, a perfectly circular head with short hair, and no trace of a neck whatsoever. He wore a signet ring with a lion on it on the first finger of his left hand, and there were wine-stains down the front of his tunic. I didn't greatly care for him, but I confess I take these irrational dislikes to people.

'Now then,' said Demeas, 'while you were in Sicily, did Aristophanes say anything at all about the desecration of the holy statues?'

'No,' I said truthfully, 'not that I can remember.'

Demeas put his head on one side. 'What did you talk about, then?' he asked.

'Well,' I replied, 'we discussed the War, and how to keep out of the way of the enemy, the play he was writing, that sort of thing.'

'So you were quite friendly with him?'

I smelt danger, and decided to hedge. 'I wouldn't say friendly,' I said, after a pause for what I hoped looked like considered thought. 'And I wouldn't say unfriendly, either. We just got on with the work in hand – getting to Catana and so forth.'

'But surely,' Demeas suggested, 'the two of you, in such close proximity, sharing such terrible dangers and with no one else to turn to but each other; surely you discussed other things.'

'I can't say we did, actually.'

'I see.' Demeas rested his chin on his knuckle for a moment. 'You know, I believe you, of course, but other people might not.'

'Other people?'

'Hypothetically. Reasonable men, if you like. They might think that under such circumstances if Aristophanes had, say, something on his conscience, something that was bothering him, it would be only natural for him to confess it to whoever he felt closest to at the time, or even just whoever happened to be there.'

'Would they?'

'Wouldn't you? And then you say, "No, Aristophanes told me nothing." Now they might well think, these men are friends, they've been through great trials together, it's natural – laudable, even – that the one should cover up for the other. That they should collude with each other; no, that's not the right word. It's on the tip of my tongue . . . '

'Conspire?'

'Not conspire exactly; but you get the general idea. But then these hypothetical reasonable men would start feeling confused, because they wouldn't know which of them was covering up for the other. And if they happened to be forming a jury at the time, they might execute both of you, just to be on the safe side. They would take the view that covering up for a blasphemer and a traitor is no better – morally – than committing the crime yourself.'

'That's the way they think, is it?'

'Sadly, yes.'

'And is it likely that a jury should be faced with this sort of dilemma?' I asked. 'In the near future, say?'

'Don't ask me,' Demeas confirmed. 'Where were you, the night the fleet sailed?'

'Here,' I said. 'Ask my wife.'

'Does she sleep at all, your wife? Or does she suffer from permanent insomnia?'

'She has been known to sleep, yes. Where were *you* the night the fleet sailed?'

'In Samos,' he replied smoothly, 'having dinner with the Athenian governor and his staff. I was investigating the smuggling of prohibited goods, and they were helping me.'

I remembered the trial. 'You're lucky to have such a good alibi,' I said.

'Alibi?' He shrugged his shoulders. 'You know, people are very hard on us public-spirited people. I don't care if I'm being immodest here, but I believe I make a substantial contribution to the preservation of our democracy.'

'Without men like you,' I said, 'there could be no democracy.'

'Exactly. And you know, I'm not a thin-skinned man, but I do get hurt sometimes by what people say.'

'People?'

'Just ordinary people, you'd be surprised. But not just ordinary people. There's always someone ready to point the finger.'

'Really?'

'Oh yes.' He looked sad. 'For instance, there was a play I went to a few years ago which contained a personal attack on me. I think it was meant to be a Comedy. Anyway, there was this man in a funny mask purporting to be me, doing all sorts of antisocial things on stage, and everyone was laughing. It was really quite upsetting, especially for my wife.'

That explained the interest in Aristophanes; the play had been one of his. It wasn't a particularly good scene, either.

'And that wasn't all,' continued Demeas, now sadder than ever. 'The very next year, I can't remember the name of the play or who wrote it, but there was a Chorus which suggested that I was no better than a tapeworm or some such creature, and that if ever the City found itself short of funds it should put me through a press as if I was an olive and squeeze out all the bribes and blood-money. There was also a reference to my domestic arrangements that I found singularly distasteful.'

That explained the interest in me. 'I don't know what gets into these people,' I said.

'Well,' said Demeas, now virtually in tears, 'it just goes to show. For the sake of a cheap laugh and a round of applause, some people are prepared to throw around the most damaging – I might say dangerous – accusations, and they don't give a damn if they ruin reputations or even lives. It's highly irresponsible, if you ask me. Why, men have been convicted of serious crimes just because the Theatre has poisoned the public mind against them. I think the people responsible have a lot to answer for.'

'You have a point, of course,' I said.

'You think so?'

'Indeed.'

'That's comforting to know,' said Demeas, and he got up to leave. 'Well,' he said, 'I won't take up any more of your time. If you remember anything . . . '

'I'll be sure to tell you.'

'You know where I live?'

'Yes indeed.'

'Well,' he said, 'I'll say good night.'

'Good night.'

Now I don't think they're as popular as they used to be, but at one time Athens used to be crawling with those teachers of philosophy, men like the celebrated Socrates and Gorgias the Sicilian, who used to give little lectures; it was three obols for a seat, and a drachma to take part, or something like that. They would present a moral dilemma, and then everyone would say how they would act under the circumstances, and the lecturer would prove beyond doubt that they were all as evil as Hecate, and they would go home highly delighted and tell their friends. I went to one of these entertainments once – I think someone bet me I couldn't keep awake – and the topic was whether it was justified to allow a wicked man who was charged with a crime he did not commit to be executed for it in order for a good man who had in fact committed the crime in question to go free. I don't remember what conclusion Socrates or whoever the lecturer was came to – it's an odd thing about those lectures, but nobody ever can seem to remember that – but the general impression I took home with me was that if ever I got into such a mess I should do whatever I liked, since virtually every course of action put forward had been shown to be fundamentally wrong.

As I closed the door and bolted it, I thought about that lecture and reflected that I had been cheated out of three obols, since here I was in a highly similar situation and I didn't have the faintest idea what to do. There were differences of course; Aristophanes was wicked and guilty, and I was good and innocent. Nevertheless, it was a close enough parallel for me to be tempted to go round to Socrates' house and demand a refund there and then.

'Who was that?' Phaedra asked, putting her head round the door of the inner room. 'One of your drinking pals from the Theatre? I hope he wasn't sick.'

'Sick is putting it mildly,' I said. 'My love, we are in a lot of trouble.'

'What do you mean, we?'

'We, as in I am going to be executed, and you are going to be left destitute when they confiscate all my property to pay the informer.'

'Oh God,' she said, 'what have you done?'

'I haven't done anything,' I snapped. 'That's the aggravating part of it.'

Phaedra sat down next to me. 'What are you supposed to have done?'

'Smashed up the statues.'

'That's nonsense,' she said, relieved that I had been worrying over nothing. 'I can vouch for that. You were in bed with me.'

I shook my head. 'I don't really think that'll be enough to convince a jury,' I said. 'Now if I could prove I had been in bed with the prosecutor, and the presiding magistrate, and the entire Council, I might just stand a chance. You, no.'

'But it's the truth,' Phaedra said. 'Do you think anyone would seriously believe that I would perjure myself just to protect you?'

'You'd be amazed,' I said. 'No, there's only one way out of it, and I can't do it.'

'What, for God's sake?'

'Don't ask.'

'Don't be idiotic,' said Phaedra. 'Tell me what's going on.'

'All right,' I said. 'That man just now was Demeas, the informer. You know him?'

'I've heard of him,' she said. 'He was behind that big trial of the people who were supposed to be smuggling in perfume from Corinth. And it wasn't from Corinth at all, you know. Any woman could have told you that. It was just the cheap stuff they make down on the coast and put up in those little bottles.'

'Fascinating,' I said. 'Anyway, Demeas has got it in for me and Aristophanes because we mentioned him in plays, and besides, we're still alive. He wants one or the other of us for his next production.'

'And?'

'And, of course, he wants the other one as his key witness. That was what he was here for just now; offering me the choice.'

'You've got a choice?'

'Yes.'

'I thought you said we were in trouble.'

I frowned. 'We are. You do speak Greek, I take it? Trouble. Serious danger. Material risk to life and property.'

'I don't know what you mean,' said Phaedra. 'You hate Aristophanes. I'd have thought you'd be overjoyed.'

'Inform on him, you mean?'

'Yes.'

'That's the problem,' I said, and I threw a handful of charcoal on the fire. 'Look, Phaedra,' I said, 'you know me. Normally I wouldn't hesitate. I'd inform on my own father to save my own neck, you know that. But not Aristophanes. I just can't.'

'But you hate him,' said Phaedra. 'He's your worst enemy in the entire world. He slept with your wife. He tried to sabotage your play. For God's sake,' she remembered, 'he's even guilty of the damned crime.'

'I know,' I said.

'And if you think,' she said, 'that he'd hesitate one minute before informing on you just because you saved his life in Sicily . . . '

'How did you know about that?' I asked.

' . . . then you're a bigger fool than you look. Don't you realise, you're a witness against him, and the rest of them, come to that?'

'Well,' I said, 'that's good, isn't it? It might stop them informing on me if they stop to think that I can do as much for them.'

Phaedra shook her head sadly. 'You just don't think, do you? You don't seriously imagine they'll believe you when you point to the chief prosecution witness and say, "Actually, it wasn't me, it was him"? That's the only way you could tell it to the jury and they wouldn't believe you.'

'True,' I said. 'It's not looking good, is it?'

'But, you idiot,' said Phaedra, 'why can't you do what Demeas wants you to? Just go to him, now, and say you'll do it? Has Aristophanes got some sort of spell on you or something?'

'Sort of,' I said. 'I promised the God I'd look after him.'

'What was that?'

'I said I promised the God. Dionysus. Why do you think I hauled his worthless body half-way across Sicily? My duty to Comic drama?'

'Is this some sort of ridiculous male all-buddies-together oath?' she replied. 'I've heard about that sort of thing.'

'No, no,' I said, 'I actually did promise the God. In person. That's why he spared my life in Sicily; so that I could look after Aristophanes.'

'Are you drunk?' said Phaedra.

'Oh, for crying out loud,' I said. 'Listen.' And I told her about the God; how I had met him in the stable during the plague, and then after *The General*, and then in the walled orchard.

'I thought so,' she said when I had finished, 'you are drunk.'

'You stupid bitch,' I said, 'I'm telling you the truth.'

'Now you listen to me,' said Phaedra, leaning forward and grabbing my tunic with both hands. 'I couldn't give a damn whether they kill you or not, but I'm not having my son grow up an oarsman, and I'm certainly not going to spend the rest of my life selling greens in the Market Square just because of some ridiculous oath you and Aristophanes may have sworn to each other in Sicily. So pull yourself together and act like a grown-up for once.'

'Phaedra,' I said, 'just let me explain, one more time— '

'Oh, you're pathetic,' she said. 'You deserve to get killed.' She let go of me, marched furiously into the inner room, and bolted the door.

'Phaedra,' I called after her.

'Later!' she shouted back through the door. 'When you've sobered up.'

I sat down by the fire and tried to think of something. But my options were limited. I tried putting myself in Aristophanes' shoes. It was a safe bet that he would get a similar visit from Demeas if I wasn't on Demeas' front step first thing tomorrow morning clamouring to give evidence. Now, would Aristophanes be put off by the fact that I actually had been a witness, and could presumably give a more convincing account of that night's activities as a result? Probably not, for the reason that Phaedra had given. Since he had been there, he could paint an equally evocative verbal picture, and since he was the accuser and I was the accused, the Athenian public would be bound to believe him. There is a theory that we have several different laws in Athens, each one dealing with a separate offence. This is not true. Whenever a man appears in the dock, nobody bothers to listen to the charge the official reads out. They know that the accused is really charged with being guilty, and that is one charge on which they will always convict. And in Athens, the sentence for being guilty is usually death by consumption of hemlock.

171

Which left only one alternative: flight. It is pathetically easy for an accused person to escape from Athens. This is not sheer fecklessness but deliberate policy, since it confirms the fugitive's guilt without wasting valuable jury time which would be better employed in the more important task of convicting the innocent. It also means that the Public Confiscator can step in quickly to seize the criminal's property; there is a lamentable tendency among people nowadays to spin out their trials in order to give their relatives time to get the bulk of their fortunes safely over the border.

So I could run for it, if I chose to do so. Where would I go? I would be faced with the horrible prospect of earning a living for myself, in Megara or Boeotia or somewhere like that. It's all very well for the Alcibiadeses of this world to jump ship and escape; they can take their pick of major cities and royal palaces, all competing to provide shelter and a pension for life to a useful and well-informed traitor. When a nobody like you or me has to escape from his city, he has to take what work he can; and unless he has a valuable skill or craft, this is likely to mean something unpleasant, probably connected with the care and upkeep of pigs or the harvesting of arable produce. We Athenians are not liked in Greece as a whole; we find it hard to get work. Now my only skill is the composition of plays, and the market for what I produce is limited to one city. Beyond that, I would be lucky to get seasonal work picking olives or grapes, and that is not my idea of life. Things have changed, and I know I'm old-fashioned, but I still believe (and everybody thought so then) that a man who has to depend on another man for his living, whether you call him a servant or an employee or whatever, is in reality nothing more than a slave, taking orders and doing what he is told. A man without land is a man without freedom, and without freedom there is no point in being alive. Even when I was on the run in Sicily, I had freedom; that was all I had.

So I wasn't going to run, and if I stayed I would have to inform on Aristophanes or die. Now I called on my soul for a little good advice, but that usually

172

eloquent spirit pretended not to hear me, and I was on my own. After a lot of thought, I saw what I had to do, and it seemed to make a sort of sense.

There had to be a reason why the God had chosen to save me, out of all those men, in the plague and the battle. I knew what that reason was; to protect the son of Philip, for as long as I lived. Now the God had so arranged matters that I had to die in order to keep him alive; but that at least explained why I had survived the plague and the battle, and in an illogical world you tend to cling to whatever explanations you can find. Now we were talking about that clever fellow Euripides a moment ago. By and large I detest his work, which is brash and modern and clever for the sake of being clever; but there is one scene of his which I must confess I like.

It's in his *Hercules*, and it comes at the point in the play where the hero, having just wiped out his family because the Goddess Hera has driven him mad in order to spite Zeus, is being comforted by his friend Theseus. Now Theseus says that Hercules has nothing to feel guilty about; the blame lies with the Gods, who made him do it. After all, says Theseus, the Gods have no moral code; they cheat and rob each other, even bind each other in chains. Hercules is furious at this, and turns on his friend. No, he says, I don't believe that the Gods bind each other in chains, or are capable of any evil; they are pure and holy, and everything they do is for the best.

So, then; whatever Dionysus was up to with me, it was for the best. This took all the weight off my shoulders – isn't that what Gods are for? It helped me to put aside my feelings of guilt at abandoning Phaedra and my son to a life of misery, for the duty a man owes to the Gods is greater than any mortal duty, and besides, the God would now have an obligation to look after Phaedra and Eutychides, for that is how the system works. I turned this solution over in my mind, and I could find no flaw in it; my only regret was that I had discovered my talent for working out the designs of the Gods too late in life to be able to make a name for myself as a Tragic poet.

As I sat there and stared into the fire, delighted with

my own cleverness, Phaedra opened the door of the inner room.

'Feeling better now?' she asked.

'Yes,' I replied.

'So you've changed your mind?'

'No.'

'I see.' She breathed out sharply. 'Because of the God?'

'Yes.'

'You're quite mad, you realise,' she said. 'I mean, your brain has actually gone.'

'If you say so.'

She sat down beside me, and neither of us said anything for a while.

'What did happen in Sicily?' she said.

I frowned. 'Is this quite the time for reminiscences?' I asked. 'Shouldn't we be discussing how to get as much of my money out of the country as we can before they send in the Confiscator?'

'That can wait,' she said. 'What did happen in Sicily?'

So I told her. It took a long time – well, you can understand why, if you've actually read this far and aren't just skipping through looking for the speeches. I found it easy to tell her, now that I had reached my decision, and she listened carefully, not interrupting except when she couldn't follow what I was saying. Occasionally I would stop, for some reason or other, and she would give me a hug and tell me to go on. It was then that I realised that I had made the right decision in accepting her, although it seemed that that decision would not turn out to be terribly important after all. When I told her about the walled orchard and the God, perhaps she understood, I don't know. When I had finished, she sat quietly for a while, picking at the hem of her dress.

'Well?' I asked.

'Well what?'

'Does it make any difference, hearing all that stuff?'

She considered this for a moment. 'It depends what you mean,' she said.

'That's a strange answer.'

'Yes, it makes a difference,' she said. 'No, it doesn't

make a difference where a difference would help. I still don't understand why you can't inform on Aristophanes.'

'Weren't you listening, then? Would you like me to go back over it?'

She shook her head. 'I don't know,' she said, 'maybe you did see the God, or maybe you thought you did; the effect would be the same. Maybe you made yourself see the God.'

'I don't follow.'

Phaedra thought for a moment and then said, 'Maybe you needed to see the God. You couldn't understand what was going on. If you didn't find an explanation for all that death and destruction you'd go mad or die. Like when you were a boy in the plague. Your soul needed some way to force you to save yourself when you'd given up and become resigned to dying; so it made you see the God. And in Sicily, it was pretty well the same thing. If you were going to survive when everyone else was dying, you had to see the God. You had to be different – special, even. There had to be a credible reason why the God should spare you and not the others. When you were a boy, that reason was that when you grew up, you knew you were going to be a great poet; that was reason enough for the God to want to save you when everyone else died. Then, in Sicily, you tried the same thing; only now you were a great poet, or as great as you were ever likely to get. It wouldn't work so well. It worked well enough to get you out of the walled orchard, but it wasn't going to sustain you across half of Sicily. And then Aristophanes turns up, and your inventive Athenian mind said yes, of course, that's it. My reason for being alive is to look after the son of Philip.'

'Clever,' I said. 'Socratic, almost. But that doesn't explain away the other time I saw Him; in the Theatre, after my play flopped. I wasn't in any danger then.'

'Oh, you just imagined it that time,' said Phaedra. 'Over-excitement, hot sun, not much sleep the night before.'

'All right then,' I said. 'How come the God was able to predict his own reappearances? How come my soul when

I was a boy was able to see that one day I'd have a play flop and end up in a walled orchard?'

Phaedra shrugged. 'Simple,' she said. 'Mental revision. You've rewritten your own memory. You've scraped off what was there before and put in something else, like the officials do when they're cheating the naval accounts.'

'You won't starve,' I said. 'You can be the first woman philosopher.'

'I thought you'd be too stupid to understand,' she said. 'Never mind, it can't be helped.'

She put her hands on my shoulders and kissed me. 'So what do you think we ought to do?' I asked. She considered this for a moment.

'I think we should go to bed,' she said. 'I don't know about you, but I'm dead to the world. Sorry, that was tactless of me. Very tired, I should have said.'

'I meant, what should we do about this Demeas business?'

'Well,' she said, 'if I were you, I'd write the funniest speech you've ever written in your life and use it as your defence at the trial. It's the only hope you've got.' Suddenly she threw her arms around me, nearly crushing my windpipe (for she was a strong woman, though you wouldn't know it to look at her). 'Eupolis, you idiot,' she said, 'I don't want you to be killed.' Then she started to cry. That nearly broke my heart, and I tried to comfort her.

'Phaedra,' I said, 'don't worry, everything will be all right. Your father will look after you and the boy, I know he will. He hasn't got a male heir, so Eutychides will be provided for. And there's plenty of time to get some of the money out; you know how long trials are taking . . . '

'Oh, you're horrible,' she sobbed. 'You're going to die, and all you think about is money. That's absolutely typical. You just don't think, do you?'

She wrenched herself out of my arms, fled into the inner room, and bolted the door again.

Chapter Eleven

The nice thing about being under sentence of death is that you stop worrying about the trivial things in life; and if, like me, you're prone to worrying, this is a great advantage.

It's all right, you haven't dropped a scroll out of the book; we haven't got to the trial yet. I was speaking figuratively. I only felt as if I was under sentence of death. Now you will say I'm exaggerating, trying to make my story more dramatic. Well, perhaps you're right. We shall see.

I went round to Aristophanes' house the next morning. I don't know what I expected to achieve, but it would have been worth trying if I had managed to see him. But the slave who answered the door said he was out of the City on business and would not be expected back for a week at the earliest. Now at first I wondered if the son of Philip had panicked and fled; this would solve everybody's problems, and I began to feel cautiously optimistic. But, to make sure, I set my slave Thrax to watch Aristophanes' house, and sure enough he reported back not long after to say that he had seen Aristophanes go out and come back half an hour later with two partridges, a sea bass and a Copaic eel. Evidently the prospect of informing on the man who had saved his life was not having a harmful effect on his appetite.

So off I went again; and again the slave told me that Aristophanes was out. He can't have remembered me from my earlier visit, since this time he told me that his master had gone off to Eleusis for a fortnight to attend the Mysteries. I asked him whether he was sure, and he said, yes, why shouldn't he be; and then I asked him if he liked sea bass. He said no. Then I gave it up as a bad job and came home.

Phaedra said I should go and see Demeas. She reckoned that I could double-cross him, by promising to give evidence on his behalf; and then, when he called me at the trial, I could swear blind that Aristophanes was as innocent as the day was long, and that Demeas had offered me money to give false evidence against him. The Athenian public love treachery but hate traitors, as the saying goes, and they might just have swallowed that and killed Demeas instead; but obviously it was too late to do that, now that Aristophanes had so clearly done a deal with Demeas, and all I could say to Phaedra was that it was a great pity she hadn't thought of that last night, when it might have done some good. Not that it would have, of course; Demeas was far too experienced at that sort of thing to be caught out so easily, and it would probably have brought about the death of both Aristophanes and me.

In spite of Phaedra's protests, I set about getting some of my money out of Athens. There were two problems. One was how to realise my assets; the other was where to send them once they were realised. There was no earthly point in sending money to any part of the Athenian Empire, since it could be recovered from there with no trouble at all by the Public Confiscator. But there was similarly no point at all in sending it into some enemy country, since then Phaedra wouldn't be able to get it back and the Spartans would probably get it and fritter it away on warships or some such nonsense. Then, when we were going through Phaedra's jewellery, we came across the pendant (gaudy but not cheap) which the Thessalian princes had given me when I went on my embassy there. We looked at each other and said, 'Well . . . ' but neither of us could think of a better idea; so I sent out Thrax again to ask an acquaintance of mine who was a Councillor if Alexander and Jason were still alive and in power. The answer came back that Alexander had murdered Jason and was ruling on his own. So I sat down and wrote Alexander a letter. I reminded him of our visit and thanked him once again for the performance of my *General*, crammed in as much theatrical gossip as I could remember or invent, and added my love and best wishes. Then, as a sort of postscript, I said that I was sending with the letter a small sum of money; if he would look after it for me until either my wife or her agent came and collected it, I would be ever so obliged to him and terribly, terribly grateful. Then, in a moment of inspiration, I said that as a tiny mark of my esteem I was sending him the original manuscript of two of my plays and a copy of the collected works of Aeschylus – luckily I had one by me, quite legibly copied and sturdily boxed up. I think it must have been those two manuscripts of mine, or maybe the Aeschylus, that did the trick, because when the time came, Alexander paid up virtually in full, and added a pair of gold earrings and an iron brooch in the form of a dung-beetle, as a present.

There was still the problem of a trustworthy messenger; but Phaedra suggested my steward from Pallene. You may remember that I had used his name for the hero of my *Maricas*. He was devoted to me, I knew, but getting on in years and not up to a long and dangerous journey. But he had a son, Philochorus (named in my honour), who was young and strong and had been on trading expeditions, so I sent for him.

Now it sounds easy enough to talk of realising assets, but of course it wasn't as simple as that, not by a long way. I had sixty-eight acres of land, almost as much as Alcibiades himself, although mine was of course more widely spread, and a fair amount of it was bare rock. Still, it was a huge estate, and there was no point even trying to sell it, as a whole or in parts. Things are very different now, of course, but in my day people simply didn't sell land, unless they were destitute or didn't have enough to live on and wanted to buy a ship or something. The best I could do was mortgage it or grant long leases, and I only managed to dispose of about eight acres that way. I could only get a fraction of its value, too; not only did the people I was trying to do business with have a fairly shrewd idea of what I was about, but the market was by now well and truly flooded, what with the confiscations and so many estates being masterless after the Sicilian campaign. I was due for my fair share of that, by the way; two cousins of mine, who I had never met, were killed in the War, and I was their nearest male relative. It seemed ironic at the time; there I was about to add nearly eighteen acres to my already quite considerable fortune, and I wouldn't live to fight the lawsuit. I assigned it in writing to my son, but without any prospect of his ever coming to contest the case.

What I could dispose of was my various other interests. I had never really appreciated how valuable they were – things like shares in ships and mines and factories aren't like land; you don't cherish every little bit of them, and show them off to your son, you just leave them to the people who know about such things and go over the receipts once a year to make sure you aren't being cheated. But when it comes to raising money in a hurry, there's nothing to compare with such things. What with the War and the disturbed state of everything, of course, nobody was wildly enthusiastic to buy, but I was able to get rid of some of them by lowering my price sufficiently. Finally, of course, there was my actual reserve of coined silver; that wasn't to be sneezed at, when all was said and done. My uncle Philodemus had brought me up to keep at least a talent in ready money at all times, and I have always done this, if possible. Not for the first time, I was grateful to him. In addition to this, Callicrates' widow sent me a loan of half a talent, from the reserve Callicrates had also maintained. I really didn't want to accept it, but she insisted; it was what he would have done, she said, if he had been alive, and to please me she accepted a mortgage on some of my land in Pallene as security.

So that was that; and when Philochorus set sail from Piraeus to Thessaly he took with him a considerable sum of money; enough to make sure Phaedra would be provided for, and to enable her to bring my son up properly.

'Knowing your luck,' said Phaedra, as we saw the ship sailing away, 'he'll get robbed by pirates.'

'Or bandits,' I said. 'Thessaly is alive with bandits.'

'Not to mention your friend Alexander,' Phaedra added. 'We must be mad, entrusting that lot to a man who's not even really Greek.'

'It won't come to that,' I said. 'Bet you Philochorus will jump ship at the first stop with the whole lot.'

'I doubt it,' she replied. 'He looked stupid enough to be honest. But that won't stop the sailors murdering him and throwing his body over the side.'

We walked home together through the City, and for some reason we were both feeling remarkably cheerful. It wasn't just because we had managed to get the money out; the whole business had been rather depressing, and we were both just glad it was over. No, I really can't say what had got into us both, but soon we were laughing and pointing funny things out to each other and making silly jokes, and people stopped and stared at us as we passed them; for in those days it was rare to see a man and a woman, especially a wife and her husband, laughing together in the street. Now, of course, things are very different, and nobody laughs at you or makes faces behind your back if you happen to mention that you are quite fond of your wife. Personally, I blame the modern craze for philosophy and this so-called New Comedy we hear so much about.

But when we reached our house, there was Demeas and a small gaggle of his faithful process-servers, gathered to bear witness that I had received the summons. He went through the legal rigmarole with the sort of polished ease that makes you realise that you are in the presence of a true craftsman, looked over the outside of the house to make sure there were no obvious structural faults that would reduce its value, and waddled away.

It was a most impressive charge. Demeas was prosecuting me for blasphemy, treason, conspiracy, damage to public and private property, communicating secrets to the enemy, assault with intent to degrade, gross bribery of officials, conspiring with persons unknown to pervert the course of justice (I liked that), disorderly and offensive conduct, and attempted murder. I had no idea what the last one was for; I could only imagine that it came free with the rest of the deal, like the extra handful you get from the olive-merchants, for luck. I later found out that he always put that in, so that if the trial looked like going against him, he would fall back on the attempted murder charge, claiming that the defendant had attacked him by night in the street in an attempt to silence him; and he took a small, elderly relative about with him wherever he went to be his witness.

I heard in due course that no date had yet been fixed for a trial. I think this was an open invitation to me to run. News of my frantic efforts to get money out of Attica most certainly reached Demeas, because he put in an offer, through agents, for a share in a ship I was selling; so he must have guessed that I was getting ready to leave. This would of course be in his interests. After all, he hadn't had to name his witnesses yet, so he wasn't committed to an account of that night's events in which Aristophanes was merely an innocent witness. If I ran, he could prosecute Aristophanes too. Aristophanes would then run, and he could move on to the next candidate; in fact, I could see nothing to stop him until he was the only man left in the whole of Attica. I'm sorry if I seem slightly obsessive about this Demeas; but it's an extraordinary thing to have someone trying to kill you for the sake of your money, especially if he isn't even a relative. I suppose that's how deer and hares feel, when we kill them not out of any personal enmity or fear but for the sake of their flesh and their skins.

Enough about him for the moment. Phaedra seemed to be taking it all very badly. If she had stormed at me for being a stubborn and irrational fool, and the sole cause of my own misfortunes, which is what I had expected from her, I could have taken that in my stride. But she did nothing of the sort. She tried to be cheerful, and she made a thoroughly bad job of it. Now, I was in a very strange mood for most of the time; one moment I was full of almost childish good spirits, making funny remarks and playing practical jokes (which is a crime against good taste of which I am not usually guilty), and the next moment I would be as miserable as a failed harvest. It didn't help to have Phaedra dragging round after me like a beggar's dog, quite obviously on the point of tears and trying her very best to cheer me up. To make matters worse, we no longer even wanted to quarrel or bicker with each other. I suppose it was a bit like the Athenians and the Spartans (explain yourself, Eupolis; whatever will you come out with next?), in that we stopped hammering away at each other and turned our combined malice on the world in general and Demeas in particular, just as the Athenians and the Spartans once stopped fighting each other to resist the Persian invaders. The parallel is not intended to be exact, since the Greek alliance drove the Persians into the sea, whereas all our jokes at his expense didn't whiten a single hair on our victim's head. But the fact remained that we were growing depressingly close to each other, and I don't think anything has ever been worse timed, not even the Athenian invasion of Egypt under the celebrated Cimon. Irony again, you see; the moment our marriage was on notice to be dissolved, courtesy of my friend Demeas, we suddenly found out that we could live together after all. Together, we could put up such a barrage of comedy that our jokes blotted out the sun, as the King's arrows did at Thermopylae; and that was with both of us only giving half our minds to the job, what with Phaedra being so depressed and me so perplexed.

About a week after Demeas proclaimed the summons, I went down to the Market Square to see if I could buy a thrush and a brace of pigeons. Because of the War it wasn't easy to find such things, but I was determined to eat pigeon at least once more before I died. Men on their deathbeds have so many regrets; so many things done that should not have been done, so many things not done that should have been done. My leading regret, at that time, was that I hadn't eaten nearly enough pigeons, and I was so busy searching for some that I didn't look where I was going, and I bumped into a fellow shopper with considerable force.

The shopper turned on me angrily. 'You clumsy fool,' he said, 'you nearly made me swallow two obols . . . '

It was Aristophanes the son of Philip. He fell silent and stared at me.

'Hello, Aristophanes,' I said. 'Buying poultry?'

Since he had a bundle of pigeons under his arm and four quails in his left hand he could scarcely deny it. 'Yes,' he replied defensively. 'What's that to you?'

'Throwing a party, I see,' I said.

'No,' he said quickly.

'You're going to eat all those birds by yourself?'

'No law against it, is there?'

Just then, his slave caught up with him. The slave was carrying six partridges, another two quails, a duck and a pheasant. He looked like a fletcher's shop.

'Hungry, are you?'

'So I'm throwing a party,' said Aristophanes. 'I can throw a party if I like, it's a democracy.'

'Am I invited?'

'No.'

I sighed. 'Be like that,' I said. 'I've just got some fresh cheese and sausages from the country which I could have brought, so it's your loss. And how are things with you?'

People were starting to point at us and whisper, and Aristophanes looked extremely embarrassed. 'Same as usual,' he said. 'Why shouldn't they be?'

'Just a friendly enquiry, that's all. I haven't seen very much of you since we got back from Sicily.'

'Well, I've been busy,' said the son of Philip. 'Which reminds me, I must— '

'I was meaning to drop in and have a chat,' I said. 'I wanted to make sure you'd got over the effects of that fever.'

'Absolutely, yes.'

'You remember, don't you? When you were dying in the mountains and I got you to safety.'

'Look, it's lovely to see you again,' said Aristophanes, 'but I'm meeting this man and— '

'I was a bit concerned,' I said, 'that you might still be a bit weak, after all that time in the olive-jar. You remember the olive-jar, don't you? The one I hid you in when I got you safely past the enemy cavalry?'

'Yes. Look— '

'And there was that bump on the head, too,' I continued. 'The one you got when I saved your life on Epipolae. When you were running away. Without your shield.'

'Goodbye.' He tried to get away, but there was a substantial ring of giggling Athenians round us now, and he couldn't.

'You know,' I went on, 'a soldier looks so ridiculous running away without a shield. I remember all those jokes of yours in your plays about poor old Cleonymus, when he dropped his at that battle. Let me see— '

That was enough for Aristophanes. He started to push his way through the crowd, and the pigeons fell from under his arm. I stooped and picked them up. 'Aristophanes,' I called out after him, 'you dropped your shield – sorry, your shopping. Don't you want it?'

There was no reply; Aristophanes was hurrying away. I shrugged my shoulders, brushed the dust off the pigeons, and went home. Outside my door, the little statue of Hermes had been smashed to pieces, and on the trunk someone had scratched 'Death to the traitor'. That deflated me after my little triumph over the son of Philip, and I went in and threw the pigeons down in front of the fire.

'Oh, well done,' said Phaedra, who was sitting carding wool. 'I knew you'd be able to get some from somewhere.'

'A present from Aristophanes,' I said, and I told her about the scene in the market. She laughed.

'We won't be hearing any more shield-dropping jokes from him for a while,' she said.

'I won't,' I replied. 'Not ever. Remember?'

I reflected immediately that this wasn't a particularly cheerful thing to say. But Phaedra arranged her face so that it resembled a smile.

'Aren't you the lucky one?' she said. 'Think of it. No more Aristophanes Comedies where you're going. No more funny slaves getting hit with sausages. No more moronic puns on place names.'

'No more parabases by Phrynichus,' I added. 'Don't forget that.'

'No more Teleclides,' she went on. 'No more Choruses

185

invoking the Gods when he can't think of anything else to put in.'

'No more houses being set on fire when he can't think of a way to end the damned thing.'

'No more automatic food scenes by Crates.'

'No more Aristomenes.'

'And never again,' said Phaedra, 'will you have to suck a pebble to stop you throwing up when Ameipsias does the scene with the old man with diarrhoea. God, you're lucky, Eupolis. I wish I were coming with you.'

I smiled. 'So do I,' I said. 'You know your Comedy, Phaedra.'

'Well I ought to,' she replied. 'I'm married to a Comic poet, remember?'

'You never used to take any interest at all.'

'I couldn't help it,' she laughed. 'God, do you remember that time when Hermippus won the prize with that thing with the whale in it? You came home with a face like mustard, hurled your stick at the wall and nearly burst into tears.'

'I call that perfectly reasonable behaviour, in the circumstances,' I said.

'I couldn't get a word out of you for a week,' she said. 'You didn't even shout, you just sat there. And then you got drunk and recited the whole of his opening Chorus in a silly voice.'

'It sounded better that way,' I remembered.

She leaned forward, putting down her wool. 'And do you remember that time when Aristophanes came third, and you held a victory party even though you hadn't even entered anything?'

'You weren't here, were you?'

'Yes I was,' she said, 'but I was sulking and wouldn't come out. And that idiot Critobulus was sick all over your new cloak.'

'God only knows what he'd been eating,' I said. 'I had to throw it away in the end.'

Phaedra was really smiling now. 'And do you remember when you won with *The Flatterers*, when you'd been expecting to be wiped out, and Aristophanes paid those men to start a fight in the audience, and you found out and paid them more? I was proud of you.'

'That was before we got back together, wasn't it?'

'I was still proud of you,' she said. 'I really wanted to be at the party, too, but of course I couldn't go. In fact, I've never been to one of your victory parties. You'd better hurry up and write another play, so I can—'

She didn't finish the sentence. I looked away.

'We've wasted each other, haven't we?' she said. 'We could have had a good time.'

'Will you get married again?' I asked.

'At my age, with a face like mine? You must be joking.'

'You'll have money,' I said, 'and besides, looks aren't everything. You could marry Hermocrates; his wife died last year and he's due for a victory soon.'

'Hermocrates?' she almost spat. 'Give me credit for a little taste.'

'Picky, aren't you?' I said. 'He's quite good-looking, if you go for that type.'

'Hermocrates,' she repeated, 'the man who presented *The Aeginetans* under the impression that it was a Comedy! I'd rather sell myrtle in the market.'

'It needn't be a Comic poet, then,' I said. 'You could marry a Tragedian. You've got the right name for a Tragedian's wife.'

'Oh no,' she said, 'a Comic poet or nothing.'

'Comic poets make very bad husbands, so they say.'

'There you are, then,' she said, 'stick to what you know. I could even try writing myself.'

'You!' I said. 'Don't make me laugh. What in God's name do women know about poetry?'

'What about Sappho, then?' she said quickly.

'Grossly overrated,' I replied, 'even for a foreigner. And half her stuff was actually written by Alcaeus. And who would you get to produce it for you?'

'Philonides,' she replied. 'I'd pretend it was one of yours.'

'You wouldn't dare.'

'There's nothing to it,' she said. 'It's a craft, like painting pots. All you have to do is study the techniques for a while and any fool could do it.'

'Rubbish.'

'We'll see.'

'No we won't. I forbid it.'

'You forbid it, do you?'

'Absolutely.'

'Well in that case,' she said, 'we'd better get these pigeons plucked.' She picked them up and called for Thrax. 'We can have some of that new cheese with them, and those sausages.'

On the very next day the date for the trial was announced; it would be in six days, at the Odeon, third case of the day. The Odeon wouldn't have been my first choice, if it had been up to me; the Archon's court has better acoustics, and the water-clock there runs noticeably longer. However, being third was a good omen, since I had led out my Chorus on the third day when I won with *Maricas*, and also with *The Flatterers*. I was mentioning this to Phaedra and she was saying that all I needed now was a good producer, when there was a knock at the door. Thrax opened it, and in came a man whose face I recognised, though I couldn't put a name to him. But as soon as he opened his mouth to wish me good morning I remembered who he was.

His name was Python, and he was a professional speaker. I had seen him scores of times, either in the Market Square hanging about with Socrates and his crowd, or at the Baths or the Gymnasium. He was one of those people who call themselves philosophers but who make their living teaching people how to speak, either in the Assembly or in court. That's another trade that's dying out, I'm delighted to say; not because it's intrinsically odious, like informing, but because it seems to attract such repulsive people.

I asked him what I could do for him, and he replied that it was more a case of what he could do for me. I think he was delighted to be able to introduce a Figure of Speech into the conversation so early, like a salesman eager to display his goods. He said that, for as little as fifty drachmas, he would undertake to prepare for me a speech of defence that would get me acquitted by a unanimous vote of the jury.

Of course I was very interested in this proposition, and I asked him to sit down and have a cup of wine. He accepted the seat but not the wine (which impressed me tremendously; here was a man who believed in keeping a clear head) and I asked him if he was sure he could get me off.

'Undoubtedly,' he said. 'Failure is unthinkable, success is guaranteed.'

I asked him if he knew what I was charged with. He said that he had gathered that it was to do with the statues.

'And what particular facet of the case makes you feel so confident?' I asked. 'To tell you the truth, I haven't much idea of what they're going to say.'

'Such knowledge would be no help but a hindrance,' said Python. 'It would clutter the mind when it should be clear. You should be not on the defensive but the offensive. That is what I generally recommend to clients.'

'So what sort of thing would you say in this speech?'

'A successful speech,' he said, leaning back in his seat and putting the tips of his fingers together, 'combines clarity and elegance, persuasion and passion, subtlety and sincerity. There must be reason with emotion, but emotion within reason. A guilty man may protest his innocence; but an innocent man must concern himself with guilt. The guilt of his accuser, for example; ought we not to consider that? I have heard that Aristophanes is to testify against you. Ask yourself this. Is it the case that this is a case where the accuser should himself be the accused? Suppose we establish your antagonist's involvement in the escapade of which he indicts you; will that suffice? No; we must then proceed to paint a pretty picture of him, to gild his guilt, so to speak, in order that the jury may see with their own eyes how brazen he patently is. Thus not only will his sword be blunted but his shield turned aside; the lamb will leap upon the lion. On this reversal of roles we cannot unreservedly rely; but already we have unburdened ourselves of the burden of proof, and condemned our enemy to plough a double furrow.'

'And what about witnesses?' I asked.

'Witnesses?'

'Witnesses.'

He seemed offended. 'I will, of course, undertake to provide all the necessary witnesses.'

'Oh, I see,' I said. 'You mean professional witnesses.'

'Of course.' He frowned. 'Tell me now,' he said, leaning forward, 'if your plough broke, would you hire a potter to mend it?'

'No.'

'Or a farrier?'

'No.'

'Or an armourer, or a basket-weaver, or a wreath-maker?'

'No.'

'You would hire a carpenter, would you not?'

'Very probably, yes.'

'And if your roof leaked you would consult a builder, and if your sandals wore out you would visit the shoemaker's shop.'

'I would indeed.'

'So you would seek the services of a professional, not an amateur?'

'I think we've established that, yes.'

'Yet whereas you would not entrust your roof to an amateur builder, or your foot to an amateur cobbler, you would entrust your life to an amateur witness?'

'Yes,' I replied. It was not the answer he expected. 'Do you know why?' I went on.

'Why?'

'Because the juries know all the professional witnesses by sight,' I said, 'and it plays merry hell with their credibility.'

He scowled at me. 'All my witnesses are credible,' he said angrily.

'Thank you,' I said, 'you're a tremendously eloquent man, really you are, but I think I can manage to get killed on my own.'

'Oh.' He looked terribly disappointed. 'You're making a great mistake, you realise.'

'Python,' I said, 'it was very kind of you to offer to help, but your stuff is strictly for civil trials – debts and minor assaults and that sort of thing. You stick to that and you'll go a long way.'

I had offended him, but that couldn't be helped. 'Well, in that case,' he said, 'I must regretfully withdraw my offer. That will be five drachmas, please.'

'Five drachmas?'

'Yes.'

'Why?'

'My dear friend,' he said, 'you don't expect me to work for nothing. You have enjoyed a lengthy conference with me, even though you have rejected my services. You don't deny that, do you?'

'I've certainly enjoyed it,' I replied, 'but not five drachmas' worth.'

'So you refuse to pay?'

'Yes.'

'You will hear more of this,' he hissed, and he stormed out of the house. Phaedra, who had been listening to all of this through the door of the inner room, came in and went on with what she had been doing.

'You weren't impressed, I take it,' she said.

'What, with that?' I laughed. 'The man's a clown.'

'Well,' said Phaedra, 'that clown has got people off worse charges than this one before now.'

'Not criminal charges he hasn't.'

'Yes,' she said, 'criminal charges. Treason. Illegal legislation. And they were guilty, too. Even the juries thought they were guilty.'

'Name one.'

She named about five; important cases, too. 'And do you know how he managed that?'

'Well it can't have been his damned professional witnesses.'

'Oh, of course not,' said Phaedra irritably. 'What gets him his results is his oratory.'

'You call that oratory?' I replied. 'That load of bath-house gibberish? I wouldn't dare put that lot in a parody; people would say I was going way over the top.'

'That's what they want these days, you fool,' said Phaedra. 'Or how come he makes a living?'

'That's a circular argument,' I pointed out cleverly.

'About the only thing that could save your life right now is a really good circular argument,' Phaedra replied. 'Look, the juries now are like the people who watch the chariot-races; they have their favourites, and that Python is one of them. They like him. They want him to win.'

'How do you know all this?' I asked. 'When did you last go to a trial?'

'Just because I'm a woman doesn't mean I'm deaf,' she replied. 'I have friends of my own, you know, and they tell me things. Look, it's beside the point how I know these things. The point is, you should get yourself a good defence speech. What have you got to lose, for God's sake?'

I took my sandals off, and lay back on the couch. 'My self-respect, for one thing,' I said. 'If you think I'm going to put my name to a lot of Socrates-talk like that, you're wrong. I'm a poet, aren't I?'

'What's that got to do with it?'

'I could write a better speech than that, in that style, and make it scan too,' I said. 'I could do it in my sleep.'

Phaedra shook her head vigorously. 'No you couldn't,' she said. 'You couldn't take it seriously.'

I lifted my head. 'What do you mean by that?'

'You'd ham it up,' said Phaedra. 'It's your instinct. You'd put in jokes, you'd make a parody of it. Which would be fine for the Theatre but no earthly use in the Odeon.'

She had a point there. 'But wait a minute,' I said. 'You're forgetting that I haven't the faintest intention of making a Python speech anyway.'

'Why not?' she said.

'Because it wouldn't work,' I replied. 'Those trials you mentioned just now. Think a minute. Weren't they all before the Sicilian thing?'

Phaedra considered this. 'All right,' she said, 'what if they were?'

'The point is,' I said, 'things aren't the same any more,

not since Sicily. If they were, do you think Python would have to go hawking his stuff door to door, like a perfume merchant?'

'He'd heard about your case and wanted the job,' she said. 'I don't think that's particularly significant.'

'Don't you? Well, I still maintain that this statues business is quite unlike anything we've had before; it's gone on longer and there's more than just money and politics in it.'

'Such as what?' Phaedra asked.

'Such as for the first time since any of us can remember, we're a defeated city,' I said. Up till now, I'd been making it up as I went along, Athenian-style, for the sake of a good discussion. But now I was thinking aloud, 'That's what's different now, Phaedra; they're scared. They've been beaten, they can't understand why, and there's no one left to blame, so they're turning on each other now. For God's sake, I'm not a politician, am I? Or a general? I haven't really got that many enemies. Since when did people like me get prosecuted on political charges? And God knows I'm not the only one. Demeas is prosecuting me because I've got money, sure, but the jury's going to convict me because they want blood. And this time the initiative isn't coming from Cleon or Hyperbolus or Pericles or anyone like that, someone with an enemy he wants to get rid of; it's the juries and the voters who started this blood-bath, all by themselves, and they won't be satisfied until there's a revolution or a civil war.'

'Oh yes?' said Phaedra. 'And have you got any evidence for all this? Or have you been chatting to the prophetic Apollo again?'

'Evidence,' I said. 'Well, for a start, there's me being prosecuted, as I've just explained.'

'That's a circular argument,' said Phaedra, happily.

'Told you I could do it,' I replied. 'Ask yourself this; who's the Leader right now?'

'Leader?'

'Leader,' I said. 'You know, in Assembly. There's an unbroken line of them, from before Themistocles' time down to Cleon and Alcibiades. So who is it now?'

'Well,' she said, 'offhand . . . '

'There isn't one, is there? And why? Because nobody's safe any longer. Oh, sure, Themistocles and Pericles and the like were prosecuted from time to time, but only by idiots like my grandfather; they were never in any danger, except from their own kind. But now the voters and the jurors are so worked up they'd convict anybody; and since there aren't any big men for them to eat any more, they're feeling hungry, and so they'll eat whatever the informers give them. Like me, for instance. And the sort of clever speeches that used to make them happy in the old days, when they were well fed and knew who their master was and where their next general was coming from; that doesn't amuse them at all any more.'

'But isn't that the point of being on a jury?' said Phaedra. 'I thought the whole attraction of it was being paid for listening to clever speeches, and then voting for the one you liked best. The bloodletting was just an additional thrill.'

'I don't think so,' I said, 'not any more. These people aren't hounds hunting for someone else's sport any more, they're wolves hunting for food. I honestly don't believe a clever speech would do any good.'

Phaedra was silent for a while. 'At least you could try,' she said at last. 'There's nothing else we can do. How would it be if you tried a really good old-fashioned speech? Put in some of the stuff you've just given me, if you can remember any of it. There's nothing an Athenian audience loves more than being insulted.'

As she said that, something seemed to fit into place inside my mind. I couldn't quite identify it, but I saw a remote possibility. I don't think Phaedra noticed, and she went on, 'Just so long as you make some sort of effort. That's what really upsets me, the way you're just accepting it all.'

I smiled. 'What else can I do?'

Phaedra frowned, then called for Thrax. 'Here's eight obols,' she said, handing him a drachma and borrowing a two-obol piece from me. 'Go down to the market and get a quart of anchovies for me, will you?' Thrax nodded and set off. 'We haven't had anchovies for a week,' she said, 'and I just feel like some.'

'Why have you changed the subject?' I asked. 'Or are you agreeing with me for once?'

'I wouldn't agree with you if you were the last man on earth,' said Phaedra, smiling. 'Let's talk about something else till Thrax gets back.'

'Such as what?'

'Oh, I don't know,' she said. 'Sing me a Chorus or something.'

I looked at her. 'You're acting very strangely,' I said. 'What are you up to?'

'I'm not up to anything,' she replied. 'Why do husbands always assume their wives are up to something when they ask them to sing?'

'But you hate my singing,' I answered. 'You always say it goes right through your head, like a nail or something.'

'All right, then,' said Phaedra, 'don't sing, if you don't want to. Tell me a story.'

'What's all this in aid of, Phaedra?'

She scowled at me. 'Just tell me a story, will you?'

'What sort of story?' I asked.

'I don't know, do I?' she replied. 'You're pathetic, you are.'

So I started to tell her the story of Jason and the Argonauts; but to make it more interesting, I told it the way Alcibiades would tell it, when drunk. This made her giggle, and she stopped being cross; which was understandable, since a major part of a Comic poet's trade in those days was making fun of Alcibiades and his lisp. I was just getting nicely into the flow of it when Thrax came back from the market. Phaedra interrupted me in mid-lisp and called him over.

'Did you get the anchovies?' she said.

'Here they are,' he said, pointing to the jar he was holding. 'Oh, and you gave me too much money,' he said, and picked three obols out of his mouth and handed them to her.

'That's the price now, is it?' she said. 'Five obols a quart?'

'It's the shortage,' Thrax replied. 'They've gone up again.'

'Never mind,' she said. 'We'll have them this evening, with the rest of the beans and some soup.'

I had to laugh. 'What's so funny?' she said innocently.

'I knew you were up to something,' I said. 'Fancy you remembering what I told you.'

'What, forget my own husband's personal prophecy from the God?' she said. 'What sort of a slut do you take me for?'

'But you said I was making it all up.'

'And so you were,' she said indulgently. 'But the fact remains that you aren't allowed to die until anchovies are three drachmas a quart. It's your sacred duty.'

'He didn't say I wasn't going to die till then,' I answered. 'Only that that's when I'd see him next.'

Phaedra got up, kissed me, and went over to the fire. 'Well argued,' she said. 'We'll make a lawyer of you yet.'

That night, I couldn't sleep. Now you will say that was soup followed by anchovies, but honestly, that wasn't all. Phaedra's little trick had impressed me, for I had forgotten that inconsistent prophecy. So perhaps it was just my imagination after all, said my soul, and it tried to go to sleep. But, I replied, you'd need to have a pretty twisted imagination to think anchovies could ever be three drachmas a quart.

My soul, which has no sense of humour, made no reply and left me to my own devices. But as I lay there, half asleep and half awake, I suddenly realised what my clever idea had been; the one that was my only hope. I prodded Phaedra in the back and said, 'Wake up.'

'Not tonight,' Phaedra replied sleepily. 'I've got indigestion.'

'It was your idea to have anchovies.'

'You know perfectly well why we had anchovies. Go to sleep.'

'Phaedra,' I said, 'I've had an idea. Listen to this.'

Chapter Twelve

They aren't terribly fashionable right now; but I have always had a weakness for Theban jokes. Possibly my favourite example of the genre is the one about the Theban who was riding to market on his donkey one day when he passed under a pear tree and saw a particularly ripe and luscious pear dangling only inches from his nose. He loosed the reins and reached up for it with both hands, at precisely the moment when his donkey was stung by a gadfly. The donkey started violently, sending the Theban sailing up in the air and into the branches of the tree, where his head and shoulders became so entangled in the general growth that he was left dangling there helplessly while his donkey recovered its composure and went on its way. There the Theban remained for the best part of the morning, until a traveller came along the road and saw him, inexplicably suspended like an enormous pear.

'For God's sake,' said the traveller, 'how did you manage to get up there?'

'How do you think?' replied the Theban. 'I fell off my donkey.'

And that, so to speak, was how I found myself in grave danger of losing my life on a charge of blasphemous treason. My position, like the Theban's, was decidedly uncomfortable, and there was no way I could comprehensibly explain how I had got there, even to Phaedra, who had heard my account of it all. You can understand, therefore, that all my other friends and acquaintances found it completely inexplicable; and, since they could not understand and I could not explain how I had got up there in the first place, they made no great effort to get me down. The eminent men I had cultivated for use in just such an emergency were either dead or out of town when I called to canvass support, and when I happened to meet them in the street on my way home from calling at their houses they disappeared like dreams at daybreak. As for witnesses, I couldn't think of a single person whose testimony might be useful to me, so I made no effort to find any.

For those of you with a morbid fascination with details, I suppose I must now set down what happened in all the stages in my trial. I've already told you about my summons; well, because of the pressure of business before the Courts, there was an unusually long interval between the summons and the appearance before the magistrate. Since this was a religious matter, the relevant official was the King Archon. For those of you who don't remember the democracy, there were three Archons – the King Archon, the Archon of the Year and the Polemarch – and they each had clearly defined legal jurisdictions, the precise natures of which I have either forgotten or never knew in the first place. Because the King Archon dealt with treason and political offences, he was one of the busiest men in Athens; but eventually the day arrived, and I duly presented myself, suitably awed, at his office. As I had expected, there was no loophole to be found in the indictment; Demeas was far too experienced at this sort of thing. He had applied to the proper magistrate at the right time of year in the proper form, and the action was properly based. So we each paid our drachma fee, and the indictment was neatly inscribed on a white tablet and hung up outside the Archon's office. We were then told when the second interlocutory would be held, and went home again, having wasted a whole day and nothing in particular to show for it. If you ask me, all these procedural steps make a farce of our legal system.

At the second hearing, as you know perfectly well, the plaintiff and the defendant have to set out the grounds on which they will prosecute and defend the case. Now I didn't want to show my hand, mainly because I had only a vague notion of what I was going to do, and I felt rather nervous about this hearing. I was tempted to try pleading No Case To Answer, just so as to avoid giving a proper defence, but cleverness of this sort, which we Athenians love, can often end in disaster, so I decided not to try it. The last thing I wanted to happen was for my defence to be struck out and judgement in default of defence to be entered against me.

There are five classes of evidence for this hearing – Laws, Witnesses, Witness Statements, Oaths and Tortures – and Demeas had them all. He turned up on the appointed day with three slaves laden down with documents, and a small army of witnesses. I had a rather battered old copy of the Laws of Solon which I had borrowed from a friend, and that was it; no witnesses, no statements, nothing. When it was my turn to present my evidence, I said that I had none; my defence would be one of mistaken identity, and since my wife was not competent to testify (being female) I had no one to swear an oath that I had been in bed all that night. The Archon, who was clearly bemused at this lack of preparation, gave the warning about penalties for withdrawal of prosecution and fixed a date for the trial itself. Demeas' evidence was sealed up in a huge casket, and the hearing ended. I remember the expression on Demeas' face; he was obviously puzzled too. Had I given up all hope, he wondered, or was I up to something? The answer, of course, was both, and therefore all I had to do to keep him mystified was to look inscrutable and only speak when somebody asked me a question.

Aristophanes was there, of course, and his demeanour throughout was rather amusing. He was acting the part of a public-spirited citizen who was doing his painful duty, and apart from making a formal denial of his allegations I let him get on with it. His account of what happened that night ran as follows: he had been walking home after a farewell party for a friend of his; he couldn't produce witnesses for this, since the friend and the other people at the party had conveniently died in Sicily. He had been passing my house when he saw me and a group of others whom he didn't recognise smashing up the statues with swords and calling on Hecate to confound the Sicilian Expedition. He tried to remonstrate with me, but I threatened to kill him and he fled. He had not brought this evidence forward until now since we had been in the War together and he had saved my life on a number of occasions; but Demeas had convinced him that it was his duty to the City to say what he knew.

Apart from him, I didn't recognise any of the other witnesses who swore that they had seen me that night. Since an Athenian jury loves the evidence of slaves extracted by torture (they enjoy hearing about the red-hot irons and so forth), Demeas had borrowed a job lot of broken-down old Thracians and Syrians from a friend of his who had a silver-mining concession, and these specimens were particularly eloquent for men who knew very little Greek. I think they had rather enjoyed being tortured, as a change from working in the mines; anyway, they had been so well rehearsed in their lines that they almost convinced me that they were telling the truth. And yet I am usually a very sceptical man, and find it hard to credit that a slave is more likely to give truthful evidence simply because a public official has been beating him up. A slave is like any other witness; either you believe him or you don't. But Solon (or whoever it was) has ordained that a slave can't testify unless he's been hung upside down and flogged within an inch of his life, and I suppose you can't pick and choose which of Solon's laws you're going to adopt. If you want the intelligent laws about wills and intestate succession, you have to put up with the code of evidence and hope that when it comes to your case, the slave in question will take the same reasonable view.

When I got home, Phaedra had a bowl of spiced wine and a basket of wheat bread waiting for me, and I peeled off my sandals and collapsed in front of the fire. I didn't want to talk, and so she didn't ask me what had happened; there was no point, since if there had been anything to report I would have told her as soon as I came through the door. Instead, we sat and looked at each other in silence for a while.

'Well?' Phaedra said at last. 'You're going through with it?'

'Yes,' I said. 'As far as I can see, it's the only real chance.'

She breathed in deeply and shook her head. 'It's your life,' she said. 'You know what I think about it.'

'Thank you very much,' I said irritably. 'You really know how to give a man confidence.'

'You asked me what I thought of the idea,' she replied, 'and I gave you my honest opinion. What did you want me to do, say it was brilliant and let you get on with it?'

'It's too late to change it now,' I said firmly. 'Once you start trying to amend pleadings, you might as well hang yourself and save the State the jury pay. And there was never any point in trying to make a case out of perjured witnesses and the like; that's Demeas' trade, and he's better at it than me.'

'I suppose so,' she said reluctantly. 'I mean, in theory it's a good idea. It's just putting it into practice that strikes me as dangerous. There's so many what-ifs.'

'Not nearly so many as there would have been if I'd tried to do it the other way,' I replied. 'This way, there's just one big what-if; what if they don't like it? And I've been dealing with that in the Theatre all my life.'

She shrugged. 'Anyway,' she said, 'like you said, it's too late now. Don't worry, I'm not going to go all sulky on you now.'

I leaned over and took her hand. 'That's a good girl,' I said.

'I hate that expression,' she said. 'Patronising, don't you think? As if I was about twelve years old and I'd just managed to make the soup without burning it. Tired?'

'Very.'

'Then eat your bread and get an early night. You've got work to do tomorrow.' She got up and poured me a cup of the spiced wine. 'Don't sit up all night, you won't be able to think properly.'

After she had gone to bed, I sat there in the dark and tried to get an opening line for my speech. I always believe that if you can get an opening line – for anything: chorus, speech, lyric, whatever – the rest will follow of its own accord. Now the beginning of a defence speech is crucial and very difficult to get right; in fact, the beginning is matched in complexity and importance only by the middle and the end. But try as I might, I couldn't get the form of words I wanted; it was either too colloquial or too formal, and I couldn't picture myself standing up in Court and actually saying it. Then the answer suddenly came to me. My problem was that I was trying to compose prose, which was something I had never tried before. All I had to do was compose it in verse and then say it like prose, and perhaps mess about with some of the words to stop it sounding too much like verse when I said it. As soon as I tried doing that, it started to flow like water from a spring. I had just rounded the thing off to my entire satisfaction when Phaedra came stumbling out of the inner room.

'For God's sake,' she yawned, 'it's the middle of the night. Leave it.'

'It's all right,' I said, 'I've got it. Go to bed, I'll be through in a moment.'

She blinked. 'You've got it?' she said. 'What do you mean?'

'My speech,' I replied impatiently. 'It's finished.'

'Oh.' She frowned. 'Just like that?'

'Yes.'

'Is it any good?'

'Do you want to hear it?'

'No.' She yawned again. 'I mean, if it's good now, it'll still be good in the morning.'

I had expected a little more enthusiasm, but I could see she was tired. 'All right then,' I said, 'I'm coming.'

'Good,' she replied.

I know it's a classic; but I don't like the *Odyssey*. In particular, I don't like the opening. Now I know it's all very clever, the way Homer keeps back the first appearance of Odysseus until the poem is well under way; this is designed to create suspense and intrigue the reader. But I can't be doing with suspense. My attention lapses. I start thinking of something else. Then, when I rejoin the poem or the play or whatever it is, I find I've missed an important bit and can't get back into it. So I won't try and build up the tension any more, although it would be easy enough to do; instead, we'll go forward to the day of the trial itself.

We left the house just before dawn and walked slowly down towards the Court. On the way, I bumped into a friend of mine called Leagoras, a neighbour at Pallene. He asked where I was going, and I told him that I was on my way to stand my trial. He asked what the charge was, and when I told him he was most surprised, and said that, since he had no business in the City that day that could not wait, he would come with me, and take a message back to Pallene when he went home should that be necessary. I thanked him, and we went on together to the Odeon.

The first case of the day was just starting, and we sat down on the benches outside to wait. It had turned out a sunny, drowsy sort of a day, the kind of day I love to spend in the country, when there is not much that needs doing. It was hard to make my mind work properly, and both Phaedra and Leagoras were no help at all; Phaedra didn't want to talk, and Leagoras was full of the news from Pallene – whose vines were doing well, who was suing who for trespass and moving boundary-stones, who had got whose daughter pregnant and so on; and although as a general rule I like listening to this sort of gossip, at least when I'm in the City, I couldn't give it the attention it needed if I was to take an interest in it. To tell you the truth, my mind was as nearly blank as it ever can be (for I am a restless man by nature) and I felt a great wave of lassitude creeping up from my feet and infiltrating every part of me. Very soon, I knew, I would fall asleep; and falling asleep in the sun does me no good at all. I wake up with a sore neck and a headache, which I generally don't lose until nightfall. This of course was the worst possible thing that could happen to a man who is about to stand his trial, with the exception of toothache or diarrhoea, and I was on the point of getting up and going for a walk to wake myself up when I saw a familiar figure walking up the street towards me.

It was no surprise to see Socrates the son of Sophroniscus hanging about the Law Courts; although he fervently denies it, he can generally be found somewhere in the neighbourhood of a good, juicy trial. He is not, strictly speaking, one of the speech-writers, like Python; but he makes a lot of money from what he calls his thinking lessons, which are little more than preparatory courses for litigants, and is always on the look-out for new clients. Since the disgrace and exile of his most prestigious pupil, the celebrated Alcibiades, business had been rather slack, and I hadn't heard his name quite so often in the Market Square or the Baths.

Phaedra and Leagoras obviously wanted to avoid him, for they tried to snuggle down inside their clothes and disappear; but I regarded Socrates' arrival as an omen from the Gods, like an eagle or an owl flying over my head. So I called out and waved to him; and sure enough he came bounding over, like a hungry dog who hears the sound of a plate on the kitchen floor.

'Good morning, Eupolis,' he said through one of those enormous grins of his. 'You're rather out of your way here, aren't you? Shouldn't you be down in the Market Square, nosing out some bits of gossip for a play?'

I smiled in such a way as to communicate lack of amusement. 'And shouldn't you be at the Lyceum?' I replied. 'You don't want to lose your pitch if there are gullible young men about, with money in their pockets.'

Socrates laughed, displaying his fine collection of yellow teeth. He never cleans them, even when he eats onions and garlic, since he purports to regard such practices as effete and not worthy of an ascetic. For an ascetic though, he's merciless on stuffed quails. 'You know better than that, son of Euchorus,' he said. 'You'll get me into trouble, saying things like that. You've been watching too many of your own plays.'

'Are you busy?' I asked, making room for him on the bench. 'I have an hour or so to kill, waiting for my case to come on, and I know you're always ready for a chat.'

'I certainly am,' he replied. 'Free of charge, seeing it's you. Only you must promise not to pirate any of my material in your lawsuit. Are you prosecuting or defending?'

'Defending,' I replied.

He nodded. 'A serious charge?'

'Fairly serious,' I replied. 'They say I was one of the men who damaged the statues.'

Socrates raised his eyebrows. 'Is that so?' he said, and sat down next to me. 'And did you?'

'No,' I said. 'I was in bed at the time with my wife here. But of course she can't give evidence, being a woman, and I can produce no one else who saw me. And that's a point that intrigues me, Socrates. Perhaps you and I could clarify it between us, if you have nothing better to do. Why is it that a woman should be forbidden to give evidence in a court of law, when men and even slaves, if tortured, are acceptable as witnesses?' I scratched my nose, then continued. 'After all, they have the same five senses as we do, and minds just like men. We listen to the evidence of men with doubtful characters, don't we, and trust ourselves to be able to assess its weight. Why can't we accept the evidence of women?'

Socrates leaned back in his seat, with his hands clasped around his left knee. 'So you are saying that there is no difference between men and women?'

'Certainly there is a difference,' I replied, 'just as there's a difference between Greeks and foreigners, and Athenians and other Greeks. But this difference doesn't make such a great difference that we should refuse to accept anything they say as the truth. I mean, when you ask your wife what's for dinner and she says dried fish, you believe her, don't you?'

'Yes,' said Socrates, settling himself more comfortably in his seat. 'Invariably.'

'And when you ask her what she did while you were out and she says she mended the hole in your tunic, you take her word, don't you? In the absence of contrary evidence, such as the smell of wine on her breath, or the bedclothes being ruffled up?'

'Indeed I do, Eupolis.'

'And yet,' I said, 'Xanthippe isn't an unnaturally truthful woman, is she? She's not under some curse, like that woman in the old story who cheated Apollo and was cursed with the inability to lie?'

'She's the same as other women in that respect,' said Socrates, plainly wondering where all this was leading. 'I couldn't say for sure.'

'But if there was a prosecution and she was a witness, she couldn't give evidence,' I said. 'Tell me why that is, I'd like to know. Then I might be able to persuade the Court to let Phaedra testify, and perhaps I wouldn't have to die after all.'

Socrates furrowed his brow for a moment. 'What is the difference, would you say,' he said, 'between women and men? The main difference, I mean, not just the obvious anatomical differences. We can take those for granted.'

It was my turn to frown. 'I suppose,' I said, 'it's that women stay in the house all day while men go out to work in the fields.'

'Exactly,' said Socrates, and he let go of his knee and sat upright. 'Now, have you ever seen a rabbit?'

'Often, Socrates, often.'

'And aren't rabbits hard to see, because of their grey fur?'

'Well,' I said, 'it's not easy to see them, unless you know what to look for.'

'And the first time you saw a rabbit,' Socrates continued, 'did you identify it for yourself, or did someone point it out to you?'

'I'm not sure,' I replied, thinking hard for a moment. 'I believe someone said, "Look, there's a rabbit" and I said, "Where?" and he pointed, and I saw it.'

'So he saw the rabbit first, and showed you what to look for?'

'As far as I can remember, yes.'

'And you had been looking in that direction,' said Socrates, 'and saw the same things as he did, but because you didn't know how to pick out a rabbit against a background of grey rocks, you hadn't identified it as a rabbit?'

'That's pretty much what happened,' I said, folding my arms in front of me, 'so far as I can recall. It was a long time ago, you understand.'

'Oh, of course,' said Socrates. 'Now, supposing you had never had a friend who knew what a rabbit looked like, do you suppose it's possible that you could have gone through life looking at stone outcrops and never known that there were rabbits all around you?'

'Perfectly possible,' I said, and scratched my ear.

'Or take speedwell,' Socrates went on. 'You know what speedwell looks like, of course.'

'I should say I do, Socrates,' I replied. 'I was brought up in the mountains, you know. It has a long, thin stalk and blue flowers.'

'But if no one had ever told you what it was,' said Socrates, looking me straight in the eye, 'if you had been abandoned on the hillside at birth and brought up by wolves, like the child in the story, you wouldn't know that the blue flower was speedwell, would you?'

'Come to think of it,' I replied, 'I don't suppose I would.'

'Now let us suppose you are walking in the hills and you look up at the sky and see black clouds. What would you expect?'

I knew the answer to that. 'Rain,' I replied.

'And why precisely would you expect rain? Because someone had told you that it rains from black clouds?'

'Yes indeed.'

'Or perhaps you found it out for yourself, by experience,' said Socrates, leaning his chin thoughtfully on the back of his hand. 'You worked out that every storm of rain you could remember was preceded by black clouds, and your mind, being rational, rejected the explanation that this was a mere coincidence.'

I nodded profoundly. 'That's what a rational mind would do,' I agreed.

'Well then,' said Socrates brightly, 'now that we've established these preliminary points, we can return to your original enquiry, about women and the Courts. Suppose there was a lawsuit, and it was vital to the evidence whether there had been a rabbit, or a sprig of speedwell, in a particular place. Would a person who couldn't identify a rabbit at sight or tell speedwell from soldanella be able to give good evidence?'

'I suppose not.'

'Exactly,' said Socrates, grinning. 'There might well have been a rabbit or a speedwell plant there, but this person would have looked straight at it and not recognised it, and would in all honesty tell the jury that he hadn't seen a rabbit or a speedwell plant. And then the jury would think that the defendant, who had just claimed there was a rabbit or a speedwell in the place in question, was a liar and not to be believed on any matter, and vote to have him put to death. Whereas if the ignorant witness had not been allowed to testify, admittedly the defendant's evidence would not be corroborated, but at least his own credit as a witness would be unimpaired. Am I right?'

'Yes indeed.'

'Now let us suppose you were in court and your defence turned on there having been a storm of rain. And imagine that, although you could find no one who had been out in the rain and thus was able to give evidence that he had got wet through, you knew that your neighbour had walked home an hour before and must have seen the dark clouds. Couldn't you expect him to testify that it had been about to rain an hour before you said it would rain, which would give at least some weight to your account of events?'

'Most certainly.'

'But supposing that your neighbour had spent all his life in one of those hot countries south of the Ethiopians where it never rains, and so had not made the mental connection between dark clouds and rain. Would his evidence be any use to you? Or would it be potentially dangerous, like the evidence of the man who couldn't recognise rabbits or speedwell?'

'Potentially dangerous, of course.'

'So we are agreed that a misleading witness is worse than no witness at all?'

'Indeed we are.'

'And that a witness who has no knowledge or experience of a thing is likely to be a misleading witness, even if he is inclined to tell the truth?'

'Absolutely.'

'And didn't we say,' said Socrates, leaning back again,

'at the very outset of our discussion, that the main difference between men and women was that men go out in the world and women stay at home; and that therefore men have knowledge and experience of the world that women inevitably lack? And isn't it true that the sort of thing that generally crops up in lawsuits as needing to be proved by evidence is exactly the sort of thing that happens out in the world, where men meet and do business and have contact with one another? The sort of thing, necessarily, that women have no knowledge or experience of, and therefore should not testify about?'

'Naturally,' I replied.

'So you agree that only men are qualified to give evidence in lawsuits, and women should be debarred?'

'I do.'

'You do realise,' said Socrates, 'that everything I've been saying up till now has been a load of old rubbish?'

'Yes, Socrates.'

'And yet you found yourself forced to agree with it?'

'Yes, Socrates.'

'Because I was talking so fast, and so fluently, and with such an air of intelligence and authority and being about to make some intelligent point, that you didn't care to interrupt me? And by the time you had worked out that I was talking nonsense it was too late to contradict me without seeming petty or just plain stupid?'

'Exactly so.'

'Well, Eupolis my friend,' said the son of Sophroniscus, rising to his feet and brushing the dust pointedly off his backside, 'that's the one and only way to win lawsuits in this City. If you can charm them with words and bewilder them with plausible ideas, you'll be all right. If not, you'll have to accept that in the absence of divine intervention you're probably going to die, and it serves you right for not consulting a competent expert, like myself. Only I wouldn't have helped you if you'd offered me all the wealth of King Gyges, after what you said about me in those so-called Comedies of yours; and neither, I expect, would any of my fellow philosophers. Good luck, Eupolis, you need it.'

'And the same to you,' I said. 'See you around.'

'I doubt it,' said Socrates over his shoulder, and he walked happily away down the street.

'What an unpleasant man,' said Phaedra. 'He'll come to a bad end one of these days.'

'I hope so,' I said. 'But at least he kept me from falling asleep, which is more than you could do.'

'I don't see what you're complaining about,' interrupted Leagoras, who had listened to our discussion with rapt attention. 'It all seemed to make perfect sense to me.'

Phaedra and I both looked at him, and he seemed rather offended. 'Don't worry about it,' I reassured him, 'it's not your fault.'

'It certainly is not,' Phaedra agreed. 'Isn't that Aristophanes over there?'

We all looked round, and saw the son of Philip, dressed in an unusually sombre gown and carrying a plain olive-wood walking-stick, following Demeas and his crowd of witnesses, slaves and other attendant Furies. A friend of my uncle's once told me of the mighty carvings his grandfather had seen in Sardis, when he went there as a young man; vast reliefs, stretching as far as the eye could see, showing the Great King of the Persians marching to war with all the nations of the earth in the van, and his hawks and his hounds and his gigantic royal umbrella. I suppose the Great King of Persia looked every bit as menacing to his subjects as Demeas did to me then, on his carvings at least. But Demeas achieved his effect without hawks and hounds and umbrellas. He had presence.

He seemed to look straight through me as he passed, as if I was already a hungry ghost twittering hopelessly on the wrong side of the river. But Aristophanes accidentally caught my eye, and gave me such a look of repressed hatred that I was quite startled. For a moment I wondered what was upsetting him so much; then it occurred to me that he blamed me for putting him in a position where he would have to make a public exhibition of himself, giving evidence against a Comic poet at a political trial. I could see his point; there is, even in Athens, a certain stigma attached to participating in one of these affairs, and there are still a few right-minded people in the City who disapprove. But even so, I took it rather hard that I should be blamed; it was Demeas' fault, after all. Perhaps I'm too sensitive. Anyway, I looked away until the procession had taken itself off to another part of the porch.

'Nervous?' whispered Phaedra in my ear.

'No,' I said truthfully, 'or at least not in the way you think. I feel like I'm about to send out a Chorus.'

'Oh, you,' she said. 'You're just vain, that's your trouble.'

I hadn't thought of that. 'Perhaps you're right,' I said. 'Or perhaps I just can't take this sort of thing seriously. There's Socrates back again, look; I expect he's going to listen to the trial.'

'You ought to charge him a drachma,' said Phaedra. 'He would, in your position.'

'Where I'm going,' I replied, 'I'll only need two coins, on my eyes.'

'That's the spirit,' said Phaedra, 'think positive. How are you feeling? Sick? Dizzy? Splitting headache?'

'That comes later,' I said, 'just before it's my turn to speak.'

Leagoras leaned across and said, 'Best of luck, Eupolis. If you don't make it, can I have your plough with the bronze handles?'

'If you can beat the bailiffs to it,' I replied, 'certainly you can. Tell them I borrowed it from you and forgot to give it back. Though they won't believe you. It's not in your nature to forget about a thing like that.'

Leagoras seemed offended again, and sat back in his seat. A moment or so after that, the herald came out and summoned Demeas and me into the Court. I kissed Phaedra on the cheek, quickly, and avoided her eyes; then I stood up, shook myself like a dog waking up at dinner-time, and walked towards the gate. I remember thinking that this is how my actors must feel, when the herald calls them on for the first scene.

The first thing I did when I got inside the Court was to examine the jury. I was looking for at least one familiar face – out of five hundred and one men, I must know at least one of them. But at first their faces were a sort of

211

brown and black porridge, and they looked like a great legendary monster such as Hercules might have faced in one of his less probable adventures. Then I caught sight of a man I recognised; I couldn't think of his name, but I had seen him recently, in the Market Square or the country. He was biting a chunk off a thick black crust of barley-bread, and he had his little wine-flask, shaped like a donkey, in his left hand, ready to soak the pap in his mouth to make it soft and malleable for his few remaining teeth. I have rarely seen a less prepossessing creature. Next to him was a tiny little man, seventy if he was a day, with a few scruffy wisps of white hair on a pointed brown skull, and he was talking very rapidly to nobody at all. I knew him for one of Cleon's Dogs, the old hard-core jurymen of the Brotherhood of the Three Obols. Many of them had recently died of old age (or, some said, of grief at the death of their master) but there were still a few to be seen, walking in along the country roads before dawn to get to the Court in time to be at the head of the jury queue when their tribe was on duty. And wasn't that one of Little Zeus' brothers, huddled up under the wall in a very old cloak? I hoped it was; surely he would be for me. Then I remembered hearing that they were all dead; there had been a little resurgence of the plague in their village in the mountains, which had wiped out the entire population except for an old man and a baby. One thing at least reassured me; they looked remarkably like all the theatre audiences I have ever inspected, with that same air of relief that the Tragedies are over mixed with impatience for the Comedy to start.

Then the indictment was read out.

'Prosecution by Demeas son of Polemarchus of Cydathene against Eupolis son of Euchorus of Pallene, on the grounds of blasphemy. Penalty proposed: death. Demeas will now speak.'

The water-clock was filled up and started to run. No one who has ever heard it from the dock will forget the sound that thing makes; someone, I can't remember who, said it reminded him of a dwarf pissing into a tin bucket. I swear they designed it on purpose to put off defendants; you sit there listening to it gurgling and plinking away, and

212

you forget all about the case that is being carefully built up around you like a wall round a besieged city. Then when your turn comes to speak you're still listening out for it, and you lose your way in the middle of your best sentence, like Theseus in the Labyrinth. I still have nightmares about it, and I wake up sweating, only to find that it's the rain trickling down off the roof, or one of the slaves skimming the milk.

Demeas started with a blistering attack. I can't remember who or what he was attacking – I don't think it was me particularly – but I could see the faces of the jurors getting grimmer and grimmer as he reminded them of this terrible injury that had been done to them. There was, I remember, a short account of the sufferings of our men in Sicily; and for someone who hadn't been there, Demeas did it very well. First the fever in the camp by the marshes; then the horror of the night on Epipolae, and the dreadful confusion and the screams of the dying; then the desperation of the battle in the harbour, and the slow misery of the march to the walled orchard. 'And of these thousands,' I remember him saying, 'so few returned to the City of the Violet Crown; what irony, men of Athens, what terrible irony that one of those apparently chosen by the God should be the sole author of all this misfortune! But I say that this was Zeus' work; he did not give this man the chance of a hero's death, but preserved him to stand his trial before you today. Witness the ease of his escape – was this not some God, my friends, leading him like a sacrifice to the altar of Justice?'

I thought of the smithy, and the cart with the olive-jar, and giggled. Unfortunately, Demeas saw this and pointed. 'Our friend thinks it's amusing, does he?' he thundered. 'Just as he thought it amusing to smash the statues of the Gods. Does the thought of our Heavenly patrons always produce this show of levity, I wonder? Does he snigger his way through the Lady's procession, or deliberately sneeze at the moment of the sacrifice?'

I wanted to know how a man could sneeze deliberately; but that would have to wait until after the trial. Anyway, Demeas rounded off his introductory remarks with a graphic description of the night of the mutilation of the statues, and started calling witnesses. I kept expecting Aristophanes to be called, but every time I saw the son of Philip prepare to get up from his place, Demeas called on another slave or hanger-on, and Aristophanes would settle back and fold his arms. At last, when I was beginning to think that Aristophanes wouldn't be used at all, Demeas called him and put him on the stand. There was a faint murmur of satisfaction from the jury, and most of them stopped eating or cutting their toenails. Someone woke up the little old man, and he leaned forward on his stick to be able to hear what was said. When Aristophanes had settled himself, Demeas cleared his throat and began. He asked his questions in the usual tone of voice, and Aristophanes answered loudly and clearly, with his chin up.

Demeas: Were you outside Eupolis' house on the night in question?
Aristophanes: I was.
Demeas: Were you just returning from a party in honour of some friends going to the War?
Aristophanes: I was.
Demeas: Did you see Eupolis smashing up statues with a Thracian sabre?
Aristophanes: I did.
Demeas: Was he alone or with others?
Aristophanes: With about ten others, whom I didn't recognise.
Demeas: Was Eupolis actively smashing statues, or simply watching the others?
Aristophanes: He was actively smashing the statues.
Demeas: Did you report this at the time?
Aristophanes: No.
Demeas: Were you afraid of what Eupolis would do to you if you reported it?
Aristophanes: I was.
Demeas: And were you subsequently in Sicily with Demosthenes and the army?
Aristophanes: I was.
Demeas: Did you and Eupolis escape through Sicily to Catana after the defeat, and did you repeatedly save Eupolis' life during that time?
Aristophanes: Yes.

Demeas: During the escape, did Eupolis freely confess that he had taken part in the desecration of the statues?
Aristophanes: Twice.
Demeas: Why are you now giving evidence against a man whose life you saved?
Aristophanes: Because I feel it is my duty as a citizen.

Now you can tell for yourselves, from this unusually long and detailed cross-examination, which lasted for at least a pint of Demeas' time, that he expected it to be his most telling evidence; normally, Demeas would have given a précis of this himself and just called Aristophanes to affirm it, but in this case he wanted to drag it out for as long as possible, to get the maximum value out of it. He was right to do so, for the jury simply lapped it up. I have never seen such attention to a cross-examination in my life. Dramatically speaking, it was shrewdly done. I speak as a professional; if you can get away with doing something in a new and shocking way, it makes a much greater impression; and in something like a trial, if you can lodge something in the jury's mind they are likely to believe it, even if you offer nothing in support.

The rest of his evidence Demeas called in the usual way, by depositions, and then he had the law read and set about winding up his case. I shall always remember what he said.

'Men of Athens,' he started off, 'ask yourselves this. What is a citizen? What does it mean to be a citizen of this City, to walk in our streets, vote in our Assembly, worship in our temples, serve in our army? What is our part in this great enterprise we call Athens? It is a man's duty to work for his city, and not to work against it. Look around this City of ours. Look at the Long Walls, which Themistocles built to protect our corn supply in time of war, to link us for ever with the sea. Look at the Council House which Solon built, to house our democracy. Look at the Nine Fountains which Pisistratus and his heirs built, to bring water into the City and defeat drought and pestilence. Look at the Walls, which our forefathers built to keep out the Persians. Look at the Acropolis, which Pericles built to be our crown and our citadel. Look at all these things, which will stand for ever, and think of the men who caused them to be. They will be remembered; yet they did no more than their duty, which is, as I have said, to work for their City. And now look at the empty streets that used to bustle with young men, and the empty houses where so many citizens lived who are now dead, buried in unmarked graves on the island of Sicily. Think who caused this desolation, and remember him; the man who brought about the destruction of our army and our fleet by his terrible blasphemy. That is a man who did not do his duty, a man who did the very opposite of his duty, by working against his City. And now prepare to do your duty, men of Athens, by voting for his condemnation and execution.'

Now that was meant to be the end of Demeas' speech; and it would have made a good finale, and perhaps cost me my life. But as it happened, Demeas had been speaking rather quickly, and so he had come to the end of his prepared material rather earlier than he had anticipated. As soon as he stopped speaking, the water-clock made one of its characteristic noises, rather like a gurgling belch, as if to tell the jury that this particular speaker was giving them short measure, and Demeas realised that he was faced with a slight problem. You see, in those days it was regarded as the mark of a good speaker that he could exactly fill up his allotted time, uttering his last syllable precisely when the last drop of water hit the bowl; and conversely, a man who finished early was regarded as being no good and therefore a liar. After all his experience of the Courts, Demeas knew just by the sound of the water-clock how much was left in it, and so started improvising a little coda to fill in the excess time. Now when I say that he improvised, I am exaggerating slightly; all practised orators are familiar with the problem, and have little timed pieces, relevant to any theme, which will last a pint or a pint and a half, or whatever the time is that they have to fill in. They have to keep changing them, of course, for fear that the jury will recognise something they've heard before and start throwing olive-stones, but generally speaking these codas are traditional in form and substance; and an orator is often judged, by the *cognoscenti*, on the quality of these set pieces. It is argued that you can't properly judge an orator's talent by his actual speech, since he may have a really awful case to present (which hinders him) or an absolutely marvellous one (which gives him an unfair advantage). But the coda is more or less standard, and is marked partly on its content and presentation, and partly on the skill with which the orator makes it relevant to the prosecution in progress.

Demeas, then, hesitated for a split second and then launched into his coda. This went as follows:

'Only one thing remains to be said, men of Athens; and, at the risk of telling you what you already know well enough, I will remind you of just why this crime is so terrible, and, more particularly, why punishing it is so important. This crime is a crime against the City, and any crime against the City, as opposed to a crime against an individual citizen, is of course an attack on democracy itself. Democracy is a joining-together of people; rather like a marriage except that in a democracy all the participants are equal. In a democracy, no individual has authority over another, because the State has authority over all. In a democracy, every man has liberty because he deliberately subordinates himself to the good of the whole, which we call the State. Now when one citizen separates himself from the whole, either actively by committing a crime against the State, or even passively, merely by being in some way different, he loses his identity as a member of that State. He loses his purpose, his function, his reason for existing. It is as if he is already dead. That is why exile is such a terrible punishment – some say greater than actual execution. Such a person is like a hand cut off from the body; the blood of communal existence no longer flows through the severed organ, and it becomes little more than a piece of meat for the dogs to chew on. We as Athenians, living in the world's only true democracy, are in truth ten thousand bodies with one common soul.

'So when one of us separates himself from the whole, not only does that person damage himself irreparably, but he offends against us and so deserves the most severe punishment. He has offended against our unity; he has, so to speak, removed a stone from the walls of Athens, and the removal of one stone can cause the collapse of the whole wall. When a man ceases to be in all respects an Athenian, he cannot be permitted to live in Athens, or indeed to live at all. If a man starts to grow in the wrong direction, he must be pruned off before he starts to warp and misdirect those around him. This is because in a democracy there must be consensus.

'Now in the case of this despicable man, who has done his best to bring about the maximum possible harm to his city, it is an easy matter to see where the best interests of the City lie. But that is not the point I am addressing myself to. I am concerned that, because this man is a Comic poet – and a good one, let me add – and has given many of you much pleasure with his witty words and spectacular Choruses, some of you may say to yourselves, "Eupolis has done wrong, and will be punished; my fellow jurors will see to that. But after all, this is a secret ballot; nobody will ever know which urn I myself put my pebble into. I think I'll vote for his acquittal; after all, he did write *Maricas*." Now that seems like an innocent whimsy, and no doubt a few of you were considering doing just that. Think again. In a democracy, not only those who do wrong and those who conspire with them or aid and comfort them are guilty and must be punished; but also those who spare them for private or individual reasons. Because this is a democracy, built on consensus and fortified with unity, we cannot allow ourselves the luxury of personal motives. If I was on your jury and my own father was in the dock and was guilty of a crime against Athens, I would have to vote against him, though all the Furies in Hell haunted me for the rest of my life. That is the great burden of living in a democracy; we must all fit the mould, or be cast aside as useless and dangerous. I say again: anyone who votes for acquittal will be as guilty as if he had done the crime himself. So vote, as I know you will, for conviction and death; only by doing so can we, as a city, lift from our shoulders the miasma of this man's blasphemy.'

As soon as he stopped speaking, the water-clock

gurgled for the last time, and the Court was absolutely silent. I wish I could capture for you the look of pleasure on the faces of those jurors. This was good, old-fashioned stuff, but spiced with those little touches of novelty that excite the palate. Each man turned to his neighbour and nodded, and I almost expected them to stand up as a Chorus and start singing the anapaests. But if I had prayed to Zeus and Dionysus and Pan, god of shepherds and confusion, and my prayers had been answered, I could not have asked for a more helpful speech. It fitted exactly what I had prepared, and only a few minor adjustments would be necessary to the speech I was carrying, like an eight-months-pregnant woman, in my mind. As the herald called out my name and told me to state my case, I felt the weight of fear slipping off my shoulders, as if I was a man who couldn't afford a mule laying down a heavy basket of olives I had carried into town from the country. I stood up, waited for the clock to be refilled, and started to speak.

Chapter Thirteen

'In all my years of attending debates,' I said, 'I don't know when I've enjoyed a speech more than the one Demeas has just made. It had the lot, didn't it? It had structure, pace, style and diversity; the only trick he missed was having a couple of slaves walking up and down handing out free hazelnuts. As soon as he had exhausted one theme, he switched straight to the next; but you didn't notice that he'd changed tack, so skilfully did he make the transition. It just seemed to flow, like the streams in the mountains when the ice melts in spring. In fact, I admire his speech so much that I can't bring myself to answer it; that would be a worse desecration of the beautiful and holy than the one I stand accused of. So I won't even try. Not a word about Demeas' speech.

'But I don't want to cheat you of your entertainment. Three obols isn't much for sitting on those cold, hard benches all day, especially for you older men, and you have a right to be diverted by some fancy speaking. So I'll make my defence quickly, and then fill up the rest of my time with some jokes or a song or something.

'Now we're all grown men here, and we know the score. I'm not talking to a party of colonials just off a wheat-ship, who think the Propylaea is a ship, or the Council Chamber is a wine shop. You know and I know that Demeas is prosecuting me because he needs the money, and Aristophanes has given evidence against me partly because he's an ungrateful arsehole and partly because he's scared shitless of Demeas, and all the other witnesses are hired by the day for a drachma down and two bushels of figs later. We also know that you're going to convict me because you want blood after Sicily, and because Demosthenes and Nicias got themselves killed before you could impeach them. Everyone here today, with the possible exception of the red-haired man in the second row from the back who hasn't got the common decency to stop eating while I'm talking for my life, also knows that my only hope of getting out of this in one piece is to give you one hell of a good speech, so that you'll let me go to show everyone how cultured and intelligent you are. And then you'll pick on some other poor sod who can't make jokes or think up fancy phrases, and glut your blood-lust on him. That's what we call a democracy, men of Athens.

'A democracy is a pack of wolves without a permanent leader. When there are plenty of sheep about, everything's well, and they congratulate themselves on how beautifully the wolf-democracy works, and maybe vote themselves all an extra hour's sleep at the new moon. But when they've eaten all the sheep, and the shepherds have banded together to hunt them out of their nests with dogs and nets, they start turning on each other and eating the fattest and the weakest. Then they find out that the wolf-democracy isn't quite what they thought it was; there's still this mystical Whole that Demeas has told us about, but the Whole consists of those wolves who haven't yet had their number called. The hunger continues, of course, and so does the democratic process. You can have a democratic process right up to the point when there are only three wolves left, and two of them can outvote the third and eat him. Then you only have two, and that's an oligarchy.

'Now this would all be perfectly laudable, if only you got something out of the democratic process, beyond satisfying your perverted craving for human blood. But you see, where the wolf image breaks down is that you don't actually get to eat your victims; you don't derive any benefit from killing them. The only people who gain are men like Demeas here, who get the informer's share of the proceeds of sale. Now you will say to me, "Eupolis, you're wrong, as usual. All your considerable wealth will be confiscated and the proceeds will go to the public purse. We've fattened you up, and now we're going to kill you." Mathematically speaking, yes, you're right. The cost of this trial is – let me see now, five hundred and one jurors at three obols a day comes to a touch under two hundred and fifty-one drachmas. The public purse will get far more out of my carcase than that, even when Demeas has had his share. As a method of raising revenue for the public purse, judicial murder beats harbour dues into a three-legged stool.

'But what makes you think that any of that money will be used to benefit you? If my wealth were divided up, so many drachmas a man, that would, I concede, be fair and equitable. But it won't be; it'll all be frittered away on the War, or public buildings, or ambassadors' wages, or hiring mercenaries, or any one of the hundreds of ways in which a community of people such as yourselves can dissipate money which they no longer regard as their own. And what benefit will you derive from that, may I ask? Don't bother thinking, I'll tell you. None. You won't get it, Athens will get it. And what's this thing we call Athens? I'll tell you. It's an enormous misunderstanding, self-perpetuating and carried on with in the hope that one day it'll sort itself out.

'It started like this. Once upon a time, long, long ago, when the world was young and people had to earn an honest living, before the Law Courts were invented, three shepherds met together in what is now the Market Square. There was a fig tree growing there, and they sheltered under its branches from the sun. But one day the fig tree died, and so the shepherds, who had grown used to meeting in that place, piled up a few rocks and bits of wood to create an artificial shade for themselves and their flocks.

'After a while, other shepherds in the area started dropping by to take shelter under this pile of rocks, and soon there was no room for all of them. So the pile was made bigger; and the bigger it got, the more people came to take advantage of it. The pile of rocks became a recognised place to meet people, trade, and discuss the season's prospects. The next thing that happened was that the pile of rocks had become a market, and a man (I can't remember his name offhand; you'd better ask Herodotus) built a house there so that he could be near the market when it opened in the morning. The next thing anybody knew, there was a little village, and the village became a town, and the town became a city. The trouble was that so many people lived in the area that there was no longer any grass for their sheep to eat, and soon all the people were looking as thin as Peison the painter. So they stopped herding sheep and started growing barley. But you can't grow barley unless you know which bit of land is yours and which bit belongs to someone else, so they had to invent property; and once you've got property you have to have laws, so laws came next. Of course, this brought them into conflict with all the people who didn't live in the City, whose land they started taking in (because there wasn't enough to go round) and therefore it became necessary to invent war.

'And so, one by one, all these things like war and law and property started appearing out of nowhere, like long-lost relatives when a will is being challenged; and soon there were dockyards and archons and taxes and prosecutions for illegal legislation and informers and politicians and street-fights and ostracism and philosophers and plague and mortgages on redemption and oratory and boundary-stones and policemen and hectemorage and hemlock and dried fish and Solon and the oligarchic tendency and the empire and silver money and figures of speech and civil war and jury-pay and the market commissioners and the Theatre and ambassadors and red ropes for Assembly and all those wonderful ingredients which go to make the boiled stew we call the Athenian democracy. And nobody could remember where they had all come from or what in hell they were there for, and nobody wanted them or knew how to cope with them; and so a commission of wise men was set up, under the chairmanship of the King Archon, to decide what to do next.

'Well, they sat and talked and argued and took votes

and prosecuted one another, but in the end they had to admit to each other that they were no nearer the truth of it all than they had been when they started. The more they thought about it, the more difficult the problem became, and soon there was talk of packing the whole thing in and emigrating *en bloc* to Sardinia.

'But, just as the Commission was on the point of coming to blows yet again, someone came up with a wonderful idea. Again, I can't remember his name, but I'm sure you know who I mean. Anyway, this gifted individual realised that all the Commission had to do to avoid being impeached and condemned to death for failing to execute its task was to claim that there was a huge conspiracy going on, prosecute a few unpopular people, and simultaneously declare war on Sparta.

'Of course it worked like a charm, and we've been following the same recipe, with subtle variations, ever since. This conspiracy about the statues, men of Athens, is nothing new; it's the same conspiracy they were wetting themselves about when my grandfather's grandfather was herding goats on Parnes. The conspirators change, sure, but the conspiracy goes on. It's aimed at the overthrow of true democracy in Attica and it's such a huge conspiracy that every single one of you is involved in it. It's a conspiracy by the people to enslave the people, and we call it Athens.

'Please don't think I'm advocating any other system of government. It's inhuman to expect a man to obey the orders of another man, be that man a king or a dictator or an oligarch or an aristocrat or a rich man or a soldier. Just imagine what it would be like if Athens was ruled by a dictator, as it was in Pisitratus' time, when they built the Nine Fountains and opened the silver mines and planted out the waste land with olives. There would be taxes, and restrictions on freedom of speech, and endless wars, and trumped-up political prosecutions, and all that sort of thing. Admittedly, we have all those already under our democratic system, but at least we know that they're democratically instituted. Like the Theban soldiers that time, when they were fighting a night-battle, and one lot of Thebans started shooting arrows at random and hitting their own men. And the men on the receiving end of the arrows were greatly distressed and didn't know what to do, until one perceptive man pulled the arrow out of his friend's belly and looked at the feathers in the flight and smiled with relief and said, "Don't worry, mate, it's one of ours."

'There is, after all, a sort of horrible Socratic logic about what you – I mean we – are doing to each other, or do I mean ourselves? The facts: the Athenians have got themselves into a terrible mess. The necessary course of action: someone must be punished. Therefore Athenians must be punished. Therefore we must punish some Athenians. I can do that sort of thing for ever. You know what I mean: if you have not lost something, you must still have it. You have not lost horns. Therefore you still have horns. There is a horse: you do not own it. There is a horse you do not own. Therefore you do not own a horse. If a man is in Megara he is not in Athens. There is a man in Megara. Therefore there is not a man in Athens. Somebody must be punished. Eupolis is somebody. Therefore Eupolis must be punished. Water will travel uphill, if you put it in a jar and carry it.

'Stick to the point, son of Euchorus, and don't try to be clever with us. But men of Athens, what do you want from me? Why have you put me here, who never did anything but write you plays, bite your enemies and fight the Sicilians for you? Don't be a fool, Eupolis, you know what we want from you. We want blood and Comedy, and not necessarily in that order.

'So how would it be if I told you what a democracy is, and then you tell me whether a man who seeks to overthrow it, as Demeas says I do, deserves to die or to be honoured with a statue, like we honour Harmodius and Aristogeiton, who killed the Dictator? Is that a suitable way to pass the time until that contraption over there finally runs dry and it's pebbles-down-the-slot time? Well, I think it is and I'm the one on trial, so if you don't like it you know what you can do.

'Democracy is a system whereby you cut off the

feet of tall men so that they're the same height as everyone else, and then say that everyone is equal. Democracy is a way of saying things so that people believe what you deny and don't believe what you assert. It's a state of mind in which you'll credit any slander about a man, however incredible, but you won't believe anything good about him, even if you see him doing it with your own eyes. A democracy is a place where the reward for doing good is death by hemlock, and the punishment for doing wrong is a pension and a statue in the square. Democracy is a system of counting where the highest common denominator is also the lowest common factor, and where two and two always make five – four, plus one extra to bribe the relevant official. A democracy is a city where the only qualification for holding power is wanting it, and the only people prepared to hold power are those who should at all costs be prevented from doing so. Democracy is where everyone can read but no one can understand; where nobody is guaranteed a square meal when he's hungry, but he can rely on a public funeral if he's killed in battle. Democracy is where everybody contributes, but nobody gets anything back. It's where a clever word at the right time can do more harm than King Xerxes' army, but where a good idea is the shortest way to prison. A democracy is a city where a Monday can be made into a Thursday by a majority vote of the citizens, and where black is white if enough people want it to be. A democracy is a way of ordering your life whereby you can't say where your next meal is coming from, but you can have the Generals executed if you're starving. Democracy is a cannibals' harvest festival, where everyone does their best to feed the hand that bites them. A democracy is a theory of logic by which everything clever is true, everything that tastes nice is good for you, everything that's somebody else's is yours, everything that's yours is liable to be confiscated. In a democracy, the impotent old men have a right to sleep with the pretty girls before the handsome young men do, and everyone has a right to pay taxes. In a democracy – only in a democracy – a man can be had up on a capital charge of which he's entirely

226

innocent, but can, if he's really clever, get off by yelling abuse at the jury.

'At least one child has been born in Athens today. He's going to grow up a citizen of the greatest democracy the world has ever seen. If he doesn't get killed in the War or by the juries, he'll live to see the end of democracy in this city – there'll be an end to it, although it'll cost a lot of people their lives, and probably be replaced by something worse. But while it lasts, the democracy will carry on the way it's always carried on. Now you all know about the mythical monsters, with the heads of lions, the bodies of goats, the backsides of gryphons and the feet of camels, who got killed by heroes in the old days. The man who overthrows democracy in Athens will kill a monster made up as follows:

'First, it has a hundred ears, all on the left side of its head. This enables it to overhear what it's not supposed to hear, and that's what it believes. It can't hear what people tell it, but then, it wouldn't do that if it could hear it. It's got ten thousand mouths, which all speak at once and which must all be fed three times a day. They often speak with their mouths full, for example when they vote for free corn distributions, which the City can't afford but which win votes. In these mouths are many long, sharp teeth, which are like the teeth of an adder; very good for biting and killing people, but useless for digesting food and chewing over the facts. The head has no eyes but a very keen sense of smell; as a result, the monster can't see where it's going or where it's being led, can't recognise its friends or avoid its enemies; but it can smell a conspiracy at a thousand yards, when the wind is in the opposite direction.

'This remarkable head is perched on the end of an enormous neck, which is permanently bent backwards at an angle. This makes it possible for the monster to see what everyone else is doing, and to stop them doing it, but it means that the monster can't see what it's doing itself. The neck ends in a pair of broad shoulders, on to which a lot of unscrupulous individuals have tied some very heavy baskets full of their own interests. These baskets are full of warships, arrows and suits of armour, and the weight of these baskets is slowly distorting the monster's spine, so that it can no longer breathe properly, and will eventually break its neck.

'Next to the shoulders is the monster's enormous belly. All the produce of the world goes into that belly; but it has no digestive organs, so all the good things that go in through the ten thousand mouths go straight out again through the vast arse, and do nobody any good at all. Because of this, the monster has permanent indigestion, which sours its temper. Next to the belly is the most enormous arse you've ever seen, which ends in a long, straggly tail. The monster spends a lot of time standing on this tail, which means that however much energy it expends in trying to go forward, it usually stays exactly where it is.

'The immense weight of this monster is supported by two spindly little legs called the Long Walls, with razor-sharp claws on the end of them. These claws are called the Assembly and the Law Courts, and the monster uses them to catch its prey. However, because of the problems the monster has in moving about, it can never move fast enough to catch anything, and so it has only two sources of food. One is a large, rancid stew, left over from the time when a man called Cimon hunted a herd of Persians across Asia Minor, let them get away, and started catching Greeks instead. He put all the Greeks he caught into the stew, and the monster has been eating them ever since. But this stew isn't enough to keep the monster going, so to supplement its diet it carves off lumps of its own flesh and eats them. For this purpose it sometimes uses the claw called Assembly, and sometimes the claw called Law Courts. The wounds which it makes by doing this don't usually heal.

'This monster is in the middle of a long and complicated food-chain, which depends on it for its continued existence. For example, the monster is crawling with parasites; informers, politicians, mercenary soldiers, foreign governments and a good many fleas. There are also many scavengers who follow the monster about, picking out the undigested goodies from its shit. Among these we may number the Spartans, the Persians and most of the other Greek states – those of them who weren't put into the stew by the celebrated Cimon.

'Because of its peculiar biology – I can't say life-cycle, because this thing doesn't breed, it eats all its own children – this creature has a harmful effect on its environment. For example, it poisons, tramples and lays waste good agricultural land all over the world, but particularly in Attica. It also pollutes the sea by discharging into it many hundreds of warships, which sail up and down burning cities, discouraging merchant trade, and then getting sunk by hostile nations. The smell of unburied bodies, rotting food, unjust accusations and fermenting rumours that hangs around the monster is so offensive that it reaches the noses of the Gods themselves, and from time to time they send a plague to try and kill it off, or sink its fleet, or wipe out its army. But the monster is very hard to kill by these methods, and until it eats up the last scraps of Cimon's stew or gets gangrene from its self-inflicted wounds it won't starve or die of disease. The greatest threat to its own survival is therefore itself, for the time being; but if a man were to be born who didn't believe all the terrifying stories about the monster's invincibility – a Sicilian, for example – he could kill it quite easily by feeding it a great fat cheese poisoned with lies, or by sailing up its arse with all the ships he'd captured from it during the war. And although the monster is very good at damaging things in general, it has no defensive armour except two long walls that serve it as legs and link it to the sea. Once those are broken down, the monster will no longer be able to stand up and will die of starvation, neglect and despair. Its fat will rot away, and when all the flesh has been stripped off its bones by the flocks of Peloponnesian and Asiatic crows which always circle over it, it's possible that a few hardworking Attic farmers may creep under the shade of its ribcage to build nests and try and grow some barley. But whether they'll succeed or not I couldn't say; because although nobody's worked the land around for years, it may be poisoned by all the blood, silver and shit that's been soaking out of the monster's pores these last hundred years or so, and so be quite incapable of producing anything.

'There is, of course, another way of dealing with this thing. We, the men of Attica, could sacrifice the monster to whichever of the Gods is sufficiently demoralised to accept such an offering, cut up its carcase and divide it up among the demes, so much fat to each one. We could then live on this fat until our vines and olives are productive again. This system could work; it worked once before, in Pisistratus' time. But then it took a dictator to overcome the monster; and although he thought he'd killed it, and could hand on the carcase to his sons to dismember in peace, the beast wasn't actually dead at all; it lifted its head and snapped up the dictator's sons in two sharp little mouths called Harmodius and Aristogeiton, and a man called Cleisthenes sewed all the bits back together again. Besides, the dictator kept back most of the meat for himself and his cronies. If you, men of Athens, were to slaughter the beast and take away its flesh to your villages in the country, that would be an end of it, and we could all live happily ever after.

'But of course you won't do anything of the sort, will you? No, you'll vote guilty, as you always do; then you'll go home and sleep soundly and dream untroubled dreams, as you always do; then you'll wake up next day and go to Assembly, as you always do; and you'll listen to some speech proposing that you send a fleet to conquer the moon, as you always do; and that fleet will be destroyed, and thirty thousand men with it, as it always is; and then you'll execute some innocent little man because he coughed during the Sacred Hymn, as you always do; and then you'll wonder why the Gods hate you worse than Styx, as you always do; and you'll execute somebody else for making the Gods angry, as you always do and always will, until the King of Sparta or the Great King of Persia comes and takes all your dangerous toys away from you. And then, when you're old and crippled, you'll tell your grandchildren that once there was a democracy in Athens, and in those days honey flowed down the middle of the streets in a great sticky torrent, and all you had to do was grab a chunk of bread and go out and mop it up. You'll have forgotten about the informers, and the riots, and the war, and the plague, and the trials of innocent men, and the inordinate quantity of blood you could buy for three obols. Then the poets and the writers of history will say that in the Golden Age of Athens there was a democracy the like of which men shall never see again, when all men were equal and worked together selflessly for the good of the State. And what will happen then, do you suppose? Why, for ever and ever there will be fools who wish they could have a democracy as perfect as the democracy they once had in Athens in Attica, and they'll fight civil wars and kill each other and paint the walls of their cities black with their blood in the name of democracy, and liberty, and the inalienable rights of man. As they always do, men of Athens, as they always will, unless someone stands up and stops the nonsense, once and for ever.

'Once upon a time there was a dictator in Athens, and his name was Pisitratus. He seized power in a coup, and abolished democracy. He levied a tax, and with the money he paid for Attica to be planted out with vines and olives, so that in future the Athenian people would have crops to sell and would be able to buy the flour they couldn't grow for themselves. And for a while everyone was happy, and the Dictator died. And his sons succeeded him, and they tried to carry on his work; but the people of Athens had food now, and they wanted entertainment. So they grew tired of the sons of Pisitratus and wanted to get rid of them; but they were too cowardly to take up arms. And one of the Dictator's sons fancied a pretty boy called Aristogeiton; but Aristogeiton had a boyfriend called Harmodius, who was pathologically jealous. So together Harmodius and Aristogeiton murdered the Dictator's son, in a particularly cowardly way: they waited until the Festival, and hid swords in their laurel-wreaths, and when the Dictator's son went by they killed him. Then, when the dangerous work had been done for them, love of liberty burnt in the blood of the Athenian people, and they shook off the yoke of tyranny. The first thing they did was set up a statue to the celebrated Harmodius and the celebrated Aristogeiton,

231

whom we honour today as the Tyrannicides. That is how we honour men who set us free by accident, prompted by an unworthy motive. How should we honour men whose sole purpose is to set us free?

'Well, well, the water-clock just burped at me and told me to get stuck into my closing remarks, and I haven't even begun my defence yet. So I think the only thing I can do in the time available to me is to change my plea to guilty. Yes, men of Athens, I confess. I did smash the statues, just as Demeas and Aristophanes the son of Philip say I did (although between you and me, it's pure coincidence). I smashed the statues, and I did it in a cold-blooded and calculated attempt to overthrow the democracy, because I want to be remembered as the true Harmodius, the man who set Athens free and gave her laws that are equal for all men. Because, like Harmodius, I will never wholly die, but live for ever in the Islands of the Blessed. Isn't that what the song says, men of Athens, the one song that every Athenian knows? I want you to convict me, I beg you to convict me; please, please vote guilty, so that I can become a martyr and have a statue in the Market Square and a drinking-song all of my very own. Please, please send me to the prison, where I can drink the hemlock that better men than I have drunk in far worse causes. I implore you, men of Athens, not for my sake only but for the sake of my wife and my little son, vote guilty and condemn me to death, because if you do you'll be condemning not only yourselves and your children but all the democrats in Attica, and then I will need no avenging Furies with torches and fancy costumes, like an Aeschylean chorus. So cast your votes, men of Athens; vote guilty, just like Demeas said. And remember: any one of you who votes innocent is no true Athenian but an enemy of our democracy and everything that it stands for.'

And that was my speech.

When I finished speaking, there was dead silence, and the only sound was the gurgling of the water-clock. Then everyone started muttering and shaking their heads, as if something very peculiar had just happened and nobody could decide whether it was a miracle or an abomination. The herald, who was looking very puzzled indeed, rose slowly to his feet and instructed the jury to cast their votes.

Now usually there's a stampede to get to the urns, with everyone pushing and shoving, and toes being trodden on and pebbles being dropped; but this time it seemed as if nobody wanted to be the first to vote; everyone was waiting for somebody else, and the herald lost patience and repeated the announcement. Then the old man I told you about earlier hoisted himself up on his walking-stick and hobbled over to the urns. There was a trickling sound and a faint plonk, as his pebble went down, and in his case at least there was no difficulty about knowing what his vote had been. The sound of a pebble going down a spout seemed to break the spell, and the jurors started casting their votes, until the Court was filled with the sound of falling pebbles, like rain on a flat roof.

For some reason, I wasn't a bit nervous. Don't imagine that I was in any way confident about the result; I had no clue whether my gamble had paid off or not. I had put my faith in the Comic dramatist's oldest gag, violent abuse of the audience; but I had seen that gag fall flat often enough to know that it's about as safe as a country bridge. Yet I was feeling perfectly calm, and the only way I can explain it is by saying that I didn't care, one way or the other. But it wasn't that carelessness I had felt in Sicily, or during the plague; that feeling that I was going to live for ever. I believe that at that moment I had lost that feeling at last. No, it was rather a feeling that I had done what I had set out to do; I had made the Big Joke, and I was satisfied with it and knew it was good, and it didn't actually matter all that much whether anyone laughed or not. Inside me, I was laughing, being a man who rarely laughs at jokes and never at his own jokes. This moment was, so to speak, the punch-line of my life, and I had delivered it to the best of my ability. If the audience failed to get the point, that was their fault for being stupid.

The votes were all cast now, and the counters were

hard at work. They counted; and then they counted again; and then they conferred with the Archon, who told them to count a third time. And now I began to laugh out loud, because the immortal Gods were obviously joining in on my joke and adding a little touch of their own, to make it superlatively funny. Finally, the Archon was satisfied, and nodded to the herald, who cleared his throat and stood up.

'The votes cast,' he said, 'are as follows. For Guilty, two hundred and fifty votes; for Not Guilty, two hundred and fifty one votes. The prisoner is therefore discharged.'

Stunned silence; then a gabble such as you only hear when there's been a serious accident, or someone has murdered somebody in the street. For my part, I nodded to the jury, said 'Thank you very much', and started to walk out of the Court, feeling rather subdued. But when I was nearly at the gate, a familiar figure stood up and barred my way. For a moment I panicked and looked round for a way to escape, but my soul told me not to be stupid, and I turned and faced the man. It was the lawyer Python, the one who had offered to write me a speech.

'Eupolis son of Euchorus,' he said in a loud voice, 'I hereby summon you in the presence of witnesses to answer at your trial for the sum of five drachmas, plus two obols interest at the usual rate, being the price of professional services rendered to you, and which you have failed on reasonable notice to pay. If you do not pay this just debt plus the interest aforesaid within five days of this day, I summon you to stand your trial at the Court of Debts at the old and new moon. I name Strephocles son of Xenocles and Pythias son of Conon, both of the deme of Cholleidae, as my witnesses that this summons was truly served.'

I borrowed five drachmas and two obols from someone and paid him; then I started laughing hysterically and had to be taken home.

Chapter Fourteen

If you can remember back that far, you may recall that this was supposed to be the history of my times, written so that the deeds of great men might not be wholly forgotten, or some such brilliant idea. Perhaps I'm just unendurably self-centred, because it seems to me that what I've written is the history of my life, with particular reference to me. Now you've probably read more of this sort of thing than I have, and so you'll know better than I do where a History is supposed to stop; or perhaps you've read this far in the ever-diminishing hope that sooner or later I'd break down and start recording all the speeches and battles and votes that took place during the period I've been covering – if so, I'd better tell you now that I'm not going to, and you can take the book back to my friend Dexitheus and explain that there's been a misunderstanding, and I expect he'll give you your drachma back, so long as you haven't spilt milk all over it or torn any of the rolls. But if this is going to be the history of my life, then it stands to reason that I can't possibly finish it until my life is over and I know what happened to me in the end; and then, of course, I won't be able to write about it, because I'll be dead. I know that sounds a bit Socratic, but there's a serious point in there somewhere. For all I know the great tragic events of my life, the truly worthy subjects for dramatic treatment, all lie ahead of me, so that everything I've covered so far – my part in the War, my trial and my acquittal – will all be notes in the margin, put in by the copier to explain references in the main text. But I want to believe that the Gods don't need me as a witness to any more remarkable events. For my part, I'm sick of writing this book; it's made me remember things I wish I had forgotten completely, and reminded me that I was just as much a fool in my youth as I am now.

So I was tempted when I started work this morning to make the moment of my acquittal the last scene in this drama, taking it as a good cue for the final chorus, a little dance by a soloist, and then straight off to the party. Certainly it seemed like one at the time, particularly to a man like myself who has an innate sense of dramatic structure. It seemed to me as I walked home that day that everything appeared to fit into place; all the actors had had the right amount to say, all their exits and entrances and changes of costume and mask had worked out all right in the end, every theme introduced could be justified in terms of the play's overall effect. Quite often, when I've written a play, I'm sitting there feeling complacent when the herald calls on my chorus and I suddenly think of the perfect joke or the perfect line of dialogue that would round off a scene or thatch over a gap; and then, of course, there's nothing I can do about it, and the poor thing is doomed to be incomplete for ever. But I had no such feeling that evening, when I peeled my sandals off my unusually damp feet and fell on to the couch in my own familiar house. The funny story about Eupolis of Pallene seemed to be over, and its protagonist appeared to be free to go.

But of course it didn't work out like that; it never does, and that's where your great poets go wrong. One day, I want to write a great big long epic poem about what happened to all the heroes of Troy after they finally got home, regained their thrones, hung up their shields in the rafters and settled down to do a little farming. I want to make all those tired old men jump through a few more hoops, just when they thought they could change into their old clothes and have a rest. I want to make Odysseus come out of retirement to deal with a catastrophic outbreak of sheep-blight in Ithaca, or to try and get the island's council to find the money to get the harbour properly repaired and the roads put in order. I want Menelaus to have to get up off his backside and do something about the shortage of seasonal labour in the Spartan olive-growing industry; though it may just be an excuse on his part to get out of the house and away from Helen, who has got very fat since she returned from Troy, and is always on at him to redecorate the inner room. I want Neoptolemus to wake up one morning to find that some bastard has stolen his best plough and left the gate of the sheep-fold open.

After my trial, the first thing I did, apart from getting a good night's sleep and eating far too much breakfast, was make an attempt to straighten out my affairs, which were in a dreadful state. The bulk of my movable fortune was up in Thessaly, and for all I knew had been spent by the delightful Alexander on chariot-races for the local chieftains. I had a number of disastrous mortgages and leases to try and wriggle out of somehow, and in addition quite a few inheritances to dispute – several distant relatives of mine had died in Sicily leaving no heirs, and my claim to their property was as good as anyone else's. In fact, when at last everything was sorted out and the best part of the money I had sent to Thessaly had quite remarkably been returned to me, I found I was better off than before, because of these inheritances. It only goes to show that the best way to get rich in a city like Athens is to live longer than anyone else.

But it all took time, and I couldn't count on any help or co-operation from anyone. The nature of my escape from Demeas made me an object of great suspicion in Athens for a while, and when I think about it, it was a miracle that I wasn't had up all over again on any one of a vast number of charges. After all, I had quite clearly recommended the overthrow of democracy in a public speech, and men have died just for hinting at less. But I reckon that saying it all in such an outspoken manner was such a grotesque and incredible thing to do that nobody could really believe that I had done it. And that's something I've noticed about communities such as ours; if you have courage, or what looks like courage, people don't like tangling with you. If you let them see you're afraid of them they'll have you; but if you make yourself look bigger than you are, they'll leave you in peace and pick on someone else. Nevertheless, it was obvious that I shouldn't push my luck. The best thing so far as I was concerned would be if the name Eupolis was completely forgotten, at least for a while.

Of course, this meant that anything so conspicuous as presenting a play was out of the question. Whatever I put in the anapaests, however innocuous, would be regarded as an incitement to civil war, and Demeas or someone like him would be after me like a dog after a lame hare. But this self-imposed exile from the Theatre turned out to be less of a hardship for me than I had anticipated, at least to begin with. I found that there was very little I wanted to say, and the urge to write Comedy had left me. At first I was surprised; I couldn't imagine being Eupolis and not wanting to compose verses. But it left a larger gap in my life than I had ever dreamed it would.

For example, as a general rule, when I can't get to sleep I don't count sheep or make lists of the names of cities beginning with each letter of the alphabet, as other men do; I compose speeches and choruses. When I'm working out of doors, I keep from getting bored by thrashing out anapaests. Even when I'm walking down the street, I tend to walk to an iambic rhythm, with a loud clop of the right foot for a spondee and a little pause to mark the caesura. Again, I find it hard to pattern my days if I haven't got a play in progress. Under normal conditions, you see, life is a battle to carve out a few uninterrupted hours for serious work from the rocky wastes of meaningless chores that surround me on all sides; without the excuse of a play to fiddle with, I have no excuse for not taking part in all those hundreds of pointless activities which all the other members of my species seem to regard as necessary and I abhor. I suppose politicians have the same trouble when they're in exile, or blacksmiths or pirates when they get too old to work.

But, for a while at least, I was happy not writing; in fact, I was happy doing nothing, which anyone who knows me would regard as a contradiction in terms. I am the sort of man who is capable of doing any amount of work, just so long as it doesn't feel like work. Anything that I've got to do makes me feel like I'm wearing lead boots. But after my acquittal, I did nothing at all, until Phaedra got quite sick of the sight of me in a chair and told me to go away and write something. But there was nothing for me to write, and I can no more write when I don't feel like it than I can be sick when I don't feel ill. I came to the conclusion that Athens was not the place for me to be, and so, four months after the trial, Phaedra and I set off for Pallene. There is, I told her, always something for a man who still has the use of his arms and legs to do in the country, and once I was in Pallene I would soon snap out of it.

I was wrong. Instead, there proved to be far more nothing for me to do. If I tried working in the fields, I would end up leaning on my mattock gazing at the hillside, until my steward politely asked me to go away because I was setting the slaves a bad example. If I went out with the goats it was even worse, and someone would have to be sent out after me to stop them straying and getting taken in and rebranded by an unscrupulous neighbour. There was one dreadful occasion, I remember, when I was entrusted with a load of figs and told to go and sell them in the market. I got the cart most of the way down the mountain; but then the axle broke, and the whole load went everywhere, with a tremendous smashing of jars and cascading of figs; and instead of swearing terribly and jumping down to see to it, I just sat there on the box of the broken cart thinking how funny it was, until someone else came up behind me and yelled at me to unblock the road so that he could get his cart through. In the end I got everything sorted out; but by then it was too late to go to market so I went back home again, and everyone was extremely surprised to see me.

One thing I did do that was constructive and useful was to spend a little more time with my son. This in itself was frowned on – it's not a father's place to go interfering with his child's upbringing before the child has reached an age where a father's influence is valuable. But those around me reckoned that, given the state I was in, I could do less damage to the efficient running of the household if I took the child up on to the hill and sat watching him crawl about. I say it was constructive and useful; I'm not meaning to imply it was constructive and useful to the boy, who probably didn't recognise me. But I enjoyed it. I'd never greatly cared for children before then – anyone you can't discuss Comic poetry with, I had always thought, is largely a waste of time. But there's nothing like spending some time with a prattling child for putting your life in perspective. To a child, you see, everything is so terribly immediate; present discomforts are insufferable, present wants and ambitions are all-important, and the most distant future imaginable is sunset. Now I was in the middle of trying to work out what I really wanted out of my life – though I didn't realise it at the time – and this new way of looking at time was a useful comparison. The way you measure time depends on what you do and who you are. A child, as I have just said, measures time by the day. A farmer thinks in three-year blocks; one year's produce in the field and two years' supplies laid up in the barn. Landless casual workers and Comic poets measure time by the year; either where this year's work is going to be, or what he's going to show at this year's Festivals. This annual approach is marginally better than the child's, but it doesn't make for stability. The other way of looking at things, which I couldn't help doing, was the way a man uses time when he's unexpectedly alive after resigning himself to dying, and that's by the minute, or the second.

But the main factor in the great rearrangement of my life was Phaedra. Almost incidentally, in the tremendous disturbances that Demeas brought into my life, I had discovered that Phaedra and I could, if we were careful, not only endure but enjoy living together. I wanted to make use of this discovery and put it to the test. For her part, Phaedra seemed mainly to want to get on with sorting out the store-cupboard or making a coverlet for the bed, and regarded all my attempts at sitting down and talking things through as irritating interruptions in her daily routine. But I persevered; and although we never had the grand debate about the nature of married life that one of those semi-philosophical writers would have inserted into the story at this point, we seemed to come to a sort of unspoken settlement; we both agreed to accept the change in our attitudes towards each other, so long as neither of us ever mentioned it out loud.

It was about this time, when I was in Pallene getting under everyone's feet, that the political situation began to change, subtly but in such a way that even I began to feel distinctly nervous. Now the last thing in the world that I want to suggest is that my speech had anything to do with it; but perhaps my acquittal was a symptom that something was changing. At any rate, the first thing that I couldn't help but notice was the institution of a wholly new arm of the legislature: a Council of Ten, set up to 'advise' the main Council. These ten men were elected, as democratically as possible, but it stands to reason that when you put a certain number of men, be it ten or a thousand, in a position of authority for any length of time, they will soon have little in common with their original mandate. One thing that amused me about the business was the fact that one of the Ten was the celebrated Sophocles, the playwright. He was well into his eighties by now, virtually blind and completely senile. He knew what he was doing, of course; he wasn't legally incapable, as he proved at a trial about this time, when his family wanted to get control of his property and he made his defence by reading out the play he had just been writing and demanding to know whether a senile man could have written that. But he no longer lived in, or even appreciably near, the real world, and he had got it into his mind that Athens was in the grip of some great tragic cycle, such as he might write a trilogy about; and that since nothing could be done to save the old place, the kindest thing would be to hasten it towards its inevitable destruction, and so precipitate its rebirth. The other nine Councillors dealt with more mundane things, such as public order and the water supply.

It was about this time, too, that the revolt in Chios began to be taken seriously, and a large force was sent to deal with it. Now I can't remember how long all this took;

and in my desire to get to the end of this story, perhaps I'm rushing forward by months or even years. To tell you the truth, I have only the vaguest recollection of the sequence of events after my trial, since I was out of them, more or less, and took little notice of what people told me. But I do remember that the institution of the Ten and the rebellion in Chios – or was it the other one, in Samos? – had a lot to do with the rise of that extraordinary fellow Pisander. I always get Pisander muddled up with Phrynichus (not Phrynichus the Comic poet, Phrynichus the General), but to be honest with you, the main characters don't matter all that much. What mattered was the change in the way people thought, and that was quite startling.

For years there had been rumours of an oligarchical tendency in Athens; young, rich men with lots of time on their hands who wanted to overthrow the democracy and seize power. This had started as a conspiracy rumour, and nobody took any notice of it unless they needed it for an impeachment or a Comic play. Now I don't know which came first, the rumour or the actual tendency, but by this time the dream was starting to take shape, and a very unpleasant shape it was, too. Up till now, oligarchs had been like giants or centaurs – you believed in them up to a point, and you knew someone whose uncle had seen one, but you never expected to meet one yourself. But now, you began to suspect that the peculiar people whose names you heard so much about, if you were the sort of person who listened to that sort of talk, might indeed be oligarchs, and you began to worry about the greatest single issue of the day, the return of the lost leader, Alcibiades.

I have deliberately not said much about Alcibiades; partly because I didn't know him well enough to talk about him, and partly because I think his importance has been vastly exaggerated. To hear some people talk, you would think the fellow was a one-man city, with fleets and armies and money of his own. Not a bit of it; he was a rather glamorous individual who spent his exile from Athens amusing himself with peripheral intrigues at the courts of Sparta and the Persian governor Tissaphernes. He may have made a great many suggestions to influential

242

men among our enemies; but I doubt whether he put a single new idea into their heads. We Athenians, believing with absolute sincerity that only Athenians can achieve things in this world, need an Athenian to be the cause of what happened next; and since Alcibiades was in the area at the time, we naturally assume that the Spartan–Persian pact, which finally did for us in the War, was something to do with some grand design or policy of the celebrated Alcibiades.

But if Alcibiades himself was of little importance, his name was another thing altogether. Wherever two or three Athenians met together to talk, his name would inevitably be mentioned; and out of that three, one would be pro-Alcibiades. Probably just to be perverse; now that it was permissible to think and talk about such things, those Athenians who loved to debate and argue (which means all Athenians) were starting to talk about and debate a change of constitution. Would an oligarchy actually be a good idea, they asked themselves? What could be said in favour of it, and what against? Now once Athenians start to talk about something, you can be sure that sooner or later they'll try doing it, particularly if it's something that hasn't been done before. In fact the greatest thing in favour of the idea of oligarchy was its novelty, coupled with a certain air of secrecy, wickedness and danger. Add to this the continued feeling of doom and despair because of Sicily, and a degree of revulsion from the excesses of the first reaction to the disaster, and you have a fine hot stew on which to feed and make yourself thoroughly ill.

Of course my name was linked with the nebulous conspiracy right from the start, because of what I had said at the trial, and as a result of this I was probably right to keep as much out of sight as I did (although, as I have explained, this was hardly policy on my part). But I'm sure the Tendency looked upon me as One of Us, and the democrats whispered about me as being One of Them. Everything in Athens is either One of Us or One of Them, and the only things that change are the definitions of Us and Them. These change regularly and out of all recognition, but nobody ever seems to notice this. Sometimes I wonder what it would have been like to have lived out my life in some more normal city, like one of those orderly little places you hear about in Crete or Euboea, where things never change and nobody takes any interest in what their city is doing because their city never does anything beyond a little unobtrusive road-mending. In a way, it would be heavenly, but I expect I should have gone mad within ten years, unless I had been born there and known no other way of life.

As it was, even in my self-imposed retirement in Pallene, I started to feel that tingling sensation that an Athenian gets when something is about to happen in politics. In my case, this sensation manifests itself most strongly in those parts of the body and the soul concerned with the composition of anapaests. Now I've never wanted to change the way people think; but I do like writing anapaests. It makes you feel involved. And you will remember that just before my trial I had thought up that marvellous idea for a play, with all the various Demes of Attica coming on as a Chorus, and all the great Leaders of the past coming back from the Other World to give advice. I think what sparked it off was that scene Aristophanes and I put together in the smithy in Syracuse, where we brought Aeschylus back to life to debate poetry with Euripides. In any case, I started thinking more and more about it when my mind was empty, and the thing seemed to gather a momentum of its own. I had made a deliberate decision *not* to write anything more for a long time, but the play was taking shape in my mind, like an unmarried girl's pregnancy, and there was nothing I could do about it. If Athens was in a crisis, I would have to write something, and that something would have to be relevant.

It was Phaedra who made me break my vow. One evening we were sitting together in my house in Pallene. She was sewing away at something, and I was staring at the hearth with my mouth open, an occupation which was rapidly becoming my profession and career. It certainly irritated my wife who tried not to look at me when I was doing it. On this particular evening, however, she seemed to lose patience with me altogether.

244

'What's got into you?' she said. 'If you don't close your mouth soon, a spider will come and weave a web over it.'

'Stop moaning,' I replied. 'There's nothing needs doing, is there?'

Phaedra looked at me for a moment. 'There's something the matter with you,' she said. 'I don't know what it is, but the sooner you get rid of it the better. You're beginning to make me feel uncomfortable.'

'I don't know what you mean,' I said, and I put my feet up on the couch and pretended to go to sleep.

'I know what you remind me of,' she said after a while. 'Do you remember that man who used to live near the fountain, the one who had the two white dogs?'

'Vaguely,' I said. 'Was his name Euthycritus?'

'I couldn't say,' Phaedra replied, 'and anyway, that's beside the point. You remember that he had a stroke?'

'That's right,' I said, 'so he did.'

'And you remember,' Phaedra went on, 'how he couldn't move or talk, but his eyes were just the same as they had been. And his wife used to get the slaves to carry him in his chair to the front door and park him there so that he could watch the people going up and down.'

'And everyone used to look the other way,' I said, 'because they couldn't look him in the eyes without cringing. I remember. Wasn't he once an athlete or something like that?'

'Possibly,' Phaedra said, biting through her cotton and putting her work down. 'Anyway, that's who you've been reminding me of these last few weeks.'

I didn't think that was funny at all. 'You do say the most ill-omened things,' I said to her. 'Fancy comparing me to a cripple.'

'Well, it's true,' she said. 'I think you'd be perfectly happy sitting in a doorway watching the shoppers.'

This startled me, because it was quite probably true. 'Have I been as bad as that?' I said.

'Yes,' replied my wife, 'or worse. You'd sit there even if there weren't any shoppers. What do you think about, for God's sake? Are you working out geometrical theories or just counting birds?'

'I'm not thinking about anything,' I said, 'except occasionally how glad I am to be alive.'

'That's odd,' she said. 'You're behaving just like a corpse. And a docile corpse, at that.'

'Aren't wives supposed to pray for inactive husbands?' I said. 'You never used to like it when I was always dashing about doing things.'

'And all that nonsense you've been talking lately,' she went on, 'about our relationship and so on. What sort of talk is that for a husband and his wife? You sound like a philosopher talking to his boyfriend.'

I frowned. 'I just wanted to get things straight,' I said.

'Things are naturally straight,' she said, 'unless you fiddle with them. You should just get on with life instead of thinking about it.'

'That's a very solemn remark,' I said, smiling mockingly at her. She frowned disapprovingly.

'You know what I mean,' she said. 'Don't start being all Chorus-like and commenting on everything I do as if I were Clytemnestra or somebody. You do a lot of that, I've noticed.'

'A lot of what?'

'Observing,' she said. 'You look at people, and listen to them, as if you were a judge at a fair. Nobody wants your assessment, thank you very much.'

'I know,' I said, 'but I can't help it, I do it naturally.'

'What you need to do,' Phaedra said, standing up and collecting her sewing things, 'is to find something to do. Otherwise you'll turn into a god or a lump of rock or something.'

'Explain,' I said.

'Well,' she said, sitting down again, 'you're just like that sometimes; a god on a mountain, or a boulder, or a tree. You just stand or sit there and watch, as if the world was a play put on for your benefit. Now when you used to write plays, this was more or less justifiable, because you made some sort of use of it all. You needed to catch how people speak and act, and make some sort of judgement for your anapaests. But now you just seem to do it for your own entertainment, and it's not natural. Either snap out of it or start writing again.'

'You're odd, too,' I said. 'I never really know whether you approve of me writing or not. You never seem to take any interest while I'm composing something. You always give the impression of being a patient wife allowing her husband to pursue his childish hobby, as if I collected seashells or carved miniature ships on scraps of ivory.'

Phaedra shrugged. 'I don't know,' she said. 'I don't think you're particularly clever, if that's what you mean, just because you can compose lines that scan. And I'm not a Comedy enthusiast, like some people are; I prefer Tragedy, personally, and I'm not a very literary person when you come right down to it. Most women aren't, actually. But I suppose you do it as well as anybody,' she said fairly, 'and probably better than most. And you've got to do something, so you might as well do this.'

I sat up and put my hands round my knees. 'So you think I ought to write a play, do you?' I said.

'Yes,' she said. 'For my sake if not for yours. Then people won't point to me in the street and say, "There goes that woman who's married to a corpse." I really can't stand much more of this godlike stuff, you know. It was different after you got back from the War, when the trial was on; you had a purpose in life then all right, and I rather liked you. But now . . .'

'All right,' I said, 'I get the message. You can't stand the sight of me just sitting here peacefully. You want me to be busy.'

'Only because it's your nature to be busy,' she replied. 'At the moment you don't really seem to exist, and that's unnerving for a girl. I never know when you're going to start walking through walls or slowly disappearing, like a dream in a poem.'

So the next day, I took the plough out over the fallow, and instead of getting to the end of the furrow and then stopping, as I had done the last time I tried it, I went straight on and did a day's work without knowing it. When I got home, I had an opening speech fully fledged in my mind, and it was the best I had ever composed. Now one thing that always worries me is whether what I'm doing now is as good as what I've done before. This is quite an obsession with me, and I end up hating things I've written because I can't seem to do as well any more. This time, though, I knew it was good. The lines seemed to have a crispness and a crackle about them, and instead of ending a line off with a conventional jingle, I had tried my best to find something new and startling, the way you do when you're just starting out in the Theatre and every word is important to you.

Shall I tell you all about that play? I've been very good so far, and not bored you with little synopses of my various brilliant dramas, so I think I'll allow myself the indulgence, just this once. The story was as follows. The Athenian State is in a crisis, because it hasn't been able to think of anything new to do since it sent a fleet to conquer the moon. So worrying is this mental sterility that our hero takes it upon himself to go down to the underworld, like Odysseus, to ask the opinions of the glorious dead.

Once he has made the journey, the first person he meets is the celebrated Myronides, the general who led Athens to victory at Tanagra, the battle I told you about which ended the previous war with Sparta in my grandfather's time. I picked on him because he seems to represent, to my generation at least, the last honest citizen and competent general of the old school. In fact he was just as much of a rogue as all those who came before and after him, but I was not concerned with absolute historical truth. No Athenian is, or we wouldn't celebrate Marathon as a victory. Anyway, Myronides acts as our hero's guide and takes him to see all the great statesmen of our history, from the immortal Solon to Pericles, and each of these gives his considered opinion about what should be done. To put each of these towering figures in his place, I made my Chorus up of the demes of Attica, with Pallene as Chorus-leader; because, when all is said and done, it is the demes and not the city which make up Athens.

I had set out to write a play, and as good a play as I possibly could; but the more I wrote, the more serious this Comedy of mine became. As you can see from what I've told you, it was a very political play; and I don't suppose I would ever have written such a work at any other time. I had set out with no clear message in my mind; but as the play progressed and I tried to think what advice Solon might actually give us in our present situation, I found a strong theme emerging and did my best to do it justice. It wasn't at all what I thought myself; but that's not really a poet's job. Aristophanes, for example, has consistently attacked the War and demanded an end to it from the moment he started to write; but he has nothing personal against the War, and at least until he went to Sicily thought very little about it. But his characters are mainly heavy-infantry farmers, and such people naturally disapprove of the War; so in order to write what he wants to write and make the sort of jokes he likes, Aristophanes must present himself as a peace-lover and a countryman, which could hardly be further from the truth. Similarly, in my case, having appointed myself the spokesman of our great political leaders, I was virtually forced to make an impassioned plea on behalf of the democracy. But, to be fair to myself, I argued for the good parts of our constitution, the parts that Solon envisaged and Themistocles and Pericles didn't manage to spoil between them. I argued that what Athens needed now was the sort of democracy where everyone was entitled to be heard so long as he spoke sense; where the majority should not oppress the minority in the way that the Few had oppressed the Many in Solon's time. Obviously (I said) you can't create that sort of system by legislation or the creation of new institutions. A democracy is the most vulnerable system of all. Furthermore, a democracy more than any other form of government tends naturally to incline towards repression, intolerance and violence, because it is the form that imposes the least restraint upon human nature. But a democracy where men restrain themselves, thereby doing to themselves what nobody else either can or should do to them, is potentially the best of all forms of government, so long as it is based on mutual tolerance and consideration and a general intention to do what is best for all, and above everything, what is possible in the circumstances.

Well, that's what I said in the play. As you know, I don't believe a word of it. I don't believe that any state the size of Athens can govern itself, whatever form of government it chooses, without causing immeasurable damage to the people who live in it. But I honestly believe that in my play I gave the City the best advice that I could, and I am proud of what I wrote then. It came out of my own experience in the way that no Comedy has ever come out of experience before, because instead of attacking and making fun of what was being done, it suggested what should be done; and instead of being hurtful to a few for the sake of pleasing many, it was designed to say what the author thought – or at least what the composite creature representing the author would have thought had such a person ever existed. And in one respect it did reflect my own personal opinion; that the demes, the villages and regions of Attica, are what matter, and that the great men and their political factions and movements are the servants of the demes and should never forget it.

'There now,' you are saying, 'that was very clever of you, Eupolis, but what happened next?' Well, I wrote the play, completing it fairly quickly by my standards, and sent it to be copied. It had occupied my attention fully all the time I had been composing it, and apart from political gossip I had taken no notice of anything else. But, as any playwright will tell you, writing the thing is the easy, relaxing part. The hard work would be getting it accepted and produced.

Chapter Fifteen

Obviously, the first thing I had to do was go and see Philonides. Now he hadn't had anything to do with the Theatre or the training of Choruses since the Sicilian disaster – I don't know if there was any deep meaning behind that, or whether it was just coincidence – and when I told him that I had a new play which I wanted to put on at the Festivals he didn't seem to want to know. He argued that he was getting old (which was true enough) and that he wasn't interested in that sort of thing any more; but I bullied him and wheedled away at him, and finally, more to get rid of me than for any other reason, he agreed to hear the play and look at a copy of the written version.

I was so confident about the play that I never had any doubts that once he saw it he would be won over completely, and as it happens I was right. As soon as he heard the entry of the Chorus, he was hooked; for unlike so many of the people who have tried to emulate him, he knew that he was first and foremost what his title said he was, a trainer of Choruses. To him, as to me, the Chorus was the heart of a play, and its costumes, movements, singing, verse-speaking and general effect were his primary concern and greatest love. He excelled at marshalling and controlling men *en bloc* and in Sparta they would have made him a general. It was because he was so good with Choruses that he was able to control and manipulate individual actors; as he himself used to say, if you can reduce a whole Chorus to tears with a single tirade, you should never have any problem imposing your will on just one man. Now Philonides could see that my Chorus of demes, if properly handled and appropriately costumed, could be the most spectacular and effective Chorus he had ever seen led out, and the temptation was too strong for him. He put up a good fight, right up to the last minute, but in the end he gave way and agreed to train this as his last and best Chorus.

The next thing was to go and see the Archon to apply for a Chorus for the Dionysia, and I must confess that I was not at all sure that I would be able to get past this obstacle. I'm convinced that I wouldn't have succeeded without Philonides' backing; as it was, I had a terrible time before I finally won through.

To start with, there was the problem of the play having been written by me. As I said just now, I was pretty thoroughly identified in the public mind with the oligarchs, because of my defence speech, and so it was natural enough for the Archon to feel that choosing a play by Eupolis was tantamount to declaring himself an oligarchic sympathiser. On the other hand, the play itself was patently for the democracy, and it was a brave man in that climate who identified himself in any way with such an outspoken statement in support of either side. There was a general feeling in the City that the mysterious leaders of the planned oligarchic coup – nobody knew who they were supposed to be, but everyone was convinced that they existed – were going around and preparing lists of diehard democrats who would have to be liquidated come the Glorious Day, and nobody wanted to be on those lists, for understandable reasons. So it was asking a lot of the Archon to demand that he choose a play that denounced oligarchy. I can only suppose that he came to the conclusion that my supposed oligarchic sympathies and my outspoken democratic views in the play cancelled each other out, and that by endorsing the play he was hedging his bets.

But those two factors weren't the only things against me. For one thing, it was a while since I had asked for a Chorus, and unless he submits work very regularly, like

Aristophanes always has, it doesn't take very long for a poet, however strong his reputation has been in the past, to be forgotten about or supplanted by some up-and-coming young pretender. Just then, there were several men who were being talked about as the New Generation of Comic poets, and there had been many applications for Choruses. Suffice to say that I was forced, for the first time, to submit to the indignity of a series of postponed decisions, and to be chosen last out of the three competitors. In fact it was a very close thing at the end, since the Archon very nearly gave the Chorus to a young man who has never been heard of since, who had put together an entirely innocuous, if not particularly good, piece of nonsense about Hercules and a cauldron of lentil soup.

But in the end I got the Chorus, and the next difficulty was putting together a cast. Now since I had been given my Chorus last, and only after a long delay, all the good actors had been snapped up by the other poets and I was left with the no-hopers and the young apprentices, who had to be trained virtually from scratch. To make matters worse, Philonides, who was getting more and more enthusiastic about the project every day, had thought up some of the most fiendishly intricate and difficult dance routines and bits of business ever seen on the Attic stage, and with not enough time to rehearse and an inexperienced and generally feckless cast, I was all for watering these masterpieces down to make sure we had at least something to show the audience come the day. But Philonides would have none of it; instead, he set out to train every actor and Chorus-member as if he had never been anywhere near the Theatre in his life. This used up huge quantities of time, money and patience, all three of which were soon in short supply, and Philonides took to venting his fury and frustration on me, which I found rather unfair. But in the end he won through, as I knew he would. There is nothing Philonides can't make a Chorus or a cast of actors do, if he's determined that they'll do it. I believe that if the Council had given Philonides a Chorus and told him to use it to sack Sparta, he'd have pulled it off, and ahead of schedule.

As I said just now, money was a considerable problem. It was just my luck to have appointed as my producer a certain Promachus, notoriously the meanest and most humourless man in Athens. For a start, he hated the very idea of being made to finance a Comic play, since he disapproved of Comedy on principle and my play in particular. It would have been difficult enough if it had been an ordinary sort of play; but with Philonides calling for the best of everything for his Chorus, and new and expensive machinery for special effects, Promachus soon declared that he was going to deposit twelve hundred drachmas with me, and that was all that could be expected from him. So in the end I found myself paying for most of the expensive things, and I didn't enjoy that particular experience at all. Of course, when the time came, Promachus took all the credit, as a producer would be entitled to do under normal circumstances, and set up a magnificent votive statue recording how much had been spent on the production (two thousand drachmas). He didn't say how much of that money had been provided by me, of course; in fact, I don't think he mentioned my name at all.

What with him, and Philonides' regular outbursts, I didn't have much time to worry about anything else, such as whether the play was really as good as I believed it was. Still, I managed to spare a few hours' anxiety for the activities of my old comrade-in-arms the son of Philip. I hadn't actually set eyes on him since the trial, but as soon as I emerged from my slumbers and started work again, I started to hear rumours that he was furiously angry with me for having been acquitted after he had given evidence against me, with all the damage to his reputation that inevitably ensued, and that he had sworn to have his revenge on me, come what may. I heard from a fairly reliable source that he had done his best to persuade the Archon to reject the play, and also that he had tried to dissuade Philonides from taking it on. I confess that I found this behaviour rather excessive, coming from a man whom I had no great cause to respect, but I didn't dare try any form of retaliation in case it made things worse. I know a man is supposed to help his friends and harm his enemies, but I couldn't be bothered just then.

I also heard that Aristophanes had got mixed up very deeply with the oligarchs, and although you could find some such rumour about anyone you cared to name at that time, I was inclined to believe it in this instance. The gist of the rumour was that he was terribly friendly with the celebrated Phrynichus, the General, and this is actually borne out by various things he says in some of his plays, for what that's worth. He was also supposed to be doing his best to ingratiate himself with Pisander, the other main ringleader; but apparently Pisander couldn't take him at any price and refused to have anything to do with him. That I can well believe, for whatever his faults Pisander wasn't without a measure of common sense, and the son of Philip would be a definite hindrance to any cause to which he attached himself. But it seems, if the rumour had anything to it, that Aristophanes was quite serious about the oligarchic cause, and wasn't just in it for the fun and the mischief. He saw himself as part of the ruling faction, up there with the best of them, and presumably once there in a position to settle some old scores, such as me. Now I can honestly say that that particular prospect didn't lose me any sleep; but I was rather concerned in case he should try anything nasty against my play. Good-natured sabotage, as I'm sure you remember, is all part of the fun of being a poet, but the whole climate in Athens at the time was such as to make you wonder what a vindictive person might not try and do. Everything seemed just that tiny bit more dangerous than ever before; it was as if the Athenian Game had got rather out of hand, and people were taking things a touch further than they would have before. This was true in everything, not just the Theatre; I don't really know how to describe it to you. You know how a game of catch can sometimes turn nasty, with the players deliberately throwing the ball at each other when they lost their tempers; well, I suppose it was like that, in a way.

Of course, violence and other forms of extreme behaviour were nothing new; but all the light-heartedness seemed to have gone out of politics and the other forms of public life in Athens, and I think this was because, as a City, we had rather lost our nerve after Sicily. Before, we were all that bit more prepared to take risks, and accept the consequences if we failed – I suppose because we were certain in our hearts that we couldn't fail, and so there would be no consequences to take. But now, Athens seemed to have become old and sour instead of young and exciting, and the endless search for novelty wasn't so much a quest for new sensations and fresh objectives as a sort of desperation, because nothing seemed to be going right any more. All the old energy was still there of course, but it was the furious energy of someone who knows he's losing, rather than the vigour of ambition. For example: we built a new fleet in next to no time, and won a few quick victories with it, which made us all feel elated and safe for a while. But we could do nothing about the revolts in our subject cities, and still less about the Spartan fortress at Deceleia on our borders, which was very slowly grinding us down. The fortress made me think back to the old days my grandfather used to talk about, before the Persians came, when the Athenians could not rest easy at nights for the thought of Aegina being still unconquered, and Themistocles urging them every day to wipe out the 'eyesore of the Piraeus'. The thought of a Spartan fortress on Attic soil would have been intolerable to the Athenians of his time, but we seemed to be able to put it to the back of our minds and get on with something else. In the meantime, to divert our attention, we thought more and more about domestic matters, including the constitution; and this sort of brooding was definitely bad for us. Hence this sourness that I've been describing. All the old, typically Athenian characteristics were still there, of course: the energy, the love of words and novelty, the random cruelty. But they were like those warships of ours which had been captured by the Syracusans; they were ours, but they were being used against us, to do us harm.

I guess it wasn't the best time to be putting on such a very political play; but I had written the thing, and it was topical, and I wanted to see it staged. But there was more to it than that; I suppose because, since my speech in my defence, I too had been thinking rather more than usual about that sort of thing. Now do you see what I mean? At the time when this story starts, your average Athenian would no more have been rethinking the democracy than he would have been rethinking the sky; the democracy was just there, and it was impossible for it to change. I may not have liked the democracy very much, ever since I was old enough to consider these things, but it simply wasn't one of the things that a man could expect to do anything about; just as, if he doesn't get on well with his family, he can't expect to be able to resign from it and join another. You can't deliberately divorce yourself from your City; your City can banish you, but even that is a most extreme measure, in many ways as drastic or more so than putting you to death. No, if something big was happening to the political system of Athens, even I couldn't stop myself from having my say.

Rehearsals became more and more frantic as Festival time drew closer, what with Philonides shouting and the actors not yet knowing their words and the fullers accidentally dyeing a whole batch of costumes purple instead of red; and the fury in the Theatre seemed to be matched by the frenzied activity outside it so that, after so many years, I can no longer separate them in my mind. I say 'activity' deliberately; nothing substantial appeared to be happening, but a great amount of energy was being expended by a great many people; and when so much heat is produced in such a small space, something, sooner or later, is likely to be broken or at least melted down. The situation in the War was no less exciting, but that seemed like a peripheral issue to us in the City, and we regarded it as little more than a source of new and rich debating-points – how would the oligarchs react to such and such, or what would the Old Guard make of the developments in Persia? This was very short-sighted of us, because we were in grave danger of losing control of our most productive subject-states. The Spartans were starting to think like sensible, rational human beings at last, instead of Homeric heroes, and they were getting ever closer to making a treaty against us with the greatest of all enemies, the King of Persia. If I hadn't been so wrapped up in the preparations for the play, I'm sure I could record a great many matters of interest to generations yet unborn about those truly fascinating few months before the Dionysia in March; as it was, I had only a vague idea of what was going on outside the City and in the War, and if I were to give you a detailed account it would be mostly hearsay, and Athenian hearsay at that. But I can tell you a little about that year's Dionysia, if that will do instead.

The main – or only – talking-point was the extraordinary set of plays that Euripides was supposed to be presenting. He was keeping very quiet about them himself, and this only fuelled the furious speculation. For at least one of them was (apparently) going to revolutionise our entire approach to Tragic drama, the Gods, and pretty well everything else. We knew that one of these plays was going to be about Helen, and that Euripides had taken his old hobby-horse, the story in Stesichorus that Helen never went to Troy but was spirited away to Egypt while Paris was left with a replica made of cloud, and used it to create some vast metaphysical question to which there was no immediately obvious answer. Then another play was going to be about Andromeda, dealing with the story in a roughly similar way; and both plays were to have happy endings and be closer in many respects to Comedy than Tragedy. Now I belong to the school of thought that many of Euripides' plays are unintentionally Comic, and so I couldn't wait to see what would happen if Euripides tried to be deliberately funny; I expected the entire audience to be in floods of tears before the entry of the Chorus. Several of the Comic poets, Aristophanes included, were desperately trying to get advance copies of these plays, by bribing the Archon's slaves or getting the actors drunk, so as to be able to include snippets of parody in their next Comedies; and even I felt a vague irritation, because Euripides hadn't had the decency to put on these grotesque farces of his in time for me to use them in my masterpiece. I had been reduced to having another go at the *Telephus*, which was the one weakness that I could think of in the whole play.

258

Of course, you will be thoroughly familiar with those two boils on Tragedy's backside, Euripides' *Helen* and *Andromeda*, and you'll be wondering what all this fuss was about. But there were some very curious things in those plays, particularly in the *Helen*, when you think of what I've been telling you about the situation at the time. For example, in the *Helen*, there's no end of praise for Sparta, mostly dragged in without any perceptible justification from the plot or the characters. If Euripides' intention was to shock the audience he certainly succeeded, and there were quite a few normally intelligent people who were very impressed. Then there was that extraordinary line about how even the most widely travelled men can't tell the difference between true gods and false ones and things which are half-divine and half-mortal. Now when a man has a reputation for obscure profundity, such as Euripides has, he can get away with saying anything at all, and people will do their very best to read something wonderful into it; and there was no shortage of idiots who took this to be a highly intelligent comment about the statues that were smashed and the expedition to Sicily. In fact I remember having the whole thing explained to me, in detail, by a barber while he was trimming my beard about a week after the Festival, and I was unable to argue with him for fear of moving my chin too much and getting my throat cut. At the time I was thoroughly convinced by what he said, as it happens; but I'm afraid I can't remember a word of it after all this time.

What with the Euripides scandal and politics and the War, therefore, nobody seemed particularly anxious to find out in advance what Eupolis was going to put on that year; in fact, the general opinion as I heard it was that Eupolis was well over the hill, hadn't written anything worth bothering with since *Maricas*, and should retire gracefully and let one of the newcomers have a chance. This sort of talk just made me all the more determined to show them all that I still had something to say, and I started making rather a nuisance of myself at rehearsals, just when Philonides and the cast had reached an uneasy truce. As a result of my interference, which

259

consisted mainly of wholly unreasonable demands that the Chorus-numbers be made even more spectacular and that the actors learn whole new speeches with less than a week before the Festivals began, we very nearly didn't have a play to put on at all. But Philonides triumphed over adversity, and just when I was ready to give up, we had a last rehearsal at which virtually everything worked. I remember walking home after that final run-through and going straight past my house because I was saying Solon's speech over to myself in my head, and I hadn't finished it by the time I reached the door.

At last the time came for the official preview, two days before the start of the Festival proper. In those days we did it slightly differently; the poets, producers, Choruses and actors went down to the Odeon (you can imagine my feelings on revisiting the place) with costumes but without masks, and the poet had to get up on a platform and announce the title of his play, with a brief summary of the plot. Naturally, nobody ever said what the play was actually about – that would have been a disastrous mistake; instead, we would put together a sort of Delphic riddle to inflame interest. I had never enjoyed this stage in the proceedings before, since I used to have no great confidence in my ability to project my voice. But, after my trial in that very building, I knew all about the acoustics in the Odeon, and it was a positive pleasure to stand up on the platform where I had made my defence and announce my Comedy. It was really a sort of declaration of defiance on my part, and to mark the occasion I had written rather a good little piece. I was well into this, and getting a very healthy reception from the audience, when a couple of men at the back of the hall started shouting and throwing olives at me. I recognised them as some of Aristophanes' regular hangers-on, who he paid to clap and shout 'Encore!' during his plays (some of them had been with him for fifteen years, and were as well known in Athens as the actors themselves). This, I reckoned, was a bit hard. It's not uncommon for a poet to organise little riots during the play itself, as I seem to remember telling you before somewhere; and I recall with great pleasure the time Cratinus got his supporters to start making a noise during one of Euripides' early efforts – he had heard that Euripides had included a speech in praise of money, and he got his people to object to this on moral grounds, with the result that the poet jumped out of his seat, ran down on to the stage and begged them to hear the rest of the play and see what a bad end the money-loving character came to. But to organise a disturbance at the preview was something entirely new; and what made it worse was that Aristophanes had somehow found out what the plot and best scenes of my play were going to be, and had told his men to shout this secret information out at the tops of their voices. But Philonides had apparently suspected something of the sort (although he hadn't seen fit to share his suspicions with me) and had hired a mob of his own. These men jumped up and started yelling that Aristophanes was part of the oligarchic conspiracy and ought to be taken to the top of the old tower in the Potters' Quarter and thrown off. So in the end Aristophanes' trick backfired on him, because Philonides' riot got far more laughs and the son of Philip was so frightened that he ran home and hid under the bed for the rest of the day.

The lots were drawn: I was to come on the second day, following Euripides' Tragedies. I was in two minds about this. On the one hand, you could be sure that the Theatre would be packed as tight as whitebait in a jar; on the other hand, the audience might be so worked up about the Tragedies that my Comedy would be virtually ignored. I'd seen that happen many times; the audience are still talking about the Tragedy, usually at the tops of their voices, when the Comic Chorus makes its entrance. Nobody has heard the opening speech, and so they haven't the faintest idea of what's going on. On balance, I decided, it would be a good thing. Nobody, not even a foreigner, would be able to ignore the opening scene of my play, with Athena coming down from Olympus on the machine.

On the first day of the Festival, I was awake long before dawn; and Phaedra and I were among the first people in the streets waiting for the procession to go by. Now not even the strange atmosphere in the City could spoil the opening day of the Dionysia. It's all different now; but in those days there was nothing like it in the world. Bear with me while I describe it; for my own satisfaction, if you like. It was very much the best side of Athens' character, and after all the terrible things I've been saying about her, I reckon it's only fair that I should give her a chance to be seen in a better light.

Shortly after dawn all the prisoners in the gaol, except for the dangerous ones, were brought out under guard to watch the procession, and the girls who had been chosen as basket-bearers were scurrying about showing off their new outfits while there was still time, before they had to take their places. The procession was always late starting; but when it came out everyone always declared, every year without fail, that it was the best one yet. The statue of the God would go by, and the basket-bearers, and then the young men chosen to sing the satirical songs and shout vulgar abuse at anyone famous they recognised in the crowd – because now the God was in charge of the City, and mere mortals, however important, had to be made to recognise that fact. Then one of the sacrificial animals – usually a large and savage bull – would always manage to escape and gore someone or other in the crowd, and there were fights and robberies and people fainting and getting trampled, and all the other ingredients of a good day out.

Then came the solemn, rather boring part, with the singing of the dithyrambs by massed choirs and everybody trying to look serious and devout and doing their level best not to cough in the wrong places. I don't know why it is, but even the most brilliant poet, when called upon to compose a dithyramb, inevitably turns out twenty minutes' worth of the most turgid rubbish you ever heard in your life, the sort of stuff that would be hissed off the stage without a moment's hesitation if it was put in a play. But, because it's the dithyramb and somehow sacred and privileged, the entire audience pretends it's the most marvellous poetry since Hesiod, and nobody says a word or throws so much as a pine-cone. But everybody is very relieved when it's over at last, and the real fun can begin.

First, there's the sticking of the pig, with all the blood and squeals, which the children always like; then the libations are poured, while most of the audience queue up in front of the sausage-sellers and chatter away to each other about the harvest. But they're all back in their seats for the procession, when the young men carry the jars of silver left over from the tribute after the City's expenses had all been paid – this was often a bit of a joke, of course; about this time the City was virtually bankrupt, but the procession went ahead all the same – and after that came the presentation of suits of armour to the sons of the men who had been killed in battle that year. Now as you can imagine, this part of the proceedings could be actively embarrassing. At the Dionysia after Sicily, for instance, there simply wasn't enough armour to go round, and they had to get the young recipients to run round the back and pass on the armour they had just been so movingly presented with to the next candidate. In the end, I believe, they all got their armour, for it's a serious matter and not even the politicians would dream of cheating; but some of them had to wait several years, and even then there were complaints that a few of the suits of armour didn't fit, or were second-hand stuff bought from the people who go around stripping the bodies of the dead after battles.

Finally, the names of the judges for the plays are drawn out of the sealed cauldrons brought down from the Acropolis during the procession, and you can picture for yourself all the producers of the plays sitting there in rapt attention as the names were announced, hoping that they had bribed the right people.

Then there would be an interval, and everyone would get up and rush out to buy more sausages, or wine, or apples, or things to throw. There would be queues outside as the foreigners who had come late tried to buy tickets, while the citizens who had only just arrived from the more remote parts of Attica strolled in past them and made sarcastic remarks. When the noise of fifteen thousand chattering and munching human beings had reached its unendurable height, the trumpet would sound and there would be the most frantic rush for seats, like an infantry line collapsing under cavalry attacks in flank and rear. Then you would see the unedifying spectacle of virtually the whole citizen body of our great democracy accusing his neighbour of stealing his seat or his cushion, or sitting on his hat, or blocking his view of the stage. In the middle of this confusion, there would be a blast on the flutes and everybody would break off in mid-recrimination as the first actor of the Festival came on to speak his prologue. This silence generally lasted only long enough for the actor to identify himself and say where the play was set; as soon as everyone realised that it was going to be yet another Orestes' Return, they would resume their arguments with their neighbours where they had left them. I imagine this is why Tragedies have prologues; I can see no other justification for them.

That was what the opening day of the Great Dionysia was like in my day. Now you will say it's just the same now, and that I've been wasting your time telling you about it, and isn't that just like a senile old man? But I must ask you to think again. Isn't it all more subdued and deliberately literary these days? Remember, we were seeing these great Tragedies, which you respect as much as Homer because you were told they were good when you were a boy, all for the first time, and we didn't know they were going to be good when we took our places in the Theatre; and bear in mind also that most of them weren't – the ones you read are the good ones. And besides, nowadays a lot of people don't even bother to go to the Festivals, whereas then it was really the only time when everyone in Attica who could possibly manage to spare three or four days was sure to be together in one place, absolutely confident that he was perfectly capable of understanding everything that was said, and that his judgement was as good as the next man's, because Athens was a democracy. That has most certainly changed, and now you have people who understand the drama, and people who know what they like, and a lot of people who say they don't like plays at all and think they're boring.

I know what you're thinking, and you're right; I am starting to sound like an old man. I think it's writing this book that's doing it. Before I started on this fool's errand, I hadn't given the old days much thought – I'm not the sort of man who likes to dwell on the past – and to a certain extent I've been thinking aloud for a lot of the time, as things occur to me that I never realised before. But we Athenians aren't terribly good at noticing the passage of time. For example; Aristophanes continued putting on the stage Choruses supposedly representing men who had fought at Marathon long after all but the last few veterans of the battle were dead and buried, but nobody in the Theatre seemed to find this strange. They still imagined that there were plenty of Marathon men still alive, and so nobody ever got around to seeking out survivors of the battle and actually asking them what happened and writing down what they said so that it would never be forgotten. Then along came men like the celebrated Herodotus, and they wrote their books and gave their recitals, and there was nobody left to say whether they had got it right or not. Which is why I started writing this, I suppose – that and the money Dexitheus offered me, of course, and the prospect of something to do over the winter. Dear God, I really am starting to ramble now, aren't I? I'd better get on with the story, before I completely lose touch with reality.

Now I've told you that I was listed to send on my Chorus after Euripides' Tragedies on the second day, and that I was in two minds whether this was good or bad. Well, I sat through the opening day like a small child who's waiting to be taken to see the market for the first time, and I hardly noticed the Tragedies. The Comedy was absolutely dire; it was one of the first of these miserable domestic farces that are so popular nowadays, all about a young man who wants to marry the girl next door but can't, for some improbable reason, and there were hardly any jokes about the politicians or the War, while the Chorus-songs had nothing to do with the plot and seemed to have been bolted on as an afterthought. I hated it, and it was very depressing to hear the audience applauding it. I take it as a personal insult when people applaud a bad Comedy, unless, of course, it's one of mine. When this travesty finally ground to a halt I went straight home instead of hanging about as I

265

usually do, talking to people I haven't seen since last year and generally enjoying being involved. Philonides came round later on, to go over a few last-minute points; but more out of politeness than for any other reason. He had everything firmly under control, rather like a good Persian governor, and needed no help from me. I asked him if he'd heard whether Aristophanes was planning any more tricks, and he looked at me very strangely and said that I was becoming obsessed with Aristophanes, so I dropped the subject. I had an early meal and went to bed, but of course I couldn't sleep. I wanted this play to win more than any other I had ever written, and I think it was at that point that I knew that if it did win, it would be my last, and I would be through with the Theatre after that. I didn't know why. I still don't.

At last it was morning, and I went over to Philonides' house at least two hours before dawn, to find that he was still in bed and not particularly pleased to see me. He was feeling generally depressed – naturally enough, considering that it was his fifty-seventh birthday – but after a cup of hot wine with honey and cheese and a mouthful of bread, he was soon rushing about like an eighteen-year-old, and then the Chorus-leaders and the actors arrived.

I shall remember that morning till I die. The Chorus-leaders were the first to arrive, and they were full of energy and enthusiasm. Then the two supporting actors came in, and they had hangovers but were otherwise intact. The protagonist, however, was nowhere to be seen. Now the man in question, one Philocharmus, was notorious for being late for everything, and so at first we didn't worry. But when there was only an hour to go until the first Tragedy and he still hadn't turned up, Philonides started sending messengers out to find him, and we sat and stared at each other, wondering what on earth was going on. Philonides was thoroughly worked up by now, and passed the time by saying what he would do to Philocharmus when he got his hands on him. But in the back of my mind I already knew what had happened to him, and so when one of Philonides' men came bursting in and blurted out what had happened, I wasn't in the least surprised.

Philocharmus (said the messenger) was in the Market Square. He was completely and hopelessly drunk, having been fed wine doctored with poppy-essence, and there was no earthly chance of sobering him up by this afternoon. The messenger said that he had met a couple of men who had seen our leading actor having a drink with a red-headed man and a tall man with freckles the previous evening, and that was all we needed to hear. Those two were the leaders of Aristophanes' claque – the same men who had made the scene at the preview. God only knows why Philocharmus hadn't recognised them. In fact, I believe he did, and that a fair amount of coined silver changed hands.

So that seemed to be that; we had no leading actor, and so no play. At least half the lines in the play were spoken by the protagonist, which was the usual thing in Comedy in my day. Philonides nearly had a stroke, mainly because it should have been his job to make sure something like this didn't happen. But I can't blame him; the people you usually have to watch are your rival Comic poets in that year's Festival, not someone who isn't even competing, and I'm sure he had taken all possible precautions against sabotage by my two immediate rivals. It hadn't entered his head that Aristophanes would carry his personal grudge against me this far.

With about half an hour to go before the start of the first Tragedy, we still hadn't thought of a plan; and I was all for going to the Archon and telling him, so that he could arrange for something to fill in the time. But Philonides would have none of it. He simply looked at me and said, 'I'm not having my best work thrown away like this. One of us will have to do it.'

I stared at him. 'You're crazy,' I said. 'I don't know the first thing about acting.'

'I know,' he said. 'And your voice is all wrong, and you move like an ox-cart with a missing wheel. And you're too short. No, you certainly can't do it. Not in a thousand years.'

We looked at each other. We had known each other for many years. Philonides had been the first man I had spoken to that day I got back from Sicily. If I had a single friend in the whole of Athens, it was Philonides. He was also perfectly capable of out-acting Thespis himself; he had a marvellous voice, a magnificent sense of timing, and the sort of authority that would make an audience sit up and take notice. But there was one drawback. He was terrified of speaking in public.

He once told me about the only time he had spoken to a large audience. It was a lawsuit, something trivial about a small debt a neighbour of his owed him, and after a lot of worrying and putting it off, he finally took it to Court. He wrote a brilliant speech for himself to deliver and learned it perfectly by heart. He rehearsed himself in it for a fortnight, doing nothing else from dawn to dusk. He went along to the Court to get used to the atmosphere of the place, took advice from seasoned litigants, and even read a couple of books on the subject. But when the day came, and the water-clock started running, he dried up completely. For all his titanic efforts, he couldn't bring himself to say a word, and the case went against him by default. Yet this was the man who could bawl out the most recalcitrant of Choruses, reduce professional actors to tears, and persuade authors to rewrite their best speeches, all by sheer force of personality. And now I was asking him to get up on the stage in the Theatre of Dionysus, for the first time, at the Great Dionysia itself, in front of perhaps eighteen thousand people, and play the leading role in a Comedy.

We sat there in silence, glaring at each other like two stray dogs in the market competing for a scrap of offal, with the terrible thought that one or other of us was going to play the leading role in a Comedy that afternoon.

'You know,' said Philonides after a very long time, 'if you held yourself a bit straighter and spoke very slowly, you could probably get away with it.'

I smiled frigidly. 'They say acting is totally different from speaking in Court,' I replied. 'For one thing, the audience is on your side. You'll probably enjoy it once you get over the early nerves.'

He ignored me as if I hadn't made a sound; it was a gift he had, and he used it to great effect when dealing with actors. 'After all,' he said, 'it's not that many years since the author regularly used to play the lead. Before the War, it was very much the done thing. Aeschylus did it all the time.'

'It was Aeschylus who put a stop to it,' I pointed out, 'when he introduced the second actor. I remember hearing someone say once that Aeschylus used to come out in a horrible rash all over his face every time he had to go on stage. He had to have a specially padded mask.'

Philonides tried a different approach. 'It must be really aggravating for you writers,' he said sweetly, 'when the audience come out after the play and all they talk about is how good so-and-so was as the hero and never even mention the poet, like the actor just made it up as he went along. And they'll never know it was you with the mask on; they'll think it was Philocharmus. So if you make a botch of it he'll get the blame, and if you're a real smash you can raise your mask at the end so that everyone can see it was you.'

'No fear,' I said vehemently. 'This is a good play, and I'm not having some idiot like me make a mess of it. Face facts, I couldn't get through the opening scene without dropping something or falling off the edge of the stage. And there's that bit where the Chorus dance in front of me; I'm so short the audience wouldn't even see me, even in the boots.'

'You're just chicken,' Philonides said desperately. He was streaming with sweat, even the backs of his hands, and his eyes had become very big.

'Yes,' I agreed. 'So are you. So which of us is going to make a fool of himself in public?'

'I've got my reputation to consider.'

'You said yourself,' I reminded him, 'they'd never recognise you under the mask.'

'Someone would be bound to recognise my voice,' he said hysterically. 'All those people I've shouted at over the years.'

'My voice is far more distinctive than yours,' I said. 'And it's not nearly so good,' I added quickly. 'You're always saying how no actor can speak lines properly. Now's your chance to show them how to do it.'

'I've retired, remember?'

'So you've got nothing to lose, have you?'

But he shook his head vigorously, until I was convinced it was about to fly off his shoulders. 'No,' he said, 'I'm not going to do it, and that's final. It's your play; if you want it salvaged, you'll have to do it yourself.'

'Listen,' I said, 'it won't be salvaging it, it'll be ruining it. No, it's obvious, there's only one thing I can do, if you won't play that part. I'll have to go to the Archon and tell him that because of your negligence and carelessness there won't be a play this afternoon. Then I'll fiddle with it a bit and put it on another year, maybe under a different name. Of course, your reputation in the Theatre will be dead meat; *you'll* never be able to work again after the news gets out; but then, that won't matter to you because you've retired, like you said.'

I stood up to go; and I had actually picked up my stick and got as far as the door before Philonides called me back. 'If you say anything like that to the Archon,' he said, 'I'll kill you, I promise. It's your precious enemy that's got us into this mess.'

'I don't seem to have much choice,' I replied. 'And look at it this way. If I go out pretending to be an actor you've trained, and I make a hash of it, as I undoubtedly will, who are they going to blame? Not me, the poet. They're going to blame the Chorus-trainer. "He's really lost his grip this time," they'll say. "Over the hill," they'll say, "just like I was telling you, he should've retired years ago." But if you do it, at least you'll only have yourself to blame. Come on, man; if some of those losers who call themselves actors can do it, you can do it, no trouble at all.'

I reckon it was that last bit that did the trick, for Philonides basically despised all actors. He sat there for what seemed like for ever, not saying a word; then quite suddenly he made a noise like a splitting wineskin and started calling me all the names under the sun. Blackmailer was one of them, I remember, and there were several variants on the theme of cowardice. I took this to mean that he would do it.

'But on one condition,' he said. 'We're going to spend

270

the rest of the day going over this thing inch by inch with a full cast, costumes, everything, until I could do it with my eyes shut; because that's probably how I will have to do it, all right?'

'All right.'

'And when it's over,' he went on, 'I want you to promise that you'll hold Aristophanes' arms for me while I break every bone in his body. Agreed?'

'It'll be a pleasure.'

He stood up, looking as if some unkind person had strapped a marble block to his back. 'A really lovely birthday this turned out to be,' he groaned. 'Right, we'll get the Chorus together and then we'll make a start.'

So I never got to see those notorious experimental plays by Euripides that have since become so famous; while they were shocking a largely unprepared audience, I was hearing Philonides through his big speech for the fifth or sixth time in the big courtyard behind a friendly corn-chandler's warehouse near the Pnyx, while a thoroughly disgusted Chorus tramped miserably backwards and forwards and calculated how much they could get away with charging me for overtime and missing the Tragedies. I'll say this for Philonides, however; although he kept breaking off every six or seven lines to call me some new name he'd just thought up, he never once suggested cutting a word of the play to make life easier for himself; nor did he make one alteration to the moves and routines he had planned with such reckless enthusiasm. And whenever he'd finished his speech and could turn to look at the Chorus, if any of them was so much as a hair's breadth out of position he would tear into him like a lion devouring a goat. If he was going to have to make an idiot of himself at his age, he said, the least everyone else could do was try and get it right for once, and anyone who cocked it up that afternoon was going to get the same as Aristophanes, or maybe even worse. Finally, after going through the play six times at top speed, he declared that he was as ready as he would ever be, and that all he needed now was a very stiff drink.

I was completely opposed to this idea, but Philonides

ignored me and sent a slave off to the wine-shop to bring him a jar of the strongest, roughest Attic wine he could find. The slave dashed away like a frightened hare, and came back with a jar covered in cobwebs and marked with the double chalk cross that usually means 'Not for sale': so I imagine he had gone somewhere where Philonides' reputation as a hard man with a bottle was properly respected. He then went off to get some water to mix with it, but he was wasting his time. Philonides just put his thumb through the wax, lifted the jar to his face, and poured. Wine went sploshing down all over his tunic, but a fair quantity of it ended up in his mouth, and he kept on gulping until I thought he must surely burst. Then he put the jar down, wiped his lips with the back of his hand, and smiled broadly. 'Right,' he said. 'Lead me to it. Someone bring that jar, I may need it again.'

We packed up the costumes, counted the Chorus to make sure everyone was there, and set off for the Theatre. When we arrived, we found we were only just in time; the Chorus of the *Helen* was just going off, to rather patchy applause, and the audience was starting to talk about what it had just seen, very loudly. I hurried over to the seat reserved for me as a competitor (the Theatre was more full than I had ever seen it before, because of the Euripides plays), evicted the foreigner and his three small children who had occupied it in my absence, and sat down to catch my breath. Just down the row from me, I could see Aristophanes son of Philip, who was staring at me as if I had at least two extra heads. I waved at him and smiled, and offered up a little prayer to Dionysus. If he got me out of this mess in one piece, I said, I would most certainly give up the Theatre for ever and never try his patience again. Then, as if the God had answered me, I felt something under my foot; it was a broken wine-flask, and it gave me a happy idea. I stooped down, picked up one of the sherds, and took the brooch out of my cloak. With the point of it I scratched a few words on the bit of broken flask and asked my neighbour to pass it down to Aristophanes. I can't remember exactly what I wrote, but it had its effect; because as soon as he read it he dropped the apple he'd been eating, gave me a look of pure hatred, and hastily left the Theatre. Now I come to think of it, I believe what I wrote was something to the effect that just before leaving home I had sent a few slaves and friends over to his house to set fire to it, and if he hurried he might be in time to stop them. The foreigner and his children took Aristophanes' seat, and since it wasn't reserved he couldn't get back into it when he returned from his fool's errand, which meant he had to watch the little of my play he eventually got to see standing at the back among the slaves and the drunks.

Philonides didn't come on until well into the first scene; so if he had still got that jar with him he had plenty of time even now to get hopelessly drunk. Although I was desperately proud of my opening dialogue I couldn't bear to watch, and if the audience laughed at all I didn't hear them. And yet there is no sensation as sweet to me as the sound of people laughing at my lines in the Theatre, so that when I hear it I can think of nothing else; so you can judge for yourself how nervous I was. But I heard Philonides' cue loud and clear, and I opened my eyes and stared at the entrance he was due to come through. For about the time it takes for an olive to fall from a tree he didn't appear; and in that brief instant I formed two mental pictures of him; one of him lying on the floor with an empty jar beside him burbling like an idiot, and another of him cowering down behind the backdrop and refusing to budge, while the slaves kicked him and called him names. Then he strode on to the stage, looking like King Theseus himself, and the audience suddenly fell silent. He seemed to hesitate for a fraction of a second, and then he launched himself into his opening speech, which is one of the best things I have ever written. His voice welled up from the stage like a spring from a split rock, making him seem twice as tall as he was, and for a while the audience were too overawed to laugh. Then the first big joke came crashing through, like a wave of the sea when there's a great storm, and the sound of laughter made the earth shake. For me it was like the first lungful of air to a suffocating man. I sucked that laughter in through every pore in my skin, and held it inside me.

It seemed to do something to Philonides, too. Just for a moment he seemed frightened, as if he had been suddenly made aware that he was not alone in the Theatre. Then it was as if he had swallowed all that enormous volume of sound and digested it, all in the time it takes to move a finger, for he thundered out the rest of the speech as if he were a god delivering a prophecy. I have never seen an audience take to an actor as they took to Philonides, and I've never ever seen an actor respond so well to a good audience. They clapped and cheered and whistled and shouted, and he got better and better. It was a long speech, that first speech of his, but time seemed to stop running while he was delivering it.

In other words, the play was a success. When the Chorus came on, there was a moment when you could have heard a coin drop, while the audience all looked twice to see if their eyes were playing tricks on them. Then they seemed to go mad, and there was such a stamping of feet that the Spartans at Deceleia must have thought that a huge army was coming to get them. But it wasn't the noise that impressed me so much as the silence when the big speeches were being delivered. Usually there's at least one idiot or drunk who talks or sings during the speeches; not this time. Except for sporadic waves of laughter or cheering, there was total quiet, and you could hear the heels of the actors' boots grinding on the floor of the stage. I have heard louder applause for a play in my time and louder laughter for a joke, but I've never heard such attentive silence in all my life. For they weren't just laughing, they were also listening, and that was what made me feel happier than I had ever felt in my entire life.

I don't remember anything about what happened after the play, or during the rest of the Festival; let alone at the Victory party after I was awarded first prize by a unanimous vote of the twelve judges. I've heard that Philonides and I got completely drunk and went all round the City reciting the speeches from the play, and wherever we went people came out of their houses and cheered us, and that we were finally carried home on the shoulders of complete strangers, fast asleep. All

I remember is waking up afterwards with a murderous hangover and vowing never to get in such a state again as long as I lived. I've kept that vow, and I've also kept my vow to Dionysus never to write another play. After the *Demes*, there seemed to be no point, for I could never have another triumph as great as that one. I did start to write a play about three years later, but the words just wouldn't flow and I gave up after the first few speeches. The desire to write Comedy had left me, and it has never come back. Shortly afterwards, of course, things were so different in Athens that I wouldn't have written anything even if I could; so, all in all, it was just as well that I wrote my last play when I did, and that Philonides overcame his nerves enough to play the leading part.

Shortly before he died, not many years later, I asked Philonides how he managed to go on, considering how unwilling he had been to do it. Had he drunk the rest of the wine, I asked him, or was it his soul telling him to be strong? He said it was neither of those things. In fact, just before the time for his cue he got such a bad attack of panic that he started taking off his mask and boots. But then (he said) he thought he saw a large man with a black beard standing behind him, looking at him with such utter contempt that he was shamed into putting the mask back on. When he looked round again, the man had disappeared and Philonides swore blind that there was nowhere he could have got to; he must just have vanished into thin air. Now at the time Philonides was suffering very badly from the fever that finally carried him off, so this may just have been his mind wandering at the end. Or perhaps it was a hallucination he'd had at the time, caused by fear and residual alcohol. But it's perfectly true that there are very few places a person can disappear into at the back of the Theatre of Dionysus, so perhaps he was telling the truth after all.

Chapter Sixteen

Towards the end of April next year, the democracy was overthrown. It was a relatively peaceful way for the world to end; four hundred leading oligarchs held a meeting outside the City at Colonus and then marched in, threw the Council out of the Council Chamber with the help of a gang of young bloods (who probably mistook the whole thing for a drinking-party), and declared that there had been a return to something they called the Ancestral Constitution. This meant, in theory, that the franchise was limited to five thousand citizens who had the necessary property qualification, but since these five thousand good and honest citizens were never actually named and nobody had the faintest idea who they were, this clearly didn't mean very much. The essence of the situation as it emerged over the next few days was that four hundred men now controlled Athens absolutely, drawing their mandate from a couple of gangs of large, taciturn men with clubs and swords. The leaders of the coup were Pisander, Phrynichus, the politician Theramenes, and Antiphon, a man who wrote speeches for the Courts (rather like my old friend Python). Apart from a few routine murders of generally unpopular people, they did very little that any reasonable man could object to, at least to start with; but that was not the point.

At the time the main Athenian army was in Samos. When they heard what was going on, they were all for sailing straight home and killing the oligarchs there and then. But before they were ready to leave, who should turn up but the celebrated Alcibiades, who had been roughing it at the court of the Persian governor, Tissaphernes the Magnificent, waiting for an opportunity to make his comeback in suitable style. He sailed in on a handsomely decorated Persian yacht, made a speech or two, persuaded the army to stay put, and sent a blood-curdling letter to the oligarchs demanding that they publish the names of the mysterious five thousand good and honest citizens who were to be the twin anchor of the ship of state. As it happens, no list was ever received by the army at Samos, but the messenger service was notoriously slow at that time of year, what with the winds and the great oar-blade shortage, and after a while the soldiers forgot all about the list and concentrated their energies on pampering their newly restored Lost Leader.

Meanwhile, the oligarchs were working flat out to cobble up some sort of end to the War, so that they could get the backing of the Spartans and the Persians for their new régime. In order to demonstrate that this was not in fact what they were doing, they set about fortifying the entrance to the Piraeus. This fooled nobody, of course; even the most innocent of us could see that their real intention was to make it possible for them to cut off the City from its grain supplies. But there was nothing we could do about it, so we let it happen. There was a wonderful feeling of helplessness in the City, something that none of us had ever known before. Things were happening and we were totally unable to interfere, we could only be passive and wait to see what would happen; and meanwhile, it was nothing to do with us, not our problem. It was a sort of euphoria, I suppose, and as such obviously impermanent. But I reckon most of us hadn't realised what was really happening – we thought it was just a weird sort of holiday, and that soon it would all be over and we could go back to being democrats again.

Sure enough, the rule of the Four Hundred ended as quickly and as effortlessly as it had started. Phrynichus was stabbed to death in the Market Square on his way to buy fish one morning, the men who were fortifying the Piraeus took this as a signal for a general holiday-cum-riot, and the oligarchs called out their supporters, in arms, into the streets. But before any serious fighting could be done, the Spartan fleet appeared off the Piraeus, apparently intending to come in and storm the City. This was obviously no coincidence; the oligarchs must have sensed a week or so before that they couldn't hold power without outside help, and sent for them. As soon as the news of the Spartan attack reached the City, the oligarchs' armed supporters manned the walls and launched our fleet, the Spartans retreated, and we chased after them. Our fleet was seriously mangled off Euboea, as it happens, but that was Foreign News, and nobody seemed to care. They were far more interested in the situation at home, which was becoming decidedly lively. For after the Spartans had gone away, a good old-fashioned (and thus illegal) Assembly was held on the Pnyx, the Four Hundred were formally deposed, and the clever lawyer Antiphon was condemned to death. And that, apparently, was that. Business as usual. We apologise for any inconvenience caused.

Wrong. The Assembly didn't vote for the restoration of the democracy; they voted for Alcibiades. In a sense, this was a wise move, since Alcibiades had our army in the palm of his hand over on Samos, and nobody, not even the most dedicated seekers after new experiences, wanted a real full-scale civil war, with Alcibiades storming the City and anointing himself King Alcibiades the First. So what they voted for was his immediate return to Athens and the establishment of – believe it or not – the rule of the five thousand good and honest citizens, which was what Alcibiades had called for when he went over to the army on Samos.

Alcibiades was understandably confused, and he stayed abroad with his army and his fleet (they were decidedly his, not ours, by this stage) while we, apparently sincerely believing that what his lordship wanted was the rule of the Good and Honest, set about making it possible. We actually appointed a Five Thousand (who in the end came to about six thousand five hundred or so, but that's Athens for you) and waited patiently for instructions. And that, not the great and mysterious *coup d'état*, was the end of democracy in Athens. People at the time blamed the odious Theramenes, who wriggled out of his involvement in the *coup* with a speed and dexterity that won him universal admiration, and set himself up as Alcibiades' vicar on earth; but I don't think his part in it was particularly significant. I honestly believe that the Athenians subconsciously realised that they didn't want the democracy any more. Since they didn't know what they did want, they made Alcibiades a god and left the whole mess up to him to solve. Alcibiades obligingly responded in a truly godlike fashion by not turning up when invoked and turning a deaf ear to their prayers, and everybody was, for the moment at least, happy. They turned their attention away from politics and started interesting themselves in the War again, to find that it had got wholly out of hand and that we were losing.

So ended the greatest and most perfect democracy the world has ever known, the ideal which generations yet unborn will strive in vain to emulate. Actually, there's more to it than that; the democracy was restored briefly, before the end of the War, amid the most horrible blood-letting that Athens has ever seen, until the Spartans disposed of it when they finally took over the City. But the monster that Cleophon and his fellow butchers created then had nothing really in common with the old democracy as it had been; it bore as much relation to the complicated organism originally spawned by Solon as my parodies do to the plays of Euripides. And I don't want to think about what happened then, because it makes me sick just to think of it. My story ends here.

So I'll just tie up a few loose ends, and then we'll call it a day. For instance; did Philonides and I ever get round to killing Aristophanes for getting our leading actor drunk, or was it just another empty promise? Well, by the time we had slept off our hangovers and regained the use of all our limbs after the Victory party, we found that our grudge against the son of Philip had faded rather. After all, not only had I won the prize for Comic drama but Philonides had won the prize for best actor – there had been a little trouble about that, since Philonides hadn't formally been entered, but it was smoothed over and he got the prize in the end – and all this good fortune was due, in a roundabout sort of way, to Aristophanes. So we let him off his beating for the time being, and decided to think up a more subtle punishment at our leisure. Then, what with one thing and another, we never got around to it, and so I suppose the matter lapsed, like an old mortgage. Later, during all the unpleasantness of the following year, when there was actual physical danger attached to any show of resistance to the new régime, Aristophanes did a couple of truly noble and courageous things, and we nearly forgave him.

Shortly before the actual *coup*, when the atmosphere in Athens was becoming very unpleasant and several outspoken people had been murdered in the street, there was talk of cancelling the Comic plays, since political comment was out of the question. But Aristophanes went marching into the Archon's office (there was still an archon, though he bore about as much relation to a proper archon as I do to Zeus the Thunderer) and demanded that he be given Choruses for both the Lenaea and the Great Dionysia. Since he still had a degree of standing in oligarchic circles, and it would have been a nuisance to have such a relatively prominent person killed, the archon agreed, and so there was a Lenaea and a Dionysia after all. And the plays that Aristophanes wrote that year were decidedly clever, too, though I wouldn't go so far as to say they were good.

He recognised that any sort of overt criticism would be impossible, so he put his mind to it and came up with a rather neat answer. There was a common joke throughout Athens at that time that the oligarchic experiment was so extreme that, when it failed, the only logical progression would be to turn the government of the State over to the women, as being marginally more bizarre even than the rule of Antiphon. Aristophanes took up this joke and based his two plays around it; but he disguised them thinly, one as literary criticism, the other as a general plea for peace. But in both plays the women take over part of the function of the State, and the way they act is remarkably close to the way the oligarchs were conducting themselves. In one play they even capture the Acropolis, as the celebrated

Cylon had done several hundred years ago, when he tried to set up a dictatorship; and there are all sorts of veiled references – to citizens being arbitrarily arrested by the police, to secret conspiracies and negotiations with the enemy to end the war at any price, to puppet magistrates and to the previous *coup* by the Whitefeet, who seized Leipsydrion. This was pretty outspoken stuff in the circumstances, but the oligarchs either wouldn't or couldn't be bothered to do anything about it. They pretended to take both plays at their face value, and let Aristophanes have his brief moment of glory. Since the *coup* went ahead as planned, I don't think many people actually did get the point of those two plays; or if they did, they ignored it.

Nevertheless the son of Philip did make a gesture, which only goes to show that deep down there is some good in all of us. But if you're hoping that Aristophanes will turn out to be all right in the end, I'm afraid you're going to be disappointed. Shortly after the *coup* he patched up his tiff with the oligarchy and was heartbroken when the Four Hundred were deposed. He soon came to terms with the men behind the Five Thousand, however, and as soon as they had got their version of the Rule of the Few sorted out, he ingratiated himself with the right people and became quite a big man for a short while. During this brief period he made several attempts to get me into trouble; for example, he tried to get me removed from the citizens' roll on the grounds that my great-great-great grandmother had been born in a small village on the wrong side of Troezen at a time when the village wasn't strictly speaking part of Attica; he managed to get me lumbered with the cost of fitting out a trireme and producing a play, both in the same year, by making out that I had volunteered; he spread rumours that I was a friend of Theramenes when Theramenes was out of favour, and that I made nasty jokes about Theramenes' wife when Theramenes was back in favour; and he pirated large chunks of a play of mine which I had composed about seven years before but scrapped, having first bribed my houseboy to steal the only surviving copy from the big cedarwood chest in my inner room.

When the Five Thousand were put down by Cleophon's rabble, Aristophanes barely escaped with his life and for a while had to go into hiding. Various friends of his put up with him for a while, but not many people can take more than a week of his company, and besides, the reward for his capture was very tempting; I guess it was running at just under four drachmas a pound for a while, until the men in power lost interest. It was then that Aristophanes found that he had nowhere to go. So he came to me, at a time when a thousand drachmas would have done me no harm at all.

I remember that it was the middle of the night, and I had just ridden down from the country because Phaedra was ill. I was desperately tired and I had fallen fast asleep in front of the hearth, still wearing my riding boots. Phaedra was asleep in the inner room; she had a bad dose of fever, and hadn't been able to sleep for two days. Then there was this diabolical hammering on the door, and I woke up as sharply as if someone had stuck a skewer through the seat of the chair.

I was terrified, as you can imagine; when you heard knocking on your door in the middle of the night in those days, you expected something horrible. But the last thing I wanted was for Phaedra to be woken up, so I hauled myself on to my feet and opened the door a tiny crack.

At first I didn't recognise the son of Philip – he had dyed his beard and brushed his hair forward over his bald forehead; but when he put his not inconsiderable weight behind the door and pushed it open, I knew who it was, and I was not at all pleased. I was about to say something or other, but I never got the chance. He thrust himself into the house and slammed the door behind him.

'For God's sake,' he said, 'what do you mean by keeping me hanging about on the doorstep for half an hour? Can't you see I'm in danger?'

I was still half asleep, and I couldn't understand. 'Danger?' I mumbled, through the mouthful of greasy wool I appeared to have woken up with. 'What are you talking about?'

'They're on to me, that's what,' he said, helping himself

to a long swig of wine straight from the ladle. 'That bastard Euxenus has sold me down the river. I got away just in time.'

'You mean someone's trying to kill you?' I said.

'Got it in one,' said the son of Philip. 'Now, where's the best place for me to hide? They may have seen me come in here, since you took so long answering the door.'

'You mean this house is likely to be searched?' I said, horrified. 'My wife is sick in there, she can't be disturbed.'

'Too late to worry about that now,' said the son of Philip. 'You should have thought about that when you were contemplating opening the damned door.'

I thought quickly, but all that came into my mind was those deceived-husband stories, where the wife hides her lover under something or in something when her husband returns unexpectedly. As it happens, Aristophanes had filled in a gap in one of his recent plays with a handful of these old chestnuts, and my semi-conscious mind couldn't think farther than that.

'For God's sake,' said Aristophanes angrily, while I was trying to think, 'make up your mind or we'll both be dead. Do you want them to catch me or something?'

It hadn't occurred to me before then, I swear to you, that here was a chance to get even with the son of Philip for a lifetime of malice and slander, and that nobody could ever blame me for it. After all, it wouldn't be my fault if Cleophon's thugs chose to kill a poet; and Aristophanes hadn't followed the correct formula for putting himself under my protection, namely clasping my knees with his hands and proclaiming himself a suppliant. He had no claim on me whatsoever, and it is a good man's duty to hurt his enemies, as the philosophers are always telling us. But once again I remembered that Aristophanes had been put under my care by the God himself; and so, rather wearily, I told him that there was a space just large enough for a man to hide in next to the kitchen boiler. It was a big open jar where we put the rubbish and the emptyings of the chamber-pots until the cart came to take them away, and since the cart hadn't been for a week there was quite a healthy build-up of material for him to hide under. He objected furiously, of course, and I was tempted to remind him of the olive-jar in Sicily; but I didn't, and eventually he crawled down into this jar, while I laid a nice thick layer of ordure over the top of him. I imagine it was quite nice and snug under there by the time I had finished, once you got used to the smell.

About ten minutes later, there was another loud knocking at the door, and I went to answer it. This time I wasn't quick enough to stop Phaedra being woken up, and she came to the door of the inner room, asking sleepily what was going on.

'Don't ask me,' I said as I slid back the bolt. 'Go back to bed, there's a good girl.'

There were five or six men at the door, with drawn swords in their hands, and they were not in the best of moods. I didn't recognise any of them; I think they were foreigners. Anyway, they demanded to know where Aristophanes son of Philip was. I told them I didn't know.

'Don't be funny with us,' said their leader, a big, grey-haired man. 'He was seen coming in here not half an hour since. Where have you got him?'

Phaedra burst out laughing, and they asked her what was so funny.

'You idiot,' she said, 'don't you know whose house this is? Eupolis is Aristophanes' worst enemy in the whole world. You don't imagine for one moment that he'd shelter that bastard, after everything he's done to this family?'

The leader of the men scowled at her. 'Shut up, you,' he said. 'We're going to search this house from top to bottom, and if we find him here you're both of you going to die. Is that clear?'

'Search away,' said Phaedra. 'I can promise you that you won't find him.'

So they searched. They tore the inner room apart, slit open the mattress, emptied the chests out all over the floor, and pulled everything down from the rafters. They sacked the rest of the house so efficiently that you would think they were Italian pirates. They went all over the courtyard and the stable, and nearly cut open the horse to see if Aristophanes was hiding inside its skin, like Odysseus in the Cyclops' cave. But for some reason they didn't empty out the trash-jar, contenting themselves with sticking my spear into it a couple of times. When they had finished, Phaedra said, 'Satisfied?'

'All right,' said the grey-haired man, 'you win. Just think yourselves lucky, that's all. And remember, we're going to keep an eye on you from now on. One step out of line, and you're dead. Got it?'

I waited for an hour after they had gone before pulling Aristophanes out from under the rubbish. One of the spear-thrusts had gone through his cloak, missing his chest by about half an inch, and he was profoundly unhappy. Not nearly as unhappy as Phaedra was, though. She stared at me as if I was mad.

'You imbecile,' she said, 'what in God's name did you want to go doing a thing like that for? You very nearly got us all killed.'

'I'm sorry,' I mumbled. 'It seemed rather clever at the time.'

Phaedra shook her head several times in utter contempt, and swept off back to bed, leaving me with a foul-smelling Comic poet to dispose of somehow. The best thing to do with him at that moment seemed to be to feed him, because he wouldn't be able to complain so effectively with his mouth full. While he was eating, I put my finger under my nose to keep out at least some of the smell, and tried to strike at least a little spark from my brains.

The best I could come up with was this. Obviously they would be keeping an eye on the house for a day or so, and it would be impossible for Aristophanes just to walk out of the front door and go quietly away. So I had to get him out in something or under something; the problem was, what? Then my eye fell on the big Bactrian carpet hanging on the wall, and I had an idea. First thing in the morning, after an extremely restless night, I put the horse in the shafts of the cart and led him round to the front of the house. My slaves then carried out the carpet, tightly rolled up and tied with rush cord. We manhandled this carpet up on to the cart, trying not to show that it was heavier than it should have been, and I took the reins and set off slowly for the country. In retrospect it was a stupid idea; had anyone been watching the house, they would immediately have started wondering why the urge to move furniture had suddenly come on me, and taken a good look inside that carpet. As it was, I had a nicely uneventful journey to Pallene; the Sicilian cavalry I was expecting to materialise from round each bend of the road never actually turned up. We unloaded the carpet into my house, cut the cords, and rolled out the son of Philip, who was fast asleep. From Pallene, I believe, he went up into the mountains and spent a month or so pretending to be a shepherd on Parnes. I wish I could have seen Aristophanes being a shepherd. It would have made up for all the trouble he had put me to.

When I got back to the City I found that Phaedra's fever had got much worse, and I knew then that she was going to die. She took a long time about it, though, and I think those were the worst few weeks of my life. I suddenly realised that I had let her slip through my hands like a precious opportunity. You know how it is; there's something you're always meaning to do, such as go up to see the wild flowers in the mountains around Phyle and take a picnic with you, but you keep putting it off, and by the time you get there everything has faded and withered, and you eat your food in silence and then go home feeling miserable. I had never found time to get to know my wife properly, and when I was forced to make a start it was too late. She was delirious with the fever half the time, and said a lot of things I hope she didn't mean; and when she came out of it, she would say exactly the opposite, telling me over and over again that I had been a good husband in the circumstances, and that she had had a better life than she had any right to expect. After a while I couldn't bear it any longer, and in my heart I wanted her to die and make an end of it. But the thought that the next day or perhaps the day after she wouldn't be there any more was completely intolerable to me, and I kept pestering her with doctors and miracle cures when all she wanted was to be left in peace. Finally she begged me not to bother her any more, and I gave up and tried to accept the situation. I stayed with her all the time, however, because both of us were terrified that if I went away for a moment she would be dead when I came back. And even then I failed her. She had just come out of a dreadful bout of delirium and appeared to be sleeping peacefully, and I was so tired that I fell asleep in my chair. I can't have slept for more than ten minutes, but as soon as I woke up I knew she had died on me. I didn't look for a while, and then when I opened my eyes I thought for a moment that she was just asleep, and that I had been imagining it. But she was dead all right, and as soon as I had made sure, I started sobbing and wailing like one of those dreadful old women who make a living as professional mourners in the City, until one of the slaves gave me a cup of wine laced with poppy essence, like the potion that Aristophanes' men gave to my leading actor Philocharmus. After that, they tell me, I went off my head for a day or so – the idiot had put too much of the poppy stuff in it, and nearly killed me too – but I don't remember any of that. All I remember was waking up with a dreadful headache and knowing that she was dead.

I buried her at Pallene, next to my father's grave, where I will be buried myself; and I had the best stone-mason in Athens set up one of those carved slabs, with a verse on it. Now being a poet I should have produced a really fine epitaph; and I thought I had. But when I saw it, it just seemed silly, so I had it chiselled off and replaced with a simple inscription recording her name and her father's name and her deme. I miss her more and more as I get older, which is strange considering that when I am honest with myself I have to admit that I didn't know her all that well. Perhaps that explains it, I don't know. I think that sometimes I forget what she was really like, and get her confused with the legendary heroines like Penelope or Laodameia, the archetypal perfect wives. She wasn't perfect, by any stretch of the imagination, but I would willingly have traded all my prizes in the Festivals, even the prize for the *Demes*, just to have known her a little better.

* * *

So now I have outlived all the good or interesting characters in this book, and you are left with me. If you do not share my undying fascination with myself, I suggest that you leave out the next bit and carry on down to the top of the last roll.

I have never been to Delphi or any of the great oracles, and so I have never been given any insights into my future, other than those the God Dionysus gave me, as I have described above. But when I went down to the Market Square this morning to buy some fish, they tried to charge me one and a half drachmas a quart for anchovies; and when I said that the price was outrageous, the fishmonger said that anchovies were on their way up, because of the War, and that he confidently expected to be charging two drachmas a quart by the end of next month. Didn't I mention we are at war again? Indeed we are, and with Sparta too, but it's nothing like the Great Peloponnesian War; it's like a fight between two extremely old men, more funny than violent.

Two drachmas a quart; what a price to pay for anchovies. When I look back over my life, I feel rather like the three men from a tiny city somewhere on the edge of the Black Sea, who had always wanted to see Athens. They were stone-masons by trade, and from every building and statue and tombstone they made, they set aside a few obols towards the cost of a trip to the City of the Violet Crown. After twenty years or so of saving in this manner they had enough put by, and so they booked a passage on a wheat-ship. All the way, as they sailed past Byzantium and along the Thracian Chersonese, they talked about what they were going to see – the temples, the Theatre, the Nine Fountains, the great civil buildings, the Propylaea, the Erechtheum. Eventually they landed at Piraeus and walked up under the Long Walls – this must all have been before the end of the War, when the Long Walls were pulled down by Lysander, the Spartan general – and into the City itself. The trouble was that they didn't know what the great monuments they had travelled so far to see actually looked like. So when they passed one marble structure, one of them would turn to the other two and say, 'That must be the Erechtheum.' And the other two would nod excitedly, and they would stand for a moment and drink in the full splendour of it. Then they would pass on and come to another magnificent pile; and another of them would say, 'No, that must be the Erechtheum.' Then they would think back over everything they had heard about Athens, and they would agree that the building in front of them was indeed the Erechtheum, and the one they had seen before must have been Solon's Council Chamber. And then they would find themselves standing in front of a still more imposing edifice (I shall run out of words meaning building in a moment, and then this story will grind to a halt) and they would all be forced to agree that *this* must be the Erechtheum. When they had been all round the City and seen everything larger and more impressive than a water-tank, they looked at each other in silence for a while. Then the eldest one said, 'Anyway, we've seen the Erechtheum. Let's go and have something to eat.'

You take my point. Everything I've seen and done has seemed to me at the time to be the crucial point of my life; and then something else has happened to me that makes me reconsider. This has made writing a coherent history of my times rather difficult. So if I have any advice for you, ground out like flour between the stones of the turning years, it is to go and have something to eat immediately, and leave the sightseeing until later. In other words, don't be what I have always been, an observer; or you will find, as I did when Phaedra died, that you've been looking in the wrong direction all your life. That was the one regret of my life, and the one thing I didn't find any Comedy in. Everything else I have laughed at, in one way or another.

One last joke, while I remember. The celebrated Socrates was put to death, along with a lot of better men, after the end of the War. He was brought to trial on a palpably trumped-up charge, his real crime being that he used to give Alcibiades lessons in clever speaking; and at his trial he remembered me and tried making a Comic defence-speech, as I had done. But this time it didn't work, and much to his surprise he was condemned to death and executed. I remember going to see him in prison while he was awaiting execution, and the poor fool still believed that he would be reprieved, right down to the last moment, when they handed him the cup of poison. He has become very fashionable since his death, and people have started writing down those great long one-sided conversations he used to have with people who couldn't get away in time. In fact, there is a strange wave of nostalgia for the War and all the celebrated men of the time. No sooner had Euripides died, up in Macedon where he went to escape from Cleophon's men, than they started reviving his plays in the Theatre. They don't revive any of my work, of course, but then, I'm still alive.

My son has been, generally speaking, an unmitigated disappointment to me, for he has taken to writing epic poetry, and nothing good will come of that. On the other hand, he married a nice girl and has two sons, and when I die he will inherit a large and well-cared-for estate, which I think he will look after. He has the makings of a good farmer, if the Muses don't get to him first. He hasn't inherited wit from either me or his mother, which is probably a blessing. He has her looks, though, and a little of my skill with words. When he was young he wanted to be a soldier. I made sure that I got to know him well enough, for fear of making the same mistake twice, but by and large I wasted my time. I have known hundreds of men like him, and they don't interest me much.

And Athens is still standing, more or less, and will probably still be there in ten thousand years' time; but it is an unimportant place now, the market town for that mountainous, unfertile district of Greece called Attica. The most important place in the world these days is probably Thebes, where the eels and the idiots come from; and if that isn't irony, I don't know what is. That is a good joke, and this is a good time to die.